"This Vulcan, Mestral," said Picard. "You're certain he was on Earth for all that time and was never discovered?"

Taurik replied, "As far as I was able to determine, his existence never became known to the world at large. It seems possible, even likely, that he was known to certain elements of the United States government and military, and perhaps similar entities from other global powers. Information on that period is somewhat fragmentary. Most of the information I was allowed to consult came from protected Starfleet archives, including the personal and official logs made by Captain James T. Kirk and Ambassador Spock during their tenure aboard the *Constitution*-class *U.S.S. Enterprise*. They provided detailed accounts of their interactions with Mestral during their various missions to twentieth-century Earth."

"James Kirk." Picard shook his head at the mention of the name. "Kirk and time travel. You know, rumors persist that the Department of Temporal Investigations was formed as a result of Captain Kirk's various entanglements with time travel."

"I have heard those rumors, sir," said the Vulcan. "You may be interested to know that when I was being debriefed by departmental agents, they neither confirmed nor denied the veracity of such unsubstantiated claims."

Picard could not help a small smile in response to the deadpan comment. "No, I don't suppose they would do such a thing."

STAR TREK
THE NEXT GENERATION®

HEARTS AND MINDS

Dayton Ward

Based on
Star Trek: The Next Generation
created by Gene Roddenberry

POCKET BOOKS
New York London Toronto Sydney New Delhi Ponval

Pocket Books
An Imprint of Simon & Schuster, Inc.
1230 Avenue of the Americas
New York, NY 10020

This book is published by Pocket Books, an imprint of Simon & Schuster, Inc., under exclusive license from CBS Studios Inc.

First Pocket Books paperback edition June 2017

Manufactured in the United States of America

10 9 8 7 6 5 4 3 2 1

ISBN 978-1-5011-4731-9
ISBN 978-1-5011-5014-2 (ebook)

For Michi, Addison, and Erin.
They know why.

HISTORIAN'S NOTE

This story takes place in late 2386, seven years after the *U.S.S. Enterprise*-E's confrontation with the Romulan praetor Shinzon (*Star Trek: Nemesis*) and a few months after the events involving the Federation, the Klingon Empire, and the renegade Klingon cult known as the Unsung (*Star Trek: The Next Generation—Prey*). These events unfold just before Trill journalist Ozla Graniv's bombshell exposé of Section 31 and its numerous clandestine activities, including the conspiracy to remove and assassinate Federation President Min Zife in 2379 (*Star Trek: Section 31—Control*).

1

***U.S.S. Enterprise* NCC-1701-E**
2386

The dart struck the center of the target, just above its two companions. A resounding beep erupted from the machine, alerting anyone within earshot that yet another bull's-eye had been scored.

"Okay, you need to stop with the voodoo or magic or whatever it is you're doing," said T'Ryssa Chen as Taurik stepped away from the white stripe on the floor that indicated where the dart thrower should stand.

Rising from his chair at the table where he sat next to Chen, Lieutenant Rennan Konya added, "That, or throw with your eyes closed. This is getting ridiculous."

Taurik moved away from the dartboard that was tucked into the Riding Club's far corner, returning to his own seat at the table. "I was given to understand that the object of the game is to quickly close out the indicated numbers. As I have already done so with numbers fifteen through twenty, all that remained was the center, or 'bull's-eye,' as Lieutenant Konya referred to it. Given the rules as laid out before the game commenced, I had no alternative but to concentrate my throws on that area of the target."

Konya did not even bother stifling his laugh, and Chen could only shake her head. Fellow crew members sitting at adjacent tables supplied their own chuckles and smiles, including Lieutenant Dina Elfiki, who raised her glass to Taurik.

"Well played, Commander."

"Don't encourage him," said Chen, eyeing the *Enterprise*'s science officer. She then pointed to Elfiki's companion, Gary Weinrib. "Don't let her encourage him. Mind your date, Lieutenant."

The gamma shift flight control officer offered a mock salute. "Aye, aye, Lieutenant."

"Oh stop it," said Elfiki, shaking her head and rolling her eyes. "You'll just make her worse.

Chen eyed Weinrib with mock suspicion. "Wait. Aren't you supposed to be on duty or something?"

"Not for four hours yet." Weinrib held up his glass. "Altair water."

"A likely story."

With the exception of unusual deviations in the crew schedule, the end of alpha shift almost always heralded an increase in patronage and good cheer in the club. Nearly every seat at the bar as well as each of the tables situated around the room was occupied, with personnel camped out at the sofas positioned before the forward viewing ports, or simply standing, drinks in hand, wherever unclaimed floor space presented itself. The Happy Bottom Riding Club—so christened by William Riker before leaving the *Enterprise* and his role as the ship's first officer to take command of his own ship, the *U.S.S. Titan*—had become one of Chen's favorite places to spend leisure time. The atmosphere here was always festive, as she and her shipmates were able to shrug off the demands of work and duty for a short while either before or after an assigned shift. It was also one of the few times during the course of any given day that she might run into friends like Dina Elfiki, whose duties often required her to be on the bridge or tucked away deep inside of the *Enterprise*'s science labs. It was the same with Taurik, who as often as not could be found toiling in the depths of the ship's engineering section or one of the numerous Jefferies tubes or maintenance crawlways running throughout the immense vessel.

With a friendly wave, Chen left Elfiki and Weinrib to their quiet conversation and returned her attention to Taurik, waiting for the Vulcan to settle into his seat before waving in the general direction of the dartboard, where Konya was setting things up for a new game.

"You're making me look bad, you know. How is it you've never played darts before tonight?"

Reaching for a glass of what Chen knew was room-temperature mineral water, Taurik replied, "Until this evening, it was not a necessary skill." After taking a sip from his water, he added, "It is a rather straightforward game. Hand-eye coordination is key, of course, as is a modicum of arm strength to deliver the dart to its intended target."

"Wait," said Konya, a trio of darts still cradled in his left hand, as he returned to the table and dropped into his seat. "Are you saying you know where you're going to put a dart every time you throw it?"

Taurik's right eyebrow cocked. "That is not what I said, Lieutenant." He paused, taking another drink. "However, upon further consideration, I am forced to concede that my remarks could be interpreted in that manner."

"So, you are saying it?" asked Konya.

"Yes."

Smiling, Konya slapped the top of the table with his free hand. "I do believe I just heard a challenge, Lieutenant Chen."

"I do believe you're correct, Lieutenant Konya."

Chen smiled, happy to see him having fun. It had only been in recent months that he had taken to coming here with her every few nights. At first it was just every so often, but he had embraced the notion of winding down at the end of a long day. It was a big step for someone like Rennan Konya, who spent long, often arduous hours immersed in his work, doing all the things for which the ship's deputy security chief was still responsible even when there was no emergency or crisis with which to contend. Konya spent a good portion of each duty day training the officers who comprised the *Enterprise*'s security division so that they would be ready to deploy against any number of response scenarios. A great deal of time was devoted to modifying procedures and simulations, and Chen knew that he was always finding ways to incorporate lessons learned during recent missions or encounters to refine the training regimen. Losses suffered by the *Enterprise* crew during the incident with the Unsung had motivated Konya and Lieutenant Aneta Šmrhová to redouble their efforts in this regard. The harsh lessons imparted by that mission, which required the ship to suspend its exploration of the Odyssean Pass and return to Federation space, hammered home the need for constant training and honing of such skills.

Perhaps this new satisfaction was providing other benefits as well. With each passing month, Konya seemed to be acting more and more like his old self, from before the Borg Invasion and the guilt and depression he had endured in the aftermath of that conflict. She knew that his sessions with the ship's counselor, Doctor Hegol Den, had proven most helpful, and Konya had confessed to her that the rekindling of their relationship had also played a large part in his overall improved state of mental well-being. She was reluctant to take any credit for the progress he had made, though it was still satisfying to know that he thought of her in such terms.

Another sure sign of Konya's improved spirits was his competitive nature reasserting itself.

"All right, Commander," said the Betazoid, tapping the table once more with the flat of his hand. He offered both a mischievous smile and the set of three darts to Taurik. "With all due respect, sir, Lieutenant Chen and I think someone needs to put their credits where their mouth is."

Placing his water glass on the table, the engineer took the darts from Konya. "Very well. If you insist."

The gentle verbal sparring and challenge had attracted notice from nearby tables. Elfiki and Weinrib along with several others had turned in their seats, angling for an unimpeded view of the dartboard.

"Are we taking bets?" asked Elfiki. "Should we start a ship's pool?"

Taurik, having moved to the white marker on the floor, appeared content to ignore the science officer's query as he regarded the board and the darts he held. He had selected one and was testing its weight in his hand when his communicator badge beeped.

"Lieutenant Commander Taurik," said the voice of the *Enterprise*'s main computer. *"You have a priority message. Eyes only, authorization code alpha echo three five. Please respond at once."*

"What the hell is that?" asked Chen, the words escaping her lips before she even realized she was speaking. She frowned, exchanging confused glances first with Konya and then Elfiki. She had heard the computer relay information about priority message traffic before, but it was usually the sort of thing reserved for the captain. For anyone else to receive something like that was out of the ordinary, to say the least.

For his part, Taurik's first response was to glance at his combadge for a moment. Then, as though noticing he was being watched by several of his shipmates, he tapped the badge. "This is Taurik. Acknowledged." He turned, extending his hand and the darts to Konya. "I am afraid I must postpone our wager."

"No problem, sir," replied the lieutenant, taking the proffered darts. "Anything we can do for you?"

Pausing, Taurik seemed to be pondering Konya's question before he shook his head. "Your offer is appreciated, Lieutenant, but this is a matter I must attend to personally." To Chen, he said, "Thank you for inviting me this evening. I trust we can repeat the experience soon."

"Taurik," Chen began, but saw in his eyes that any attempt to pry more information from him would be fruitless. She recognized the way his demeanor changed when he had something new and important demanding his full attention.

Without saying anything further, the Vulcan turned and departed the lounge, leaving Konya to move back to the table and return to his seat. His own expression was a mask of confusion.

"I'm not the only one who thought that was weird, right?"

Alone in his ready room, Jean-Luc Picard regarded the computer terminal perched near the corner of his desk. On the screen, below the seal of the United Federation of Planets, flashed the words PRIORITY ALERT – CAPTAIN'S EYES ONLY. VOICE PRINT AUTHORIZATION REQUIRED.

The tone indicating the activation of the ship's intercom sounded, prying Picard's eyes from the monitor as the cue was followed by the voice of the *Enterprise*'s first officer, Commander Worf.

"Bridge to Captain Picard."

"Go ahead, Number One."

"Sir, Lieutenant Šmrhová has completed her check of the communications logs. There is no record of the message being received. However, a file matching the message's date stamp was loaded into the ship's command-protected memory banks. The date suggests it was copied to our system during our last visit to Earth Station McKinley."

Everything about the order packet was unusual, beginning with how Picard had become aware of it. Notification of the message had come not from his chief of security, Lieutenant Šmrhová, who would have received all incoming communications traffic from her station on the bridge. Instead, the advisory was issued by the ship's main computer, directly informing him not of an inbound message meant for his sole attention, but instead a preprogrammed order packet. Now evidence suggested the orders had been lurking within the computer's memory banks for nearly three months.

Why?

"Number One, you're certain the file comes from a legitimate source?"

Worf replied, *"Lieutenant Šmrhová assures me that the packet contains an authorized Starfleet encryption algorithm, designed for voice-print access and keyed to you, Captain. Neither she nor anyone else has examined the file's contents."*

Drawing a deep breath, Picard released it in calm, deliberate fashion. The action did little to assuage the tension that seemed to have settled upon him. He felt its weight, along with mounting suspicion. He did not like secrets, and neither did he appreciate whatever games someone at Starfleet Command had apparently decided was necessary in this instance.

"Has Lieutenant Šmrhová completed her sensor sweep?"

"Affirmative," replied the first officer. *"We are alone out here and standing by to resume our course."*

Pursing his lips, Picard considered his next steps, particularly in light of the current situation. While reviewing the waiting message was a priority, the manner of its delivery was still troubling. For weeks, the *Enterprise* had been pursuing without incident its ongoing charting of the Odyssean Pass, the area of space to which the starship had been assigned to explore months earlier. Time spent studying a rogue comet as well as two uninhabited solar systems had been a welcome change of pace, including a brief shore leave on a particularly inviting Class-M planet that the crew had all to themselves. After the ship's science officer, Lieutenant Elfiki, had informed him that scan data of the Pass collected by unmanned survey probes had revealed the existence of a planet in another nearby system that showed signs of civilization, Picard decided it was time to get back to work. Long-range sensors seemed to reinforce the early scans, with the detection of weak broadcast transmissions and even indications of interplanetary spacecraft activity.

The *Enterprise* had been on course for less than two hours when the computer's message came, informing Picard not to proceed with entering the system until he had reviewed the encrypted orders packet. The question now plaguing him was whether the orders and the system were related in some way. How was that even possible? So far as Picard knew, beyond the automated sensor drones from decades earlier, no one from Earth or the Federation had ever visited this region.

Curiouser and curiouser.

"Maintain present position. Yellow alert until further notice, Number One. I'll apprise you further as I'm able. Picard out." With the connection severed, the captain returned his full attention to the computer screen and its blinking message.

There's no sense putting this off any longer.

"Computer," he said, reaching to pivot the computer terminal so that it now directly faced him, "decode and play message. Voice print authorization: Picard four seven alpha tango."

The image on the screen shifted from the Federation seal to the visage of Admiral Leonard James Akaar. At one hundred nineteen Earth years of age, the Capellan was still a vibrant, muscular man, his broad chest and shoulders straining the cut of his Starfleet dress uniform. His once-blond shoulder-length hair had largely surrendered to pale gray and his skin was deeply lined, but his eyes were still bright with determination and purpose. Staring out from what Picard recognized as the admiral's office at Starfleet Headquarters in San Francisco on Earth, Akaar was leaning toward his desk, his large hands clasped before him.

"Hello, Jean-Luc. I apologize for this unusual means of communicating orders to you, and I know you must have many questions. Rest assured that the reasons for my methods are due to the sensitivity of the matter on which you'll

soon be briefed, and because I trust you to proceed with all proper discretion and delicacy. It involves a matter that has only recently come to my attention, mostly by chance. We might never have known about it, if not for the simple reason that Starfleet decided the Odyssean Pass was a place we needed to explore, and you're only hearing this message because of the specific planet you've chosen to investigate."

Listening to the recorded message and feeling the first hints of irritation beginning to stir within him, Picard shook his head. Why the games? If he could be trusted to "proceed with all proper discretion and delicacy," then why could he not receive an actual briefing from Akaar before the *Enterprise* had left? It was obvious that it involved something the *Enterprise* had encountered during their journey through the Odyssean Pass, or else it was something they would soon face on the planet that had attracted his curiosity, but what was the connection?

"As I already said," continued Akaar, *"I know you must have any number of questions, and if I know you as well as I think I do, you're glaring at me right now and wanting to punch your computer screen."*

"It's not the worst idea," muttered Picard.

"This is the sort of thing that requires hands-on care. Since I can't be there, I've handed that job over to another member of your crew; someone I know you trust, and with good reason. He's already proven his loyalty and his prudence on a related matter, and I think he's the ideal person for handling something this sensitive. You should be hearing from him in due course, and I urge you to listen to everything he has to—"

The intercom sounded again, and Picard paused the playback in time to hear Worf's voice for a second time.

"Bridge to Captain Picard. I apologize for the interrup-

tion, sir, but Lieutenant Commander Taurik has come to the bridge and is requesting to speak with you in private. He says it's urgent, sir."

"Taurik?" Looking at Admiral Akaar's frozen image, Picard frowned. "Have you enlisted him into this scheme of yours?"

"I beg your pardon, sir?"

Realizing he had spoken the question aloud, Picard pressed a control on the terminal to darken the screen. "Send him in, Number One."

A moment later, his ready room door slid aside to reveal the *Enterprise*'s assistant chief engineer. The Vulcan stood just beyond the threshold, his back ramrod straight and with hands clasped behind his back.

"Thank you for seeing me, Captain. I apologize for calling on you, as I know your shift has ended."

Picard's eyes narrowed. "I'm the captain, Mister Taurik. I'm never really off duty." He waved for the Vulcan to enter the room so the door could close behind him. "Let me guess: you're Admiral Akaar's point man on whatever this is about." He gestured to his computer screen.

Nodding, Taurik replied. "Yes, Captain. I was personally briefed by Admiral Akaar during our time in Federation space. It was a most . . . illuminating discussion."

"Perhaps you'd care to share the details with me?" Pointing to the chairs positioned before his desk, Picard indicated for Taurik to join him.

"Thank you, sir." Taking the seat to Picard's left, Taurik seemed to relax not the slightest bit as he settled into the chair. "First, Admiral Akaar wanted me to tell you that our present circumstances are not due to an external threat, and neither are they a reflection on you or any member of the *Enterprise*'s crew."

"So why are we here, Commander?"

To his surprise, Picard observed that Taurik appeared . . . nervous? The engineer glanced over his shoulder, as though expecting Worf or someone else to come barging in at any moment. Though Taurik's hands were clasped and resting in his lap, Picard noted how he was almost fidgeting in a most un-Vulcan manner.

"As it was explained to me, sir," said Taurik after a moment, "the *Enterprise*'s next mission and the problems we may soon be facing stem from decisions and actions that were undertaken more than three centuries ago . . ."

BEGINNINGS

2

Near Bloomingdale, Georgia
March 16, 2031

Finding the ship was easy. The trail of fallen, burned pine trees on either side of a shallow, curving trench of scorched, overturned soil simplified that part of the problem.

Moving step by cautious step from the relative safety of the trees south of the crash area, Gunnery Sergeant Erika Figueroa stopped her advance, inspecting the newly carved trough for signs of other activity. She switched the optical gun sight mounted atop her M4A3 carbine assault rifle to thermal mode, peering through the illuminated reticule and noting the pockets of heat that marked the ship's violent passing. Other areas along the ground that were farther away from the craft's final resting place retained some residual warmth, but much of the disturbed terrain had already cooled in the night air.

Lucky dirt.

Despite the first official day of spring being just four days away and the notable lack of humidity that would soon plague this part of eastern Georgia in the coming months, sweat still ran down Figueroa's chest and back beneath her black T-shirt and uniform jacket. Recent rains had made the ground here soft, and she felt the soles of her combat boots sinking slightly into the damp soil. On the far side of the ragged furrow, just visible within the first line of trees that had escaped destruction, she saw half of her six-person team moving with a deliberate caution similar to her own.

"Smitty, any radiation?" she asked. Despite her speaking in soft tones, it was still sufficient to be picked up by the transceiver tucked into her right ear, and transmitted over her team's secured communications frequency.

"That's a negative, Gunny," replied Sergeant Matthew Smith, Figueroa's assistant team leader, from the other side of the crash line, and through the thermal optic of the heads-up display built into her helmet's eye shield, she could see him raise his left hand and wave in her direction. *"Everything's in the green."*

All of them had received extensive familiarization in the areas of nuclear, biological, and chemical warfare and defense as just one more component of their multifaceted training. Smith was the team's undisputed NBC expert, and the one tasked with carrying one of the unit's two compact Geiger counters. The spare was in a pouch on Figueroa's tactical vest, along with a similar device for detecting hazardous chemical and biological agents.

Glancing over her shoulder, Figueroa raised her left hand and signaled toward the trees ahead of her. "Keep moving," she said. "Let's get on with this. We still don't know what we're dealing with."

Her team was but one aspect of a larger response following a tactical alert after radar stations controlled by the United States Space Command detected the presence of an unidentified craft flying along the country's east coast earlier in the evening. A pair of F-35A joint strike fighters dispatched from Langley Air Force Base in Virginia had intercepted the craft in minutes, at which point the craft had deviated from its slow, seemingly meandering course south along the Atlantic coastline and initiated aggressive action against the two fighter jets. At last report, a rescue team had already found the pilot from one plane that had endured an attack by some form of energy-dampening beam. The second pilot had better luck, firing on the ship and disabling it with a missile that sent the craft tumbling toward the ground just after sunset, where it eventually devastated a sizable chunk of Georgia forest northwest of Savannah.

As for Figueroa and the other five members of her team, they had been activated from their base of operations at Camp Lejeune in North Carolina and dropped into this area via parachute from a Marine Corps transport plane. Support craft including a helicopter for extraction was en route, but for the next hour or so and as the hour crept toward midnight, Figueroa and her people were on their own.

"Walkabout, this is Homestead," said a male voice in her ear, employing the code names selected for the night's activities. *"What's your status? Do you have eyes on the target?"*

"Getting there, Homestead," replied Figueroa, minding her footing as she stepped over the rotting trunk of a fallen pine tree. "Just making sure it's a decent neighborhood."

"We're on a tight schedule, Walkabout. We need to pick up the pace."

"We do, huh? Is there something *we* don't yet know about down here?"

Figueroa knew that the support team monitoring their communications from the mission operations center at Camp Lejeune had already heard the few words she and her people had exchanged, and everything was couched in euphemisms such as "neighborhood" to denote the crash site and other distracting language in the unlikely event someone else might be tapping into their transmissions. The personnel back at Lejeune also had direct access to the visual feeds provided by the heads-up displays in the team's helmets. Therefore, and despite their apparent impatience, they were about as informed as they could be regarding the current and evolving situation without actually being forced to traipse through the dense Georgia forest.

Damned keyboard commandos.

Over the encrypted comm frequency, the voice replied, *"Given the neighborhood, local law enforcement is already mobilizing assets to investigate. We estimate no more than six zero mikes before you have company."*

"Crowd control's on the way, right?" According to the terse pre-mission briefing she received while en route to the target location, Figueroa had been assured that additional support personnel with the authority and ability to cordon off the crash site would be in place no more than an hour after her team's entry into the area. She knew that they were on borrowed time. Even though the unidentified craft had crashed in a secluded area of forest north of quiet out-of-the-way Savannah, its fiery descent would not have gone unnoticed. Given its population of fewer than 2,500 people and a small emergency response capability, Figueroa guessed that keeping local police and fire department personnel out of the area would be a simple matter, provided the proper support assets found their way here first. Otherwise, she might be in for an interesting conversation with a disgruntled town police chief who had been roused from bed in the middle of the night.

One problem at a time, Gunny. Let's do this.

Looking once more over her shoulder, she caught sight of Corporal Eric Tate and Lance Corporal Jason Bayley, who stood silent and unmoving in the darkness, several meters apart and waiting for her signal to continue their advance. Ahead of them, illuminated by moonlight on this cloudless March evening, a dark shape sat at the end of the trench. The ship had come to rest with its angular front sitting between the trunks of two massive pine trees and all but buried by the dirt it had churned up during its landing. Fewer trees had been uprooted or chopped off at varying heights as the craft's plunge through the forest had slowed, though a few of the larger pines had still paid the price for being obstacles to the downed vessel.

"Homestead," said Figueroa, "we have visual on the target. Commencing our initial approach."

"Understood, Walkabout. Proceed with caution."

Instead of replying, Figueroa turned back toward Tate and Bayley and made a show of rolling her eyes. The response earned her wide smiles from her subordinates.

Maneuvering around fallen trees and other torn up vegetation was becoming less problematic the closer they moved to the ship. The worst of the damage was farther back at the point of the ship's initial contact with the forest before plowing into the soft earth, uprooting or crushing everything in its path before sliding to a halt. For the first time since finding the crash site, Figueroa stepped from the concealment offered by the trees around her and onto open ground. The muzzle of her M4 led the way as she proceeded forward, eyes scanning the large, unfamiliar object ahead and the area surrounding it. Dark panels at the craft's rear indicated a form of engine bell, but they looked nothing like anything Figueroa might see at the tail end of a rocket, or even some of the other odd vessels she had encountered since joining her current unit. She noted the numerous dents and gashes in the ship's dull, unpolished hull, doubtless incurred during its headlong flight through the trees.

"No markings," said Sergeant Smith, who was mirroring Figueroa's movements as he advanced toward the craft along its right side. He was close enough now that she could hear his voice from the far side of the trough at the same time as his words piped through her transceiver. *"Anybody recognize its shape? I've never seen anything like it."*

A chorus of replies from the rest of the team confirmed what Figueroa was already thinking. "Looks like we've got us a new player." Adjusting the filters on her helmet's HUD, she looked from left to right across the crude clearing the ship had created as part of its landing. The display's thermal optics showed her nothing but the other members of her team.

"Gunny," said Corporal Tate, and when she looked to her left, she saw the young Marine aiming his rifle toward the ship. "Open hatch."

Even without the helmet's enhanced vision capabilities, Figueroa was able to make out the darker oval along the craft's port side. Raising the barrel of her rifle so that she now was aiming at the portal, she searched for signs of life but saw nothing.

"Everybody do another sweep. Double-check our flanks and rear." Even as she gave the order, she was moving toward the craft's open entry. With every muscle tensed, it was an extra moment before she noticed her fingers were beginning to tingle from gripping her rifle so tightly, and an ache in her teeth told her she was clenching her jaw. Coming abreast of the open hatchway, Figueroa angled the muzzle of her rifle through the portal, searching for signs of life or danger. The inside of the craft was as unfamiliar to her as its exterior, filled with surfaces that might be inert control consoles. At the same time she realized there had been a fire inside the ship, she recoiled at the smell of burned . . . *something*, and her gut told her that someone or something had died as a result.

"We've got a live one over here!"

Turning from the open hatchway, Figueroa saw Tate and Bayley moving toward a cluster of trees, aiming their rifles at something she could not see. The two Marines came at their target from the sides, converging as they moved forward, and then she saw what had grabbed their attention.

Son of a bitch.

Lying on the ground, the figure was dressed in some kind of dark suit that covered it from head to toe, and it was obvious from the clothing's design that it was intended as some kind of protective garment. From her vantage point, Figueroa guessed from its silhouette it was at the very least humanlike if not actually human, but she had learned from experience with her current unit that all might not always be what it appeared to be. The suit, or whatever it was, also shrouded its wearer's head, including an opaque face shield that concealed its features. As she drew closer, she saw that it was moving, but it was obvious to her that it was also injured. It seemed to be paying no heed to Tate or Bayley, who were yelling at it and ordering it not to move.

"It probably can't understand a thing you're saying."

Figueroa lifted the muzzle of her rifle to point at the object of her subordinates' attention. The people who had dispatched her team to recover whatever might be found at this location possessed technology that might be able to help them communicate with this . . . whatever it was. While she was curious about all of that, the priority for now was taking this individual into custody. Studying the figure through her thermal optics, she grunted in annoyance while observing the protective garment must also insulate body heat. That explained why she and the rest of her team had not seen it before, but it also made her wonder if it had any other friends out here.

Oh, good. Paranoia. Just what we want right now.

"Homestead, we're definitely going to need a crew in here. The target isn't in our catalog," she said, employing still more evasive language to alert her support team that whatever this ship might be, it was absolutely not like anything they had seen before.

"Copy that, Walkabout," replied her support liaison. *"Assets are en route. Estimated time of arriv—"*

"Gunny!"

The shout from Corporal Tate cut off the rest of the reply, coming an instant before weapons fire erupted from the other side of the ship. Backing away from the hatchway and moving to the vessel's rear, she saw Sergeant Smith aiming into the trees and firing off another burst from his rifle. To his right, the other two members of her team, Lance Corporals Martin Esparza and Alyssa Schmidt, had their weapons up and pointing toward the forest, though neither of the younger Marines had fired.

"Hold your fire!" shouted Figueroa, just as her HUD's thermal optics picked up something moving between the trees. The heat signature was too small to be a man and seemed to be floating above the ground, and it took her a few seconds to realize that whoever or whatever it was had to be wearing some kind of protective clothing similar to their new friend, but its head or part of its upper body was still exposed. Whatever it was, it was moving pretty damned fast.

"Tate," she said, "you and Bayley keep an eye on your find. The rest of you follow me." Seeing the bobbing mass through her face shield, she started toward the trees.

"Excuse me."

The voice, calm and composed, caught Figueroa completely off guard and made her turn toward its source. She was able to see what she thought might be a man standing near the side of the newly plowed trench and wearing dark clothing.

"What the hell?"

The words had barely escaped Figueroa's lips before everything vanished in a brilliant white light.

You fool! How could you be so stupid?

A red ember of pain burned in his left side, just beneath his armpit, and even though he pressed a hand against the wound, Jonathan McAllister still felt warm wetness seeping between and around his fingers. Genetically enhanced muscles helped in that regard, pushing him with speed and sure footing over the uneven terrain, while improved vision allowed him to see in the darkness even with the overhead tree canopy shielding the forest floor from the limited moonlight.

Despite his injuries, he was still able to move with a degree of stealth, but McAllister could already feel himself beginning to slow down as his steps became more uncertain. The single bullet from the Marine's weapon had caught him by surprise, knocking him off his feet. Then had come the shouts as the shooter alerted his friends that an intruder was in their midst.

That would be you, Agent 6889.

There had been precious little time to react to his discovery, and even less to cover his tracks as he plunged headlong into the forest, hoping to use the dense trees and his own protective garment to mask his movements and his body heat from the thermal sights carried by the Marines. He had heard the shouts from behind him as the small military unit pulled itself together before setting off in pursuit. He did not have much time.

Likewise, the time allotted to him to respond to this situation had also been anything but generous. The craft—which even the Beta 7 supercomputer at his disposal was unable to identify—had been spotted and shot down while McAllister was in the midst of finishing up another assignment in China. The mission to sabotage the uranium-enrichment facility located near the coastal city of Fuzhou was yet another task given to him and his fellow Aegis agent, Natalie Koroma, along with a warning that time was of the essence and the covert action needed to be carried out as quickly as possible.

The reasons for their employers wanting the facility taken out had not been made clear, at least not with any great deal of specificity. Likewise, the parameters for neutralizing the plant's enrichment abilities had largely been left to the agents to determine. Over the past few years, along with decades of training in preparation for his assignment here on Earth, McAllister had learned two very simple facts about his benefactors: the Aegis tended to be very tight-lipped and left the details of the missions they directed to their onsite agents. Along with Koroma and other agents who had preceded them—Cynthia Foster, Ian Pendleton, Elizabeth Anderson, Ryan Vitali, and Gary Seven—and aided by people like Roberta Lincoln and Rain Robinson who had devoted their lives to the Aegis mission, McAllister knew what was expected of him and that he might not always be given complete information or the "full picture" about what his benefactors were trying to accomplish. It was an odd, occasionally irritating way to do business, he had long ago decided, and one hell of a way to shepherd a planet and its civilization toward a prosperous new age.

Same story, different day.

As for this new problem, the first priority was determining the alien spacecraft's origin. That it had defied even the Beta 7's attempts to identify it was troubling, but that might be due to a simple unfamiliarity with the vessel itself. A proper scan of the ship and its occupants would provide more than enough information for the advanced computer to make a determination, even if that required the machine to contact its remote monitors on the Aegis homeworld. He had at least been able to conduct a scan and send that information to the Beta 7. With luck, the computer would have answers for him by the time he returned to his and Koroma's base of operations on the Isle of Arran in Scotland.

The second problem was in denying anyone else access to these mysterious visitors. That was the more challenging aspect of McAllister's mission, and he had failed it. Now the only thing left for him to do was make a run for it and hope he could elude his pursuers long enough to call for extraction. Once he was back on Arran and his injuries treated, he and Koroma could devise an alternate plan for dealing with the new arrivals, along with the Marines and anyone else who would shortly be taking an active interest in them.

Not so fast, Jonny.

Feeling a wave of dizziness beginning to rush over him, McAllister stumbled and reached toward a nearby tree in an attempt to steady himself. His eyes started to blur, and the forest around him seemed to dance at the edges of his vision. The pain in his side had subsided to a dull, constant ache, and his pulse rushed in his ears. His breaths were coming in short, shallow gasps, and it was becoming more difficult to inhale. Despite his effort, he ended up falling against the massive trunk of the towering pine tree.

I think he got a lung. Damn.

He needed to get out of here, and fast. If the Marines found him, McAllister knew he would have to face tough questions he did not want to answer. His capture would only force Koroma to devote time and effort to rescuing him that might be better spent carrying out another mission of greater importance to the Aegis and, by extension, the people of Earth. Further, there was the problem of the bullet hole in his chest, the bleeding that did not appear to be stopping, and his increasingly labored breathing.

You're in a bad way, Agent. Call for extraction.

Not wanting to ease his right hand's pressure on his wound, McAllister fumbled with his other hand for the left breast pocket of his dark jacket. He tore open the pocket's Velcro flap and reached for his servo. The futuristic device, engineered to resemble and even operate like an ordinary if somewhat outdated fountain pen, was his primary lifeline. He needed to trigger its emergency recall function in case he lost consciousness so that the transport system could find and pull him back to Arran.

McAllister's hand found nothing. The servo was gone.

A check of his other pockets told him that the device was no longer on his person. He must have dropped it back when he was shot. If the servo was discovered by one of the Marines, they might not understand at first what they had found, thinking it to be a simple pen. They might accidentally activate one of its many advanced features, perhaps harming themselves or another innocent bystander. McAllister could not allow that to happen.

Of only slightly less importance was the possibility that the servo might be delivered to someone higher up in the Marines' chain of command; someone who could recognize the device for what it was. Within the governments of the major powers around the world, a select few individuals were aware of the Aegis agents and their mission. These were trusted allies, cultivated over many years to be informants and in some cases partners as Koroma and McAllister carried out their various missions. Some of these people had knowledge of the agents and their activities going back decades, recruited or otherwise befriended by predecessors such as Gary Seven and Roberta Lincoln. What McAllister could not count on was any of those confidants being the ones who came into possession of strange items like his servo.

"Damn it," he said, pushing the words between gritted teeth. He had to go back.

Think, Jonny.

He did not need to attempt finding the servo. There was the emergency burst transmitter, surgically implanted within his right ankle bone. It was encased in a substance that mimicked the properties of human bone so as to be invisible to various types of metal or frequency scanners and trackers. All he had to do was push on the right spot and a short encrypted signal would be sent to the Beta 7, triggering immediate extraction. Once he was home, he could instruct the computer to deactivate or even destroy his wayward servo before it fell into the wrong hands or hurt someone.

So how come my ankle looks so far away?

Sagging against the tree, McAllister allowed himself to slide to the ground, bracing himself with his left hand in an attempt to keep from toppling over. He was not entirely successful, and the sudden movement as he lurched to one side reignited the pain in his chest. The bullet. Where was the bullet? There had been no exit wound, so far as he could tell, which meant the round had lodged itself somewhere inside him. What other organs had it damaged?

His breathing had grown even more difficult, and now his eyelids felt heavy. McAllister pushed himself back up to a sitting position, wincing at the stab of pain beneath his blood-soaked right hand. The new pain forced a sharp inhalation of breath, which he was only half able to complete. Spots danced in his eyes, and for a moment he was certain he would vomit. His vision was narrowing, closing in on him, and all he wanted to do was go to sleep.

Then McAllister felt a hand on his shoulder.

"Jonathan."

It was a deep voice, one McAllister recognized, and enough to jar him back from the haze threatening to swallow him. He jerked his head up, forcing his eyes to focus long enough to see the face of the person who had found him. It was a man, dressed in dark clothing all but identical to his own. His gray-and-black hair was worn in a style that had not changed in all the years McAllister had known him, and which he knew was just long enough to hide the tips of the other man's pointed ears.

"Mestral?"

3

U.S.S. Enterprise
2386

Leaning back in his chair, Picard considered what he had heard. Much of it sounded as though it might have leaped from the pages of fiction, and yet he harbored no doubts that what Taurik was telling him was absolutely true.

"A Vulcan, living in secret on Earth for more than a century before first contact," he said. "I've read stories like this to my son, Commander."

He had spent many a night reading from just such a novel to his son, René Jacques Robert François Picard. Now the boy was devouring all manner of books on his own, but he still sought out this particular title from his father's book shelf. Despite a fascination with the human space program of the late twentieth and twenty-first centuries, Picard preferred reading nonfiction accounts of those eras, and his taste in fiction normally ran to classic literature. The novel, published more than a hundred years ago, presented itself as the real, "secret" first meeting between humans and Vulcans in the twenty-first century, which supposedly occurred decades before the encounter noted in modern history books.

Taurik nodded. "I am aware of the novel to which you refer Captain, and have read it myself." He cocked an eyebrow. "It is a most interesting story, despite its having no basis in reality."

"For the same reason I still read *The War of the Worlds*

and *Sunrise on Zeta Minor*, Commander." Picard offered a gentle smile. "My son is rather taken with those as well. As for this Mestral, you're certain he was on Earth for all that time and never discovered?"

Taurik replied, "As far as I was able to determine, his existence never became known to the world at large. It seems possible, even likely, that he was known to certain elements of the United States government and military, and perhaps similar entities from other global powers. Information on that period is somewhat fragmentary. Most of the information I was allowed to consult came from protected Starfleet archives, including the personal and official logs made by Captain James T. Kirk and Ambassador Spock during their tenure aboard the *Constitution*-class *U.S.S. Enterprise*. They provided detailed accounts of their interactions with Mestral during missions to twentieth-century Earth."

"James Kirk." Picard shook his head at the mention of the name. "You know, rumors persist that the Department of Temporal Investigations was formed as a result of Captain Kirk's various entanglements with time travel."

"I have heard those rumors, sir," said the Vulcan. "You may be interested to know that when I was being debriefed by departmental agents, they neither confirmed nor denied the veracity of such unsubstantiated claims."

Picard could not help a small smile in response to the deadpan comment. "No, I don't suppose they would do such a thing." Leaning forward in his chair, he rested his hands on his desk. "You do raise an interesting point, Commander. I know you were questioned at length about the information you gleaned from the computer of the Raqilan weapon ship, and its impact on possible future events. Does this have anything to do with that?"

"Sir, I am not at liberty to discuss details of what I found in those computer files," replied the engineer. "However, I can tell you that this has nothing to do with the Raqilan or their weapon ship from the future."

Nodding, Picard allowed himself a slight sigh. "Well, I suppose that much, at least, is good to know."

In truth, he had been anticipating a conversation with Taurik since the end of the *Enterprise*'s bizarre encounter with the *Poklori gil dara*, an immense space-based weapon constructed by a race calling themselves the Raqilan. The *Enterprise* had discovered the massive vessel, seemingly abandoned, in interstellar space. Sent from the future to a point in time decades in the past, the ship's crew remained in hibernation after its onboard computer failed to revive them at the proper time. Instead, the craft drifted for decades until it was found by the *Enterprise*. During their investigation of the vessel and its systems, Taurik accessed its main computer and stumbled across what he had only described as "information pertaining to future events." He had not said as much, but it was easy to infer from the Vulcan's refusal to share what he found that Taurik believed the impact to future history was significant. After quarantining and encrypting the data within the *Enterprise*'s main computer, Taurik had notified Starfleet Command and the Department of Temporal Investigations about his discovery.

DTI's original intention was to dispatch a team of agents to the Odyssean Pass for the express purpose of debriefing Taurik, but those plans changed when the *Enterprise* was summoned back to Federation space in order to assist Admirals Akaar and Riker with "the Unsung," a cult of renegade Klingons who had begun causing trouble for both interstellar powers. Never prone to waste time—and hating anyone who made jokes about such things—DTI agents had taken the opportunity to bring Taurik to their headquarters, where he was subjected to extensive periods of questioning that, so far as Picard was told, covered the Raqilan affair in excruciating detail.

"I take it the department is—or was—well aware of this Mestral and his activities on Earth?" asked Picard.

Taurik replied, "They only went into detail with respect to this specific matter, but I gathered from their comments that they were only aware of his presence on Earth due to Captain Kirk's report."

"And these other people you mentioned," said Picard. "These Aegis agents. You're certain that they were working on Earth for an extended period as well?"

Taurik nodded. "The presence of the Aegis was also discovered by Captain Kirk, through a Starfleet-sanctioned temporal incursion to twentieth-century Earth. Interestingly, I was unable to find information about that specific mission in our memory banks."

"I'm not surprised, given the nature of the mission and its obvious risks." Even the records of his own ship and crew's encounters with various temporal phenomena were almost always stored in protected archives within the *Enterprise*'s main computer, with access available only after authorization from himself or Commander Worf. Attempting to retrieve archived logs or reports of another starship's run-in with similar time-related oddities almost always triggered a host of alerts and hand wringing from someone at Starfleet Command and the DTI.

Taurik said, "According to the information I was given, Captain, this group had representatives on Earth beginning in the mid-twentieth century. Their goal seemed to be one of indirect influence on various world affairs, in the hopes of assisting your people through one of the most turbulent periods in Earth's history: the development of nuclear weapons, their rapid proliferation, and eventual widespread use during your Third World War."

"You said indirect influence," replied Picard. "So, they weren't there to prevent any of these events from transpiring?"

"They did prevent certain events from occurring, or ensured that others *did* occur. Most of their actions could be described as course corrections of one sort or another, sir; intended to keep humanity on what might now be looked upon as a predetermined path."

Picard was unsure what to make of that. A group of outsiders, working in the shadows? Surreptitiously guiding the people of Earth toward . . . what, exactly?

"Are you saying they precipitated World War III?"

"It is impossible to know for certain, sir," replied Taurik, "but based on the information we have about the various Aegis operatives and their known actions, I would doubt it. A more accurate conclusion might be that the conflict was inevitable from their point of view, but the actions they took mitigated the severity of its lasting impact and perhaps even set the stage for the events that came later."

Even as he started to respond to the engineer's comments, Picard stopped himself. Was what Taurik described all that different from Starfleet's observance of the Prime Directive? How many primitive societies had he observed? On some occasions, circumstances had required him and his crew to act on behalf of the unknowing civilization. Then there were the rarer instances when he was obliged to stand by and do nothing, even in the face of calamity. Such occurrences haunted him, even as he struggled to remind himself that the Prime Directive—the mandate for Starfleet and the Federation to refrain from becoming involved in a less-advanced society's natural progression—was a laudable goal with noble intentions. Picard had seen firsthand the results of sidestepping or violating the directive. While there were times when it was the right thing to do, there also were the few, indelible occasions when such action had ended in total disaster.

Had Earth actually suffered at the hands of such interference? Or had humans simply chosen their own fate as a consequence of their collective childishness, while the observers were forced to stand by and watch as war engulfed the planet? As horrific as it sounded to him, Picard preferred the latter scenario. At least in that regard, humans had learned their own violent lesson, ultimately emerging from the hell they created to become a mature society and eventual member of a vast interstellar collective, the United Federation of Planets.

That was what he wanted to believe.

Rising from his chair, Picard moved from behind his desk to the replicator set into the ready room's rear bulkhead. After instructing the computer to produce a cup of hot Earl Grey tea, he glanced over his shoulder to Taurik. "Considering the sensitivity of this information, I'm surprised the DTI provided you with such insight. In my experience, that sort of accommodation is unusual, to say the least."

Taurik turned in his seat so that he faced Picard. "Given the somewhat unique nature of my situation, the agents who debriefed me seemed happy to offer this information to facilitate my speaking with you. I have been granted a status of 'provisional liaison' to the DTI and the admiral. However, I was told that time travel or other temporal activities are in no way involved with our current mission. My orders in this regard are to monitor our activities and report anything I feel might have a bearing on the advanced knowledge I possess. As a consequence, Admiral Akaar has also used this as an opportunity to inform me about our current situation, so that I could in turn brief you."

"There's obviously a connection between what you've told me and where we're headed," said Picard. "What is it?"

"I have not yet been fully briefed on that aspect of our mission, sir. Admiral Akaar has given me only the information I need to facilitate this discussion, while assuring me that I will receive additional details as warranted."

Picard did not like the sound of that. "Based on whatever you report to him."

"That is correct, Captain."

Retrieving his tea, Picard did not return to his seat, but instead moved to the narrow viewing port set into the bulkhead behind his desk. From this vantage point, he was afforded a view of the distant stars, distorted though they may be by the subspace field generated by the *Enterprise* as it moved at warp. "Provisional liaison," he said, after a moment. "That sounds like a fancy term for 'errand boy.' I can't say I'm pleased with the notion of Admiral Akaar placing an informant among my crew, Commander." As he was facing the port, Picard was able to see Taurik's reaction thanks to his reflection in the transparasteel barrier. Despite his staid emotional control, the Vulcan engineer still managed to shift in his seat, as though trying to make himself more comfortable.

"I do not believe that is my role, Captain."

Now annoyed, Picard attempted to force back the abrupt feeling as he sipped from his tea. The tactic was not working, and he seemed to have lost his taste for the beverage anyway. Turning from the window, he set the cup and saucer upon his desk.

"Nevertheless, that's the role you've been asked to play. Why did you not report this to me sooner?"

His composed features once more in place, Taurik replied, "Admiral Akaar ordered me not to do so, sir."

Annoyance was now warming toward actual anger as Picard returned to his seat. He reached for one of the padds on his desk, holding it in his right hand while tapping the device's edge against his left palm. Was it a way to occupy his hands while his mind processed what he had heard, or was it an unconscious means of allowing him to ensure his own self-control was firmly in place before he said something he might later regret?

"I don't fault you, Commander. You're following the orders of a superior officer, but rest assured that Admiral Akaar and I will be discussing this at length. That will be all, Mister Taurik."

The engineer rose from his seat, bringing himself to his full height and dropping his hands to his sides. It was not quite the position of attention a fresh-faced Academy cadet might adopt, but still provided a level of formality and respect Picard could appreciate.

"I apologize if I have given offense, Captain, or if my actions communicate a lack of trust. I was merely—"

"That will be *all*, Commander. *Dismissed.*" There was

an edge in his voice that he had not intended, but Picard said nothing as the Vulcan offered a formal nod before pivoting on his heel and marching out of the ready room. Picard waited until the door closed and he was once more alone in his sanctuary before allowing a groan of anger to escape his lips.

"Damn you, Akaar."

That out of his system, he said in a louder voice, "Picard to bridge."

"Worf here, sir," replied his first officer.

"I require an encrypted subspace communications link with Admiral Akaar at Starfleet Command. Priority one." During its initial journey from Earth to the Odyssean Pass months earlier, the *Enterprise* had deployed a series of subspace relay stations at regular intervals. That endeavor continued the longer the starship remained in this region, extending the Federation's communications network farther than had been done in quite some time. It was but one more aspect of Starfleet's renewed commitment to deep-space exploration and the ongoing effort to expand knowledge, and also made it easier to "call home" when circumstances warranted.

There was only the briefest of pauses before the Klingon replied, *"Aye, sir. According to the ship's computer, it is oh-three-forty-eight hours in San Francisco."*

"I did not inquire as to the time, Mister Worf. I want the link established immediately. Make it so."

Picard paused, catching himself. It was not his crew's fault that he was angry at a flag officer hundreds of light-years away from the *Enterprise*. Taking out his irritation on his subordinates was unfair and poor leadership.

Pull yourself together, Captain. Save it for the admiral.

While he waited for the communications request to

be processed and the link established with Earth, Picard retrieved a fresh cup of tea from his replicator and was back in his seat when Worf's voice filtered through the intercom.

"Subspace link established, Captain. Admiral Akaar is ready for you."

"Excellent, Number One. Thank you."

On his desktop computer, Picard watched the Federation seal disappear for a second time, replaced once again by the aged visage of Leonard James Akaar. Despite the early hour, the admiral was wearing his Starfleet uniform and showed no signs of having been roused from slumber. It was an interesting detail, Picard decided.

"Hello, Jean-Luc. I've been expecting you to make contact."

"Obviously." Picard made no attempt to school his tone, instead allowing his festering irritation to lace the single word.

"I take it you've talked with Commander Taurik." There was no humor in the older man's face, which was fine with Picard. He was in no mood for that sort of thing anyway.

"Yes, I've spoken with him, Admiral. Briefly, considering that he appears to have no real information about why he's been placed in his current position. Sir, why did you feel it necessary to take a member of my crew and enlist him as your eyes and ears aboard my ship?"

From the way his eyes narrowed as he listened to the question, it was evident that Akaar was expecting this line of questioning. This only served to heighten Picard's annoyance.

"It was deemed a matter of Starfleet security to keep this information contained to as small a group as possible."

Picard leaned closer to the computer screen. "It was 'deemed'? Admiral, you are the head of Starfleet. Nothing is deemed anything unless *you* authorize it."

"Very well." There was now a hint of irritation in Akaar's voice, as though responding to Picard's own elevated emotions. *"I gave the order, based on recommendations from the Department of Temporal Investigations. You, better than most people, should understand and appreciate how seriously they take any potential contamination of the timeline. That said, I made the decision, and I'm the one who briefed Taurik directly. So, are you questioning my decision or my motives?"*

"I'm questioning both, Admiral." There was no hesitation, no doubt on Picard's part. He wanted his feelings on the matter made clear, without any possible confusion. "I'm questioning why you or anyone else felt the need to act in this manner. Is it a matter of trust or confidence? Are we believed to be a risk to Federation security?"

"Now hold on, Captain. I—"

"No, I most certainly will not hold on, sir!"

The outburst was enough to echo off the ready room walls and sufficient to reduce Akaar to stunned silence. Picard was certain his words had to have been heard by his bridge crew, but he did not care. Instead, he glowered at the admiral and saw the surprise in the elder man's face. He had struck a nerve. So be it.

"After everything this ship and crew have done, after everything *I* have done, this is how you choose to proceed? When Taurik made it known that he had encountered whatever information he saw about the future, he acted immediately and in accordance with all appropriate regulations to contain the situation. I fully supported him in that action. We've done all that can be asked, and more, acting in the best interests of Federation security *and* the safety of my ship and crew. Apparently, that's insufficient, but instead of telling us what more can be done, you choose instead to keep us in the dark and plant an informant in our midst. I won't stand for it, Admiral. Not for a moment."

Now it was Akaar's turn to lean closer to his computer screen. *"Are you countermanding my orders, Captain?"*

"No. Taurik may continue to observe and report whatever he feels appropriate, to you or the Department of Temporal Investigations, but no report will leave this vessel without my authorization. Further, I don't appreciate a member of my crew being placed in a position where they may have to choose whose orders they're going to follow, and without being given the information needed to make a proper decision. Taurik isn't even fully aware of why you've given him this assignment, and now he's trying to navigate the obstacles you've thrown in his path. There may come a time when he sees his loyalties as divided. Should that happen, Admiral, have you authorized him to undermine *my* authority as captain of this ship?"

It was a verbal trap, and Picard knew Akaar recognized it as such, just as he intended. Challenging the authority of any starship commander was a serious matter, and both men knew it. This was particularly true of vessels like the *Enterprise*, which operated far from the comfortable environs of Federation space and whose captains therefore enjoyed great latitude and autonomy in order to respond to any number of situations where waiting for guidance from back home was impractical if not impossible.

Then there was Picard himself. He rarely trumpeted his own record or list of achievements, but the simple fact was that after more than fifty years wearing a captain's rank and with most of those years spent in command of starships, he believed he had damned well earned the consideration the current situation seemed to be lacking. He suspected Akaar knew this, as well, even if the admiral did not like being bullied into admitting as much.

"*All right, Captain,*" he said. "*We'll do it your way, for now, but just so we're clear with each other: this conversation isn't over.*"

Not even bothering to hide his disdain, Picard replied, "And just so we're clear, Admiral: I wasn't asking your permission. If I can't be trusted to command my ship with the best interests of my crew, or Starfleet, or the Federation at heart, then relieve me. Otherwise, let me do my job. I won't stand for half measures."

Akaar bristled at that comment, but did not reply to it. Instead, he said, "*We'll discuss this later. Akaar out.*"

The communication ended before Picard could say anything else, not that anything more was required. He had made his position clear, and the admiral would either accept it, or not. Whatever happened next, Picard was certain of one thing: he and Akaar would settle this matter, and soon—one way or another.

Now, however, Picard had a more immediate concern: Taurik, and the knowledge he possessed not about the future, but rather Earth's past.

4

"Bring us to full stop. Maintain this position."

Rising from his chair, Picard moved around the flight controller and operations manager positions situated at the front of the *Enterprise* bridge's command area so that nothing stood between him and the main viewscreen. The current image, magnified thanks to the screen interpreting data collected by the starship's array of sensors and scanners, showed a pale brown and dull blue world. Even the clouds obscuring portions of the land masses and oceans seemed dreary.

Behind him and just off his right hand, Lieutenant Joanna Faur reported, "Full stop, Captain." The flight controller tapped another set of controls at her console. "Holding position."

"Sensors," said Picard. "Are we alone out here?"

From where he sat at the operations manager's station to Faur's left, Glinn Ravel Dygan replied, "Sensors show no activity in the immediate vicinity, sir. I am detecting indications of interplanetary travel. Seven small vessels with minimal crew complements, each moving at sublight velocities. There are also artificial satellites orbiting the fourth planet, though they're also pretty small and fragile. I would liken them to first-generation space stations placed in orbit around Cardassia Prime, or perhaps even Earth during your late twentieth and early twenty-first centuries." The young Cardassian exchange officer turned in his seat. "Earth's stations of this type were far more robust than those of my people, sir."

Standing at the bridge's primary tactical station behind and to the left of Picard's command chair, Lieutenant Aneta Šmrhová added, "The ships are armed, but their weapons are fairly primitive. Even if they were able to intercept us at this distance, they wouldn't pose a significant threat."

"Nor should we," replied Picard. He was uninterested in any sort of confrontation, but given his lack of knowledge about this star system or its inhabitants, it was prudent to examine and prepare for all possibilities. To that end, he had opted against approaching the system's lone inhabited planet, preferring instead to linger at the solar system's outer boundary while the *Enterprise*'s sensors did their work. This would allow them to conduct a discreet if incomplete surveillance until he was more comfortable with the situation and decided it was safe enough to move closer for a more thorough survey of the planet.

Turning from the viewscreen, he regarded T'Ryssa Chen, who stood next to Dina Elfiki at the science station on his right. "Lieutenant, what do the *official records* say about this system?" As he asked the question, he was unable to keep himself from casting a brief glance to Taurik, who stood silently near the bridge's aft engineering stations. For his part, the Vulcan simply raised his right eyebrow.

"The library computer's file is pretty thin, sir," replied Chen. "According to our records, the unmanned probe that surveyed this region designated this as System 3962 in the Federation stellar cartography database. It was among the first mapped by the probes sent to chart the Odyssean Pass. The system contains eight planets, but none are reported as being inhabited, or even having a Class-M atmosphere."

For the second time, Picard glanced in Taurik's direction. "Isn't that interesting? Lieutenant Elfiki, what do our sensors show about the fourth planet now?"

Tapping a control and studying something on her console, the young science officer replied, "It's definitely Class-M, sir. I estimate a population of approximately thirty million higher-order life-forms on the planet, along with a few hundred on its only natural satellite as well as a dozen or so stations in orbit. However, there are approximately one hundred other, smaller constructs also deployed around the planet that aren't inhabited. Some look to be communications satellite relays, but all of them appear to be equipped with some form of energy weapon."

"An orbital defense network?" asked Commander Worf, from where he sat to the right of Picard's chair.

Elfiki frowned. "Maybe, but some of our scan readings aren't conclusive, sir. There's a high degree of background radiation in various concentrations across the planet that's causing a bit of interference, but it's not anything I can't filter out with a little time." She gestured toward the image of the planet on the viewscreen. "There are numerous unaffected areas down there, such as at higher elevations or along coastal regions, which not coincidentally is where the bulk of the surface life signs are located. However, there's still radiation in the atmosphere. Something major happened here, sir. I'm guessing two hundred fifty to three hundred years ago, give or take a couple of decades." She frowned. "Sir, there was nothing about these radiation levels or possible global conflict or other catastrophe in any of the records I was able to find."

"Mister Taurik," said Picard, though this time he

made a point of not looking in the Vulcan's direction. "Do you have anything to add?" In his peripheral vision, he saw the engineer move away from the engineering station so that he now stood abreast of Worf.

"The planet's indigenous inhabitants call this the Vorlyntal system, and refer to their own world as Sralanya. They identify their species as Eizand."

That was enough to make Worf scowl as he regarded Taurik. Rising from his seat, the first officer glared at the Vulcan. "How do you know this?"

Picard held up a hand. "All in good time, Number One. Commander Taurik, please continue."

He knew that the engineer now possessed at least some further information about the *Enterprise*'s intended destination; he had made a preliminary report to Admiral Akaar following the conversation in his ready room, and presumably had been authorized or briefed with additional details. Taurik had reported as much to Picard following that communication, and while the captain was certain the junior officer would not lie to him, Taurik nevertheless might opt to keep some things to himself unless asked directly. Once again, Picard considered the awkward position into which Taurik had been placed by the head of Starfleet, and once more he sensed irritation welling up within him.

Taurik said, "Almost all of the information collected by the unmanned sensor probes regarding this system was originally entered into official records, but later expunged and reclassified as top secret."

"So you're saying that someone in Starfleet ordered that information pulled from our data banks?" asked Chen.

Shaking his head, Taurik replied, "No. I am saying that this information was pulled from all such records and moved to a classified archive. The intention at the time was to keep it stored in secret until time and circumstances warranted its access. Even then, such authorization could only be granted by the Starfleet commander-in-chief."

"Admiral Akaar," said Worf, before turning to Picard. "Sir?"

Picard replied, "Yes, Number One. Admiral Akaar."

He had considered updating his first officer with the information Taurik had already given him, but instead had decided on prudence, wanting to see how the next steps in this odd mission began to play out. He did not like keeping his people in the dark, about anything, and normally bristled when orders required him to do so. This was particularly true when it came to Worf, or any first officer, so far as Picard was concerned. He believed that the person serving as a starship captain's figurative right hand could only truly function in that role if they possessed as much information as possible at any given time. Under normal circumstances, Picard would already have briefed the commander, but there was still too much that was unknown. If this turned out to be some kind of unsanctioned mission that might cause embarrassment or worse for the Federation, he wanted to insulate his people from any fallout. He did not believe Leonard James Akaar would place him or his crew in such a situation. It had occurred to Picard that the admiral might also be receiving higher direction, and perhaps it was that guidance that was not born of noble intentions. There was nothing about this situation that made Picard comfortable, and he needed more information before he brought Worf or anyone else into the fold.

"I do not understand," said the first officer. "Such an action would suggest the Federation or Starfleet is deliberately concealing information about this planet. That suggests it represents a threat that we wish to keep from being publicly known, or else we have had earlier dealings with its people."

Taurik replied, "I believe it to be the latter, Commander."

"But you are not certain?"

Looking first to Picard, the engineer shook his head. "Admiral Akaar has not yet deemed it appropriate to share that information with me, sir."

Picard noted the shift in the Klingon's body language as he absorbed this response. A subtle glance was enough to communicate that Worf understood the position his captain seemed to occupy, even if he took issue with how he, along with the rest of the bridge crew, was being brought into the loop.

"It seems we're dealing with a matter of extreme delicacy, Number One, and the admiral prefers to take things slowly, at least for now." He turned to Taurik. "However, given the fact that Akaar is not here, I don't know that I like having to wait for information to be parceled out." His patience for these games, whatever their intentions, was wearing thin.

An alert tone sounded from the tactical station, and he looked over to see Lieutenant Šmrhová frowning as she studied whatever was being sent to her console. The security chief tapped several controls before directing her attention to Picard.

"Captain, sensors are picking up three vessels traveling at low warp, on what appears to be an intercept course out from the planet. At their current speed, approximately warp one point eight, they'll be here in less than an hour."

Picard scowled. "They know we're here."

So much for remaining discreet.

Nodding, Šmrhová replied, "Looks that way, sir. Each of the ships is carrying sensor equipment, but well below our capabilities, and they've got energy weapons that are similar to the planet's satellite network. They're also carrying a crude form of nuclear projectiles. Six missiles each. We've got them outgunned, but I wouldn't want us being hit by one of those without our shields."

"Let's have a look at them, Lieutenant."

The image of Sralanya disappeared from the screen, replaced by a trio of ships traveling at warp speed, their velocity well below the threshold of the *Enterprise*'s sensors to locate and examine. Each was rectangular, long and narrow, and Picard observed that the ships were constructed from components fitted together along a spine. One of the ships contained eight segments, while its companions were smaller, comprised of six sections, and a few of the modules differed in size and shape from their counterparts, suggesting that they had been used because matching sections could not be found. The rear two components of each craft were also the anchor points for smaller, narrower cylinders that extended beyond the rear of their respective ships.

To Picard, none of the vessels looked particularly robust, seemingly cobbled together from pieces of other ships, and perhaps even using equipment never intended for space travel. Each possessed a similar neutral gray hull coloring in what to him seemed an obvious attempt to make the ships appear uniform despite the apparent inconsistencies in their construction. Still, in some ways they reminded him of the first low-warp, long-haul interstellar cargo freighters that once connected Earth with its initial handful of colonies in the twenty-second century, though even those vessels had a utilitarian aesthetic he found appealing. These ships, while not unsightly, still affected an air of having been constructed through sheer necessity, using whatever materials could be found.

"They're scanning us, sir," reported Šmrhová. "Nothing obtrusive. Our sensors show it's more like lidar or ranging scanners, to verify our location. They could be targeting us."

Casting a glance over his shoulder to Picard before speaking, Worf asked, "What is the range of their weapons?"

"The missiles don't have warp propulsion, so they're not a threat until the ships get a lot closer. The energy weapons are a different story, but not at this distance."

"We'll maintain our current alert level for the time being," said Picard, not wanting to appear provocative without just cause. Stepping away from the viewscreen, he moved toward his chair. "How many people are aboard those ships, Lieutenant?"

"They have small crews, sir. Less than thirty life-forms each. Most of the interior space is devoted to propulsion, weapons, and especially storage." Šmrhová shrugged. "These might be some kind of long-range cargo vessels that double as patrol ships."

Picard said, "That wouldn't be unusual. After all, Starfleet interplanetary missions in the late twenty-first and early twenty-second centuries performed similar duties." Indeed, the capabilities of the first Starfleet vessels shuttling between Earth and other planets of its own home system were comparable and in some ways less advanced than what they were now seeing. He gestured to the screen. "Do they possess ship-to-ship communications?"

"Looks that way, sir," replied Šmrhová. "But they're not transmitting anything, even back to their homeworld, so it might take some time for the computer to compose an algorithm and a database for the universal translator."

"I believe I can help with that, Lieutenant," said Taurik, and Picard realized the Vulcan had been silent during the last few moments.

"Really?" asked Šmrhová, not even bothering to hide her surprise.

Taurik nodded, stepping closer to the tactical console. "Computer, decrypt and transfer all data from protected file Taurik Three One Delta Five to primary and secondary language memory banks. Voice authorization six eight six epsilon."

A moment later, the feminine voice of the *Enterprise*'s main computer replied, *"Decryption and transfer complete. Eizand linguistic database now installed in all language banks."*

"That's some trick," said Chen, stepping over to the command stations.

Directing his attention to Picard, Taurik replied, "I cannot take credit. This was information sent to me by Admiral Akaar."

"How very thoughtful of him." Picard fought to keep his voice neutral, but could not help the sarcastic remark. He had not been aware of that level of information being imparted by the admiral to Taurik, which meant that Akaar was still exerting influence on his "provisional liaison."

I guess I'll need to have another talk with the commander, and *the admiral.*

Rather than say anything further to Taurik, Picard instead turned back to the viewscreen. "Open a channel."

"Frequency open, sir," reported Šmrhová.

Rising from his chair, Picard pulled at the front of his uniform jacket before announcing for the intercom, "This is Captain Jean-Luc Picard of the *Starship Enterprise*, representing the United Federation of Planets. We've detected the approach of your vessels. We are on a mission of peaceful exploration and are new to this area of space. We welcome the opportunity to meet with you."

When nothing happened after a moment, Šmrhová said, "They're receiving our hail, Captain. Shall I resend the greeting?"

"No," replied Picard. "Let's give them time to absorb all of this." Having participated in numerous first-contact situations over the course of his career, he always tried to wonder what the representatives of the other party were thinking during the opening moments of such a meeting. Fear? Uncertainty? Anticipation or hope? Picard had seen all of those reactions and everything in between, but he still did not consider himself an expert in these situations. There were too many variables, too many unknowns in any first contact with a new species, and that was before adding in the odd dynamic of this perhaps not even being such an encounter. It was obvious that Starfleet and perhaps members of the Federation government possessed knowledge of this system and the Eizand, but to what extent?

I suppose we'll soon find out.

"We're receiving a response, sir," said Šmrhová. "It's on a low-frequency band, but I can make the necessary adjustments. Signal is audio and visual. There's also another communications frequency in operation, but it's not aimed at us. Instead, it's being directed back to the planet, Sralanya, via a string of communications relay stations scattered throughout the solar system."

Looking up from her science station, Elfiki added, "I've been giving those a look, Captain. They're definitely a form of communications network. Almost like an early version of our subspace relays. Even from their present distance away from their planet, they can still relay communications in near-real time. They're maintaining an open frequency with someone back home. It's encrypted, but with enough time I can get past that."

"Very interesting," said Picard. Who might be monitoring the ships and their actions? A senior military or government leader? Both scenarios made sense, but from this distance, the ramifications of such observations appeared minimal.

Nodding in approval at the reports, he nodded toward the viewscreen. "Lieutenant Elfiki, proceed with your decryption efforts. Lieutenant Šmrhová, let's meet the welcoming committee."

The image on the main viewscreen shifted to reveal a thin, pale humanoid dressed in a dark blue garment that to Picard appeared to be a uniform, with silver highlights along its shoulders and in a circular pattern over its right breast. Its skin was a dull white, speckled with raised, dark spots across its face and head, which was bald. A heavy brow, long, thin nose, and a narrow jaw and chin gave the alien a hawklike appearance as it stared at Picard with small, white eyes. The sides of the alien's head were smooth, with only slight bulges beneath the skin that seemed to protect openings that might be for auditory canals. It said nothing for a moment, though its gaze locked on Picard and he felt as though he were being studied or sized up as a potential adversary. Only the alien stood in sharp relief, with the rest of whatever room in which he stood being rendered out of focus, doubtless as a measure to prevent Picard—or anyone else—from gleaning too much in the way of information or clues as to shipboard systems or other protected assets.

"Captain Picard, I am Alonijal, commander of the planetary security vessel Novradir.*"* The voice was a deep baritone, suggesting a male gender. *"On behalf of the people of Sralanya, I order you to remain at your present position. Any attempt to approach our planet will be viewed as an act of aggression."*

Making sure that his hands were visible as his arms hung at his sides, Picard replied, "Commander Alonijal, it is not my intention to approach your planet until or unless invited. As I said before, my crew and I are on a mission of peaceful exploration. It is our desire to make new friends, not enemies."

"And yet you trespass within our space, skulking about under stealth as though confident that we would not see you." The Eizand's eyes narrowed, his gaze remaining fixed on Picard. *"It is a poor way to offer greetings, Captain."*

"Yes, I can certainly understand how you might perceive it that way. We were studying your planet while attempting to determine how best to make formal contact with your leaders, as we certainly don't wish to alarm your people." Picard paused, deciding to offer a small smile. "That you have initiated contact with us does simplify matters a great deal."

Alonijal did not react to that statement, instead looking past Picard as though taking note of the other bridge officers he could see. There was a moment's hesitation as the Eizand studied first Glinn Dygan and then Worf, before returning his attention to Picard.

"You seem to represent a number of different species, Captain. Where did you say you came from?"

Sensing an opportunity, Picard gestured to Chen, who nodded before stepping closer to the viewscreen.

"We represent the United Federation of Planets, Commander. It's an interstellar cooperative of many worlds scattered across our area of the galaxy. We have come together over the course of many years in the interests of fostering mutual peace and support, and we each share the resources and cultures of our individual world with the others. As we continue to explore the galaxy, we always seek to extend the hand of friendship to whoever we might encounter."

"This is Lieutenant Chen," said Picard. "She represents just one of those many worlds." He moved close enough so that he could place a hand on Glinn Dygan's shoulder. "Indeed, my ship is home to beings from nearly thirty different planets. This officer is from a planet called Cardassia Prime." Glancing away from the screen, he gestured to Worf. "My second-in-command represents the Klingon Empire. Both of these officers hail from worlds that once were our enemy, but which are now allies. I, along with a significant number of my crew, hail from another world called Earth."

Any trace of curiosity, let alone warmth, vanished from Alonijal's face. His stare turned glowering, even accusatory, as he regarded Picard.

"Did you say Earth*?"*

Forcing himself not to look away from the viewscreen, Picard fought to make sure his features remained composed. "Yes, that's right."

Without warning, Alonijal's visage disappeared from the viewscreen, replaced with the image of the planet Sralanya and leaving Picard to regard his bridge officers.

"The transmission hasn't been cut, sir," said Šmrhová. "The connection's still active, but they're blocking our seeing or hearing them. I'm also picking up increased chatter on the frequency they're using to stay connected with their homeworld."

"Was it something we said?" asked Chen. "And how do they know about Earth?"

Frowning, Picard glanced to Taurik. "An interesting question." He turned to Šmrhová. "Is there any change in their posture?"

The security chief replied, "They're maintaining course and speed, sir. No signs of weapons activations. Their ships don't have deflector shields, though they are fitted with a form of ablative armor."

Worf said, "That other communication, sir. Alonijal may be requesting or receiving new information or instructions."

"My thoughts exactly, Number One." In and of itself, the action was not unusual, but Picard would have preferred some insight as to what was being discussed. He was about to ask Elfiki about the progress of her decryption efforts when Alonijal's image returned to the viewscreen. Picard noted the Eizand's expression was hard and fixed as he stared outward from his bridge or office or whatever room he currently occupied, the interior of which was once again blurred. His hands, held in front of him during the initial moments of their conversation, were now clasped behind his back.

"I have been in contact with my superiors, and I have been directed to escort you to Sralanya."

Doing his best to keep his voice level, Picard replied, "May I ask for what purpose?"

Alonijal's thin lips tightened and his pale eyes narrowed, as though he were contemplating not answering the question. Instead, he said, *"Our leader wishes to speak with you, directly."*

It was the response he was hoping for, but Picard chose not to allow any reaction to this development. "That's very good news, Commander. I appreciate that this sort of first-contact meeting can be rather stressful, but I assure you that we will proceed as your leader thinks best."

"This is not our first time being contacted by outsiders, Captain." Pausing, Alonijal directed his gaze to something Picard could not see, before facing forward once more. Maintaining his detached, suspicious demeanor, he said, *"Upon our arrival at your location, my ships will maneuver into position to escort you. Any action against any of my vessels will force me to retaliate."*

"I assure you I will take no such action," replied Picard. Then, because he felt the need to establish some boundaries before the Eizand ships arrived, he added, "However, I also will have no choice but to respond to anything I perceive as provocative. Let us both take steps to ensure that no undue actions occur here today, Commander."

There was an obvious bristling at Picard's veiled warning, and Alonijal's only response was curt. *"Agreed,"* he snapped, before vanishing once more from the viewscreen.

"I don't think he likes us very much," said Chen.

Returning to his command chair, Picard released a small grunt. "Apparently not. Commander Worf, your evaluation?"

"It is obvious they do not trust us," replied the Klingon.

"Understandable, given the circumstances." Picard glanced over his shoulder. "Mister Taurik, do you have any additional insights you wish to share?"

Stepping away from the bridge's rear engineering stations, Taurik replied, "Not at this time, sir."

"Perhaps you or Admiral Akaar might see fit to enlighten us as to how these people are aware of Earth's existence. Something tells me that's going to weigh heavily during our meeting with their leader."

The engineer said, "I will make an immediate inquiry to the admiral, sir."

"Grand."

How was it possible that these people had come to know about Earth? Had they encountered one of the survey probes mapping the Odyssean Pass, decades earlier? According to the Starfleet data records, there had been no prior contact with the Eizand, but given Admiral Akaar's cryptic messages and his meeting with Taurik, it was obvious to Picard that there was more here than would ever be found in any official report.

His fingertips making their own random tapping patterns on his chair's armrests, the captain considered the image of Sralanya that once again dominated the viewscreen. So many questions, he decided. Were the answers to be found on this lone, unassuming world?

We'll find out, soon enough.

5

Isle of Arran, Off the Coast of Scotland
March 17, 2031

"It was touch and go there for a while, but I think he'll pull through."

Turning from the fireplace and its welcome, soothing heat, Mestral saw Natalie Koroma descending the wooden stairs that led to the farmhouse's sleeping rooms as well as what passed for its infirmary.

"Is he conscious?" asked Mestral.

Koroma grimaced, running one hand across the top of her head and her shoulder-length black hair as she moved to stand next to him by the fire. "I gave him a pretty strong sedative. He'll likely be out for at least sixteen hours. The rest will do him good."

As she spoke, Mestral heard the fatigue in her voice, which seemed to bring out more of the accent that sometimes laced her speech. To the practiced ear, it was easy to identify her as hailing from the area of West Africa now known as Sierra Leone, though so far as he knew, Koroma had only visited that region, making her the first of her family line in centuries to do so. Her ancestors, like others taken from Earth and other worlds by the Aegis, had spent uncounted generations in preparation for their deployment in service to the mysterious organization and its largely unknown though seemingly benign goals.

"Sleep is an oft-overlooked aspect of the healing process."

"Maybe you can teach him one of those Vulcan healing trances." Koroma smiled. "Better yet, teach me. I could use a nap that lasts about a week." Covering her mouth, she stifled a yawn. "Sorry."

"No apologies are needed. If you wish to retire for a brief rest, I can work with the Beta 7 to obtain information and help us with our next course of action." For the first time, Mestral noted the flecks marking the ebony skin of her right cheek. "Are you all right?" he asked, gesturing to indicate her face.

Reaching up to wipe her cheek, she looked at her fingers and scowled. "McAllister's blood. He lost a lot of it, but the medical computer was able to synthesize enough plasma to stabilize him. It was pretty close, though. If you hadn't found him when you did . . ." She let the sentence fade. Clearing her throat after a moment, she said, "I've done all I can for him here, but the internal damage is still pretty extensive. Even if we weren't out here in the middle of nowhere, we can't really take him anywhere without attracting attention."

"What do you propose?" asked Mestral, his question accented by the crackle of a burning ember from the fireplace.

Koroma shook off another yawn. "At this point, I think the best plan is to send him home. For-real home, I mean." She gestured toward the ceiling, though Mestral was able to infer her true meaning.

"The Aegis homeworld." It occurred to him that he had never heard the mysterious planet even referred to by a proper name. He had inquired about that on rare occasions, going all the way back to his first shared experiences with Gary Seven and Roberta Lincoln in the late 1960s. Although he always was polite during such discussions, the enigmatic Mister Seven had chosen to leave unanswered questions of that sort, right up to the point he left Earth.

Mister Seven. I wonder where you might be, and if you are doing well.

It had been thirty-five years since Gary Seven decided to leave Earth. At the time, he had been approaching the high end of a human's typical life span, though he at least continued to benefit from generations of genetic enhancement. It was likely that he would far outlive any twenty-first-century contemporaries here on Earth, but growing older still came with costs. To that end, Seven had elected in 1996 to depart for a lower-gravity planet that was more forgiving of his aging body. He had left his friend and protégée, Roberta Lincoln, here to "mind the store," as he put it, and the human woman—who did not enjoy the advantages of selective breeding and genetic engineering—had continued the Aegis mission on Earth for many more years before she too had retired. Mestral had witnessed these transitions, up to and including the latest transfer five years ago to Natalie Koroma and Jonathan McAllister.

Indeed, Mestral's first encounter with the Aegis had come more than a decade after his own arrival on Earth. Formerly a member of a Vulcan survey crew sent to study Earth at a point well before it reached the ability to carry out interstellar travel, he and his companions had crashed in the mountains of Pennsylvania in the fall of 1957. They had spent months living and working in secret while attempting to blend in with the local humans until a rescue ship arrived from Vulcan. Fascinated by humans and their largely untapped potential, Mestral had opted to stay on Earth so that he might witness their continued progress and the feats he suspected they one day would accomplish. After he had convinced his surviving companions of his sincere desire to stay on Earth and bear witness to these historic milestones, they had agreed to report him as having died during their ship's crash. In the decades since that incident, Mestral had done his best to keep a low profile, hiding his true identity and origins. Only through random chance—at least, in his estimation—had he come across evidence of advanced beings living and working on Earth, and his life was forever changed by such knowledge.

Two of those advanced beings, Koroma and McAllister, were products of the Aegis's long-term training program. Each was a descendant of humans taken from Earth thousands of years ago and, like Gary Seven, prepared over the course of generations for their assignment on Earth. Here, they continued the mission begun by their predecessor agents, working to assist human civilization in navigating a path that would one day see it evolve into a society ready to join an interstellar community.

As for the unidentified parties who comprised the Aegis, they and their own planet would continue to remain unsolved mysteries. Even if Seven or any of the other agents had deigned to share its name, it was all but useless without access to detailed star charts, and Mestral doubted the world was listed among the Vulcan stellar cartographic information he had taken from the computer banks of his crashed vessel. His other source for comprehensive data had been the Beta 7 and its predecessors, and the advanced computer was certainly unwilling or forbidden to help him in this regard.

"It's the best option for Jonathan in the long run," said Koroma. "They can completely heal his injuries and have him back to us in no time. Maybe by then we'll have some more intel about this ship." Stepping away from the fireplace, she called out, "Computer on."

In response to her instructions, a portion of the stone wall on the room's opposite side lowered into the floor, revealing an advanced computer console consisting of a trio of touch-sensitive interfaces and a quartet of display screens. A large black panel dominated the wall console's upper left corner, displaying a seemingly random pattern of multicolored lines and dots scrolling back and forth across its surface.

"Computer on," replied the Beta 7 in its characteristic feminine voice. In keeping with its sophisticated artificial intelligence software, the computer's tones and speech pattern sounded almost human, though Mestral was still able to detect a hint of mechanized and automated delivery even in the short response. He had been affiliated with Koroma and her predecessors long enough to have seen the computer's previous iterations, and each version was more advanced than its older counterparts. Part of that progress was to give the machines an even greater range of human-sounding speech and delivery in their spoken interactions with the agents they supported.

Holding her hand over her mouth to cover a third yawn, Koroma said, "Report on scan readings provided by Agent 6889. Have you identified the alien ship?"

"Affirmative, Agent 5746," replied the computer using Koroma's own official Aegis designation. *"Vessel is a long-range scout craft. Place of origin: Sralanya, fourth planet of the Vorlyntal star system. Inhabited by a sentient species, the*

Eizand. Technologically advanced. Ship is equipped with rudimentary interstellar propulsion, and interior scans indicate crew hibernation support systems for long-duration travel. Bio-scan readings of ship occupants indicate Eizand physiology. Crew of three. Two dead, one alive."

Accompanying the Beta 7's report was a page of text on one of the console's screens, including what Mestral recognized as coordinates, though like the solar system and planet they represented, the displayed figures were not at all familiar to him.

"I do not believe my people have ever encountered this world or species," he said. "At least, we had not prior to my departure from Vulcan."

Koroma shook her head. "Doesn't ring a bell with me either." She tapped the Beta 7's control console. "But our bosses seem to know who they are. Computer, what do we know about that area of space?"

"The Vorlyntal star system is located within an unexplored region, between territories currently claimed by the Klingon and Romulan Empires. The system is not aligned with any of the major interstellar powers."

Frowning, Koroma looked away from the monitor to regard Mestral. "That's an awfully long way to travel to come here. It would take years, even at low warp speeds, which is why the ship looks to have been equipped with hibernation systems, and we still don't have a reason. Why would they come all this way?"

"Logical choices would include searching for resources," replied Mestral, "or perhaps a planet of similar environmental makeup as their own world in order to establish a colony. They may even be seeking allies; someone to assist them against an enemy."

"If that's the case, then they certainly came to the wrong planet. We're barely able to wander around our own solar system, let alone travel to someone else's."

Mestral was well aware of all of this, having borne witness to the dawn of Earth's "Space Age." Following the 1960s efforts by the United States and the Union of Soviet Socialist Republics to land astronauts on Earth's moon, and after the Space Shuttle missions spanning thirty years as well as the continued semipermanent presence of humans in space stations orbiting the planet, crewed spaceflight to other worlds in the Sol system had been very limited. The first bold steps in that direction had occurred rather recently, in stark contrast to the predictions offered by futurists, fiction writers, and films and television programs that since the early years of the previous century had depicted humanity pushing outward into the cosmos at some point in the "not too distant future."

It had been little more than a decade since the first such missions to the system's other planets had begun, with the *Ares* program concentrating on Earth's nearest neighbor, Mars, while the *U.S.S. Lewis & Clark* had completed the first manned mission to Saturn and back in the early 2020s. The third *Ares* mission was scheduled to be completed in the coming months, with a fourth and fifth mission already in the planning stages for launch within the next three years. Despite these accomplishments, and others that would follow, Earth and humankind were still decades away from being able to launch a truly interstellar exploration initiative. They were confined to their own solar system, and a threat to no one beyond its boundaries.

Stepping closer to the console, Koroma swiped her hand across one of the touch-sensitive interfaces. "Jonathan wasn't able to complete a scan of the ship's computer, so unless we can access it remotely or get back to it, we're out of luck."

Mestral had participated in training for missions of this sort, though the truth was neither Koroma nor McAllister had encountered an alien spacecraft since beginning their assignment. Still, it was not possible to conclude that ships of extraterrestrial original had visited this planet without being detected by the Beta 7 or its predecessor computer. Further, Mestral knew that there were any number of organizations and other groups scattered around the world that were eager to possess such vessels and the technology they might contain.

Including McAllister's servo.

She had not found the device among her colleague's clothing and other items retrieved from his pockets. Was the advanced tool simply lost in the Georgia forest, or in the hands of the American military or one of the government's numerous intelligence agencies? Her attempts to locate it via the Beta 7 were unsuccessful, either because the servo was damaged, disassembled, or somehow shielded against attempts at communication or tracking. The computer would continue its attempts to locate the device, but Koroma figured it was a lost cause.

Setting aside that thought, she returned her attention to the Eizand craft. "Computer, attempt a link to the ship's onboard systems and access to its data storage facilities."

"Stand by."

He expected the computer to take at least a moment or two to complete any connection to the alien spacecraft. Instead, Mestral was surprised when the Beta 7 came back with a response in short order.

"Unable to establish link. The craft has been moved from its previous location."

Koroma exchanged glances with Mestral, though she added a roll of her eyes. "Yeah, that was predictable. So scan for it. They couldn't have gone too far with it this fast." She paused, her eyes narrowing. "Could they? How long was I with Jonathan?"

"Four hours, seventeen minutes, thirty-six seconds," replied Mestral. It was nearly nine o'clock in the morning, local time, but still the middle of the night on the east coast of the United States. Could the American military unit sent to investigate the downed spacecraft have moved the ship to a secure location in such a short amount of time? That seemed unlikely. "Is it possible the vessel has been destroyed?"

Frowning, Koroma replied, "That'd be out of character. We know the American government's been working to find and warehouse any alien technology they can find. Seems odd that they'd pass up a golden opportunity like this. Computer, are you reading any signs of a detonation or other means of destroying the Eizand ship?"

"Negative, Agent 5746."

"Okay," said Koroma, "so it's not where it was, and we can't find it. That means someone from one of those dark corners of the American military or government has a new trick up their sleeve."

Mestral nodded. "Then perhaps it is fortunate we have allies in a few of those corners as well."

6

Fort Benning, Georgia
March 17, 2031

As the elevator continued its descent, Kirsten Heffron quit counting floors once her ears popped.

Unlike those found in just about any other structure requiring such conveyances, the interior of the elevator car was barren of anything that might be useful to a passenger. The control panel to the right of the door lacked a key pad or buttons, but instead featured only a slot for an encoded key card. No other features were necessary, as this elevator existed for a single reason: ferrying riders from the control station on the surface to the underground facility directly below that unassuming structure. There were no other stops, and the car's movements were controlled by computer interfaces at both ends of the shaft. The key card slot along with its counterpart in the operations room of the topside control center was an access control measure, which seemed superfluous to Heffron. If an unauthorized person attempted to use the elevator, guards in the control station would either detain or neutralize them as the situation warranted.

Thankfully, Heffron's key card worked.

She felt the car's descent slowing and drew a deep breath, making sure her first action upon the doors opening would not be to utter a loud, echoing yawn. She had been roused from sleep hours earlier when the alien spacecraft had first been detected; it was a rude interruption to restless sleep to cap off a long work day, and she was beginning to feel the effects of prolonged activity.

You, slowing down? The hell you say.

The elevator arrived at its destination and the doors parted, revealing a concrete corridor. Standing at the threshold was a man dressed in an army major's Class-A uniform. Like her, he also looked a bit worse for wear, which she could understand, as that was the eternal burden of anyone cursed to be her aide.

"Good morning, Director," offered Major Donovan Kincaid, in his normal businesslike manner. A graduate of the United States Military Academy at West Point, Kincaid carried himself with the usual air of self-assurance and bearing one expected from a graduate of that renowned institution. As usual and despite the dark circles beneath his eyes, the man's uniform was the epitome of the required army standard, down to a pair of shoes that were polished like obsidian glass. How was he able to do that, at all hours of the day or night?

Oh, be quiet. You were like that once.

"It's still early, Donny. Let's not get ahead of ourselves." She offered a smile to accentuate the small joke. Stepping from the elevator, she acknowledged with a nod the pair of army noncommissioned officers flanking the entrance, each decked out in tactical gear and armed with M4A3 carbine rifles. "Please tell me coffee has found its way down here to the center of the Earth."

Kincaid's expression warmed the slightest bit. "On the way, Director. Black, I presume?"

"And strong enough to cause heart flutter. I'm guessing it's going to be one of those days." She started walking the length of the corridor, and Kincaid fell into step on her left side. "Anything new?"

"No, Director," replied her aide, his tone once more all business. "The EBE hasn't said a thing since the recovery team brought it in."

Heffron grunted, expecting that. "What about the team who found the ship? The Marines? Are they all right?"

"Doc says he expects them to make a full recovery. All six of them were found unconscious near the ship, and have no memory of what happened. The team leader, Gunnery Sergeant Erika Figueroa, says the last thing she remembers is reaching the spacecraft, and then waking up after being found by the support team we sent in after them. Her people all have similar stories. Something or someone put them down, but without any obvious intent to hurt them. We've seen this kind of thing before."

Yes, we have.

Heffron could not help a quick glance to see her aide's expression of confusion. While her aide's statement was correct, she suspected he was thinking along lines dissimilar to her own. Kincaid was almost certainly wondering about the technology used by these new specimens of EBE or "extraterrestrial biological entity," in the rather turgid vernacular that so characterized nearly any government organization. On the other hand, she was considering whether the Marines being disabled might be in any way connected to the mysterious "agents" she had encountered on rare occasions. Operating in much the same manner as covert operatives working under her own command, these unknown agents had seen fit to insert themselves into various activities conducted by her people over the years. Their identities, sponsor, and true motives remained unknown, but based on their words and deeds, they appeared to be benevolent and even concerned with helping not just the United States but the entire world.

Heffron had first become aware of such individuals thirty-five years ago, while still a young active-duty Marine Corps officer assigned to a clandestine group working from within a classified sublevel deep beneath the Pentagon. Back then she was the aide, working for the group's commanding officer, General Daniel Wheeler. That unit—the one she now oversaw—had since its inception continued the work begun by the shadow organization to which she answered, Majestic 12. Begun in the late 1940s following the crash of an alien spacecraft near Roswell, New Mexico, MJ-12 and a small number of tenant and offshoot units had operated under a simple mandate: protect the United States and the entire world from possible extraterrestrial invasion. Several of the smaller subordinate groups had come and gone over the years, while Majestic itself had remained hidden among the shadows, its existence known to only a small handful of outsiders. Now, at age sixty-three, Heffron commanded one such "subsidiary," answering to a director within MJ-12 who in turn received his orders directly from the president of the United States.

Another pair of army guards in full tactical gear stood at the end of the corridor, flanking a heavy metal door with no knob or handle. A card slot and biometric interface panel set into the wall was the only visible means of gaining entry, and Kincaid gestured to one of the guards to open it. The sentry, an Asian man, nodded without speaking and produced a key card from the pocket of his equipment vest. Heffron heard the sound of metal bolts sliding aside before the reinforced security hatch swung outward.

It had been years since she had last been in this room, but it mostly tracked with her memories of past visits. She would have preferred a location that did not require such a lengthy commute as Washington, D.C., to southwestern Georgia, but Fort Benning was the closest military installation to the crash site that had both work and storage facilities within MJ-12's operational envelope. Even as she entered this room, she knew that elsewhere, but not too far away, scientists and engineers were already working in another subterranean bunker as they examined the alien spacecraft that had been transported well before dawn to Benning via a pair of U.S. Army aerial crane helicopters. Heffron tried to imagine the level of precision flying that maneuver had entailed, and shook her head.

Those pilots need raises.

The room into which she stepped was nothing more than a square of concrete, its walls, floor, and ceiling all painted a featureless gray. A pair of fluorescent lights hung from the ceiling, doing little to alleviate the room's utter dullness. It was the same shade of gray that so characterized far too many rooms, corridors, buildings, ships, and whatever else the military could cast in that color. It was as though the Department of Defense and its ancillary organizations were defied by law from purchasing any other shade of paint. Heffron did note that the array of equipment housed within the room had been kept up to date, with the computer workstations continuing their trend toward smaller, sleeker models. Communications and monitoring equipment arrayed atop a long table on the room's far side also looked more sophisticated than she recalled. As always, the chamber's most prominent feature was the large window set into the far wall, which afforded her a view of still another room that looked all but identical to the one in which Heffron now stood. However, it was the other chamber that was far more interesting to her, thanks to its lone occupant: the extraterrestrial biological entity.

The alien.

Strapped to an upright metal panel that was welded to the floor and featured iron restraints to secure his arms, legs, and head, the male—Heffron had been informed of its apparent gender—was staring straight ahead, toward the window that from his point of view appeared as nothing but a mirror. Approximating the size and general physiology of an adult human male, the alien possessed a white-gray skin covered in dark spots. Even from where she stood looking at him, several feet on the other side of the window, Heffron could see that the dark markings were not ornamental or merely variations in pigmentations. Those areas were raised, as though covering protuberances of bone that lay closer to the surface, like a knuckle or ankle bone. Long, thin fingers extended from his hands, and it took her a moment to notice that what might be the alien's thumbs looked to sprout from the middle of his palms. He possessed no hair, not even eyebrows, and a pronounced brow that dropped down to form an extended, tapered nose that cast the alien's narrow, pale white eyes in shadow. There were no ears to speak of, though Heffron saw raised areas around openings on either side of his head. His jaw line was tapered, though not quite to a point. The alien's clothing was what Heffron knew was the same utilitarian, dark-red single-piece garment he had been wearing at the time of his capture, though she saw that a piece of its left sleeve was missing, likely cut away and removed for analysis by a forensic team. The clothing was also scorched and torn in several places, and Heffron could see where bandages had been applied to abraded or burned skin.

"He hasn't moved or uttered a single thing since he was put in there," said Kincaid. "Hasn't asked for anything to eat or drink, or to go to the bathroom, nothing." The major shrugged. "Hell, if not for the medical team and their initial exam, I wouldn't even know if he did eat, or drink, or go to the bathroom."

Heffron's gaze shifted to the array of monitors placed just below the windowsill. Working with data transmitted to them from a host of sensors set into the walls of the other room, the screens showed various images of the alien and provided insight into such things as his pulse and respiration rate, body temperature, and even indications of the wounds he had suffered in the crash. For humans, biometric readings of this sort would be used to determine whether a person was lying, or under severe physical stress or pain. That functionality had been successfully translated on rare occasions when an extraterrestrial was in the room, but for the moment there was no way to be certain such methods would work on their current guest. All of the present readings, so far as she could tell, indicated the alien was at rest, if not outright unconscious or even comatose, leading her to wonder if he had no real comprehension of his current circumstances, or simply did not care. He had offered no resistance since his capture, though Heffron knew that a team of soldiers with rifles and other means of subduing or neutralizing him was standing just outside the door set into the room's opposite wall, out of earshot but ready with one call on the intercom to charge the room if needed.

Her attention still on the alien, Heffron asked, "What about the ship? Have we learned anything interesting?"

Kincaid replied, "The engineers are really only just getting started, but they've still managed to provide a few interesting bits. They've already identified the weapon used against the planes that intercepted it. Some kind of targeted electromagnetic pulse generator. Basically turned the fighter into a flying rock. It's actually something we've had people working on for a few years, but we're nowhere near anything with this kind of precision. The R&D kids will love getting their hands on this one."

Nodding at the report, Heffron offered a small, knowing grunt. One of the positive aspects of Majestic 12's oversight of captured or recovered alien technology over the years was the resourcefulness demonstrated by the contingent of scientists and engineers, and other specialists from a variety of technological disciplines, that comprised the clandestine agency's research and development division. Reverse engineering such technology would keep those people busy for years if not decades to come. While the list of items they had been able to re-create was small, it was by no means insignificant. She wondered what they might do once they really had a chance to dig into this newly acquired spacecraft and begin extracting the secrets it contained.

"Are we ready in here?" she asked, eyeing the computer workstation and its attending lieutenant.

The young air force officer, whose name tag identified him as "Cushman" and who to Heffron looked all of sixteen years old rather than mid-twenties as she guessed his age, shifted in his seat. "As ready as we can make it, Director. The engineering team that made the first breach of the ship's computer system was able to glean some linguistic data that we fed into our system." He pointed toward the window and the alien in the next room. "According to the preliminary report, they were monitoring our communications and broadcast transmissions and building their own language files. That was a big help. It's still slow going, but we think we have an alphabet and an initial database we can use to get started."

Another of MJ-12's ongoing research and development efforts was attempting to understand and interface with computer and communications equipment found aboard the various recovered craft. While not always successful, these endeavors occasionally provided insight into a ship's point of origin within the cosmos. A larger benefit, at least in Heffron's opinion, was the wealth of information Majestic had acquired with respect to how visitors from other worlds performed their own covert reconnaissance of Earth.

In her mind, this offered deeper, often alarming insight into humanity's vulnerabilities in the face of potential invasion.

This seemed particularly true when it came to the monitoring of electronic traffic. It seemed a common tactic, with extraterrestrials availing themselves of the countless trillions of bits and bytes of information coursing around the world thanks to the internet and satellite communications networks. As Heffron and others saw it, conducting comprehensive studies of the planet long before exposing themselves to risk by attempting a landing, let alone contact with any humans, provided an enormous strategic advantage. She knew of at least a half dozen different instances where data recovered from the onboard computer of an alien craft revealed an extensive catalog of Earth's myriad spoken and written languages, along with processes to facilitate translation into the visitors' native tongues. In one case, a computer record had included a comprehensive assessment of what later proved to be a fictitious language created for characters of a science fiction television series.

"All right," said Heffron. "Let's do this. Fire it up." She waited until Lieutenant Cushman offered a thumbs-up gesture before stepping closer to the window and the small instrument pad set into the wall just below its frame. She pressed one of the buttons and the lights in the other room brightened. Another button controlled the reflection and tint on the window's opposite side, turning it from reflective to transparent. Knowing she was now visible to the alien, Heffron waited for the alien to acknowledge any of these changes, but quickly realized that if she was hoping for an emotional reaction, she might be here a while.

"Hello," she said after pressing another control and activating the intercom system connecting the two rooms. "My name is Director Heffron. We know from a preliminary investigation of your vessel that you've built a computer database to help you learn our languages. Can you understand me?" As she spoke, she hoped her voice sounded more confident to the alien's ears—or whatever he used to detect and decipher sounds—than it did to her own.

The alien said nothing.

"We know that you were traveling with two companions," she continued. "I'm sorry for their deaths, and if you tell us how to properly handle their remains, we will make every effort to do so." She pointed toward him. "We attempted to treat your injuries, but if there's something more, or different, that we can do, we are willing to assist you." Feeling Kincaid's and Cushman's gaze on her, she tapped the button on the small panel that muted the intercom. "There's no sense starting off with strong-arm tactics. May as well see what cooperation gets us." She knew that if passive questioning techniques failed to produce any useful information, Majestic 12 was prepared to employ harsher methods of interrogation. She preferred to avoid such measures, but the situation might well be taken out of her hands, depending on any perceived urgency their current guest represented.

The mobile phone sitting next to Cushman's desk vibrated, and the lieutenant answered it. He said nothing, but Heffron saw him glancing in her direction. At one point, he frowned, reaching for a pen.

"Any idea how to spell that?" he asked, scribbling something Heffron could not read. Then he ended the call with, "Got it, sir. I'll tell her immediately. Thank you." Returning the phone to the desk, he swiveled in his chair.

"That was R and D, Director. Computer forensics techs are having a little more luck. They've found what they think is the ship's navigational database. Star charts, coordinates, that sort of thing, including a record of the vessel's flight." He glanced at his notes. "I have no idea how to say this, but their planet is called . . . Srah lanya? Something like that, in the Vorlyntal system. According to the techs, it's pretty far from here, as in years and years even at faster-than-light speeds." He shrugged. "I've been involved in a few of these sessions, Director, and I've never heard of that one."

Exchanging glances with Kincaid, Heffron returned to the window and reactivated the intercom as she studied the alien. "Does the planet name Srah lanya mean anything to you? The Vorlyntal star system?"

"Sralanya," said the alien, emphasizing the second syllable. "Vorlyntal," he added, in this case accenting the first part of the word. Heffron watched his eyes narrow in obvious suspicion, and she looked once more to the biometric monitors. The mere mention of the name had been enough to elevate his heart rate, if only a slight bit.

"Is that your home planet?" she asked. "That's where you come from? I'm told that it's very far from our world. Why would you travel such a great distance to our planet? Is there something you want or need? Do you believe our people pose a threat to yours?" Heffron forced herself to maintain her composure even when the alien said nothing further, and his bio readings returned to their former levels.

One cool son of a bitch.

"Director," said Kincaid, "you and I both know from experience that there are usually a few reasons why someone from another world might travel so far to look us over. They're curious about us, or they're looking to make friends. Or they want something from our planet, or . . ."

Nodding, Heffron sighed. "Or they want the planet. Why can't they just be looking to take a leak or something before getting back on the highway for someplace more interesting?" She had never been able to accept the idea that in the entire universe, Earth might be the only planet that could make someone go out of their way to come here and have a look around. That belief had only been strengthened during her tenure with Majestic 12 and the group she led. Her firsthand encounters with beings from other worlds, and even those few humans who seemed to have contact with such individuals, had only served to strengthen her convictions in this regard.

Speaking of humans with special friends, this is probably a good time to call one of them.

It had been some time since she had spoken with the two "agents" who had succeeded Roberta Lincoln as representatives of a still-unknown organization that, according to the older blond woman Heffron met in 1996, sought to help guide humanity away from a path of potential self-destruction. Her former commanding officer, General Wheeler, had without qualification trusted Lincoln and her employer, an equally mysterious man named Gary Seven, owing to an encounter with the agents more than a decade before Heffron had even known of Majestic 12's existence. On rare occasions, Seven and Lincoln had provided Wheeler with information or access to technology that was far beyond anything Heffron would have thought possible, usually in service to helping Wheeler and his people accomplish some difficult or seemingly impossible task. While their motives remained unexplained, their actions had earned her trust. Both Seven and Lincoln were gone, having retired or simply moved on to some other concern, and in their place were two younger agents, Natalie Koroma and Jonathan McAllister, for whom their predecessors had vouched. The method of contacting these agents was the same as it had been with Seven and Lincoln: the odd silver pen she kept at close hand nearly every hour of every day.

"Let's take a break," said Heffron after a moment. Pressing the control to return the observation window to its mirrored effect for their guest's benefit, she made sure the intercom was deactivated before turning to Kincaid. "I need to use a phone. Somewhere private."

The major gestured toward the door. "This way, Director."

Heffron let her aide lead her out of the room and back up the corridor they had used to enter the underground complex, guiding her to a secondary passageway that she recalled from memory led to a large control room and a suite of offices. Several of the private workspaces were assigned to officers in charge of the operations here, while a pair of smaller rooms was reserved for visiting personnel like herself. The two offices were furnished in identical fashion, with a desk and chairs, a couch along the far wall, and a computer terminal and an encrypted phone station on the desk.

"I'll be a few minutes," she said to Kincaid as he paused at the threshold to the office and allowed her to walk in alone. "Why don't you find us some of that coffee?"

Nodding, the younger man reached for the doorknob to pull it closed. "I'll take care of it."

She waited until he closed the door, watching him through the narrow window slit set into its metal frame as he wandered away from the office on his way to whatever passed for a kitchen down here. Moving to the desk, she took the opportunity to give the room a surreptitious once-over, searching for any obvious signs of monitoring. It was an old habit, she knew, and in all likelihood a fruitless gesture, as most modern surveillance equipment was so small and nondescript that the chances of spotting such a device without proper scanning equipment was all but impossible. With her back to the door, she made a show of reaching for the encrypted phone's receiver and activating a secure communications line, while her free hand moved inside her jacket and retrieved the unassuming silver fountain pen from an inner pocket.

It had been a source of temptation over the years to have the device disassembled and its functionality studied, but Roberta Lincoln had cautioned her against such action many years ago, warning Heffron that it was just as possible she or someone else might injure themselves while tampering with the "servo," as the blond agent had called it.

As Lincoln had taught her, Heffron pressed the concealed control to activate the servo's communications function. Instead of the telltale beep she expected, she instead heard nothing but a faint metallic click. Frowning, she made a second attempt and received the same results.

"It's just a fountain pen, Director."

Startled by the voice behind her, Heffron whirled to see Major Kincaid standing in the now open doorway. How had he done that without her hearing him?

"What do you want?" she snapped.

The major offered a grim smile. "Answers, Director Heffron." He gestured to the pen in her hand. "We've known about that interesting little device of yours for quite some time now. You've been carrying that replica for months. The real one is in one of our labs, where it's been studied quite thoroughly by our research engineers. We just didn't want anyone knowing we'd done that; not you, and certainly not the people who gave it to you."

Eyeing the pen, Heffron scowled, but said nothing. It was obvious that Kincaid knew at least something about the device that she thought she had kept a well-guarded secret. Instead, she focused on what else her aide had said.

"Who's we?" Her eyes narrowing, she pointed the pen at him. "You're with Majestic? What did they do, send you to spy on me?"

Kincaid smiled. "I've been spying on you since the day I was assigned to you, Director. Majestic's had their eye on you for a while. They've suspected you've been colluding with aliens for some time, but they had no proof." Once more, he indicated the pen in her hand. "Well, almost no proof. We've been waiting for whoever gave it to you to make contact, and now they have, which means it's time for us to put the next phase of our plan into motion."

Sure she would not like the answer, Heffron asked, "And what plan is that?"

"The same as it's always been, Director." The smile faded, and Kincaid's expression turned cold. "Protecting our planet, by any means necessary."

7

U.S.S. Enterprise 2386

Deep and ugly, the scars of war ran rampant across the planet.

Though Picard had witnessed this sort of damage defacing more worlds than he cared to admit, the devastation marring Sralanya's surface was as disturbing as it was extensive. Vast expanses of browns and greens signifying terrain that had not yet been displaced by industrialization were interrupted by huge dark blemishes that pockmarked dozens of areas on the planet's four continents. Standing before the bridge's main viewscreen, he knew that the seemingly random patterns indicated whatever remained of cities and other built-up population centers. How many people had lived in those areas? How many lives had been snuffed out in an instant, wiped from existence by the hellish fury unleashed by weapons of great destruction?

In some ways, the scene before him reminded him of the photographs taken by astronauts trapped aboard space stations orbiting Earth, who had watched helplessly as the first waves of intercontinental ballistic missiles swept across the globe. Those spacefarers, marooned once contact with ground support facilities was lost during the opening days of the Third World War, had borne witness to the apocalypse, documenting the destruction caused by nuclear weapons and the aftermath. Their photos, video logs, and written journals, retrieved decades later, ended up providing a uniquely detached chronicle to the conflict. Did the citizens of Sralanya have similar records of this dark chapter from their own history?

"We've achieved standard orbit, sir," reported Lieutenant Joanna Faur from the conn position. "There seems to be a lot of interest in our arrival."

Picard turned from the screen and began moving back toward his command chair. He had tried and failed to keep his seat during the uneventful transit to the planet, waiting for something more troublesome to happen. Nothing had occurred, which only served to make him more anxious. Was this truly a peace overture, or simply a ruse designed to place the *Enterprise* into some compromising position? At this point, it was hard to say. Aside from a brief, terse exchange upon the arrival of these three vessels before they had moved into a triangular formation with the *Enterprise* at its center, there had been no communications with Alonijal during the journey, which had occurred at low warp and while holding to a strict, uncompromising course in to the planet. This suggested to Picard that the Eizand vessels might have difficulty with offensive or defensive actions while travelling at warp. If true, that was a helpful bit of information that might come in handy later on, should the current situation take an unpleasant turn.

"Lieutenant Šmrhová?" he asked, standing before his seat. "What are your sensors showing?"

The security chief replied, "Several of the closer satellites in the global network have definitely taken a liking to us, sir. Scans show that they tracked our movements all the way in. I'm not picking up any signs of targeting scanners or weapons being activated."

Having occupied himself with the secondary tactical console during the brief journey to the planet, Worf added, "Like their vessels, the satellites do not have any sort of deflector shields, though they are fitted with a form of armored plating that will not be effective against our weapons."

"What about the energy weapons they carry?" asked Picard.

Šmrhová replied, "From the scans, they're a form of targeted electromagnetic pulse generator, sir. Basically, whatever they hit loses power, at least temporarily. If they hit us with our shields up, we'd likely experience a power drain, and concentrated fire might well be able to overload our shield generators, but as Commander Worf said, they're no match for our weapons."

"Let's hope we don't have to test one another's capabilities. We're not looking for a fight after all." Turning back to the viewscreen, he gestured toward the image of the planet. "Lieutenant Elfiki, what can you tell us about the devastation? How long ago do you believe this happened?"

Straightening her posture from where she stood behind her console on the bridge's starboard side and facing Picard, Elfiki said, "Based on the residual radiation levels and other atmospheric and environmental conditions, I'd say somewhere around three hundred years ago, sir, give or take a decade or two. Major cities seemed to be the primary targets and thus were hardest hit. Judging from impact areas, some of the larger cities were struck by multiple weapons that likely left few if any survivors. Then there's the fallout that would've been carried by the wind or water to adjacent regions. Low-lying regions fared a lot worse, but very few areas of the planet escaped completely unscathed."

"Is there any way to determine the number of casualties?" asked Chen.

"I can only guess, based on the apparent size of the various population centers and their accompanying sprawl, and then add a percentage based on what we know about the aftereffects of such weapons." Elfiki's expression fell. "We could be talking more than a billion people lost, and that's probably a conservative estimate."

"It's unbelievable," said Chen. "And only a fraction of that number left to fight for simple survival in the aftermath of global calamity." She shook her head. "I've read about the nuclear wars on Earth, Vulcan, and other planets, and I've always wondered whether those who died in the initial attacks were the lucky ones. I mean, at least they were spared from whatever came later."

Picard had already entertained similar thoughts. Despite the magnitude of loss here, it saddened him to think that it still paled in comparison to the wanton, pervasive destruction he had witnessed with his own eyes. Sixty-three billion lives had been snuffed out by the Borg during their last—and final—invasion. Billions more had been left with no world to call home, forced to relocate to planets that had escaped obliteration. Nearly half of Starfleet had been destroyed or suffered damage repelling the invasion. The Borg had been stopped, and the threat they represented to the entire galaxy was forever quashed, but the costs of that victory were tremendous, and ongoing. Even now, more than five years later, the Federation and its allies continued to address the aftermath of that conflict. It would take many more years before those wounds faded, but Picard knew they would never truly heal.

Such was also true for the people of Sralanya. Three

centuries after whatever war had marred their world, the descendants of those original survivors lived. The obvious visual evidence was that they had found the strength to push past the darkness of those early years in the wake of utter devastation and begin what surely would have been a long, difficult rebuilding process. Perhaps pieces of this fragmented society had even found ways to thrive in the new world they were forced to create, but Picard knew they would never escape the tragic legacy they had inherited.

"Current conditions?" he asked.

Elfiki replied, "Sensors show twenty-six areas with large population concentrations, sir. Definitely cities of a sort, but not nearly as expansive in size or density, mostly along what are now the coastlines and well away from any of the larger areas of destruction or contamination. Based on the readings, none of these buildings are more than a couple of centuries old, and most are much newer. There are also other areas of the planet that might be massive excavation efforts, consistent with extensive mining and drilling for various natural resources. Scans of those areas show trace elements of a number of metals and minerals and large subterranean pockets from which they likely extracted fossil fuels. Coal, petroleum, natural gas, that sort of thing, but the planet's reserves of such materials are pretty depleted, sir. The modern cities are dependent on solar and geothermal energy production, and a couple employ nuclear reactors."

"Commander Taurik," said Picard, without turning from the screen, "I don't suppose Admiral Akaar has offered any further information on this topic?" He knew the engineer had not been in contact with the admiral since the arrival of Alonijal's ships, but Picard had decided this was a good test to see if the commander might be withholding information and parsing it out only when prompted. It still galled him to think one of his officers might behave in such a manner, and he forced himself to remember the difficult position into which Akaar had placed Taurik. Pondering that notion only served to stoke Picard's irritation, but he pushed aside such feelings.

Taurik replied, "No, Captain. The admiral offered no specific information regarding the planet's population prior to . . . whatever transpired here."

Despite his attempt to maintain his bearing, the halt in the engineer's response was still noticeable. Picard could not believe for a moment that Taurik might be lying. Was it uncertainty? Discomfort at the role he was required to play? For the moment, there was no way to know.

"Captain," said Šmrhová, "we're receiving an incoming message from the planet's surface. It's being transmitted from within one of the larger cities."

Chen added, "Here we go."

"Indeed." Picard straightened his uniform jacket, squaring himself before the main viewer. "On-screen, Lieutenant."

Uncertain what to expect, he was pleasantly surprised to see what he believed was an Eizand female, standing before a large window that afforded a view of a cityscape. The image was clear enough that he was able to make out the hodgepodge collection of buildings and other structures, none of which seemed to harbor any distinct architectural features but instead looked rather plain and utilitarian. Beyond the city lay mountains and clear, inviting blue sky. As for the Eizand, she stood tall and regal, wearing a striking teal-green dress or robe highlighted with an intricate gold pattern. The garment's darker color and ornamentation accented the female's pale, hairless skin. She raised her hands in apparent greeting, and Picard saw that the long, thin phalanges extending from her palms were each adorned with several gold rings.

"I am Hilonu, presider of the Tevent Coalition, the largest city-state on the plant of Sralanya. It therefore falls to me to welcome you to our world. You are Captain Picard, I presume?"

Trying not to dwell too much on what to his ears sounded like an odd introduction despite the Eizand's gentle voice, Picard replied, "Yes, Presider Hilonu. I bring you greetings on behalf of the United Federation of Planets. We are new to this region of space, on a mission of exploration. It's my great honor to meet you, and I hope we can establish a peaceful dialogue."

Her gaze fixed on Picard, Hilonu said, *"Peaceful exploration, and yet your massive vessel bristles with weapons capable of raining destruction down upon our planet."* Before Picard could respond to that, she added, *"Of course, I cannot imagine anyone with such intentions wasting time with pleasantries."*

For the first time, her expression softened, and she allowed her eyes to shift from him to the rest of the bridge that was visible over the connection. *"Commander Alonijal was correct, in that you seem to represent a multitude of species and worlds. I hope you will understand, Captain, that this is a great deal to absorb all at once."*

"I understand completely, Presider." Buoyed by the opening Hilonu seemed to have provided, Picard said, "Commander Alonijal did share with me that we are not the first visitors from other worlds that you have encountered. That's actually rather a relief for me, as it does make this process somewhat easier. Whenever we make first contact with another species, it is customary for the highest-ranking individual to request an audience with the leader or leaders of that society. In this case, I am that individual, and it would be my privilege to speak with you in person, should you be willing to do so."

Once more, the Eizand's expression hardened. *"And if I decline such a request?"*

"Then we shall leave your space as peacefully as we came, and never return, at least until such time as you reach out to us, and I will regret the opportunity lost this day."

In all his years as a Starfleet captain, Picard had represented the Federation during first contact with dozens of new worlds and civilizations. Only a handful of those had refused the offer to open a dialogue, and most of those eventually had sought out the Federation following that initial meeting. On each of those occasions where the leader of a people had rejected an offer to meet, Picard felt disappointment, as though he had failed to carry out this most important responsibility entrusted to him. On the other hand, there also was value in demonstrating to the newly contacted people and their leader that Starfleet and the Federation could be trusted, even if it meant holding to his word that he would leave if asked. It was far less satisfying, though in his mind no less important.

"Very well, Captain," said Hilonu after a moment. *"I will grant your request. Talking with you should prove most illuminating."* She gestured toward Picard. *"And please, if you would be so kind as to bring along members of your*

crew who represent other worlds and cultures, that would be most satisfactory."

Something about her responses still felt off to Picard. There was no curiosity or wonder in Hilonu's voice or mannerisms, but neither was she treating this dialogue as a common occurrence. There was a trace of something else in the way she spoke. Not just wariness or even distrust, which he could understand and appreciate, but also a hint of . . . resentment? That seemed illogical, but very little about this entire affair made sense. As Picard saw it, the only way to get a better handle on the situation was to take charge as best he could, and extract answers from anything and any place he could find, using any means at his disposal.

"Excellent. I look forward to meeting you, Presider."

After the conversation ended, while both Elfiki and Šmrhová verified the location provided by Hilonu as the designated meeting place, Picard turned to Chen.

"What do you make of that, Lieutenant?"

The young contact specialist replied, "There's definitely more below the surface with her than she's letting on, sir. I can't put my finger on it, but something's up."

Pleased to have his gut instinct validated even in some small way, Picard nodded. "My thoughts exactly. You'll accompany me to the surface, along with Lieutenant Elfiki and Glinn Dygan. I think that should provide a bit of diversity for Presider Hilonu."

"Captain," said Worf, stepping around the secondary tactical console, "I would prefer to beam down first with a security detail and ensure the meeting place is secure."

Picard replied, "That might be misinterpreted as a lack of trust, Number One. I'm afraid I'm going to exercise captain's prerogative this time." Before his first officer could retort, he held up his hand and offered a small smile. "However, a two-person security detail won't go unnoticed or unappreciated."

His posture stiffening, and despite his obvious reticence at his captain pulling rank, Worf said, "Aye, sir. I will see to the away team preparations."

Stepping away from the engineering stations and approaching the command area, Taurik said, "Captain, I request permission to accompany you to the surface."

"I appreciate the offer, Commander, but I don't see the need for an engineer on this occasion." Picard knew why the Vulcan was asking, and he was hoping Taurik might understand and respect his subtle hint.

His hopes were misplaced.

"Sir, in light of my . . . additional duties, I think it would be prudent for me to join you."

Feeling his irritation with Taurik and his entire situation beginning to return, Picard asked, "Are you questioning my orders, Commander?"

The Vulcan replied, "No, sir. With respect, I was attempting to point out that my presence on the away team might provide me with an opportunity to gather more information, which I could then forward to Admiral Akaar. I believe it is what he would want, sir."

Before he could give them conscious thought, before he could do anything to mitigate or even preempt his response, the words were out of Picard's mouth. "I'm not interested in what Admiral Akaar wants in this instance, Commander." He made no attempt to soften his tone as he glared at the engineer. "Further, I will not have my decisions questioned by a subordinate on the bridge of my ship. You are relieved of duty, Mister Taurik, and confined to quarters until further notice." Then, even though it was unnecessary, and knowing he would regret it, he added, "Once there, you are free to apprise Admiral Akaar of your change in status."

He could hear and see the reactions to his abrupt directive from everyone on the bridge. Even Worf, often as stoic and unreadable as any Vulcan, reacted with widened eyes. He opened his mouth as if to say something, but stopped himself. Instead, he directed his own attention to Taurik, who for his part had weathered Picard's dressing-down in his usual composed manner. Not even an eyebrow raised in reaction to the orders he had just received.

"Understood, Captain."

Without another word or furtive glances directed to any of the other bridge officers, Taurik turned and made his way to the starboard turbolift, disappearing into the car as the doors closed behind him. Picard waited until he was gone before turning back to the viewscreen, which once more displayed an image of the planet Sralanya. His anger—some if not most of it unjustified and directed at the wrong person, he knew—had already begun to ebb. He drew a deep, calming breath and felt his emotions coming back under his control.

Damn it.

Only after another moment did he sense Worf moving to stand beside him.

"Is there anything I can do for you, Captain?" The unspoken addendum to that question may as well have been broadcast over the ship's intercom.

Waiting until he had taken and exhaled another calming breath, Picard replied, "No, Commander. I will deal with that matter at a more appropriate time, but for now we have other priorities."

He tried, and failed, to push Taurik and his annoyance with Admiral Akaar from his mind. Instead, they lingered, bleeding into his other thoughts as he considered what he was about to do. Perhaps the Vulcan would be useful during the upcoming meeting with Hilonu, but there were still too many unknowns regarding him, Akaar, and whatever it was about this world that had not yet been revealed.

On the screen, the planet and its secrets beckoned.

8

Classified Location
March 21, 2031

Though it had no windows, the room was comfortable enough. It had an actual bed with a decent mattress and warm blankets, and the floor was carpeted. There was a dining table and chairs, and a sofa and recliner were positioned before an entertainment system. A case of bookshelves on one wall afforded her a decent selection of books and recent periodicals. She even had her own private bathroom. In many ways, her accommodation, the sort normally reserved for high-value individuals placed in protective custody, was better than a good number of the roadside hotels and motels she had used over the years.

It was still a prison.

Sitting at the table, Kirsten Heffron sipped the coffee that, along with her breakfast, had been made to her precise specifications, as the room possessed no kitchen facilities. In a fit of immaturity and rebellion as she entered her fourth full day of captivity, she had requested in excruciating detail how she wanted her meal prepared, including the ten ingredients she had specified for her omelet as well as the temperature of the steak that was to accompany it. She asked for grits instead of oatmeal, grapefruit juice rather than orange, as well as the bread she wanted for her toast—along with whipped butter.

Every parameter of her breakfast order was fulfilled to

the letter, and Heffron figured all she had accomplished was to elevate the misery of at least one poor kid with no stripes and the bad luck to be assigned to this site's mess hall. Her original plan was to not even bother eating the meal, but Heffron could not help succumbing to its pleasant aroma. She doubted her hosts would lace her food with any illicit substances. They had it in their power to subdue her at any time.

Besides, the damned steak was delicious.

The sound of the door unlocking caused Heffron to shift in her seat, and she saw the door swinging outward. She caught a fleeting glimpse of an air force sergeant in tactical dress, complete with rifle, standing on the opposite side of the corridor before another figure blocked her view. Her jaw tightened as she recognized Major Donovan Kincaid entering her room. The man had dispensed with his army officer's uniform and now wore a tailored if unremarkable charcoal-gray business suit with matching silk tie over a white dress shirt. Heffron could not help noticing that his shoes were still well polished.

"Major Kincaid," she said, raising her coffee mug in greeting.

Smiling, the man replied, "I'm afraid that was a cover identity, Director. My real name is Gerald Markham. I'm with Majestic's operations division."

That made sense, Heffron conceded. Even within MJ-12's very tightly maintained security envelope, the operations division was a maze of compartmented secrets all its own. To the best of her knowledge, she had never before met anyone affiliated with that section of the clandestine organization.

Probably the whole point.

"Did you forget I was in here?" she asked. When

Kincaid—Markham—moved to take a seat at the table, she waited until he was situated before adding, "Make yourself at home."

Markham chose to ignore the remark. "I hope you're being treated well."

"It's not the Waldorf, but I've stayed in worse. When's checkout again?"

That prompted a small smile as Markham leaned back in his seat and crossed his legs. Resting his left forearm on the table, he began a slow, rhythmic tapping with his forefinger on its polished surface. He said nothing for several moments, but instead only stared at her in silence. It was an old trick, one Heffron had used during more than one interrogation or other conversation where she wanted to make the other party nervous or uncertain.

"Is this going to take a while?" she asked. "There's a movie I want to watch." She knew she should have just said nothing and quietly returned his stare. From experience, she knew that once the subject of the interrogation began talking, it was a short road from there to getting them to confess to anything and everything. It bothered her that she had given to Markham anything he might later try to use against her, but the simple truth was that she was already bored of their conversation, brief as it had been, and wanted to kick things into a higher gear.

Let's get on with this, already.

For his part, Markham seemed to agree. "Before this goes very far, Director, I want you to know that I do like and respect you, despite my duties requiring me to deceive you. Further, you're very well respected within our organization. I hope you know and believe that."

Heffron waved to indicate the room around them.

"So, this is the deluxe treatment for high rollers, then? I would've thought my rewards points would get me something a little fancier. Oh, and by the way? Don't think I didn't notice the lack of minibar. Where are we, anyway? I don't recall seeing that little tidbit on the brochure."

From the moment she awakened from her drug-induced slumber and found herself in her new accommodations, she guessed she had been remanded to a secure yet unofficial holding facility. Otherwise known as "black sites," numerous such installations of varying sizes and functions were operated around the world by the governments of the United States and other major powers. A few were located within the borders of U.S. territory, while many more were situated outside those boundaries, both literally and figuratively. There was nothing about this room, which so far was all she had seen of this particular complex, to identify her location. Being sent to such a facility usually meant that the one being incarcerated for all intents and purposes ceased to exist. Heffron had visited a few such prisons and authorized the transfer of detainees—human and otherwise—to them on more than one occasion. She knew how this process worked.

You are in one very deep, dark hole, Director.

Again, Markham smiled at the comments. "I've always liked your sense of humor, even when it was misplaced or otherwise inappropriate. I can't tell you how many times I was forced to hold back laughing when you said something that got under the skin of a superior. You never showed any fear or even the slightest concern for retribution. I admire that."

"You could've just sent me an email," she replied. "You know, instead of going to all this trouble."

"Unfortunately, we've arrived at something of a problem." Markham sat up straight in his chair, adjusting himself so that he now faced her directly. His other arm came to rest atop the dining table, and he clasped his hands in front of him. "Simply put, there are those within the organization who are concerned that you've been in contact with individuals not of this world."

Heffron eyed him. "I believe the term used when you took me into custody was 'colluding.' Did I misremember that? I sometimes forget the details when I'm accused of treason."

His tone now taking on an edge, Markham replied, "No one's leveled any formal accusations, Director. Not yet."

Ignoring the veiled threat, Heffron took a deliberate sip of her coffee. "You've had me here for four days. Is there a backlog of suspected traitors and other threats to national security that you're still processing?"

"We've been busy," snapped Markham, and Heffron forced herself not to show any reaction to the minor lapse in bearing. It was enough that she was finding a way to irritate him. That might be useful at some point.

Instead, she said, "The alien and his spacecraft. I trust they're well?"

"The alien has been remanded to another site, where he's undergoing a battery of tests and questioning." As though anticipating her next response, Markham held up a hand. "Don't worry, he's being treated in humane fashion, at least for now, in keeping with your established preferences for coddling those who threaten our way of life."

Heffron set down her coffee cup. "So, you've concluded he's a threat?"

"By himself?" Markham shook his head. "No. From what we've been able to learn, he's just a cog in a much larger machine, who doesn't even believe what he's been sent to do is wrong."

Despite her attempts to appear aloof, Heffron could not help asking, "And what might that be?"

The finger tapping began again as Markham paused, as though considering the merits and detriments of sharing information with her. Heffron knew that he likely was wondering if she might ever see the outside of this facility.

It's not a bad question, you know.

Markham said, "According to the answers he gave during a more comprehensive period of questioning than when you last saw him, his name is Brinalri, and he represents a race who call themselves the Eizand. As previously reported, our engineers working with the ship and its navigational charts have verified that he and his companions came from a planet called Sralanya, in the Vorlyntal star system. It's a rather unimaginable distance from here, but their ship was equipped with a form of faster-than-light propulsion that we quite honestly don't understand, along with systems that enabled the crew to sleep during what was still a lengthy journey."

"So, what brings them here?" asked Heffron. Her mind was already racing ahead to one of the usual possibilities, attempting to marry one to Markham's previous remarks about the alien, Brinalri. "Wait, let me guess. They like our planet."

"They like our planet very much, apparently. In fact, they like it so much that they want to relocate their entire civilization here. According to Brinalri, their own planet is dying, although we're still talking centuries before it can no longer sustain life, but they're apparently not waiting around for the situation to become dire. The Eizand dispatched a number of ships similar to the one that visited us, to search for suitable planets that might act as a second home for their people, and Earth is apparently on their list of ideal candidates. The fact that someone's already living here doesn't seem to raise much concern."

Heffron considered the implications of that statement. "You think they'd invade Earth, wipe us out, and move in?" It was an interesting, if frightening, proposition, but one that did not bear the weight of intense scrutiny. "This isn't a movie, Markham. There's a whole universe out there, and we both know there are other planets that support life. How can Earth be the only planet capable of sustaining these people? It seems ridiculous."

"It has something to do with the particular combination of atmospheric and other environmental factors," replied Markham, "along with the variety of natural resources, on Earth as well as the other planets of our solar system. Apparently, we're a rather appealing sort of top-shelf interstellar buffet or something."

"That doesn't explain what they plan to do if they decide Earth is the right planet for them." Heffron leaned forward. "Are we talking about an invasion?"

Drawing a deep breath, Markham replied, "We don't know. Brinalri doesn't seem to know, at least from the answers he gave us, and there's nothing in his ship's computer to indicate anything, one way or another. In fact, according to the latest reports from our engineering teams, they didn't even have a chance to dispatch any sort of message back to their own planet before they crashed here. There's been no communication back home. So far as we can tell, we don't believe Brinalri's people even know where he is."

"Does anybody besides me think we may be jumping to conclusions, here, Mister Markham?" Before the Majestic agent could respond, Heffron held up her hand. "Look, I get the need for caution, and maybe even a little paranoia. I've spent the bulk of my adult life in a job that preaches that sort of thing, remember? But there's a time for that, and a time for restraint. This alien doesn't pose a threat right now, so we should be taking the time to understand as much of his technology as possible. Maybe find a way to communicate with his home planet. Who knows? This could be an opportunity to extend a hand in friendship."

"Have you always been this naive?" asked Markham. "Or has your mind been corrupted through years of dealing with others not of this planet?"

For the first time, Heffron allowed herself a small smile. "So, we've circled back around to that?" She shrugged. "Fine. Ask your questions, Mister Markham."

The agent leaned forward, staring at her. "Who are you working for?"

"The same people you do."

"Where are your loyalties?"

"My country. This planet. I also like my cat, except when he's throwing up on my carpet instead of the tile that's two feet away."

Reaching into his jacket, Markham pulled out what Heffron recognized as a silver fountain pen. Hers, she guessed. The servo, given to her years ago by Roberta Lincoln.

"Don't worry," he said. "It's just the shell. The innards are still safe in one of our research labs. A fascinating device, really. The level of microminiaturization is extraordinary. If we can ever figure out how it works, it'll be another technological leap like the others we've enjoyed thanks to these periodic visits from other worlds. Interestingly, one of its components activated, just a few days ago. Indeed, it occurred the very night we recovered the Eizand craft. The engineers tell me it was the pen's communications device, as though its owners were trying to contact you. I find that a rather interesting coincidence, all things considered."

It occurred to Heffron that since Markham had dropped his Donovan Kincaid facade, his speech and word selection had become much more articulate, more so than while playing his assumed identity. He comported himself just like the other senior-level Majestic 12 personnel she had encountered over the years. Why had she not noticed that before? Was it part of their training, or was MJ-12 just in the habit of recruiting annoying people into their ranks?

Markham held up the pen. "Who does this belong to? Who gave it to you?"

Having had a few days to contemplate her answers to such questions, Heffron had decided that the truth would be the wisest course. She at first worried that anything she shared might endanger the people who had entrusted her with the servo, but after further thought concluded they may well have anticipated such an eventuality. After decades spent living and working in secret, they would have contingency plans for discovery that would include the risk of exposure either through direct contact or via someone with whom they had a relationship.

"The people who gave that to me are part of a private organization that has a vested interest in seeing us avoid various pitfalls, both ones we've already navigated and ones that might present problems in the future. I guess you could say they're activists, of a sort."

As she expected, Markham was unable to suppress a fleeting expression of surprise in response to her forthright answer. He blinked a couple of times and even swallowed as though dealing with a lump in his throat.

"That's rather . . . candid," he said. "Who are they?"

"They'd prefer their identities be kept secret. To be honest, I don't even know the real names of everyone involved or where they are." She had some information, but very little in the way of specifics. Knowing how this conversation was going to play out over the next few minutes—and mindful that in this case truth really was stranger than fiction—Heffron was choosing to parse her answers in the hopes of not overwhelming her host, or causing him to veer too far away from believing her. In addition to not really needing to worry about the agents who had seen fit to include her in their small circle of trusted friends, Heffron held no desire for any interviews with Markham to deteriorate to something unpleasant.

Shifting in his seat, Markham was trying to present himself as someone who already had the answers to the questions he was posing. Heffron knew better, but said nothing. It was obvious he was trying to determine whether she was being cooperative, or playing some kind of game with him.

"I know how this works," she said. "We both know you're being polite right now, and that we have methods you can use to get me to answer any question you ask. Setting aside the fact that I don't appreciate being played, what with your whole 'Major Kincaid' bit, I appreciate that you've opted to keep things civil to this point. That's why I'm attempting to work with you here. The people who gave me that pen have representatives here, on Earth. Human representatives. Not aliens in disguise or people brainwashed for some nefarious purpose. *Humans*, who honestly want to see us not destroy ourselves through our own stupidity. I've dealt with them enough to know they're on the level. They've even helped us a few times, behind the scenes. I'm betting they've done a lot more I don't even know about."

"How long have they been here?" asked Markham. His attempts at appearing detached had failed. Despite his efforts, he was fascinated by what she was telling him.

"Since the 1950s. Not the same humans, of course, but somebody from the group they represent has been here, keeping an eye on things."

Markham set the pen down on the table, and for the third time began tapping a finger. "And in all that time, what exactly have they done to help us?"

"They've prevented a world war on a couple of occasions." In broad strokes, working from the limited information provided to her by Roberta Lincoln and her successors, Heffron recounted a few of the higher profile endeavors in which the covert agents had taken part. "It might've been all over for us, way back in 1968, if not for them. Remember the rocket that blew up in the atmosphere? It was really a top-secret nuclear weapons platform that malfunctioned and fell back to Earth. If it had detonated over Russia, they would've retaliated against us, and that would've been all she wrote."

"You're saying these agents prevented that from happening?"

Heffron nodded. "That, and they did so in a way that got everybody on all sides of the table to reconsider the risks of deploying such weapons." The practice had not been eliminated altogether, but the United States and Russia had at least curtailed their plans for establishing a "nuclear umbrella" around the planet. As years progressed and relations between the two nations thawed—interrupted on occasion by brief bouts of regression back to the older ways of thinking and posturing—the need for ever-increasing nuclear arsenals had begun to fade. Both powers still possessed the means of obliterating the planet several times over, but there was an order to things. At least, insomuch as stability could be given to a situation born of chaos and, arguably, insanity.

"Assuming I believe any of this," said Markham after a moment, "what would be their motivation? Why do that, while wars rage across the planet? How many conflicts have we had between 1968 and today?"

"Too many." Born the year the incident with the rocket had taken place, Heffron had never known her father, who was killed in Vietnam the following year. An older brother had later died during a terrorist attack against U.S. Marines in Beirut, Lebanon, in 1983. None of this prevented her from earning a commission in the Marine Corps, but like many if not most who chose the profession of arms, she longed for a world that required far fewer people to venture into harm's way for the sake of political ideology.

"How many of those conflicts could these friends of yours have stopped?" asked Markham. "Are the deaths associated with them their fault or ours?"

"Ours. We're the ones deciding to wage the wars,

remember?" Heffron sighed. "As I already told you, they're trying to help us. Not watch over us like a parent or babysitter, but offer a nudge or two on occasion. The same way a child has to fail in order to really learn the value of effort and commitment, so do we. Maybe there'll come a day when we're not fighting each other, but I figure it's not something anybody else can just hand to us. We'll have to earn it for ourselves."

Markham shook his head. "Or perhaps they're grooming us for their own purposes, which they've not shared with you."

"Two people? Grooming an entire planet?" Even as she spoke the words, Heffron regretted the slip, as she had been trying to avoid specifics about her mysterious benefactors. Markham seemed to appreciate her answers to this point, but now she noted the subtle changes in his posture and the set to his jaw.

Shit.

"Let's talk more about these two people."

Considering the man's request, Heffron once more weighed her earlier decision about the level of cooperation she had decided to offer. Perhaps a bit of prudence was in order just now.

"I'm not in regular contact with them, if that's what you're asking. They don't come just because I blow a whistle." She had to pause to recall the details of her previous meeting with the agents. "It's been years since I last heard from them. We touched base soon after the Bell Riots and when we started to close the first of the Sanctuary Districts."

There had been concern among various government entities, including Majestic 12, that the districts—areas of major American cities where the homeless, mentally ill, and other indigent members of the society had been interned—were ideal hiding places for extraterrestrials moving covertly among the human population. Rumors persisted of aliens lurking within several of the districts and working to trigger a revolt of the people against their own government, though such wild conspiracies had never borne any fruit. Natalie Koroma and Jonathan McAllister, using whatever advanced resources they had at their disposal, had assured Heffron that no such uprising was in the offing.

"Were they behind that as well?" asked Markham.

"Not that I'm aware of."

"Do you initiate contact in these instances?"

"I've never had to initiate contact." Only when she said the words aloud did she realize the full truth of that statement. "I honestly never thought of that before today. It's like they always just knew that it was a good time to reach out."

Markham's eyes narrowed. "But you were going to contact them the other night."

"Yes. After our initial interview with Brinalri and the reports from the team who found him and his ship, I wanted to know if they were the ones who subdued the Marines."

"Why would they do that?"

Heffron knew she was now moving into dangerous territory. "On occasions, when an alien craft has landed here, they've taken steps to ensure the visitors are able to get away undetected. In rarer instances, they've been required to . . . neutralize them." She knew from experience that the agents used violence and lethal force as absolute last resorts, which in her mind only served to strengthen their benevolent intentions.

"I want to meet these friends of yours," said Markham.

Gesturing to the pen that still lay on the table near his right hand, Heffron replied, "Knock yourself out."

To his credit, Markham smiled. "No, I don't think so. They attempted to contact you, remember? I suspect they're aware by now that you are not available, after failing to respond to their call. I think we'll just wait to see what they do next."

"We could be waiting a while," said Heffron. "They're not in the habit of just charging into a situation blind. They'll take their time finding me."

His smile fading, Markham replied, "Then I suppose we'll have to use that time to find out every last thing you know about them, Director Heffron. Your days of collaborating with potential enemies of this planet are over."

Heffron sighed.

I'm definitely in a very deep, very dark hole.

9

U.S.S. Enterprise
2386

"Are you all right?"

Sitting on the sofa in the main room of his family quarters, Picard did not realize at first that his wife was talking to him. When it finally registered that he was being rude, he blinked several times and looked up from the padd resting in his lap. Displayed on the device's screen were shipboard systems and status reports that he had read and already forgotten.

"I'm sorry. What did you say?"

Beverly Crusher stood before him, arms crossed and studying him with that same expression she reserved for patients she knew were being less than forthcoming with her as she attempted to provide treatment. Her right eyebrow was cocked in almost Vulcan fashion, though Picard also saw the faintest hint of a smile at the corners of her mouth.

"I said, are you all right? I heard about what happened with Taurik. Want to talk about it?"

"The gossip still travels rather quickly, doesn't it?" Picard shifted his position on the couch so that there was room for Beverly to sit next to him, and he laid the padd on the ledge behind him. The action allowed him to see Sralanya, the curve of the planet just visible outside the ports as the *Enterprise* held to its standard orbital path.

"Well, it's not every day the captain has a meltdown

on the bridge of his own ship." Beverly settled onto the couch. "At least, not without there being some kind of alien probe or mind control or other outside force at work."

"It was *not* a meltdown." He was not proud of how he had handled Taurik or that entire affair in the presence of his bridge crew, but Picard would not concede to the notion that he had lost control of his emotions, even for the briefest of moments. "A junior officer challenged my authority, in the presence of other subordinates. I couldn't allow that to go unanswered."

Tucking her legs beneath her, Beverly said, "I know, and for what it's worth, I agree with you. Whatever his intentions, Taurik was out of line at that moment, but you can't really blame him for everything, Jean-Luc."

Picard adjusted his position once more so that he could now rest his head on the back of the couch. "I know. This matter with Admiral Akaar is something I need to deal with, and quickly. I will, after this business with the Eizand is concluded."

"But if Taurik knows something about these people and whatever happened here centuries ago, doesn't it make sense to have him with you on the away team?"

"No." The word came out with more force than he intended, and Picard caught himself. Placing a hand on her leg, he smiled. "I'm sorry. No, until I have a chance to speak with Presider Hilonu, I don't want anything that might influence that dialogue. If Akaar wanted me to know something before I beamed down, he'd have told Taurik. That hasn't happened, so I'm left to wonder if even he has all of the facts about what happened here."

It was a thought that had been bothering him for hours. How much about this planet and its people did

Akaar—and Starfleet, and even the Federation Council, by extension—truly know? If Taurik was any indication, there was still much to be learned, and Picard had no reason to believe the Vulcan was deliberately withholding information. He got the sense that everyone was waiting for him to solve the puzzle of this world and its mysterious connection to Earth.

When I said I wanted to go back to being an explorer, this isn't really what I had in mind.

"You don't think Taurik's aboard to undermine you on behalf of Akaar, do you?" asked Beverly. "I mean, I know the admiral's methods can be unconventional, but this doesn't sound like him at all."

Picard replied, "The admiral is more than capable of playing his cards very close to his vest, and it's a tactic that's served him well."

In the aftermath of President Nanietta Bacco's murder and the whirlwind of events that had transpired during the search for her assassins, Leonard James Akaar was one of the few people who began to identify trouble within Starfleet and the Federation government. To that end, he had enlisted William Riker, another officer with a gift for unorthodox strategy and thinking, to help him search for the truth. Promoting Picard's former first officer from captain to admiral had given Riker more latitude to move about and hunt for the answers needed to uncover the conspiracy and ultimately rescue the Federation from traveling down a path of darkness from which there might be no escape. Their efforts, along with those of the *Enterprise* and others, succeeded in exonerating those who were falsely accused of the crime while exposing the conspirators. At the center of the entire sordid affair was Ishan Anjar, the Bajoran who rose to power as the president pro tempore while the Federation prepared to hold elections to select Bacco's permanent successor. Akaar and Riker, to say nothing of Beverly Crusher herself, were directly responsible for revealing Ishan as an imposter as well as a Cardassian collaborator during their occupation of Bajor. These staggering disclosures saw to it that Ishan was removed from office in disgrace, clearing the way for the legitimate election of the Andorian Kellessar zh'Tarash as the new Federation president.

"Okay, so he's a good tactician," said Beverly. "What do you think Akaar is doing now?"

Picard shook his head. "I don't think it's anything sinister. Given whatever it is that Taurik found in the computer files we extracted from the Raqilan weapon ship, I think this is Akaar's way of playing things safe, at least for the time being." So far as he knew, he had done nothing personally to arouse the admiral's suspicion or his ire. Was it simple paranoia, or was there something more at work here?

We'll find out sooner or later.

A glance to the chronometer on the desk across the room told him that his brief respite was nearly at an end. Stifling the urge to yawn, he pushed himself from the couch.

"I need to go," he said as he turned and headed for the small room where he knew his son was napping. "I'll say goodbye to René before I leave." Seeing the look of caution on Beverly's face, he held up a hand and smiled. "Don't worry. I won't wake him."

He paused at the bedroom's entrance, looking to where his son lay unmoving on the bed. Blankets were kicked aside and one leg dangled over an edge, and his hands were cast atop his head as though his entire body were conspiring to take up as much space on the bed as possible. Picard listened to the sound of the boy's low, steady breathing and watched the rhythmic rise and fall of his chest, and with a pang of envy tried to recall when he had last enjoyed such total, peaceful slumber.

"Why don't you go down to the planet," he said as Beverly moved to stand next to him, "and I'll stay here with him."

"You want me to negotiate an interplanetary relations treaty or whatever you're going to do down there, while you tend to my patients?" Beverly shrugged. "Deal. I could use the change of scenery."

Picard wrapped his arm around her shoulders. "I wonder what Admiral Akaar would have to say about that?"

T'Ryssa Chen did not even wait for the door to slide open before she was pushing her way into Taurik's quarters.

"What the hell is going on?" Realizing the door was still open and her voice might be carrying into the corridor, she moved away from it and allowed it to close. In a lower voice, she said, "Sorry. Now, what the hell is actually going on?"

Standing in the middle of the room, his hands clasped behind his back, Taurik regarded her. "Come in."

"Don't start with me." Chen held up a hand as though to forestall whatever meaningless attempt at detachment Taurik might next offer. "We're supposed to be friends, but you never told me you were working for Admiral Akaar. How long has that been going on? Since your last visit to Earth?"

She knew that he had been debriefed by officials at

Starfleet Headquarters during their recent return to Federation space. Those meetings had, according to unsubstantiated rumor, involved agents from the Department of Temporal Investigations, following the events with the Raqilan weapon ship and Taurik's apparent discovery of information detailing events that would not happen for years if not decades. For his part, Taurik had taken numerous steps to isolate himself and the potentially dangerous information he had found in the weapon ship's computer banks, refusing to discuss it with her or anyone else, including Captain Picard. In fact, he had weathered several of her attempts to goad him into talking about it, steadfastly refusing to offer even the slightest hint about what he had seen. His integrity and resolve could be damned infuriating at times, but what did any of that have to do with Akaar?

"I was under orders not to reveal the nature of my assignment," replied Taurik. "Even Captain Picard was not aware of this development until earlier today. It was deemed by Admiral Akaar a matter of utmost secrecy."

Unimpressed, Chen scowled. "Well, I think it's safe to say that the secret's out." Hoping to grab a quick meal before beaming to the planet's surface, she had made a cursory pass through the officer's mess after being dismissed from the bridge, and speculation was already running rampant among the members of the crew. "You're not really some kind of spy, working for Akaar, are you?"

"That is at best a mischaracterization of the assignment I have been given." Despite his Vulcan discipline and training, Chen saw that her comments had an effect. She noted the tensing of his jaw even as he stared at her. "Our current mission involves matters of a sensitive nature, much of which the admiral has not yet revealed to me. I have already discussed this matter with Captain Picard, and we have reached . . . an understanding."

Chen snorted. "Yeah, I saw that. So did everyone on the bridge. Taurik, I've never seen the captain that angry, even when he's mad at *me*. So, whatever this is that you've got going on, it's obviously something he's taking very seriously and very personally." She desperately wanted to ask him what all of this was about, but she knew that he would not tell her, thanks to orders of confidentiality and whatever other secrecy agreements to which he was bound.

"I regret that my actions, or any perception that I am withholding information, are responsible for his reactions. I have no desire to disrespect him or circumvent his authority." He paused, breaking his gaze from hers, and began to pace the length of his quarters' living area. "I find myself conflicted, T'Ryssa. To the best of my knowledge, Admiral Akaar has not given me any unlawful orders. He has not instructed me to disobey Captain Picard or do anything that might undermine him in any way. And yet, the very nature of my assignment makes it appear inevitable that I will be forced to choose between conflicting obligations. Captain Picard has already warned me about this possibility. All I can do is my utmost to keep both him and Admiral Akaar informed. Anything beyond that is out of my control."

It was obvious to Chen that her friend had spent a great deal of time pondering the dilemma his assignment presented, and she knew he would do his best to proceed with integrity, but would he place Admiral Akaar's needs over the captain's? She found it hard to believe.

"Look, Taurik, I don't think the admiral's a bad guy, but what he's done here is incredibly unfair to you and Captain Picard. It's obvious the captain feels that way, too, or else you wouldn't be sitting here, relieved of duty and sent to bed without supper."

Taurik eyed her quizzically. "I do not believe my replicator has been deactivated."

Rolling her eyes, Chen sighed. "You know what I mean." She folded her arms across her chest. "So, what are you going to do now?"

"I will remain in my quarters until Captain Picard rescinds his order. I am in the process of preparing a new report for Admiral Akaar, which includes another request for more information that I can in turn share with the captain."

Chen shrugged. "Well, that might get you back on the captain's good side."

"I do not seek to curry favor," replied Taurik. "I am merely carrying out my duties as I am able, even with the restrictions placed upon me."

"Whatever you have to tell yourself." Chen smiled, hoping to take out some of the sting from her sarcastic remark. She saw by the slight curling of the corner of his mouth that he understood her intentions.

Before she could say anything else, the tone of the ship's intercom sounded, followed by the voice of Commander Worf calling for the members of the away team accompanying Captain Picard to report to the transporter room.

"That's my cue," she said.

As he regarded her, Taurik's expression softened. "Be careful, T'Ryssa."

Was he trying to tell her something, without really

telling her something? Chen decided that the more reasonable explanation was that she was just being paranoid. Still, there was something in her friend's eyes that gave her pause.

"Hey, I'll be with the captain. What could possibly go wrong?"

10

Sralanya
2386

Even as the residual tingle of the fading transporter beam played across his skin, Picard noted their rather large welcoming committee was already on station, waiting. Six Eizand, three males and three females, stood at the edge of a circular grassy quad that had been designated as the away team's landing point, flanking a seventh individual whom the captain recognized as Hilonu. Her six companions were likely her security detail, dressed as they were in matching dark maroon garments that Picard instinctively knew were military or police uniforms. Each carried a sidearm in a holster worn on the hip, with the weapon's stock or grip facing forward. Hilonu had exchanged her green dress for one of azure blue contoured to her figure, and which Picard saw was accented in much the same fashion as her previous ensemble with gold patterns woven through the fabric. Behind Hilonu and her flanking detail were another eight Eizand, a mixture of males and females dressed in what Picard took to be formal civilian attire, consisting of robes and loose-fitting blouses and trousers of varying colors, with each garment featuring its own version of gold or silver patterns around the neck or shirt and pant cuffs.

A quick glance around him affirmed his earlier thoughts about the city itself. Beyond the courtyard where the team had materialized, a large park filled with trees and other vegetation—most of it growing at odd angles and featuring leaves and bulbs of varying colors—acted as a buffer between the surrounding buildings. While the city itself was by no means beautiful, Picard still sensed a vitality and purpose all around him. The structures appeared to prioritize pure function over anything else, with very little in the way of aesthetic embellishments. Most of the buildings were squat, gray or brown in color, and rose only eight to ten stories above the ground while covering entire city blocks. Some of the structures were connected by elevated walkways, and the streets—composed of a white-gray material with flecks of some mineral that reflected the late afternoon sunlight—were wide and filled with an assortment of ground vehicles that looked to operate on a form of antigravity or repulsor-lift technology. Despite the obvious activity unfolding all around them, Picard noted a lack of background noise he might expect from a thriving urban environment. A sweet, pleasant scent hung in the air, reminding him of raspberries or honeysuckle.

Returning his attention to their hosts, he stepped forward. "Presider Hilonu, we meet at last."

Crossing her forearms before her, the Eizand leader offered a slight bow, tilting her head so that it almost touched her chest. "Welcome to Sralanya, Captain Picard, and the city of Ponval, capital of the Tevent Coalition." She gestured toward her entourage. "Please do not be alarmed. These are my security escorts. Protocol requires them to accompany me whenever I leave our assembly chamber or my home." Her expression brightened in what Picard thought was her first genuine display of emotion. "It is but one of the many burdens of my office."

"Indeed," said Picard. "I can sympathize, as regulations call for me to have a similar escort whenever I leave my ship." He used the reply to introduce the other members of his away team—T'Ryssa Chen, Dina Elfiki, Glinn Ravel Dygan, and security officers T'Sona and Austin Braddock.

Taking a moment to study the other strangers in her midst, Hilonu said, "I see that at least three of your party are of species different from yours, Captain."

"That's correct. Lieutenants Chen and T'Sona represent the planet Vulcan, though Lieutenant Chen is of mixed heritage, with a Vulcan father and a human mother."

Hilonu stepped away from her security detail, extending her hands toward Glinn Dygan. "I have never seen a being like you. What do you call yourself?"

"We call ourselves Cardassians, Presider," replied Dygan. He nodded toward Picard. "In fact, my people were once enemies of the Federation. We waged war against each other, and later we fought alongside one another against a common foe."

"It is nice to see that such disparate peoples can come together in times of strife, and later in pursuit of shared goals and opportunity." As she spoke, Hilonu directed her gaze to Picard. "Was that always the case with the people of your world, Captain?"

"Not always, Presider. We definitely endured a great many growing pains once we achieved space travel capability." He extended a hand toward Chen and T'Sona. "The people of Vulcan were our first interstellar allies, and we learned much from them, including many things we were doing wrong in our haste to explore space. They made us aware of the countless planets where life exists and gave us some of our first and harshest lessons about interacting with those worlds." Again, he smiled. "Even with their help, it took us a while to find our way."

"Intriguing," said Hilonu, once more adopting that same detached manner she had employed during their first conversation. "I look forward to hearing more, Captain."

Recalling a request made by Lieutenant Elfiki prior to their beaming down, Picard said, "Presider, I wonder if it might be possible for the members of my team to tour your city." He gestured toward the group of onlookers who still stood behind Hilonu and her security detail. "Under escort, of course. It's obvious that a great calamity once befell your world, and we're most interested to learn how your people survived its aftermath." He paused, looking at the city that surrounded them. "You appear to have made remarkable progress, despite the challenges you've faced."

"Our plight fascinates you." Hilonu seemed to ponder her own words for a moment before adding, "Yes, we have endured a great deal rebuilding our society. We have tried to make things better for our people, but there are those who do not believe in what we are attempting to do, or who have lost faith in us. Indeed, we still deal with dissenters on a frequent basis, but our efforts continue." She sighed. "One day, I hope we will earn back the trust we have lost."

Then, as though deciding this was not appropriate conversation for visitors, Hilonu said, "As it happens, we anticipated your request, and we are happy to accommodate it. Perhaps we can learn something from one another."

He should have been buoyed by her comments, but

instead Picard found himself parsing her words, searching for hidden meaning. That earlier suggestion of antipathy still seemed to be present, though Hilonu offered no other obvious indications of such feelings. Perhaps the Eizand simply did not like outsiders of any sort, but to Picard it seemed too pat an answer.

Only one way to find out.

Leaving Elfiki in charge of the rest of the away team with instructions to remain in regular contact, Picard along with Lieutenant T'Sona accompanied Hilonu and her security detail from the courtyard. Their route took them to a stone walking path that wound through the park. Her escorts set up a protective cordon around her but allowed him to fall into step beside the presider.

"This area is really quite lovely," he said, once more eyeing the nearby trees and other foliage. "I think I could find myself spending quite a bit of time here."

Hilonu replied, "I often come here in an attempt to relieve the stresses of my duties. It is a wonderful place for quiet contemplation." She pointed ahead of them. "There is a small pond ahead, and I often sit on one of the benches there, reading or simply closing my eyes for a short time. Then disappointment sets in when I am required to return to my duties."

Picard was reminded of the Starfleet Academy campus, so lovingly tended by the seemingly ageless groundskeeper, Boothby, whom he had befriended so long ago during his earliest days as a cadet. Picard had found similar solace in those gardens and quiet spaces.

"The park was a deliberate choice on the part of the city's builders," said the Eizand leader. "They wanted those who lived here to remember that our planet was once home to great beauty. It could be so again, and we did not have to remain confined to these cities that are all that remain of our race." She shook her head. "We were meant for more than that. Many areas of Sralanya still carry the scars of the war, but efforts are under way to reclaim those regions and hopefully restore them. It is a task that began well before I was born and will continue long after I die, but it is worth it. Many of our people have devoted their entire lives to the cause, and it is a source of great pride."

"I can imagine," replied Picard. "My planet endured a similar conflict, centuries ago, and it required the same level of commitment to help it heal the wounds it had suffered."

Hilonu turned to look at him. "Your people waged war on themselves?" When he offered a silent nod as reply, her expression turned to one of sadness. "A horrible thing, is it not?"

Emerging from the park, the presider's escorts led the way across a raised walkway toward one of the larger buildings surrounded by a fenced enclosure. The procession continued across to the structure's entrance, at which point Hilonu moved to the front of the group as it passed through the large, arched doorways. The building's exterior may have been as drab as its neighbors, while inside was a different story. Polished tile covered the floor, and large columns rose toward a high ceiling, upon which was a colorful, abstract mosaic. The oversized foyer reminded Picard of a museum or art gallery more than the office of a political official.

Even that opulence was overshadowed by the appointments of Hilonu's own office. The presider's inner sanctum, located on the building's uppermost floor, was filled with ornate furniture, artwork, and sculptures representing a variety of styles—at least so far as Picard could tell—and had a commanding view of the park they had just traversed. From this vantage point, Picard was able to make out ground and small air vehicles moving about the streets of Ponval and over, around, and even through the various buildings. There was a definite energy here, and even a beauty, he thought, amending his earlier feelings.

As Hilonu moved to a curved desk positioned in the room's far corner and the young Eizand male standing next to it, Picard and T'Sona stood near the entrance, waiting for an invitation to join the presider. He watched as the other Eizand, obviously an assistant, handed her a type of tablet, which she began to scrutinize. Outside the office, the security detail was breaking up, with two members of the group moving to stand near the doorway while their companions, along with Hilonu's assistant, disappeared down the long corridor. Facing away from the office, neither of the remaining guards appeared to give him any notice before the door closed.

"If Presider Hilonu's office is any indication," said T'Sona, "it appears the Eizand are quite fond of the decorative arts."

Picard nodded. "So it would seem." A longtime admirer of such things, he had already added this to the list of topics he hoped might occupy the time he spent with Hilonu. Covering a diverse range of subjects, he had learned, was a fine means of navigating the often uncertain waters of dialogue and diplomacy when interacting with the leaders of a newly contacted species. Anything that might serve to highlight commonalities was always useful, in his experience, and an appreciation of the arts, literature, and other cultural pursuits was one of his favorite subjects.

"Captain," said Hilonu, and Picard turned from T'Sona to see the Eizand leader gesturing toward him. A nod from him was enough for the Vulcan security officer to understand that she should remain by the door as he crossed the office. Hilonu had moved from behind her desk to a curved sofa situated before the large window and its view of the park, and she indicated for him to sit with her.

"I apologize for keeping you waiting, but I was reviewing a report from our constabulary. It seems a group of dissenters ransacked one of our offices. There is no way to know if they took anything of value, as they burned the building to cover their activities." She shook her head. "Just when I think there will be a brief moment's peace, something like this happens."

Picard said, "Presider, if there is something you need to be doing, we can meet at a more appropriate time."

"No. I have a dedicated staff seeing to matters such as this. Besides, I imagine you have a number of questions, and I'm anxious to hear them."

Picard nodded. "Indeed. Obviously, we're quite interested in your people and how you came to be where you are today. It seems that the history of your world has at least some parallels to mine and a great many others."

Waving toward the window, Hilonu said, "This city and the others like it represent most of what remains of the Eizand people, Captain. Our numbers are much stronger than they were even just a few generations ago, but in the immediate aftermath of the war, our civilization was on the brink of vanishing altogether." She paused, looking away from him and casting her gaze toward the window and the city beyond.

"Even before the last war, we were mired in problems that largely were of our own making. There are representatives from more than two dozen city-states that survived the war, but only three had amassed enough territory and resources to affect affairs on a planetary scale. My people, the Tevent, along with the Galj and Yilondra, were by far the largest nations on Sralanya. Naturally, most of the conflicts between our different peoples arose from the usual sorts of disputes, and were the same things we thought defined us: the land we claimed, and the things to which we thought we were entitled, or thought we needed more than anyone else. Matters of faith and the deities and beliefs embraced by our different cultures seemed like a convenient way to sow divisions between us."

"Yours is not a unique story, I'm afraid," said Picard. "Quite the contrary, it is an all-too-familiar tale; one that for a time defined the people of my world." He nodded to where Lieutenant T'Sona remained by the door. "Even Vulcan, whose civilization I would consider one to which we all might aspire, at least in some ways, was once gripped by the same sorts of conflicts. They corrected their society's downward spiral, and later helped mine emerge from the darkness into which we'd plunged ourselves. If not for them, I honestly don't know what might have become of my own people, but I likely wouldn't be sitting here talking with you today."

For the first time since meeting them in the courtyard, Hilonu smiled, but Picard noted it seemed a grudging one. "Perhaps we are not so different from one another as I originally believed." Once more directing her attention to the window, she said, "So, we quarreled over land and natural resources to feed our ever growing, industrialized existence. We ripped into the planet that had given birth to us and claimed its riches as our own, consuming them with nary a second thought as to the impacts of our pillaging on the atmosphere, our oceans, even ourselves. Then, as those resources began to dwindle and it became evident that whatever was left would be the focus of future conflicts, the wars became more heated, the tactics more underhanded. While the Tevent, the Galj, and the Yilondra at first ignored one another in their quest to expand territory, we soon reached the point where we were all that was left standing in each other's way. That's when the skirmishes and wars began in earnest."

Something beeped on her desk, and she rose from the couch. Hilonu reached for the tablet her assistant had given her, likely studying one of any number of reports and updates she doubtless received on any given day. It then occurred to him that it was the first such notification she had received since their arrival in her office, and he wondered if he should take anything from that.

Aren't you being a bit paranoid, Jean-Luc?

Returning the tablet to her desk, she crossed back to the couch. "It soon became apparent that we would have to take action, as a people, to ensure our survival. Some of our brightest scientific minds had already been making all manner of dire predictions, warning us about our continued abuse of the planet's natural resources and the impact on the environment. Several initiatives were put forth, including radical programs to curb our dependence on the very fuel sources that were causing the damage. Other, more extreme scenarios also were developed, including an increased emphasis on travel to other worlds in our star system. It was hoped that those planets or their moons or whatever other objects might be found would harbor resources we could exploit." Again, her expression fell. "Apparently, it was not enough that we were killing our own planet. Now we wanted to take our shortsightedness to the stars. There even were those who thought it would be better for us to find another world suitable for relocating our entire civilization. Hence, the development of ships that could travel at the speeds necessary to reach beyond our system."

"Faster-than-light propulsion," said Picard. "You had warp capability generations ago?"

Hilonu nodded. "Before the war, our level of technological advancement was quite impressive, though perhaps not as much as that which you currently enjoy." She smiled, adding, "Like something out of a child's storybook, yes? Ships that we could hurl toward the stars, in search of a new chance for our people. Surely, your own culture's fascination with space travel began in similar fashion."

"Indeed it did." Interstellar spaceflight had long been commonplace centuries before his birth, though Picard remained fascinated with that period of human history when such an ability had not yet been achieved. Some of his favorite stories from childhood involved those initial, tentative voyages from Earth, first to its own Moon and then, eventually, to the other planets of the Sol system and beyond, until that momentous day when humanity, embodied for a brief moment by one man, Zefram Cochrane, achieved the fanciful goal of propelling a spacecraft faster than light itself.

With a bit of help, of course.

"We began with automated probes," said Hilonu, "dispatching them toward distant stars that deep-space telescopes indicated might have planets capable of sustaining us. Probes that returned with promising data collected during their journey were then followed up with larger, crewed vessels sent to investigate further. Most of those vessels returned, but we did lose contact with a few. In those cases, we sent other ships to determine what might have happened. Contact with one of those rescue missions was also lost, but then the ship was returned home." She stopped, turning so that she could level an accusatory glare at Picard.

"The planet that vessel was sent to study was yours, Captain."

AFTEREFFECTS

11

The Pentagon, Washington, D.C.
November 5, 2032

"Is the rescue mission still on schedule? Do you anticipate any problems with the ship making it there on time?"

Sitting behind the desk in his office, fourteen stories below the Pentagon's ground level, Gerald Markham watched the press conference unfolding on the high-definition flat-screen monitor mounted on the far wall. On the screen, Amy Sisson, Director of the National Aeronautics and Space Administration, stared intently at the reporter who had just posed the question. Tall and trim of build with a runner's physique, she stood with confidence behind a podium in the media room of the Johnson Space Center in Houston, Texas. As befitting a senior official for a government organization, she wore her brown hair in a shoulder-length style while dressed in what Markham thought of as a traditional ensemble of gray pants and matching jacket over a white silk blouse. In another nod to convention, pins representing the American flag and the NASA emblem decorated her left lapel, while a third pin denoted a gold shooting star. It was this third device, Markham knew, that carried the most weight with the people in this room, as it symbolized the fact that prior to her ascension to the agency's leadership ranks, she had been an astronaut; someone uniquely qualified to discuss matters pertaining to astronauts.

Including, unfortunately, dead ones, and those marooned on other planets.

His feet resting on the corner of his desk, Markham watched as Sisson, with the same aplomb with which she had begun the press conference, now fielded its eighth question. It was really the tenth or eleventh, but as some variation of it had already been asked twice, Markham wasn't counting it as such.

"As I already said, Ethan," replied Sisson to the reporter who had offered this latest twist on the well-tread query, *"the* Theseus *is still on course back from the asteroid belt and has commenced its deceleration in preparation for insertion into Mars orbit, which is scheduled to take place at four seventeen a.m. Central Standard Time on Sunday, November seventh. Once orbit is established, the ship's landing vehicle will make its descent to the* Ares IV *mission site, where the* Theseus *landing crew will retrieve astronauts Kumagawa and Novakovich. It's probably a good time to remind everybody that the astronauts are not in any immediate danger. The habitation module at the* Ares *mission site has more than enough supplies to sustain them until the arrival of the rescue ship. Once everyone's safely back aboard, the* Theseus *will leave Mars orbit and commence its acceleration on a course back to Earth."*

"How long will the trip home take?" asked another male reporter.

Sisson's response was immediate. *"Approximately two hundred fourteen days. We anticipate no delays or alterations to this schedule, barring any other unforeseen circumstances."*

The reporter offered a follow-up question. *"What sort of circumstances might those be?"*

"I don't know, Stan. That's why I called them 'unfore-

seen.' This is space travel we're talking about. Talk to me in two hundred fifteen days, and we'll see how things went."

"Ouch," said Heather Burden, Markham's assistant director and one of his closest friends and confidants. "They're going to roast her for that one." Dressed in dark slacks and a light-blue collared blouse, Burden sat in one of the two padded chairs positioned before Markham's desk. She had shrugged off the jacket that went with her pants, tossing it and her briefcase onto the sofa that sat along the office's far wall, and had been waiting for him, with the television already tuned to the press conference being carried on the NASA channel as well as most of the major news networks. From that and the way she wore her brown hair loosely about her shoulders, Burden gave the appearance of being done with her work and ready to go home, but Markham knew that such escape was still hours away.

Shifting in his chair to make himself more comfortable, he replied, "But it's the truth. Leave it to someone who's been up there to cut through the crap. You'd think journalists of all people would get that. Some things never change."

Dealing with a routine mission mishap or even the loss of an unmanned probe was one thing, as evidenced by how short the public memory was with respect to such expensive failures as the *Voyager 6* and *Nomad* probes, both lost in attempts to push exploration efforts beyond the solar system. Standing tall in the face of actual tragedy was something else altogether.

This was not the first time Markham had watched a NASA official handling an event of this sort. He was too young to remember the press conferences and memorial services that had come following the loss of the Space

Shuttle *Challenger* in 1986, but he had been a teenager when a similar tragedy befell the *Challenger*'s sister ship, *Columbia*, in 2003. Since that time, there had been training accidents, and deaths of astronauts from other causes unrelated to their chosen profession, but there had been only one mission-related incident in nearly two decades that had resulted in lives lost.

Until last month.

"Has there been any new information about Lieutenant Kelly?" asked another reporter in the front row as Sisson pointed to him.

"We still don't know anything about the anomaly that came into contact with the Ares IV *command module. Our satellite tracking was unable to confirm whether the ship was destroyed or somehow caught up in the anomaly as it continued on its straight-line course past Mars. There's no evidence of an explosion, and none of the Mars satellites have detected or encountered any debris, so right now we're leaning toward the latter theory."*

Hands shot up in response to Sisson's answer and she called on another reporter, who was dividing her attention between her tablet and the director.

"Do you think Lieutenant Kelly might still be alive?"

Markham saw Sisson's jaw clench, and knew that she realized almost any answer to this question was only going to spawn a host of new queries. He also could tell that despite any feelings she might harbor, she had prepared for this moment.

"We're still conducting our investigation, and we'll continue to do everything we can until we have all the answers as to what happened to Lieutenant Kelly. However, it's important to remember that the scene of the accident is fifty million miles away. This is going to take some time, and

we'll want to be as thorough as possible, for the sake of Lieutenant Kelly's family as well as how we plan for future Mars missions and the safety of the men and women who will be making those journeys."

"So the Ares *missions aren't on hold?"* asked a third journalist, a woman Markham recognized as being a science reporter for the *Washington Post.*

"The Ares V *mission is still in the planning stages and not scheduled to launch for two years. And don't forget that we have other projects and missions in various stages of planning that will take our people to the other planets and even beyond the solar system. All of those objectives are still being pursued. We've got time to carry out a thorough investigation without placing these programs in limbo. As we gather more information, the decision to delay or cancel future* Ares *missions is still on the table, but right now I see no reason to make such a decision. At the moment, our priorities are the rescue of astronauts Rose Kumagawa and Andrei Novakovich, and finding out what happened to Lieutenant John Kelly."*

"I like her," said Burden, her attention still on the screen as Sisson fielded another question. "Why haven't you recruited her yet?" Taking a dark band she had been wearing around her wrist, she pulled back her brown hair and secured it in a ponytail.

Lifting his feet from his desk, Markham chuckled as he rose from his seat. "I've considered it, the same way we've considered recruiting every NASA director since 1958." He moved to the counter set into the wall to his right, which contained a wet bar and small refrigerator. After pulling two glasses and a bottle of Scotch from one of the overhead cabinets, he returned to his desk. With the Scotch bottle still in his hand, he gestured to the monitor, where Sisson was answering another question. "Not all of them are suited for what we do, but she's one of the best candidates to come along in a while."

He knew everything about Amy Sisson, thanks to the extensive dossier that had been prepared for him by the Majestic 12 information analysts and which contained data from numerous sources both public and clandestine. She was, according to her file, the youngest person ever to hold the position of NASA director, and she had wasted no time putting her fingerprints on the organization. Under her leadership, the first *Ares* missions to Mars had been accomplished ahead of schedule and well within budget projections, delivering far more than even the most generous estimates in terms of return on the project's staggering financial investment.

"She looks tired," observed Burden, her gaze still fixed on the screen. "Can't say I blame her, though. Not after the month she's had."

Pouring a portion of the Scotch into a glass for Burden before preparing one for himself, Markham retook his seat. "No kidding. She's been carrying this on her shoulders from the moment it happened. If I was her, I'd be in a coma, and happy about it." He gestured with his glass toward the screen. "She's taking it personally. According to her file, she and Kelly were friends, though they never had any missions together. Not that it matters. Astronauts are a tight bunch."

From watching the interviews Sisson had given to dozens of news organizations around the world in the wake of the *Ares IV* incident, Markham knew that everything surrounding the accident—if indeed it was an accident—was weighing on her, and that even as she spoke to this gaggle of reporters she was riding herd on every person at NASA who might be able to contribute anything toward finding out what had happened at Mars. It was the first loss of an astronaut since her appointment as director, and by all accounts she was sparing no expense or effort when it came to learning the truth. No fool, Sisson obviously was aware that she and the entire agency would be subjected to unrelenting public and political scrutiny as people sought explanations for the apparent tragedy before looking to assign blame. Markham also could tell from her demeanor that the director did not care about any of that, but instead was focused on the issue at hand. This was more to her than one of her employees or subordinates dying on the job; John Kelly was a brother-in-arms, after a fashion, and Markham knew that Sisson and everyone who worked for her would not rest until they knew why Kelly had been taken from them. Sisson likely felt she owed an explanation not just to the man's family and every astronaut under her leadership, but to everyone, period.

"Did you ever want to be an astronaut?" he asked, before sipping from his drink.

Burden shook her head. "No. I wanted to be a game designer."

That surprised Markham, as it was not a fact included in her personnel file. "Really? How the hell did you end up here?"

He was familiar with most of her story. Younger than him by more than a decade, Heather Burden had in short order become an invaluable member of his team and his own inner circle. Previously, she had been assigned to the Raven Rock facility as part of just one of the organizations overseen by Majestic 12. That was before the subordinate group's renaming and relocation to the Pentagon for reasons of security as well as in response to the latest evolution of its ongoing mandate of investigating and protecting the United States and perhaps the entire world against extraterrestrial threats. At Raven Rock, Burden had overseen an investigative team of military and civilian personnel. She had been charged with verifying or debunking reports of alien activity around the country, all while avoiding the attention of rival nations fielding agents with similar missions, along with the media and the public at large. Her record of achievement was exemplary, and she even was part of the team that had located the Eizand spacecraft last year. It was that action in particular that had brought her to Markham's attention, and he had personally seen to it that Burden was brought in as a member of his revamped group, which did not possess a formal name, but instead was attached to the top-secret project to which he had been assigned as leader.

"Recruited by the NSA out of college. They liked my language and software scores. You know the rest." She shrugged. "If I had it to do over again, I think I'd have gone with the game thing. What about you?"

Markham chuckled. "I absolutely wanted to be an astronaut." Long before fate and circumstances had seen to it that his view of space and the wonder it held was quashed by the harsh reality of this job, Markham had been a space enthusiast. Born well after the earliest efforts to place manned spacecraft on the Moon and send the first automated or remote-guided probes to the solar system's other planets and beyond, he had still reveled in the history of those achievements. Names like Yeager, Shepard, Glenn, and Armstrong had fueled his dreams even as he grew up watching space shuttle launches along with science fiction films and television programs, and reading the works of authors like Heinlein, Clarke, Butler, and Cherryh. He knew it was unlikely that he would ever climb aboard a shuttle or whatever type of spacecraft might succeed those vessels. Still, he dreamed of such things well into adulthood and even after seeking an officer's commission in the United States Air Force. As a captain, he worked his way to a duty assignment with the Space Command headquarters at Peterson Air Force Base in Colorado, where fate and circumstance saw to it that he was recruited by Majestic 12.

Once Markham was brought into a realm so secret that it had operated almost without notice since its inception in 1947, his eyes were forever opened to things he had only envisioned thanks to a favorite novel or film. When he joined the group, MJ-12 was but the top of a pyramid that extended through numerous departments and agencies throughout the government of the United States, while enjoying partnerships with similar organizations embedded within the leadership bodies of several major nations. Despite once being adversaries, during the Cold War and the period of global instability that had defined the 1990s and the opening decades of the twenty-first century, these covert agencies had learned over time that they all faced a common foe; not one that originated anywhere on Earth, but instead lurked among the stars.

"Somebody like Sisson would be perfect for us," said Burden. She had finished her Scotch and was helping herself to the bottle on Markham's desk.

Markham nodded. "Under most circumstances, she would." He gestured toward the screen. "On the other hand, she's the person NASA needs right now. They're going to be under scrutiny for months, and she's perfect for handling that the way it needs to be handled." He grimaced. "Not from the public, of course. They'll forget about this sooner or later. Sure, they'll remember the anniversary of Kelly's death, and there'll be mention of him the next time an *Ares* mission goes up, but otherwise? Some idiot celebrity or another Washington scandal will grab their attention, or maybe we'll just go and throw ourselves into another war that doesn't need fighting."

As much as he loathed the fickle, wandering attention spans that seemed to typify the average citizen, Markham also knew that it was this apparent indifference that gave people like him and Burden and organizations like MJ-12 the perfect cover. Unless or until they did something that unavoidably attracted notice, they were able to operate almost with impunity as they went about their work. Still, it was often frustrating to think that he, and Burden along with everyone who toiled in secret, likely would never be recognized for their sacrifices and the very real contributions they made toward the security of every man, woman, and child on this planet.

Quit whining, he reminded himself. *You knew what the job was when you took it.*

"Besides, she's too high-profile at the moment. It's precisely because she'll be heading up the *Ares IV* investigation that we can't bring her into the fold. There's too much risk that any connection to us might get picked up by a reporter who decides one day that it might be fun to do some actual journalism." Markham shook his head. "No. For now, NASA and the rest of us need Sisson right where she is."

Sipping from her drink, Burden seemed to contemplate this for a moment before saying, "You know

NASA's own investigation isn't going to turn up anything. How can it? They don't have the resources to really figure out what happened out there. Hell, even we don't have that. Not really."

"No, but we've got enough to put forth some theories that NASA won't, at least not publicly."

After more than seventy years, it was inevitable that the space agency would come across proof that humans were not alone in the cosmos, or even alone while sending spacecraft into Earth orbit or to the solar system's other planets. On the occasions when astronauts, or a satellite or other unmanned survey probe, had captured evidence of extraterrestrial activity, the person serving as NASA director was informed about aspects of Majestic 12's mission that were relevant to the given situation, at which time they were forever linked to the covert organization and forbidden from publicly mentioning or discussing it in any manner. So far, there had been no reason to bring Amy Sisson in for such a briefing, but Markham knew that might change.

Pressing a button on the small keypad set into the top of his desk muted the television on the screen, and Markham asked, "Where are we on our look into this?"

Burden, as though sensing that the tenor of their private meeting had changed, placed her glass on the desk and straightened in her chair. "We still don't know what it was that hit the *Ares IV* command module, but according to our own satellite data, it certainly didn't act like any sort of natural phenomenon." She held up a hand. "That is, anything we've seen before. NASA's Mars satellites show what looks to be a huge ball of energy coming out of nowhere and closing on the ship's position, and then the ship just disappears. According to Lieutenant

Kelly's description, it was more than a thousand meters in diameter. Even if he'd had any sort of real warning, there was no way he would've been able to maneuver *Ares IV* out of the way in time."

Pondering this while studying the remnants of Scotch in his glass, Markham said, "That's what NASA's satellites tell us. What about ours?" As part of Majestic 12's overall mission of attempting to keep tabs on everything happening on or above the Earth, a series of top-secret launches over the decades had seen to it that the covert agency now had its own network of satellites orbiting not only Earth but also the Moon and now Mars—for communications as well as other purposes, only a few of which took advantage of reverse-engineered components from captured extraterrestrial spacecraft. If NASA opted to revitalize manned missions to Jupiter or even back to Saturn in the coming years, MJ-12 would likely place additional equipment at or near those planets as well. Such a network had been in the planning stages following the *U.S.S. Lewis & Clark*'s journey to Saturn and the odd circumstances surrounding that mission back in 2020 that had involved contact with a mysterious probe of alien origin. That NASA, in the form of the official who had preceded Amy Sisson as the agency's director, had chosen to concentrate short-term exploration goals on Mars rather than the outer planets had shelved any Majestic plans for Saturn.

Thank God. It's a hell of long way out there, for one thing.

Having retrieved a data tablet from her briefcase, Burden had returned to her seat and was swiping at the device's screen. "Our satellite coverage is much more comprehensive than anything NASA or any of the other civilian space agencies have up there, so we've got imagery they'll never see. This thing, whatever it was, moved in a straight line, Gerry. That suggests something artificial; something guided . . . by something *else*."

"That's what I was afraid you'd say." Reaching up to rub the bridge of his nose, Markham sighed. "I don't suppose this thing's behavior is consistent with anything we've seen before?"

Burden replied, "Its energy readings were off the scale. Definitely not like anything that's shown itself around here." She frowned. "To be honest, given its energy output, I'm thinking it probably is some kind of natural phenomenon. I just can't see any kind of ship putting out that kind of power without being a whole lot bigger. At least, not if you compare it to the sorts of ships we've seen."

"But you can't rule it out."

Shaking her head, Burden narrowed her eyes. "No, I can't rule it out." She turned to look back at the television, where Director Sisson was still answering press questions. "It's going to take months to even begin to answer all the questions. Like you said, Mars is a damned long way away for this kind of thing."

"We've been collecting bits and pieces of alien technology for decades, and yet we've never been able to figure out the systems that allowed them to travel here in the first place. I mean, can you imagine what we could accomplish if we could get to Mars in five minutes instead of five months?"

"If we do figure it out," replied Burden, "are you applying to NASA?"

"Damned right. It has to be more fun than this." After a moment, he offered a small, humorless smile.

"You'd think after all these years, I'd be used to having conversations like this, but there are still times when I stop and think to myself, 'Your job is the weirdest thing ever.' Do you ever feel like that?"

Burden smirked. "Every morning when the alarm goes off."

His smile fading, Markham said, "All right, now for the big money question: Do you think there's any chance this could be related to our friends the Eizand?"

Once more, the assistant director frowned. "Again, I can't rule it out. There's nothing to tie this to anything we've seen from the Eizand, but there's also nothing that explicitly rules it out, either. The simple truth is that we just don't have enough information to make that kind of determination. Not yet, but we're definitely trying to cover all the angles." She shook her head. "It'd be nice to run this past Brinalri."

Markham almost flinched at the sound of the name. The Eizand specimen had died after an escape attempt during an interrogation seven months earlier, the first time the alien had attempted such a bold move during his captivity. His death, like the rest of his existence, was a closely guarded secret even within Majestic 12's sphere of influence. The body had been dissected by forensic examiners, with samples of bone and organs sent to different MJ-12 labs around the country for continued study.

How much more could we have learned from him. What a waste.

"We're out of luck on that score," said Markham, trying to push aside the irksome thoughts. "I'm going to want a report for Majestic and the White House within forty-eight hours." As though anticipating her protest,

Markham raised a hand. "Doesn't have to be the whole book; just whatever chapters you have by then. I've been getting heat from the president and upstairs about this since Kelly disappeared."

The senior level of Majestic 12's leadership cadre, known casually as "upstairs," was uncertain that the *Ares IV* accident might be related to the Eizand. Looking for anything they could use to justify ramping up various proposals that were in the planning stages, they now were turning their attention to Gerald Markham and the rest of the group known simply as Initiative 2031. The latest in a series of compartmented organizations dating back to the founding of Majestic 12 in 1947, I-31 was the successor to such programs as Project Blue Book from the 1950s and '60s, or its 1980s counterpart, Project Cygnus. This new iteration had been put into motion following last year's capture of the Eizand spacecraft, after MJ-12 scientists and engineers discovered during their inspection of the craft that its crew had transmitted a distress signal prior to making planetfall. The original ship was still being studied and disassembled in a secret subterranean facility beneath Minot Air Force Base in North Dakota, with the top priorities being understanding and possibly reverse-engineering the Eizand faster-than-light propulsion technology. Progress on that front had been limited, but the engineers spearheading that effort had reported advancement so far as interfacing with the craft's onboard computer systems. The entire endeavor, Markham was told, could take years to complete.

Meanwhile, that Eizand crew had friends, who will probably come looking for them, if they haven't already.

Not looking up from her tablet as she swiped at its

screen, Burden asked, "What about NASA? They don't even know what they're looking for, but they might get lucky." She held up the tablet. "There's still the rescue mission, after all."

Thinking of astronauts Rose Kumagawa and Andrei Novakovich, currently stranded on Mars and awaiting rescue by the *Theseus* spacecraft and perhaps at the mercy of whatever unexplained force had taken John Kelly and the *Ares IV* command module, Markham sighed. "There's that. Obviously, we'll have to keep a close eye on their investigation. We can't have them stumbling onto something and releasing it to the press or the web before we have a chance to sanitize it."

As a transparent government agency, NASA was duty-bound to release any information, including photographs or video, of anything uncovered during the course of its investigation. Majestic 12—and I-31 by extension—were free of such mandates.

"Anything else I should be doing?" asked Burden as she rose from her seat.

Markham slumped back in his chair. Suddenly, he felt tired. "Yes. Pray whatever hit *Ares IV* is some kind of natural phenomenon, because if it really is the Eizand or somebody else, then we may have a very big problem."

For a moment, he wondered if the people he had been trying to find—the mysterious "agents" about whom former Majestic director Kirsten Heffron had told him so much and yet so frustratingly little—might know anything about this incident. It was a possibility he could not rule out, and it had been some time since he had last spoken with Heffron, who remained in MJ-12 custody. Perhaps it was time to initiate a new line of questioning with her. Markham was certain she could have no knowledge of the *Ares IV* incident, though perhaps there was some morsel of information about her "friends" that she had managed to keep to herself despite Majestic's best efforts.

We'll have to see about that.

12

Classified Location
November 5, 2032

Switching off the television monitor, Kirsten Heffron tossed the unit's remote control onto the dining table, listening to the plastic device clatter as it dropped onto the hard surface. The NASA press conference had concluded, and Director Amy Sisson left the podium despite the barrage of questions still being tossed her way. Heffron did not blame the other woman, as the questions now being offered were repeats or restatements of queries the director had already answered. It took a person of considerable patience to tolerate that sort of nonsense, and it was obvious from her composed demeanor that Sisson was well suited for such babysitting.

Better her than me.

She turned from the monitor, surveying the rest of the pair of rooms that served as her living quarters. A definite improvement from the underground metal room to which she had been consigned during the initial weeks of her incarceration, her current accommodations were comfortable if not lavish. If she positioned herself at just the right angle while gazing through the window forming the rear wall of her "cottage," Heffron could pretend there were no guards standing watch at various points atop nearby buildings and along the walking paths connecting the different structures. Moving to the window, she ignored the two sentries within her field of vision and focused instead on the gardener tending to a row of hedges outside the cottage across from hers. For a brief moment, here and there, Heffron could almost forget this wasn't a real apartment complex or neighborhood, but instead the prison where she likely would spend the rest of her life.

"Be it ever so humble," she said aloud.

"There's no place like home?" replied a voice behind her.

Spinning on her heel, Heffron turned to see Doctor William Davison standing in the now-open front doorway leading from her cottage. A tall, bald, gaunt man, whose skin looked as though it might burst into flames upon exposure to sunlight, he wore his usual white lab coat over a black button-down shirt and khaki trousers. The shirt was open at the collar, and Heffron could see the metal chain around his neck that she knew carried a magnetic key card. He wore narrow oval glasses with shaded lenses, giving him a somewhat sinister look that she was certain was by design.

"I really hate when you do that," she said, making no effort to hide her disdain. "Would it kill you to knock first?" The doors to the cottages, which possessed no handles or hinges and were controlled by security keypads, slid aside with almost no sound. It was a feature she did not appreciate, though her captors tended not to abuse the power they wielded over her except on rare occasions.

I wonder what's so special about today?

Davison smiled. "You don't have anything to hide. Do you, Miss Heffron?"

"You tell me. You're the ones with cameras and listening devices hiding in the walls, or you can just snoop around in here while you've got me off doing something else. If you're going to bother me while I'm home, I'd at least like a chance to find something I could use to kill you before I open the door."

"And that is why I don't knock first." Without waiting for an invitation, Davison stepped farther into the room and allowed the door to slide shut behind him. Noting Heffron's robe and pajamas, he said, "Please get dressed. We have a busy day."

"Sightseeing?" Heffron stuck her hands in her robe's pockets. "You never take me anywhere, you know. I think our relationship might be going stale."

Offering another smile, Davison even chuckled at her comment. "I must commend you, Miss Heffron. Your spirit and humor have remained undiminished throughout your stay with us. Considering everything we've put you through, it's really quite remarkable."

"Were you expecting me to feel guilty or something? All you did was pump me full of drugs and make me answer an endless barrage of questions. Everything I told you was against my will. My conscience is clear."

"Of course, which is why we've attempted to make you as comfortable as possible." Davison clasped his hands behind his back. "Surely this community is far preferable to the black site in which you were previously interred?"

Loath as she was to do so, Heffron had to agree with the man. The still-unknown location that was her involuntary home during the first weeks of her imprisonment at the hands of Gerald Markham and Majestic 12 had been little more than a subterranean bunker. Situated deep enough beneath the earth that the entire facility—including any luckless individuals it harbored—could likely be sealed off, buried, and forgotten if it or its contents ever became inconvenient to Markham or anyone else connected to MJ-12. She had heard rumors to that effect regarding other, similar sites, but they along with so many other tales about Majestic's various activities remained unsubstantiated.

In contrast, this "community" was more appealing, at least one some level. She had no idea of her current location, but the mild climate throughout the year as well as the indigenous flora hinted at somewhere tropical, perhaps the Caribbean or South Pacific. Heffron knew that MJ-12 had facilities in both of those regions and elsewhere around the world, dating back to the organization's operations during the Cold War, in particular the 1960s and 1970s during the height of the conflict in Vietnam. Further, the governments of the United States and other prominent world powers had operated places like this for decades, first as refuges for covert agents and other individuals whose lives were at risk after careers spent making enemies around the globe. Later, someone had decided that if high-stakes assets needed to be incarcerated for "reasons of national security," it made better sense to treat such individuals with care and dignity, if for no other reason than as a measure of respect for past service. Heffron had heard of these installations, but had never seen or visited one until becoming a guest.

Wherever they were, Markham and her other masters were certain she could not escape, leaving her in the custody and care of "resident behavioral specialists" like William Davison and others here. The interrogations had concluded some months earlier—eight or nine, if Heffron remembered correctly—and since then she had been left largely alone save for infrequent, erratic visits from Markham. In the meantime, she was free to move about this community and partake of its numerous amenities. There were rules of conduct for "residents," such as the directive to remain within the community's perimeter, which was easy thanks to the electrified fence that surrounded the property. She was allowed to interact with the other residents, though with surveillance a constant concern, most of her fellow inmates tended to avoid discussing things like why they were here or anything connected to their prior lives that may have contributed to their incarceration. As prisons went, Heffron knew there were worse places.

"All right," she said, not moving from where she still stood by the window. "What's on the schedule for today?"

Moving around the cottage's main room, Davison examined the paltry collection of items she had used to decorate her quarters. There were no pictures or anything of a personal nature that had belonged to her prior to her arrival here, but she had taken advantage of the community's library and commissary to find a few books and other items to add some color and flavor to the place. Having nothing of any sentimental value was a good thing, Heffron knew. If she had to leave or was taken from this place, there would be nothing to carry, nothing to concern her, and nothing she would miss. When or if she left this place, she wanted to leave it all, and if that meant torching the entire community to the ground, that would be a nice bonus.

Davison seemed to understand her feelings.

"It's moving day," he said, turning from a wedge-shaped bookshelf that occupied the room's far corner. "You only need to get dressed. Your personal effects, such as they are, will be transported to your new home."

After they have a chance to pick through everything.

Her masters would never pass up an opportunity to rummage through her meager belongings in search of contraband or even something she may have fashioned into a weapon. Such inspections were as frequent as they were random, never giving any resident a chance to muster even the slightest hope that they may be getting away with anything their captors did not notice.

Eyeing the doctor with open skepticism, Heffron asked, "Where are we going?"

"We wouldn't want to spoil the surprise, would we? However, rest assured that you're being transferred to a community very similar to this one. Our hope is to make your stay with us as comfortable as possible."

Heffron snorted. "I'm partial to Maui." When that drew no response from Davison, she added, "Let me guess, more questions? What's left to ask? Haven't you already pulled everything you want out of me?"

Her initial interview sessions with Gerald Markham and other Majestic 12 agents had been straightforward, but her interrogators had quickly lost patience with her unwillingness to answer far too many of their questions. In particular, Markham and the others had been focused on learning about her relationships with supposed extraterrestrials. Heffron had been surprised to learn the extent of the information MJ-12 possessed on this topic, especially her past interactions with the enigmatic individuals who had revealed their presence to her and her predecessor, General Daniel Wheeler. Like Wheeler, who had passed away almost twenty years ago following his retirement from the Air Force, Heffron had known very little about the true identities of Gary Seven and Roberta Lincoln. Upon her first meeting with them while still serving under General Wheeler, both Seven and Lincoln had assured her that they were human, though Heffron always suspected there was more to the older man than met the eye. She had pondered that point on numerous occasions over the years, wondering whether the "organization" Seven and Lincoln claimed to represent really were extraterrestrial in origin, as Seven had claimed. Such questions were never answered, but even the limited demonstrations of advanced technology her mysterious "friends" had employed continued to fuel such theories.

As years passed, Seven and Lincoln reduced the frequency of their often-unannounced visits, and Heffron eventually learned that others had assumed their responsibilities. Natalie Koroma and Jonathan McAllister along with another, a reserved man she only knew as Mestral—all humans so far as she could tell—would drop in on her at irregular and infrequent intervals, usually at her home in Falls Church, Virginia, and well away from the prying eyes of Majestic 12 and its various subordinate organization. The tips they provided her with respect to alien activity on Earth were limited and always accurate to the finest detail, sufficient for Heffron to deploy forces to deal with the situation they presented. She knew this restrained imparting of information was for her own benefit and protection, but that did not lessen her frustration while wondering what other secrets these "agents" possessed, and how else they might be able to help not only the United States but the entire world to defend itself against alien invasion. What else did they know? How long had they and their predecessors been carrying out their work, toiling behind the scenes of history? What other acts, subtle or overt, had they committed while supposedly holding to their mission to aid humanity in its progress toward improving civilization here on Earth?

Heffron had tried and failed to answer those questions, but her incarceration under the watchful eye of Gerald Markham and the interrogations to which she had been subjected had proven that her mysterious benefactors were correct to insulate her. With the assistance of various pharmaceuticals—some of which may well have been extraterrestrial in origin thanks to technology and other items plundered from those alien spacecraft recovered over the decades of Majestic 12's existence—Markham and his people had extracted from her everything she knew of Gary Seven and those other agents. Even with her early attempts at cooperating with Markham and the later, drug-enhanced interview sessions, she had not been forced to betray them too deeply. Beyond their names and the fact that they seemed to possess advanced technology and a wisdom about Earth and humanity that almost certainly had been augmented by an otherworldly perspective, Heffron knew almost nothing about them. Markham had found the servo once given to her by Roberta Lincoln and ordered it disassembled for study, but so far as Heffron knew the senior Majestic official had been unsuccessful at unlocking the device's secrets. He wanted more information, much more, but she was unable to provide it, and Markham had been forced into a sort of waiting game, hoping that the agents might see fit to attempt locating Heffron.

"Director Markham did not share with me his reasons for wanting you moved," said Davison. "Surely you understand the necessity for security."

Heffron rolled her eyes. "Whatever." Gesturing to herself and her robe, she said, "I'm going to change now. Tell one of your spies to tear himself away from his monitors and get me some coffee." Given her prolonged incarceration, she had given up the notion of enjoying much in the way of privacy, and at her age she had abandoned any pretense of modesty. Her one exception had been her bathroom, from which she had pried the concealed cameras and microphones and left them on her small dining table for Davison to find. After the third such demonstration, the doctor had promised the devices would not be replaced, and so far as she could tell he had held to his word.

"Breakfast is already on the way," he replied. "It will be here when you're ready."

"Stop it. You're spoiling me." Leaving the sarcastic remark to hang in the air between them, Heffron began moving toward her bedroom, but stopped at the sound of the chime connected to her cottage's front door.

Davison smiled. "The staff is ahead of schedule, it seems."

Stepping toward the entrance, the doctor pressed a control on the keypad set into the wall just to the door's left, and the door itself slid aside to reveal two people. A man and a woman, each dressed in nondescript gray suits. Whereas the woman's white dress shirt was open at the collar, her companion wore a tie along with a gray fedora. It took Heffron an extra second to recognize the new arrivals, but then she remembered that she only knew of one person who wore such a hat.

Son of a bitch.

"Who are you?" asked Davison, his expression turning to one of suspicion. Instead of responding, the woman held up what appeared to be a silver pen, which emitted a muted electronic tone as she aimed its pointed end toward the doctor. Before Davison could say anything else, the pen released another odd, metallic snapping sound and his body went rigid.

"You're tired," said Natalie Koroma, still holding her servo. "You should sit on the couch and take a nap."

"A nap," repeated Davison as he turned and walked to the room's far side, and Heffron watched as he stretched out on the sofa and closed his eyes.

Koroma's companion, Mestral, stepped through the open doorway, extending his hand. "Director Heffron, it is time for you to leave this place." Despite the composed demeanor that she remembered from their prior meetings, Heffron still heard a slight hint of urgency in the strange man's voice.

"Sounds good to me," replied Heffron. "I wondered if you might come looking for me. I guess I should've expected it."

Mestral replied, "Ascertaining your precise location proved most difficult. Your former associates' efforts at concealing your movements were quite exceptional."

"We figure they have to be onto us," added Koroma. "At least somewhat."

Heffron said, "They know your names, and the fact that you visit me on occasion and you may have some advanced tech at your disposal. I'm sorry I gave them that much."

"Don't beat yourself up about it," replied Koroma, her attention divided between Heffron and scanning the area outside the cottage. "We've withheld a lot of information from you for your own protection, but you're about to get the full story, after we get you out of here."

Glancing down at her robe and pajamas, Heffron asked, "Do I have time to—"

"No," snapped Koroma, holding up her servo. "I

disabled the surveillance devices covering your cottage, but it won't take them long to figure out something's up."

Before Heffron could protest, any response she might offer faded as an alarm began blaring somewhere nearby, accompanied by shouts that already seemed to be very close and getting closer.

Koroma grunted in annoyance. "Like I said."

Mestral nodded. "It would be prudent at this juncture to make a hasty exit."

Despite being worried that she might die in her pajamas, Heffron decided that it was preferable to remaining here for one second longer than necessary. "Then let's get moving. How do we get out of here?"

"We've got it covered," said Koroma, smiling as she once more held up her servo.

Master Chief Petty Officer Ross Bullock was the first through the open door, the muzzle of his Glock pistol leading the way as he entered the cottage. Sidestepping to his right as he crossed the threshold, he swept the room in a practiced, left-to-right fashion that allowed him to sight down the pistol's barrel and search for threats. To his left, he saw Petty Officer Jeni Frontera, dressed like him in a black utility uniform with accompanying tactical vest, mimicking his movements as she covered the room's other side. The only sign of habitation inside the cottage was the prone form of Doctor William Davison, who lay snoring on the sofa positioned against the room's far wall.

"Clear," he said.

Frontera was still aiming her Glock at the bedroom. "Look at this!"

Stepping toward her while raising his pistol to where she was pointing, Bullock saw a fading ring of bright blue haze framed in the doorway leading to the other room. Only then did he notice a faint tingling sensation on his exposed skin.

"Feel that?" He held up his left arm, which was bare to the elbow thanks to his uniform top's rolled sleeves.

"Yeah," replied Frontera. A moment later, she frowned. "It's gone now."

Bullock gestured with his pistol toward the bedroom. "So's that blue mist, or whatever the hell it was." Stepping closer, he pointed his Glock's muzzle through the open doorway, checking the room beyond but finding no one. Only the unmade bed offered any immediate evidence that anyone had been living here.

"She's gone," he said.

Frontera had already pulled her tactical radio from one of the clips on her vest's shoulder harness. "This is Frontera. Lock down the entire community. We've got a runaway."

"We're not going to find her," said Bullock. "She's already long gone."

"That's impossible," replied his partner as she returned the radio to its clip on her vest. "Where the hell could she have gone? And you're saying she got past Madsen and Cooley out there?"

She hooked her thumb over her shoulder, pointing back the way they had come, indicating where she and Bullock had found Petty Officers Daniel Madsen and John Cooley, both unconscious—more like sleeping, just like Doctor Davison—and sitting propped against a pair of oak trees in the garden less than a hundred feet from here.

"No," said Bullock. "She definitely had help."

Scowling, Frontera regarded him with open skepticism. "What do you know that you're not telling me?"

"A lot."

As senior enlisted member of the community's military security detachment, Bullock was briefed into numerous aspects of their assignment here, more so than his subordinates, including Jeni Frontera. Much like the organization to which he was attached, and the senior leadership of the organization overseeing this facility, information was subject to numerous levels of compartmentalization and distributed on a strict need-to-know basis. As a relatively junior member of the security contingent, Frontera was given only the details of this facility and its occupants that were required for her to carry out her duties, which largely were limited to guarding and overseeing the community's high-value occupants.

"Come on, Ross," said Frontera, and Bullock noted her growing annoyance. "What the hell is going on? I mean, I knew Heffron was an important person, which is why she was here, but nobody's supposed to *know* she's here." Her eyes widened, as though a sudden thought had just occurred to her. "You think this was an inside job?"

Bullock holstered his Glock. "No, but it was definitely someone who knows what they're doing." Despite possessing more information than his partner about Director Kirsten Heffron and the reasons for her stay here, there still were some things he did not know with respect to their distinguished guest. "All I was told is that people would be looking for her, and that they weren't garden-variety spies or even special ops assets. Whoever they are, they've got some serious backing and resources, and they'd stop at nothing to find Heffron." He gestured around the room before nodding toward Davison. "Looks like the bosses weren't kidding."

"But how?" asked Frontera. "This place isn't even on the map. *Any* map."

Bullock grunted in agreement. The top-secret, high-security asset community or "H-SAC," in Majestic 12 parlance, occupied a small, unnamed island in the Pacific, hundreds of miles from the nearest cluster of human habitation. Access to the island was via ship or helicopter and the occasional small plane that was all the facility's short, narrow landing strip could accommodate. Relentlessly patrolled and guarded, and blanketed by a full suite of state-of-the art surveillance and anti-intrusion systems, the island should have been impenetrable.

And yet, someone had walked right into this cottage and spirited away the community's most valuable resident. Whoever had found and apparently taken Kirsten Heffron, they were way ahead of even the most advanced spy tech on the planet, to be able to find this facility and target a specific individual for extraction.

Well, maybe not walked.

The thought echoed in Bullock's mind as his gaze fell once more upon the doorway leading from the bedroom, and he considered the blue mist or haze he had seen there moments before. Were Heffron's rescuers sporting some sort of very advanced technology? Could it be alien in origin? Perhaps her liberators *were* aliens. It's not as though the possibility were out of left field, after all. Seven years attached to Majestic's military security forces had taught Bullock that much.

"Like I said: serious backing and resources." Reaching

into the pocket of his uniform top, he extracted a mobile phone and selected a preprogrammed number from its directory. His call was answered on the first ring.

"Control," said a male voice. "What's your status?"

"The asset is gone," replied Bullock. "I think it's them, sir; the ones you told us about. They found her."

13

Sralanya
2386

"For the safety and security of all our people, we are forced to answer these unprovoked actions against our planet. We cannot tolerate interlopers or invaders from other worlds, including yours."

The video was grainy, shifting and jumping almost with every word, and the three figures displayed on the wall-mounted monitor were blurry and indistinct, but Picard had little doubt that he was looking at a trio of humans. A male and a female positioned side by side in high-backed seats within the cramped confines of what could be a spacecraft's cockpit. Behind them was a third, a male situated at a ninety-degree angle from his companions. The restricted space was packed with consoles and other instruments, and Picard could only speculate as to their functions. As for the people, all three wore a form of pressure or space suit, though the image's poor quality left Picard room for doubt. Still, there was something familiar about the clothing. He recalled what he knew of manned space missions from Earth's late twentieth and early twenty-first centuries and decided the suits worn by these individuals could be similar.

None of that helped him begin to make sense of what he was seeing.

"These people actually piloted your ship here from Earth?" Picard asked the question while keeping his attention fixed on the monitor. The image on it had been paused, offering him only a slightly less distorted look at the three people. They were human, he decided, or at least *humanoid.*

What the hell is this about?

"You heard the message for yourself, Captain," said Presider Hilonu, who had stood in silence as Picard watched the video and listened to the broadcast, which had been delivered in several Earth languages. "There also was a version rendered in the primary language of my people and the native tongue of the crew who originally piloted the craft. There were some deviations and gaps in the message, likely owing to the primitive nature of the translation method, but the meaning was quite clear, as was their origin, Captain." Hilonu indicated the monitor with one hand. "They were human, just like you."

Unable to tear his eyes from the screen, Picard asked, "How old is this footage?"

"It has existed since well before my birth, Captain, as well as that of my parents, their parents, and their parents before them. According to our historical records and based on our ability to translate how we compute the passage of time compared to your own units of measure, the ship returned to Sralanya approximately three hundred and twenty of your years ago."

Shaking his head in disbelief, Picard finally forced himself to turn from the monitor so that he could face the Eizand leader. "Presider Hilonu, I promise you that I have no idea what this is about or how this possibly could have happened. Three hundred and twenty years ago, my people were standing on the verge of a devastating conflict that would decimate significant portions of our planet. Hundreds of millions of people would die in that war, and our civilization would approach the brink of collapse. Only through an unlikely act of extraordinary courage and no small amount of luck were we handed a lifeline, which we used to pull ourselves back from that precipice. Our ability to travel beyond the confines of our own solar system was in its infancy, and would not improve until years after we learned that life truly did exist on worlds other than our own. At that time, we simply did not possess the means or technology to travel from my planet to yours."

Naturally, Picard chose not to mention that he had seen the aftereffects of the Third World War and the damage to the planet of his birth with his own eyes, thanks to the *Enterprise*'s being forced to follow a Borg sphere back through time after an attack on Earth more than a decade ago. That incident had resulted in the starship emerging from a temporal rift in the mid-twenty-first century, nearly ten years after the end of the global conflict that had brought humankind to its knees, and only hours before the legendary Zefram Cochrane made his historic first warp-powered space flight. Preventing that achievement would have ensured Earth's isolation from the rest of the galaxy, rather than prompting the initial formal meeting between humans and Vulcans in 2063 and ushering in a new age of technological advancement and cultural enlightenment. Instead, the Borg would have assimilated the entire planet and its war-weary population, forever consigning them to the living death—and hell—that was assimilation into the Borg Collective. It had fallen to Picard and his crew to secure humanity's future, and its destiny.

And that only served to sharpen the Borg's attention on us, didn't it?

Pushing away the unwelcome thoughts lest he become trapped within them, Picard turned back to the monitor. "Presider, if your people did visit my world, then this evidence suggests that human crew was somehow able to acquire an understanding of your technology in order to make the journey. What I don't understand is how they managed such a feat or what would compel them to do so in the first place." Realizing an important point he was overlooking, he asked, "And what about your people? The ship's original crew? What happened to them?"

Her hands clasped before her, Hilonu replied, "From what the human pilots told the authorities after they were taken into custody, the ship's original complement was captured by military forces on your world. They were subjected to interrogation, scientific study, and even torture as their captors attempted to learn everything possible about them and our planet. Your ancestors were apparently quite paranoid about invasion by another spacefaring race, Captain."

On this point, Picard could not argue. "There was a time when my people were gripped by a number of irrational fears, Presider, and it was because of such fear that we nearly destroyed ourselves." He gestured to where Lieutenant T'Sona stood near the office's row of windows, silent and vigilant with her hands clasped behind her back. "If not for the Vulcans, humanity might very well have extinguished itself centuries ago."

Glancing away from Picard to T'Sona, Hilonu said, "Lieutenant, do you have any thoughts on this matter?"

"Captain Picard speaks the truth, Presider," replied

the security officer. "My people had been observing Earth for many years prior to establishing formal contact and relations. We witnessed the war that ravaged their world, and nearly annihilated their entire civilization."

"You observed all of this and did nothing?" asked Hilonu. "I do not understand."

T'Sona said, "At the time, Vulcans conducting such survey missions were required to avoid all contact with the observed planet or its people, and were strictly prohibited from interfering in their culture or affairs in any way. It is a policy that has carried forward to this day, and which Earth and other civilizations agreed to uphold when we came together to form the United Federation of Planets. Starfleet officers in particular swear an oath never to violate this order."

"We call it our Prime Directive, Presider," added Picard. "It's a law that we take very seriously and strive always to uphold." He sighed. "To be perfectly honest with you, there have been times when I've been tempted to violate that directive, or been forced to stand by and observe what I thought might have been a preventable tragedy from unfolding. There also have been times when I have indeed disobeyed the order, because I felt a particular situation was not in keeping with the directive's intentions. It is a noble concept, but flawed. However, it is far more preferable than willfully infringing upon another world's sovereignty while in pursuit of our own agenda."

For the first time since revealing the video footage, Hilonu offered a small smile. "I sense a strength of character in you, Captain; an integrity I can admire. As a leader of my people, I have learned to trust my instincts, which tell me you are a person of principle. You are, so far as I can tell, a worthy representative of your Federation." Stepping away from him, she returned to the wall screen and reached for the small control pad mounted next to the screen. "Would that your example was one followed by more of your people, or that this 'Prime Directive' was a law your civilization chose to adopt far earlier." She waved one hand toward the screen. "Instead, your ancestors chose to impose their will upon us through force of arms."

"Are you saying that they attacked you?" Picard had to force the words from his mouth, contemplating even as he spoke them aloud the horrific potential they described.

Closing her eyes for a moment, Hilonu nodded. "Yes. It was a carefully orchestrated assault, focusing on a handful of our most prominent cities across our planet. The Tevent Coalition and each of the other major political powers were targeted for orbital bombardment with powerful mass-destruction weapons. Within moments, those cities lay in ruin and millions of our people were dead, but as terrible as that attack was, it was what came afterward that truly wounded our world. However, it was our own shortsightedness that was to blame for what happened next, as several of our nations had long ago entrusted our security against one another to automation. In the face of attack from an undefined enemy, those systems reacted as they had been instructed to do."

It took Picard a moment to realize what the presider meant. When realization dawned, he felt his jaw slacken in disbelief. "No."

"Automated attack response systems," said T'Sona. "It is not an uncommon scenario. In the event of a mass-casualty attack by a major power, the targeted party would have procedures to initiate preprogrammed counterattacks as an immediate response. Such protocols were designed to be initiated in the absence of anyone to rescind any existing default instructions, thereby ensuring a response to any sort of large-scale offensive. These scenarios often resulted in widespread destruction to both sides of the given conflict. The very idea of an exchange on that level possibly taking place was usually more than sufficient to compel any governments who might be party to such an occurrence to do everything in their power to ensure it never happened."

Picard said, "The term was 'mutually assured destruction,' Lieutenant." In his youth, he had read reports and other historical records accumulated from other worlds thanks to nearly two centuries of deep-space exploration and encounters with various alien species. Later, as a Starfleet officer, he had seen firsthand the aftermath of such insanity. At the forefront of all those terrifying examples was Earth itself, which nearly crumbled beneath the weight of this very folly as the planet was thrust into the horrors of its third and final global war.

"The term seems most applicable in our case, Captain," said Hilonu. "With communications fragmented in the wake of the initial orbital attacks, there were few if any government or military officials in a position to revoke the automated retaliation procedures. Numerous missiles, each equipped with nuclear warheads, were launched by each of the surviving major powers. Science and technological advancement had seen to it that the radiation produced by these weapons was minimal. That is the only reason there were any survivors left to attempt rebuilding our society, and why I stand before you today. However, those advances also ensured that the missiles' destructive capability was unparalleled. The devastation was massive, with casualties climbing into the hundreds of millions within a single day. Even now, generations removed from the conflict, we still do not know for sure how many Eizand were lost."

Picard, feeling unsteady as he listened to the presider recount her people's calamitous history, forced himself to remain silent and still and ignored the sudden dryness in his throat. Hearing this recitation of destruction and death was becoming too difficult to bear.

Imagine having to live through it.

"What happened after that?" he asked.

Her expression flat and unreadable as she stepped away from the wall monitor and toward her desk, Hilonu replied, "I imagine the events that transpired are not that dissimilar to the aftermath of other such wars you may have witnessed or studied, Captain. Those nations that still possessed functioning military forces, the Tevent Coalition included, seized whatever opportunities presented themselves. Clashes erupted across the planet as armies moved to secure footholds in enemy territory. Border expansion and resource hoarding drove a number of low-intensity conflicts in the years immediately following the global war." Once more the presider indicated the paused image on the viewscreen. "Our history and our legacy is one of strife and suffering, thanks to the events of one single dark day."

We cannot tolerate interlopers or invaders from other worlds, including yours.

Recalling the ominous last words of the recorded message, Picard stared at the frozen, grainy image of the three humans. Who were they? Under what authority had they come to be here and for what purpose? Attack? The very idea seemed ill-considered at best and ludicrous at worst. A single vessel, even one obtained from the Eizand or some other spacefaring race and armed with nuclear weapons, was still just one ship against an entire planet. While it might inflict some damage to its target, the odds were still in the world's favor, and that was before taking into account any sort of space-based defenses the Eizand had harbored back when this was supposed to have occurred.

There's more to this story. There has to be.

"What about the ship?" asked T'Sona. "Assuming it actually made it to Earth, it would fall to twentieth- or twenty-first-century human scientists and engineers to study it to the extent that its technology could be understood and employed. Was it armed with weapons capable of initiating the assault you describe?"

Hilonu shook her head. "No. We have armed some vessels dispatched for deep-space exploration missions, but the ships that were part of that original initiative were not so equipped. The weapons it brought to our world were not of our making, Lieutenant." She turned her gaze to Picard, and when she spoke again her voice took on a harder edge. "Once we captured the ship and its crew, our military interrogators quickly determined that the pilots and the weapons they carried came from your world, Captain."

It was not an accusation, Picard realized. The words were spoken without hesitation or doubt, but instead as a statement of unequivocal fact. They gave voice to a truth known to Hilonu all through her life and carried by those who had come before her. Whatever narrative had formed over the course of the generations born into the future set into motion on that terrible day was entrenched, as much in the presider's own mind as it likely was for a great many of the Eizand people. Perhaps they all held similar views, which meant many of them almost certainly harbored at least something approaching an innate resentment toward anyone who might evoke memories or knowledge of the tragic events that had shaped their civilization.

No wonder she looks at you the way she does. Despite her best efforts to remain civil, she likely can't stand the sight of you. You're the face of the people who tried to destroy her world.

"Presider," said Picard, "I hope you can believe me when I tell you I have no knowledge of these events, how they came to be, or who might be responsible. However, you have my solemn word that I will do everything I can to learn the truth of what happened here."

Again, the Eizand leader offered a small, almost humble smile. Casting a glance toward the top of her desk, she reached for a keypad set into its surface and pressed a recessed green control that emitted a sharp tone.

"I sense that you are a good person, Captain; a decent person. However, that does not change what I must now do."

Behind him, Picard heard the door leading from Hilonu's office opening, and he shifted his stance to look in that direction. He was in time to see a trio of Eizand entering the room, each dressed in the dark maroon uniforms he now recognized as denoting members of the presider's security detail. All three officers—two males and a female—were brandishing the sidearms normally worn on their hips, and the male leading the group was aiming his weapon at Picard.

"Captain."

T'Sona's voice was sharp and commanding despite her normal Vulcan composure. Moving in immediate reaction to the apparent threat, the lieutenant lunged toward the closest Eizand guard, who saw her approach but was not fast enough to defend against it. Her left hand closed around the guard's right wrist, arresting the movement of his pistol before it could be aimed at her. At the same time, her right hand clamped down upon the juncture of the Eizand's neck and shoulder and Picard saw the guard's body go limp as he succumbed to the nerve pinch. Allowing the body to fall to the office's carpeted floor, T'Sona stepped away from the unconscious guard and reached for her own phaser just as the other two Eizand officers were turning in response to her actions.

"Lieutenant! No!"

The warning came too late as the Vulcan drew her phaser from its holder on her hip and raised the weapon toward the guards. This time, the Eizand were faster, firing their own pistols at her before she could even take aim. Picard flinched at the metallic snap that filled the room, and he was sure he felt displaced air washing over him as the weapons unleashed their charges. Both pistols spat forth hellish blobs of red-white energy that struck T'Sona in the chest and hip. The force of the salvos was enough to push the lieutenant off her feet and thrust her backward into the nearby wall. She struck the flat, unyielding surface with a sickly thud and Picard saw her eyes widen in apparent surprise. Falling from her hand, her phaser dropped to the floor as her body followed suit, crumpling into a heap against the wall before T'Sona pitched forward and landed face-first on the room's thick carpet.

"Cease fire!" shouted Hilonu, her words barely audible over the echo of the weapons' reports.

Ignoring her and the guards, Picard rushed to where T'Sona lay unmoving on the carpet. He reached her even as he sensed the two security officers closing on him, but he paid them no mind as he rolled the Vulcan onto her back. His breath caught in his throat as he beheld the ghastly burns and wounds that marred the front of the lieutenant's uniform, including the ripped and scorched flesh beneath the clothing. He did not need to look at her open, unseeing eyes to confirm that she was dead.

Anger welling up within him, Picard pushed himself to his feet, pivoting around until he locked gazes with Hilonu and leveled an accusatory finger. "Was that truly necessary? She only disabled your guard. He'll recover, but she was defending me, as her duty compelled her to do." He forced himself to remain still, offering no resistance as the remaining male guard and his female companion moved so that they now flanked him. The male, standing on Picard's left, reached with his free hand to snatch the captain's communicator badge from his chest. Picard allowed himself only an instant of regret as he considered the lifeline the combadge represented, connecting him to the *Enterprise.*

"My guards were also protecting me, Captain," replied Hilonu, "and they are authorized to use deadly force to do so."

Movement to his right made Picard look in that direction and see the female Eizand guard removing T'Sona's communicator badge and phaser from her body. Picard schooled his features, willing himself to offer no outward sign of the rage and regret building within him. Instead, he returned his attention to Hilonu and locked eyes with the leader.

"If you had wanted to take us into custody, you could've done so at any time without inciting violence." He thought he saw a hint of what might be genuine regret in the presider's eyes, but it was fleeting before she composed herself.

"It is possible that we are simply not yet as advanced and open-minded as you are, Captain. After all, we are recovering from a global calamity just as your people once had to do. Perhaps, in time, we will learn to curb our baser instincts while in pursuit of harmony and peace with our interstellar neighbors."

Moving from behind her desk, Hilonu stepped toward Picard, her expression once more fixed and impassive. "For now, however, I have a solemn duty to perform on behalf of the Tevent Coalition and all the people of Sralanya. I am empowered to see to it that all of those lost in the war along with their descendants who have given so much to prevent our civilization from sliding into ruin receive some measure of justice."

Feeling a knot forming deep in his stomach, Picard asked, "And just what justice do you seek, Presider?"

Hilonu's eyes narrowed, and now Picard saw genuine fury behind them.

"Captain, as a representative of Earth, you are charged with wanton acts of aggression against the Eizand people and the planet Sralanya."

14

There was a time when T'Ryssa Chen had been very particular about her vacation destinations. Risa was a natural first choice, at least before the Borg had all but annihilated the planet, and Pacifica and Betazed were nice places to get away from it all, at least for a while. Even areas of Vulcan, like T'Paal or the Lake Yuron region, had their appeal. She would never have considered taking any sort of leave to a city like Ponval, which she might once have viewed as far too industrial and workaday—in other words, boring—for her tastes.

That was then. Today, however, anything that offered a chance to leave the *Enterprise* in favor of fresh air and warm sunlight, if only for a few hours, was like stepping into paradise.

"Thank you again for allowing us to tour your city," she said to Sonthal, the leader of the four Tevent Coalition security officers who had been detailed to accompany the away team.

"It is a privilege to serve, Lieutenant," replied the Eizand. He, like the others, had been walking behind the away team, though he had positioned himself in proximity to Dina Elfiki. The escorts, all male, were dressed in matching maroon uniforms, holstered sidearms, and small devices attached to the side of their heads that Elfiki had confirmed with her tricorder as being compact communications devices. The guards had said little since the group's departure from Presider Hilonu's offices, though they had answered every question put to them without hesitation. However, the officers' formality with respect to any interaction with her or the others still gave Chen cause to wonder if she and her companions were actually welcome here.

"I scanned the streets and the walking paths," she said. "They're all connected to a solar energy collection network, which channels and redirects the generated power to things like street lamps and other external fixtures. The crystalline pieces embedded in the road or sidewalk surface are the collectors." She smiled. "Better than a lot of batteries I've seen. It's really quite impressive."

"Yes," replied the guard. Then, as though understanding that more information might be desired or required, he added, "Similar collection systems are also incorporated into the roofs of homes, all public buildings, and many private businesses. The individual systems collect sufficient power to meet the needs of the particular structure, and the rest is channeled to distribution nodes for use throughout the city."

"And it's clean, too," added Dina Elfiki, who was walking beside her on yet another stone path winding through yet another peaceful, well-maintained park situated in the middle of still another cluster of drab, gray buildings. "You can't beat that."

Sonthal seemed unimpressed with their admiration. "The system meets our needs."

This guy is going to be fun all day, thought Chen. The guards had been polite and professional the entire time, though they seemed determined to keep a distance, proverbially and literally, from their charges.

"Any places you'd recommend for lunch?" she asked, attempting once more to put their escorts at ease. "Our preliminary scans indicated a number of your foods were compatible with our digestive systems. I'd love to try some of the preferred local cuisine."

Sonthal replied, "I will consult with my supervisor and determine a suitable dining location."

Swing and a miss, T'Rys.

"We're not on shore leave, you know," said Elfiki, indicating the tricorder Chen wore in its holster on her left hip. "You're supposed to be scanning things and putting together thoughts and ideas so that you can report to the captain."

"You're the science officer," replied Chen. "Scans and readings are your thing. I'm the contact specialist, remember? I'm specializing in contact, and right now that means soaking in the ambiance."

Elfiki chuckled. "Right."

"That obvious, huh?"

"Like a red alert siren at two in the morning."

"What can I say? As big as that ship is, it's still a ship." She gestured to the garden around them. "The arboretum and the holodecks can only take you so far. They'll never beat the real thing."

Offering her a sidelong glance, Elfiki said, "So now you're a nature lover? I've seen your quarters. Every plant you've ever touched has died. Even the artificial ones."

"That doesn't mean I can't admire the simple beauty that's all around us, or the work of people who know what they're doing and are able to . . . you know . . . not kill things."

Behind them, Glinn Ravel Dygan said, "I must concur with Lieutenant Chen. There is nothing quite like walking the open spaces with the dirt of a real planet beneath your feet. As a boy, I used to run and play in the forest near my home. It is something I missed once I entered the service, and to be honest I was beginning to feel . . . confined . . . aboard the *Enterprise*."

"That's right," said Chen. "This is your first away team in a while, isn't it?"

Dygan nodded. "Indeed it is. Given my role aboard ship, such excursions are rarely justified. I must remember to thank Captain Picard again for the opportunity."

Glancing over her shoulder, Chen said, "What about you, Braddock? You're an outdoorsy type, right? Didn't you say you liked to camp when you were a kid?"

Tall and muscular, Lieutenant Austin Braddock was looking through the trees to his right, and only when he brought his gaze back around to Chen did he seem to notice she was talking to him. Chen realized that—like the trained security officer he was—Braddock had been keeping pace behind his companions, with his attention focused on their surroundings rather than the conversation taking place immediately in front of him.

"Sorry, Lieutenant. What was the question?"

"Camping," repeated Chen. "You said you did a lot of camping as a kid."

Braddock nodded. "My father and I would go camping on Luna and Mars whenever he was home on leave. The fishing on Lake Armstrong was something else."

"Were you a hunter in your youth?" asked Dygan. "My father hunted when I was a child on Cardassia Prime, but it is not something for which I ever developed an interest."

Shaking his head, Braddock said, "I never even picked up any sort of phaser or other rifle until I joined Starfleet." The brawny blond-haired man shrugged. "We never owned one, and it was just something I never had a chance to try."

Chen smiled. “And yet, you hold the ship’s marksmanship record.”

“My instructors thought I was a natural.”

“Don’t let him fool you with that false modesty,” said Elfiki. “He still holds most of the records at Starfleet Security School, too. Braddock here’s one of the best sharpshooters I’ve ever seen.”

Braddock replied, “I just did what the instructors taught me to do.” Then he revealed a small, mischievous smile. “But yeah, I do all right.”

“There it is,” said Elfiki. “I knew that modesty bit was an act.”

It was not really an act, Chen knew. The quiet, reserved security officer possessed a demonstrable aversion to discussing his various accomplishments, in particular those achievements tied to his talents as a marksman. Though he and the rest of the *Enterprise*’s security contingent were well trained to handle any number of situations that might threaten the ship or the crew, in space or on some alien world, Austin Braddock excelled in these areas. His skill and experience had saved the captain and various other members of the crew on numerous occasions, and he was most often selected by Lieutenant Aneta Šmrhová or her deputy chief of security, Rennan Konya, to assist Kirsten Cruzen whenever a larger team of specialists was needed during an away team mission. Tempering his exceptional proficiency was a genuine humbleness that made him immensely likeable to Chen and—so far as she knew—just about any other member of the crew who knew him.

“Might we venture into some of the public spaces?” asked Glinn Dygan, after the away team and their escorts had walked in silence for a few moments.

They had come to the edge of the park, and Chen now could see Eizand moving about via ground vehicle or on foot, with the crowds more dense in this part of Ponval than what she had witnessed closer to the capital building. She noted people sitting in patio areas outside several of the buildings, and took these to be patrons at various dining establishments.

"Is this some kind of retail district?"

Behind her, Chen heard Sonthal reply, "Yes. You will find merchants scattered throughout the city, but this section is zoned specifically for such pursuits. It is quite popular with local residents as well as visitors from the other cities."

Elfiki said, "Looks pretty interesting. Can we have a tour of that area?"

Turning to face Sonthal, Chen saw that his attention seemed focused elsewhere, and it took her a moment to realize the Eizand security officer's left hand was pressed to the communications device on the side of his head. He glanced in her direction before his gaze shifted to the other members of his detail, and Chen noted how each of them also seemed to be listening to something on their own comm units.

"Everything okay?"

The Eizand lowered his hand before turning to Elfiki. "Lieutenant, I have been instructed to take you into custody." When Braddock moved toward her, Sonthal held up a hand. "Please do not make this any more difficult than it needs to be. Your security officer will be required to surrender his weapon."

Noting the tension on Braddock's face as the other members of Sonthal's escort contingent separated and began positioning themselves to form a perimeter around the away team, Chen said, "Hang on a second, here. Let's everybody just calm down a bit. Sonthal, what's going on?"

"I am not authorized to discuss the matter with you, Lieutenant." The Eizand's left hand dropped to the grip of the sidearm that still rested in its holster on his right hip. "Please comply with my instructions, or we will be compelled to employ more forceful methods for taking you into custody."

It was one of his security officers who moved first.

Chen saw the young Eizand male pulling his weapon from the holster on his left hip, retrieving the sidearm across his body with his opposite hand and bringing it up to aim at her. The pistol's muzzle never made it that far before it was stopped by Glinn Dygan, who moved much faster than Chen would ever have expected. Reaching out with one hand, the Cardassian arrested the Eizand's weapon in midbrandishing, yanking it free of the other officer with startling strength and speed.

"Dygan!" snapped Elfiki. "No!"

Her warning was too late as Dygan used his free hand to push the Eizand security officer backward, forcing him from the walking path and making him trip over a cluster of nearby rocks. The escort stumbled and fell to the grass, though he was agile and was already regaining his footing.

Tapping her communicator badge, Chen snapped, "Chen to *Enterprise*! We're in trouble down here!"

That was all the time she had before Sonthal and his companions rushed in, weapons drawn and aiming at the away team. Braddock, the only one armed with a phaser, was rushed by two of the guards while Sonthal and the guard who had tussled with Dygan moved to cover the rest of the team. With Sonthal's pistol aimed at his head, the Cardassian exchange officer allowed the weapon he had taken to fall from his fingers, and he raised his hands to show he would offer no further resistance.

"Enterprise *to away team,"* said Commander Worf over the connection Chen had established, his deep voice erupting from Chen's combadge. *"Report!"*

Any reply she might have offered died as the muzzle of Sonthal's weapon pointed at her face. Without saying anything, the Eizand officer reached forward and plucked the badge from her uniform tunic. Then she watched as he dropped the device to the walking path and stomped it with his boot. His companions followed his example, removing and neutralizing the badges from the rest of the team.

"You will come with us," said Sonthal, "and do so peacefully."

Elfiki, her hands raised as one of the guards removed her tricorder from her waist, asked, "What are you going to do with us?"

With neither his weapon nor his gaze wavering from Chen, the security officer replied, "That is not for me to decide. My orders are to move you to a secure holding facility and await further instructions."

"You understand our ship is still up there," said Chen. "They know something's going on down here. They won't just stand by and do nothing."

The Eizand nodded. "Yes, we know what your people are capable of doing." He gestured with the weapon for Chen and the others to turn and begin walking.

"How's that ambiance treating you now?" asked Elfiki, though Chen saw that the science officer's attempt at gallows humor was not working even for her.

Reaching toward her friend, Chen laid a hand on her shoulder. "It'll be okay. If they really wanted to hurt us, they could've done it already."

Behind her, Glinn Dygan said, "You were able to apprise Commander Worf of the situation, Lieutenant. He is doubtless taking action as we speak. This matter will surely be resolved in short order, and hopefully with few if any complications for either side. We will be fine."

"It's not us I'm worried about," said Braddock from where he was walking next to Dygan. "What about the captain?"

Chen sighed. "Good question."

Something told her she was not going to like the answer.

15

U.S.S. Enterprise
2386

Rising from the command chair, Commander Worf moved closer to the forward bridge stations, centering himself between Lieutenant Joanna Faur at flight control and Ensign Jill Rosado, the relief officer who now sat at the ops station while Glinn Ravel Dygan was off the ship. Every muscle in his body was tensing in reaction to the curt, harried communication just received seconds ago from the surface of Sralanya.

"Replay the message, Lieutenant," he said.

Standing behind him at the primary tactical station, Lieutenant Aneta Šmrhová replied, "Aye, sir." Worf heard her tapping a short command sequence to her workstation before the anxious voice of Lieutenant T'Ryssa Chen erupted from the intercom.

"Chen to Enterprise*! We're in trouble down here!"*

After a moment, Šmrhová said, "I've double-checked everything, Commander. That's the whole message. We didn't even have time to respond to the initial hail before the signal was lost. I've scanned for Lieutenant Chen's communicator, as well as Elfiki's, Braddock's, and Dygan's. None of them are active."

"Contact the captain," snapped Worf. "And scan the surface for Vulcan, human, and Cardassian life signs. Lock transporters on them and prepare to beam them aboard on my command." He already knew that residual radiation in the planet's atmosphere had required Commander La Forge and his engineering team to make some modifications not only to the transporters but also the ship's sensors, but the *Enterprise*'s chief engineer had assured both Captain Picard and Worf that the adjustments were minor and would not hamper the operation of either system.

"Commander," said Šmrhová after a moment. "I'm not able to make contact with Captain Picard or Lieutenant T'Sona either. Every combadge from the away team is inactive." An almost musical sequence of alert tones emanated from her console, and the security chief frowned. "Now we're being hailed from the planet's surface, but not from the captain or the away team." She looked up from her console. "It's coming from the seat of the Tevent Coalition government, sir: Presider Hilonu."

Not liking where his instincts were already telling him this was going, Worf turned to face the bridge's main viewscreen and drew himself to his full height. "On-screen, Lieutenant."

In response to his order, the curvature of Sralanya as viewed from the *Enterprise*'s high orbit above the planet disappeared, replaced with the image of the statuesque Eizand leader. She was dressed in an almost regal-looking jade-green gown that flowed from her shoulders, its material reflecting whatever gentle lighting was being cast upon her from somewhere off screen.

"This is Commander Worf, first officer of the *Enterprise*." Remembering to keep his tone neutral, he said with as much diplomacy as he could muster, "Presider Hilonu, we have received what we believe may be a distress call from one of our people on the planet's surface. Our attempts to contact this individual and other members of our team have been unsuccessful. I would like to speak with Captain Picard."

Her hands clasped before her, the presider replied, *"I am afraid that is not possible just now, Commander. Your captain and the other members of his entourage have been taken into custody, where they will remain until the business of Eizand justice is concluded."*

"Justice?" Despite his self-imposed pledge to remain composed, Worf frowned at her, and he even felt a momentary twitch as he almost released a snarl of disapproval. Holding that in check, he said, "I do not understand."

"All will be made clear in due course," said Hilonu. *"For now, you should take whatever steps are necessary to communicate to your superiors that Captain Picard will serve as the representative of the civilization that attempted to destroy ours. He will stand trial for Earth's crimes against Sralanya and the Eizand people."*

Worf turned to Šmrhová and signaled for her to mute the connection. "Have you located the captain and the others?"

The security chief replied, "I've got the captain and the away team, sir, but the readings are muddled. I'm not even sure if I have everyone, as I'm only counting five life signs instead of six."

"Who's not accounted for?"

The security chief replied, "Either Chen or T'Sona, sir. I'm only picking up one Vulcan biosign, but I can't get a clear enough scan to distinguish between them. It looks like the away team's been taken somewhere that's at least partially shielded from our scans. If I'm reading this correctly, they're in an underground facility of some kind, and there's a combination of materials in the surrounding rock as well as disruption from power distribution lines in close proximity that's interfering with our readings." She looked up from her console. "Sir, I don't know if what I've got is strong enough for a transporter lock."

Turning back to the screen, Worf gestured for the communications channel's audio to be restored as he eyed Hilonu. "Presider, if you do not allow me to speak with Captain Picard, you will leave me no choice but to attempt retrieving them by any means at my disposal."

"Do not attempt any more landings or other actions against us, Commander," warned the presider. *"Captain Picard has already enlightened me about your various rules and regulations when it comes to interfering with sovereign worlds. If provoked, we will defend ourselves."*

Worf stepped closer to the viewscreen. "Provoked? Presider Hilonu, you have arrested our captain and members of our crew, one of whom I am unable to locate. You have threatened our people with legal action and have so far failed to provide any evidence that points to their culpability." He almost surprised himself with how easily the oratorical skills he had cultivated as an ambassador came back to him, allowing him to speak in a manner far more dignified than he might prefer as a warrior or even a Starfleet officer. "Unless or until specific charges are presented, I am duty bound to see to the safety of every member of this crew."

Appearing unfazed by his response, Hilonu remained stoic on the screen. *"Formal charges will be presented in short order. Until then, Commander, I urge you to employ restraint, for the sake of everyone involved."*

The connection ended and the presider's image disappeared from the screen, replaced once more by the view of Sralanya. Worf pondered the planet for a moment, considering his options. Not for the first time, he fumed in silence at the thought that he was here, safe from immediate danger, while his captain awaited whatever fate Hilonu and Eizand justice might have planned for him. Commanding officer's prerogative notwithstanding, Worf knew it was he who should be down there with the away team.

What would Captain Picard do if he were standing here? Depending on the circumstances, he might exercise the very moderation Hilonu had recommended, though his decision would be driven by whatever information he possessed with regard to the condition of any personnel still on the surface. If the presider had permitted Picard to speak to him, Worf could imagine the captain ordering him to wait for further instructions, provided he felt that he and the others were in no immediate danger. If that were indeed the case, Picard would almost certainly err on the side of diplomacy in the hopes of resolving the situation in as amicable a fashion as he could forge.

Unfortunately, Worf did not have access to the captain. All he had to inform any decision he might make was what Hilonu had told him. Without taking some action, there was no way to ascertain the captain's and the away team's condition. They could be injured, for all he knew. The inability to locate at least one member of the team, T'Ryssa Chen or T'Sona, was troubling.

He could not stand here and do nothing.

"Lieutenant Šmrhová, would moving us closer resolve your sensor readings?"

The security chief replied, "It couldn't hurt, sir. However, we're not alone up here. There is the network of satellites and space stations, but so far they all seem to be maintaining their own orbital paths. That said, those within our line of sight around the planet's curvature are tracking our location and movements. They may not take kindly to us doing anything crazy, and they do have those EMP generators. We should probably give them a wide berth."

Worf nodded. "Understood." Stepping backward until he once more stood just behind the forward bridge stations, Worf said, "Lieutenant Faur, break from standard orbit and lower our track until Lieutenant Šmrhová's scans improve. Plot a course that steers us clear of any of the space stations or satellites."

"Aye, sir." The conn officer tapped several controls on her console's flat surface. "The computer's fashioned a course for us. Breaking from standard orbit."

With the sort of confidence that could only come from someone possessing tested skill and experience, Faur moved her hands across the workstation. On the main viewscreen, the lieutenant's actions had an immediate effect, as Worf watched the curve of Sralanya shift and disappear from view as the *Enterprise*'s orbital path changed. From where he stood behind her, the first officer was able to see her console's graphical representation of Sralanya and the starship's position relative to it. A series of small red icons represented the network of satellites and other space-based habitats circling the planet, and he noted how the course plotted by Faur and the ship's computer would at first take the *Enterprise* away from the planet before maneuvering the vessel into a new trajectory that would keep it well away from any of the artificial constructs and perhaps even convey to the people of Sralanya that no affront or harm was intended. Within moments, Faur had guided the starship into its new, lower orbit, and Worf listened as she and Šmrhová coordinated their efforts.

"Sensor readings are definitely clearing," the security chief reported a moment later, but Worf could still detect a note of skepticism in her voice. "I'm able to detect five members of the away team, but the scans are still encountering interference."

Faur said, "I don't know how much lower I can take us without picking up some buffeting from the atmosphere."

"Bridge to engineering," said Worf. "Commander La Forge, we require more power to the sensor array."

His voice filtering through the bridge's intercom system, the *Enterprise*'s chief engineer replied, *"We're already on it, Commander. It's not just a question of power, though. We think the combination of lingering background radiation and the mineral composition of the subsurface rock and soil are what's causing the problem. I may have to make some more adjustments to filter out the interference."*

"Do so quickly," said Worf. "We are attempting to locate and retrieve Captain Picard and the away team."

"Understood."

Behind him, Worf heard a telltale tone from Šmrhová's tactical console. He recognized the alert as meaning the sensors had detected a potential threat to the ship, and he turned to see her frowning as she studied the readings before her.

"Sir, several of the satellites and two of the larger constructs are breaking from their orbits." Pausing, she tapped a short sequence of commands to her station before adding, "They're moving to intercept us. According to my scans, they're activating their onboard weapons systems. The closest is at one hundred seventy-six kilometers and closing."

"Yellow alert," snapped Worf, returning his attention to the viewscreen. "Shields up. Lieutenant Faur, prepare to break orbit. Šmrhová, open a channel to those satellites and Presider Hilonu's office."

Once the security chief reported that the frequency was open, Worf said, "This is Commander Worf of the *Starship Enterprise*. Our sensors have detected the movement of your satellites in our direction. If they continue on their present course, I will have no choice but to deem their intentions as hostile and take whatever action I deem appropriate to protect this vessel and its crew."

After a moment, Šmrhová said, "No response, sir, but they're definitely receiving us." When another tone sounded from her console, she added, "Twelve satellites and two of the larger stations have broken from their previous orbital tracks and are definitely moving toward us. I'm picking up a communications frequency shared between them. I'm not sure, but I think each of the two stations is controlling six of the smaller satellites. It's definitely looking like a coordinated effort."

Watching the graphic on Faur's console that showed the satellites maneuvering closer to the *Enterprise*, Worf knew he had but seconds to make a decision, but what was the best course of action here? He hated the idea of running, especially with the captain and the away team on the surface, but he also had to consider the larger situation. While he was confident the ship's phasers were more than a match for whatever the Eizand weapons might offer, did he really want to complicate matters by lashing out, even in defense of his vessel and crew? What would Picard do in this situation?

A tactical withdrawal is not a retreat if it is undertaken without being forced.

It was something Picard, as consummate a strategist in Worf's estimation as he was an explorer and a diplomat, had said more than once. What always seemed to make the captain so effective in battle was his reluctance to resort to violence, but not fearing to utilize every available resource once that became the only option. He was as shrewd as he was prudent in this regard, and Worf had learned as much about the proper conduct of war from Jean-Luc Picard as he had from every instructor at Starfleet Command School and every Klingon commander he had ever studied.

Then there were the other facets of this particular situation. With Picard and the away team still in Eizand custody somewhere on or below the planet's surface, a display of superior weaponry might provoke some form of punitive action against them. Further, Sralanya was not a declared enemy, and with Picard unreachable, it fell to Worf to represent Starfleet and the Federation in the best possible light. While he was certain a more aggressive response to the away team's capture would result in its retrieval and return to the ship, the damage to relations between the Federation and this newly discovered world could be irreparable. For the moment, all of this could be the result of a simple yet massive and unfortunate misunderstanding. It was Worf's job to determine whether that was true and how to resolve the issue for the benefit of everyone involved, including the Eizand.

Evaluating all of that, Worf knew he had only one real option.

"Lieutenant Faur, break orbit. Ready phasers to disable those satellites, but not destroy, if they get too close."

He was just deciding what "too close" might mean when another alarm sounded. This one burst from the intercom system, accompanied by red alert indicators flaring to life around the bridge.

Standing over the master systems display table in the *Enterprise*'s main engineering room, Geordi La Forge felt the slightest reverberation in the deck beneath his feet. Tucked deep inside the central portion of the starship's secondary hull, insulated by surrounding decks, conduits, and layers of hull plating, this sensation along with the sudden illumination of the shield generator indicators on the oversized display were the only things telling La Forge that the ship had just been attacked.

"Look at that," said Lieutenant Veldon, one of his junior engineers, who currently was manning the MSD and the adjacent wall display that dominated the engineering section's primary operations area. A Benzite, Veldon wore a special respirator harness around her neck that produced a steady vapor comprised of elements native to her home planet's atmosphere, making her more comfortable in the Class-M environment favored by most humanoids and commonplace aboard Starfleet vessels. "Starboard shields are down eighteen percent."

La Forge, his attention divided between the wall display and table, was already tapping lengthy strings of instructions across the MSD's control interfaces. The damage reports showed him that the impacts against the *Enterprise*'s starboard deflector shields had come from attacks launched by two of the Eizand satellites. Not constant beams, the salvos instead had come in the form of powerful resonance bursts from the electromagnetic pulse generators housed within each of the unmanned vehicles. He had been studying the devices since the first sensor data had been collected upon the starship's insertion into orbit of Sralanya, and had concluded that the ship would only be at risk if subjected to attacks by several of the satellites working in concert. That notion seemed unlikely, given how Captain Picard had facilitated communications with one of the Eizand leaders and arranged for face-to-face meetings on the planet.

Unlikely, but not impossible, and now here we are.

He tapped his communicator badge. "La Forge to bridge."

"Bridge," replied Commander Worf, and the chief engineer noted that the Klingon's voice sounded tighter and more curt than usual.

"Worf, those EMP generators are already having an effect on our shields. We're rerouting power to compensate, but I don't recommend we let them keep taking shots at us." As he made his report, La Forge tapped another control, activating a connection to the *Enterprise*'s sensor array. From the MSD, he had access to all of the telemetry being collected by the starship's host of scanning equipment, just as if he was overseeing those operations from the science or tactical consoles on the bridge. Thanks to this, he now was able to see that still more of the satellites were already maneuvering into position even as the starship was undertaking a new course to move it farther from Sralanya. A scan of the devices had revealed that none possessed the capability to leave the planet's orbit on their own, so retreat was still a viable option for the *Enterprise* and would give La Forge and his team time to come up with a means of dealing with the satellites, perhaps without being forced to destroy them.

"I don't know how much we can take if they gang up on us, Worf." From what he could discern from the readouts, the ship was continuing to withdraw, but was doing so at a speed La Forge thought was too slow. There was only one reason for such a strategy: Worf was unwilling to leave Captain Picard and the away team on the surface, and was doing everything he could to balance his concern for them against the safety of the ship. Knowing the first officer as he did, La Forge was certain the conflict of priorities would be weighing on his friend.

"We are attempting to—"

The rest of Worf's reply was lost as everything around La Forge bucked in response to a new assault on the ship's shields. Static flooded the open communications frequency and every light source in engineering flickered. The deck shuddered beneath him and La Forge grabbed the edge of the MSD table to keep himself steady as the *Enterprise* absorbed the brunt of the new attack. Still standing on the other side of the table, Lieutenant Veldon pointed to the technical schematic displayed on the table's center screen.

"Commander, shield strength has dropped another twenty-six percent."

"Damn it. Reroute power from nonessential systems. I want to stay ahead of this. Bridge, what's the story up there?"

The Klingon replied, *"Seven of the satellites launched a simultaneous attack."*

"I can see that." La Forge studied the schematic, noting the blinking amber line that traced around the computer-generated dorsal view of the *Enterprise* and represented its deflector shields. "We're already down below fifty percent on shield strength. We're rerouting power, but now it'll take more time to get us back to full capacity."

No sooner did he speak the words than the ship trembled from another assault, and this time the alarm sirens blared all through the engineering section. Glancing up from the MSD, La Forge saw several members of his staff moving between workstations, diagnosing the slew of new reports and alert messages streaming across numerous consoles and displays around the room.

"Shields at seventeen percent," reported Veldon.

His fingers almost a blur as he entered a rapid-fire string of commands to the various interface panels on the table's flat surface, La Forge said, "I'm pulling power from the warp engines. That should buy us some time." Another indicator flashed on the MSD, and he saw that the ship's phasers had just been fired.

In a louder voice, he said, "Worf, we can reroute power for the shields, but it's a temporary measure. We need some breathing room if I'm going to get this under control."

Over the still-open comm frequency, Worf said, *"Acknowledged. We disabled two of the satellites, but more are coming. We're moving the ship to a safe distance."*

A moment later, other displays on the table marked the *Enterprise*'s new course away from the planet and its increase in speed to half impulse, which was more than enough to break orbit and push the starship well out of range of its attackers.

Having heard the bitter tone of defeat in his friend's voice, La Forge said, "We'll figure this out, and we'll get the away team back."

"Keep me apprised of your progress. Worf out."

The connection severed before the chief engineer could say anything else, but in truth there was little if anything left to say. He and his people had a job to do.

"He seems rather upset," said Veldon, the vapor from her respirator drifting up and over her face.

"That's one way to put it," replied La Forge. Feeling the first hints of a headache beginning to form behind his eyes, he rubbed his temples and willed himself to ignore the warning signs and focus on the task at hand. "We've got a lot of work to do, so we should probably get started."

16

Isle of Arran
November 20, 2032

Kirsten Heffron decided she could get used to this.

Sipping coffee, she sat in a wooden rocking chair, admiring the lush, gently sloping farmland that extended some distance from the front porch of the farmhouse that was the unlikely headquarters of the equally improbable people who had rescued her from Majestic 12's clutches. In the distance, the pale pink glow of dawn approached from beyond the hills. She always enjoyed coffee or tea while watching the sunrise, and while it was a favorite and refreshing way to start a new day, it was also a luxury in which she had rarely indulged in recent years. It was another of life's simple pleasures that often fell by the wayside as she became ever more involved in the demands of her job.

Not anymore. For better or worse, those days are probably over.

The more she mulled that thought, the more Heffron realized she did not care. She had served her country to the best of her ability, and her country had repaid her with betrayal. That would not happen again; not so long as she had any say in the matter. Retirement, even if forced upon her, would be something she would enjoy free of guilt from this point forward, and it began with reacquainting herself with the things she missed from simpler, happier times.

After a long, hot bath—a treat she had afforded herself at least once each day since her rescue and the likes of which she was denied during her extended captivity with only a shower provided in her various holding cells and "community" cottages—Heffron had wrapped herself in comfortable sweats and a robe. The ensemble, along with an assortment of her other clothing and several personal items, was a gift from her benefactors, who liberated them from the storage facility where MJ-12 had placed her belongings after taking her into custody. Heffron was pleased to note that the jeans in particular were of much looser fit than the last time she had worn them. It was nice to see that incarceration had at least one tangible benefit.

Doesn't mean I'm in any hurry to go back.

As for the farmhouse and the island on which it sat, Heffron was forced to admit that she had never even heard of this place before arriving here via the most unlikely of transportation methods. The woman, Natalie Koroma, had never mentioned it during any of their handful of previous meetings. In fact, the mysterious woman had never provided even the slightest hint as to where she might live or work, no doubt a deliberate choice on her part to keep her identity secret. It was but one more piece of the bizarre puzzle surrounding Koroma and her colleagues that Heffron could never solve, as she had no idea what the completed picture might look like.

"Good morning, Director Heffron."

Her colleagues. Holy crap.

Looking up at the sound of the voice, Heffron saw Mestral standing on the farmhouse's front porch, just outside its main door. Despite the early hour, he was already dressed and groomed in what she had learned was his usual impeccable fashion in a dark gray suit, white dress shirt, and gray-blue tie. Only his hat was missing, affording Heffron a look at his black-gray hair and the tips of his pointed ears. The hat came off for the first time shortly after her arrival with him and Koroma following their rescue of her from the MJ-12 "custodial community." That was when Heffron learned the truth of Mestral's identity and origins as a visitor from another world, Vulcan.

"Good morning, Mestral. You can dispense with the title. I was fired, remember? I'm not a director anymore."

She was at first concerned about his story of having lived on Earth in secret since 1957 following the crash of his scout ship in rural Pennsylvania. The ability to hide with such success from the apparatus that was Majestic 12 and its various tenant organizations over the ensuing decades was a bit disturbing on some level, though mitigated by the obvious evidence that Mestral was not a threat to the planet or humanity. Just the time they had spent together in this most remote of safe houses had been enough to convince her of the Vulcan's sincerity. Several evenings had been spent sitting by the fireplace in the house's great room as she listened to Mestral recount his journeys from place to place, observing like the scientist he was all manner of human technological and societal development while doing his best to remain anonymous.

Heffron also learned that he even had been allied with one of MJ-12's now long-defunct initiatives, Project Blue Book, during the 1950s and 1960s, aiding case officers from the United States Air Force to investigate alleged sightings and encounters with extraterrestrial visitors long before she was born. Mestral described several of these tales as he worked with people whose names Heffron vaguely recalled from archived reports and other documents detailing Majestic's activities over the decades. All of this came before his chance encounter with the predecessors to Natalie Koroma, Gary Seven and Roberta Lincoln, whom Heffron herself had met decades ago, and his decision to assist these mysterious Aegis agents with their own assignment here on Earth. She was at first taken aback by the seeming arrogance and presumption that aliens from another world would take such an active interest in Earth. Once Seven and Lincoln explained the purpose of their mission, and the very real stake they had in its success due to their own human heritage, Heffron began to appreciate the scope of the effort to which they had committed themselves. Seven in particular was, figuratively and literally, a rare, special breed of person, one of scores of humans born on a planet untold thousands of light-years across the galaxy and trained over the course of generations for this task. He had devoted his entire existence to the betterment of Earth and humanity. As for Roberta Lincoln, she had abandoned any semblance of a normal life in order to join Seven's cause, consigning herself to toil in obscurity toward a goal that she might not even live to see realized.

Sounds familiar, doesn't it?

The quiet evening talks with Mestral had been most illuminating, as she learned ever more about people like Seven and Lincoln, and Natalie Koroma and Jonathan McAllister—the latter having been injured with such severity that his time here on Earth had been cut short.

Each of them, like her and the uncounted men and women who had pledged themselves to the mission of Majestic 12 over the decades, had answered a higher calling to service, but even that duty seemed to pale in comparison to that undertaken by Seven and his colleagues. It was during these contemplative sessions with her new Vulcan friend that Heffron was forced to admit with no small amount of regret and even shame that, from Mestral's point of view, humans had not always comported themselves in the best manner, and for all the amazing leaps in science and technology, there remained significant work to be done in the area of learning how to live in peace and harmony with one another. While there had been some advancement, there seemed to be very little *progress*. Despite their apparently unlimited potential, were humans ultimately a lost cause?

Let's hope not.

"I knew you'd be up already," she said, shifting in the rocker as Mestral moved from the door toward an adjacent seat. "But if I didn't know any better, I'd think you were getting ready to head off somewhere."

Mestral lowered himself into the other rocking chair. "I am preparing to depart for Washington. Since we liberated you from the Majestic facility, we have been attempting to monitor their activities with respect to you. We investigate any communications where you are mentioned and follow up on any actions stemming from those missives. We have discovered them to be quite guarded with any information pertaining to you, but we are confident they have not ceased their efforts to find you."

Nodding, Heffron sipped her coffee. After a moment, she said, "I don't expect Markham to ever stop, not while there's any chance of tracking me down. If it takes him the rest of his life and he has to search every inch of this planet on foot, he'll keep looking until he finds me." She paused, regarding the sun, which was just now beginning to creep over the distant hills. "I guess this means I can't go home for a while, if ever."

"That is unlikely, at least until such time as your standing with Majestic 12 can be revised to a status that is agreeable to all involved parties, especially yourself."

Smiling, Heffron chuckled. "You mean something we can all live with? I'd be happy to just be able to go home and be left alone to enjoy retirement. Maybe take some of that money I've stashed away all these years and buy a house on a beach somewhere where a cabana boy has a fresh drink any time I hold out my hand. I could live with that."

It's good to have goals, right?

"What about Brinalri?" she asked.

Mestral replied, "I was unable to ascertain his current location. However, I have accessed a series of electronic messages that refer in vague terms to a prisoner having died during an escape attempt. No identities or revealing characteristics were included in the message, though there were questions and confusion regarding proper disposal of remains, which were inconsistent with my understanding of common human practices pertaining to such matters. This suggests the subject of the missives was not human."

"Damn it." Heffron shook her head. "He came all that distance across space, and for what? To die in some hole in the ground that most people will never know even existed."

Whatever reply Mestral may have delivered went unspoken when the front door opened and Natalie Koroma stepped onto the porch. She was dressed in faded jeans, a teal button-down blouse, and black running shoes, and her black hair was pulled into a ponytail. As usual, she wore no makeup, and Heffron noted the concern in the young Aegis agent's eyes.

"We've got company."

Both Heffron and Mestral pushed themselves from their rockers, and Heffron could not resist looking out from the porch to the lush green grass covering the gentle slope of the hills. What was she expecting to see? Teams of Majestic agents storming the farmhouse? A squadron of attack helicopters maneuvering for a strafing run?

"You're sure?" she asked, shrugging off her robe and leaving her dressed in her sweatpants and matching shirt.

Koroma nodded. "Yeah. The Beta 7 picked up unusual ship traffic off the coast on the far side of the island. Definitely out of the ordinary, and that's before you add in the military comm signals the computer detected."

"Uh-oh." Heffron felt a cold chill beginning to course down her spine.

"Exactly." Koroma looked to Mestral. "The signals are encrypted, but the Beta 7's chewing on them right now. We need to start our evac plan."

Stepping toward the door, the Vulcan replied, "Understood."

Heffron followed the two agents back into the farmhouse and watched as Koroma moved past the fireplace, where logs where already burning and warming the room, to where the Beta 7 supercomputer was visible. The stone wall that shielded the mechanism had dropped into the floor to reveal the array of controls and monitors. It was obvious that the machine was far more advanced than even state-of-the-art military computers. Quite comfortable operating the equipment used by her and her people as a consequence of her work, Heffron could appreciate the Beta 7's design and interfaces. She was confident that with its voice recognition protocols and artificial intelligence algorithms to assist her, she could be well-versed in its operation after just a week or two of training. Then she might well avail herself of the computer's vast wealth of information, to say nothing of its apparently direct access to the enigmatic benefactors who supported Koroma and Mestral, provided them with their equipment and other resources, and watched from afar as events unfolded here on Earth.

"Computer, what've you got?" asked Koroma.

With a feminine voice Heffron almost found soothing, the Beta 7 replied, *"One armored transport helicopter, likely V-22 Osprey or variant, moving in this direction. Estimated time of arrival, two minutes, thirteen seconds."*

"How does it know that?" asked Heffron.

"Communication signals are being transmitted between the inbound vehicle and its support ship."

Mestral asked, "How many people are aboard the helicopter?"

"Unknown."

Koroma said, "You can bet it's more than three. I don't remember the details, but I think Ospreys can carry twenty to twenty-four fully-loaded combat troops, but I'm betting they're coming to snatch us, so they'll need room for us." She shrugged. "Figure twelve to fifteen troops, at minimum."

"What do we do?" asked Heffron.

Any reply Koroma or Mestral might have made was lost when every light and piece of electrical equipment in the house went dark or inert. Even the Beta 7's control panel and displays deactivated, its sudden loss of power startling Heffron.

"Uh-oh," said Koroma. "This can't be good."

A low hum broke the near silence inside the house, accompanied by a soft blue glow that played across Mestral's face and emanated from a device he had extracted from a pocket of his suit. It was small and rectangular, and the Vulcan was holding it before him like a camera.

"Some form of electromagnetic pulse was employed against us," he said. "It has temporarily incapacitated all unshielded electrical equipment in the immediate area, including the house and the barn."

"That's bad, right?" asked Heffron.

Koroma shook her head. "The Beta 7 shut itself down as a safety precaution. It'll be back in a couple of minutes."

"I believe our visitors will not grant us that interval," said Mestral.

"No kidding." Koroma waved toward the front of the house. "If we can get to the barn, we can still use the transporter."

Feeling adrenaline beginning to pump into her bloodstream in anticipation of the coming intruders, Heffron considered what the next few minutes would require. The mysterious "transporter" used by Koroma and Mestral to bring her here was secreted in the barn behind the farmhouse. Like the Beta 7, it was hidden behind a stone wall designed to protect it from outsiders. Heffron guessed that twenty to thirty meters of open ground separated the farmhouse's back porch and the barn.

A long way to go if somebody's hunting you.

"Do you have any weapons?" When Koroma did not answer but instead eyed her with doubt, Heffron could see the disapproval in the agent's eyes. "Tell me you have some kind of weapons locker here."

Koroma drew a deep breath before nodding. "Yes." She pointed to a closet in the room's far corner, which Heffron had assumed was a coat closet of some kind.

"Really?"

"It's just me and Mestral," replied Koroma. "And we both prefer not to use firearms, if necessary."

"That's nice," said Heffron. "I want one anyway." Hearing footsteps behind her, she turned to see Mestral carrying an unfamiliar pistol-like object in each hand. To her, they resembled stun guns of the sort employed by law enforcement and the military.

Scowling, she asked, "What are those?"

"Nonlethal measures," replied the Vulcan. "They fire bolts of energy that disrupt neural impulses in humanoid targets, rendering them unconscious."

"And they work?"

"They are most effective."

Heffron shrugged, extending her hand so that Mestral could give her one of the weapons. "Good enough for now." If she ended up using the thing against whoever was coming after them, she would be sure to avail herself of whatever armaments they might be carrying.

"Look, I appreciate everything you've done for me," she said, dividing her attention between the odd weapon in her hands and Mestral and Koroma. "But you need to know that there's no way I'm letting Majestic take me again. They'll have to kill me." She delivered the last words with what she hoped was an emphasis that communicated her unspoken meaning.

Because I'm sure as hell going to kill them if that's what it takes, but I'm not going back.

"What if they're waiting for us outside?" she asked.

Koroma smiled, bobbing her eyebrows. "We're not going outside."

Allowing herself a small sigh of relief, Heffron returned the smile. She should have known the agents would have some kind of contingency plan even for something like this.

Then, her breath caught in her throat as she heard voices from somewhere outside. They were faint, but not too distant.

Oh, damn.

"Where the hell are they?"

Dressed like the eleven men and women he commanded in black military fatigues and carrying an M4A3 assault rifle, Gerald Markham knelt behind a small rock cluster jutting from the damp grass along the sloping hillside and peered through the weapon's optical sight. Even with thermal mode activated, the sight's illuminated aperture showed him no sign of anyone moving inside the stone farmhouse or the barn behind it. On the other hand, it did reveal to him the herds of sheep scattered among the distant hills, most of them roaming about in the early morning and availing themselves of the rich green grass all around them.

"Oscar Three Sierra," he said for the benefit of the

comm unit tucked into his right ear. "This is Leader. Do you see anything?"

A quiet voice, belonging to Lieutenant Derrick Sapp of the United States Air Force and detailed to Majestic 12's security force, replied, *"That's a negative, Leader. All quiet. You suppose we spooked them?"*

Markham hated to admit as much. This assault—at least on a general level—had been in the planning stages for more than a year, ever since Markham had become aware of Kirsten Heffron's relationship with the mysterious beings who seemed eager to guide and inform her from the shadows. Who were these people? Where did they come from, and who did they represent? A foreign power, or a party from another world, as Heffron believed and had admitted during more than one of her interrogation sessions?

The plan to find Heffron—and, by extension, her rescuers—had solidified after the director's liberation from Majestic's high-security asset community located on a small, unnamed, and otherwise uninhabited island east of Guam. The island did not even appear on maps, and MJ-12's information technology and communications oversight divisions ensured that any photography collected by orbiting satellites was scrubbed of imagery that might reveal the location of its network of clandestine installations. This had led Markham to wonder how Heffron's saviors had even managed to find the H-SAC in the first place. Perhaps they had access to MJ-12 information or even personnel, which by itself was disturbing.

You can't do anything about that now. You're here. They're here. Find them.

It had taken them nearly a week to trace and confirm the source of the still unexplained transmission that had been tracked from the H-SAC to this location. Satellite imagery provided insight into the seemingly innocuous farmhouse, which sat all alone on this island off the coast of Scotland. As far as Markham and his people could tell, aside from the sheep and whoever lived in the house, this area of the island was uninhabited, isolated from the few thousand people comprising Arran's population. That, at least, made things easier so far as launching a military strike on the target location, which presented its own set of challenges. Despite being located in the middle of nowhere, it was determined that the house and surrounding area employed a full suite of intrusion detection systems, including some technology with which Markham was not familiar. Nothing like it was known to be available anywhere, or on the drawing board in the case of the military or even Majestic. Satellites also had detected subsurface thermal blooms indicating a power source of some kind, which by themselves would not be unusual, but coupled with the transmission raised flags of concern for Markham. This had to be the base of operations for the agents who had rescued Heffron, and there was a distinct possibility that seizing it would yield him and his people access to a new source of advanced, even alien technology that could be exploited for any number of reasons.

Taking out the power source had been an easy enough feat, thanks to the targeted electromagnetic pulse generator Markham's team had brought along. MJ-12 scientists made quick work of studying the device taken from the Eizand craft captured over a year earlier, training Markham and a select group of agents in its use. This was the first time it had been employed against a live target in the field, and so far it had performed as expected.

Too bad it can't scan for bodies. That'd be nice right about now.

Shifting his position, Markham turned his attention to his companion, an air force sergeant named Scott Reu. "Power's still off, right?"

The sergeant, crouching like Markham behind the rise, indicated the pulse generator strapped to his chest. He pointed to a gauge set into the device's shell. "According to this, it's all quiet."

"Damn it," said Markham, spitting out the words. "They must have known we were coming. Probably picked us up on radar or something." Until he got inside the farmhouse and had a look at whatever technology was hidden there, he had no way to know what sort of advanced detection equipment these people might possess. Laying claim to the house would be a nice prize, but only in consolation. For this mission to be a success, they needed to capture Miss Heffron and her benefactors.

"Hang on," said Reu, his attention on the pulse generator's controls. "I've got something." He pointed to the barn. "Something's up in there."

Peering once more through his rifle's thermal sight, Markham studied the barn, but saw no signs of habitation or even the warmth that might be cast off from powered equipment in operation. He was about to shift the rifle to look at another part of the structure when something orange and red flitted across his sight's reticule. Then he saw two more.

Son of a bitch.

"They're in the barn." Into his comm unit, Markham said, "All teams, move on the barn. Go."

17

Isle of Arran
November 20, 2032

Emerging from the tunnel beneath the barn's rearmost stall, Kirsten Heffron took Natalie Koroma's proffered hand and allowed the agent to pull her the rest of the way up the ladder. Heffron could not help noting that the younger woman was able to lift her with a single hand and little effort.

"You work out?" she asked.

Koroma replied, "Exercise, a healthy diet, and generations of genetic engineering to produce a superior breed of human. That's what's in the brochure, anyway."

"Probably too late for me, then."

Despite the tense nature of their current circumstances, the younger woman seemed to appreciate the inappropriate humor and released a small grunt of amusement. "Probably, but give it a thousand years or so."

Mestral pushed himself out of the tunnel opening and regained his feet. The scanner he had produced back in the farmhouse was once more active, and the Vulcan was pondering whatever information it was relaying to him. "Twelve life readings, converging on this location from multiple avenues of approach, and each heavily armed."

"That's our cue," said Koroma, moving toward the rear of the otherwise unoccupied barn and the stone wall at the structure's rear. "Computer on. Activate evacuation protocol."

In response to her command, part of the wall slid aside to reveal a smaller version of the Beta 7 interface, which Heffron remembered from her arrival here two weeks earlier. This was the first time she had been in the barn since that initial exposure to the advanced machine in full operation. Lights and bands of streaking color played across the console's main display screen, and the computer emitted a string of almost musical electronic tones as it processed whatever commands Koroma had put into motion. Next to the console was the heavy metal vault door she had glimpsed her first night here. The wheel on the door spun counterclockwise and the door opened as though of its own volition, revealing an empty chamber inside.

"Is the programming ready?" asked Koroma.

The Beta 7 replied, *"Programming complete. Preselected destination confirmed."*

Something exploded behind them, near the front of the barn, and Heffron flinched at the abrupt sound and flash of light. Turning toward the sound, she saw that a large hole had been blown through one of the barn's massive double doors, and thin beams of green were now shining through the resulting smoke.

"Get back," whispered Koroma, just before Heffron felt herself pushed against the wall behind her. Then she saw the agent raise her right hand up and away from her, the servo she held aiming toward a heavy cross beam supporting the barn's loft. Without another word, Koroma fired the slim weapon. There was no beam or loud report, but instead just a sharp metallic snap, followed immediately by a large chunk of the wooden beam disintegrating. That was enough to split the support and it collapsed, bringing with it a large portion of the loft's decking and the hay stacked atop it.

The green beams disappeared, and Heffron heard muffled shouts of warning and other distinct commands being issued by at least two different people. Was it her imagination, or did one of the voices belong to Gerald Markham?

I wouldn't doubt it. He likely caught six kinds of hell for letting me get away.

"Computer," said Koroma, "stand by to execute fail-safe emergency protocols as soon as we're gone."

The Beta 7 replied, *"Acknowledged. Initiating protocols."*

"What does that mean?" asked Heffron.

"Sanitation," replied the agent, her attention still focused on the front of the barn as she searched for new threats. "No traces left behind. Once we leave here, there's no coming back."

Her eyes widening in surprise, Heffron swallowed a sudden lump in her throat. "Well, that ought to slow them down."

"They did track us to this location," said Mestral. "Until we learn how they accomplished that, we are still at risk of being found again."

"One problem at a time," snapped Koroma. "Let's get the hell out of here."

Flickering light from outside the barn caught Heffron's attention and she saw what had to be a flashlight beam piercing the gloom from the breached doorway. It seemed their attackers were no longer concerned with stealth. When a shadow appeared in the hole marring the barn door, Heffron reacted without thinking. The weapon in her hand raised and aimed for the opening and she fired. A burst of green-yellow energy spat from the odd pistol, lancing across the barn and through the hole. She heard someone outside gasp in shock or pain before the shadow fell away from the door.

The reaction was immediate, with a storm of metallic snaps erupting from beyond the doorway as dozens of holes were punched through the structure's wooden walls. A hand in her back sent Heffron tumbling to the barn's dirt and hay floor as bullets pierced the air above her. To her right, Mestral had dropped to the ground, flattening himself while at the same time aiming his own stun pistol toward the front of the building that had become a shooting gallery. A noise from her left side made Heffron look to see Koroma diving behind several bales of stacked hay, with bullets chewing into the uncertain barrier as the agent rolled out of sight.

"If they damage the computer," warned Mestral, between two quick bursts from his weapon, "we will not be able to utilize the transport system."

Rolling onto her side, Heffron gestured toward the barn's front entrance. "Tell *them* that."

From where she had sought protection behind the hay bales, Koroma poked her head into view. "Mestral, get her out of here. I'll watch our backs."

The agent punctuated her order by aiming her servo and firing again, this time toward the opening in the barn's front door. Heffron could not see who or what she might be engaging, but she heard shouts of warning in response to the strike. With her other hand, Koroma reached behind her back and produced from her waistband a stun pistol similar to the ones Heffron and Mestral carried. Pointing the weapons in different directions as though attempting to cover possible avenues of approach and attack, Koroma rose from her crouch. She left her place of concealment, moving with controlled haste farther into the barn and toward the Beta 7 and the transport vault.

A noise from somewhere above them caught Heffron's attention, and she looked up to see shadows flitting in the slats of the barn's walls, near its slanted metal roof. Then she heard the sound again, and realization took hold.

Holy shit.

"They're coming in through the—"

The rest of her warning was drowned out by an explosion that accompanied a hole being punched through the barn's roof. Heffron flinched at the echo of the detonation as it bounced off the structure's interior. She looked up to see a figure in dark clothing descending a rope through the jagged opening. A second person followed on another line.

Even as the two assailants dropped toward the barn's floor, Koroma was reacting. Her servo and the stun pistol in her other hand took aim and fired, each catching one of the figures just as their feet touched the ground. Their bodies went limp, sagging against the D-ring connectors linking them to the ropes they had used for their descent.

"Move!" she shouted, without turning away from the source of the new danger.

Ahead of her, Heffron saw more shadows at the edge of the hole in the roof, as well as at the door. Early morning sunlight glinted off metal, and the stun pistol in her hand raised in automatic response.

Weapons fire erupted once more within the barn, and this time Heffron felt something drilling through her left shoulder, spinning her off her feet, and sending her falling against a thick wooden support column.

Pain erupted in her upper chest, and when she tried to grab on to the column for support she found her left arm would only hang limp at her side. White heat radiated from what she now saw was a red stain darkening her sweatshirt, and she sank to her knees.

"Damn it!"

The shout came from Koroma, scampering from where she had taken up position behind another of the columns as she moved toward Heffron.

"Director," said Mestral, before Heffron felt hands under her arms and the Vulcan helping her to her feet.

Stuffing the stun pistol into her waistband, Heffron used her good hand to hold on to Mestral. Behind him, she saw that the vault door was open, and a cloud of bright blue mist roiled inside the small chamber. She picked up the low-pitched hum of the futuristic machine as it prepared to carry out its task and transport them to safety. Feeling another hand on her arm, she turned to see Koroma. The agent still wielded her servo in her other hand, her attention focused toward the breaches in the barn door and ceiling.

"Time to go," said the agent. "You two first."

Even if she had wanted to argue, Heffron did not have the strength to resist. Instead, she allowed Mestral to guide her toward the transport vault as Koroma took up one final defensive position, covering her companions' escape. As she crossed the threshold into the vault, Heffron turned and looked down the length of the barn just as another dark figure connected to a rope dropped down from the hole in the roof. His weapon, some sort of short-barreled assault rifle, barked as it fired, sending bullets flying in multiple directions.

Several of the rounds found Koroma, her body shuddering with each impact. She staggered backward before tripping over her own feet and crumpling to the dirt floor. When she came to rest on her right side, her limbs were splayed in an awkward fashion, and she did not move.

"No!"

Even as the first tendrils of the transport vault's unexplained energies began to embrace her, Heffron saw from the blank expression on the other woman's face and her open yet unseeing eyes that Natalie Koroma was dead.

Then everything vanished in a blue whirlwind.

"Cease fire! Cease fire, you idiots!"

Storming into the barn behind two of his soldiers who at his order had broken through the structure's compromised front door, Gerald Markham saw that his order had come too late, and the damage was done. Not Kirsten Heffron, but instead a younger woman lay unmoving on the barn's dirt floor.

Damn it.

At the far end of the dilapidated barn, Markham saw the heavy metal vault door that was just closing. Behind it, visible for only a fleeting second, was a hint of blue fog, an almost electrical phenomenon that was already fading even before the door finished hiding it from view.

That has to be it, thought Markham, his attention riveted not only on the door but also the adjacent computer console. The teleportation equipment that he knew these people had at their command. It was here for the taking. Both it and the console were set into a wall of irregular stones and mortar, which seemed out of place for a structure such as this. Markham knew from his reconnoiter of the area that the barn backed up to an earthen embankment, which served to help hide not only the advanced machinery but also its power source. None of that, he recalled, had shown up on any of the satellite thermal imagery he had ordered for this entire area.

That no longer mattered, of course. Now he had the actual equipment in hand, ready for study and exploitation. Ever since first hearing about these mysterious "agents" from Kirsten Heffron, Markham was convinced that these people had to possess some form of advanced technology. Was it alien in origin? From what he saw before him, he could not make that determination, but he would soon have qualified scientists and engineers to answer that question, along with all of the others he had been harboring for so long.

Finally.

"Sir," said a voice from behind him, and Markham glanced over his shoulder to see Sergeant Reu standing a few paces away, holding his M4 rifle slung low and next to his right hip. "We've secured the house. There's nobody home."

"Get your people out of there, Sergeant," replied Markham, returning his gaze to the computer equipment. "I've got a team on the way to conduct a complete investigation of the entire site. What about your men who were dropped during the fight?"

Reu said, "Medics say they're just stunned, sir. Lucky for us, the weapons employed by the targets were obviously nonlethal."

The observation made Markham frown, realizing that he had all but forgotten about the fallen woman. Turning to where she still lay on the ground, he shook his head. "Yeah. Lucky us. Have your troops establish a perimeter and await further instructions."

"On it." Reu stepped away so that he could speak into a tactical radio clipped to his equipment harness.

Markham glanced again to the computer console, anxious to examine it, but instead he moved to stand over the dead woman. Based on her appearance and from the information provided by Heffron, he knew this had to be Natalie Koroma. It was almost certainly an alias, if these "agents" conducted themselves with any sort of training or common sense, and everything Markham learned about them suggested this to be true. A full autopsy conducted by pathologists and other forensic technicians would use all MJ-12 resources at their disposal to confirm the woman's identity. Perhaps that information would uncover links to other individuals, be they fellow agents or civilians who like Kirsten Heffron had benefited from their knowledge and assistance over the years. Such connections would, Markham hoped, lead to even more examples of the advanced technology that these people employed, and maybe even to those who provided it.

"It's a damned shame you didn't live," he said, his gaze lingering on Koroma's unmoving form. "I bet we'd have learned a hell of a lot from you." He was still angry that the agent had been caught in the crossfire. He did not blame Sergeant Reu or the rest of the team for acting to defend themselves when it became obvious that their quarry would not surrender without a fight, and neither was he grief stricken that the troublesome agent would no longer present problems for him or Majestic. Instead, he simply was disappointed at the opportunity lost to acquire more information.

She still has friends. We'll find them.

Feeble light from one of the bulbs illuminating

the barn's interior flickered off something lying on the ground next to Koroma's body, and as Markham stepped closer he saw that it was a silver fountain pen. He allowed himself a grim smile as he recognized the agent's servo. Kneeling next to the fallen woman, he retrieved the device, judging its weight in his hand. Was it his imagination, or was it somewhat heavier than the one confiscated from Heffron a year ago? Majestic engineers had disassembled and studied that device, determining that it harbored a microminiaturized communications transceiver far more powerful than anything created even by the United States military or MJ-12 itself. Markham knew that the servo also had defensive capabilities, as evidenced by the unconscious soldiers being treated outside the barn. What other secrets did it conceal? Along with everything else tucked into this building and the adjacent house, the research department would have a field day playing with this specimen.

Without warning, the servo turned red hot in his hand.

"Son of a bitch!" Dropping the pen, Markham jerked his hand toward him, instinctively pressing it against his side and wincing at the momentary flash of pain coursing across his skin. Examining his palm, he saw that it was reddened, but the initial discomfort was already fading.

"Are you all right, sir?" Reu asked. The sergeant lurched toward him, extending his free hand as if to help.

Markham scowled at the dropped servo where it had fallen. The device's outer silver shell was now black, and as he watched, it stretched and swelled before bursting into uncounted pieces. Some of the fragments, glowing with extreme heat, landed on stray pieces of hay littering the barn floor, setting them alight.

"Damned thing had a self-destruct," he said, shaking his hand to mitigate the lingering effects of the servo's reaction. "Definitely an attention getter."

What else did they booby-trap?

"Oh, damn." Looking away from the servo's remnants, Markham turned his attention on the computer console, which was still active at least on some level. Several lines of multicolored light coursed across one of its monitors, and another display showed a seemingly random cascade of scrolling text. Staring at the information being presented, Markham noted that it was rendered in either a human or computer language he did not recognize.

A muffled explosion from somewhere outside made Markham and Reu exchange surprised glances. The sound was followed by shouts of alarm before a new voice shouted from the front of the barn.

"Everybody out! The house was rigged to blow!"

Seeing the MJ-12 soldier standing in the doorway, Markham grabbed at Reu's arm and pushed him in that direction. "Get your people out of here!"

The sergeant ran for the door with Markham on his heels, and both men exited the barn in time to see the farmhouse collapsing in on itself. Wood and stone fell inward, dropping into a hole that had opened up beneath the entire structure. More explosions were emanating from within the falling building, with thick clouds of dark smoke billowing into the early morning sky. Markham was still following Reu away from the barn when another explosion made him flinch. This one came from behind him, and he felt the rush of displaced air washing over him as he stumbled over the uneven ground before dropping to one knee on the dirt. Reu stopped, turning and extending his free hand to Markham before raising his head and looking toward the barn.

"Holy shit."

The sergeant let his proffered hand drop to his side, and Markham was forced to push himself to his feet. Facing the barn, he was in time to see the building's wooden shell crumbling to the ground, falling into a hole not unlike the one that was continuing to consume the house.

Removing his tactical radio from its clip on his equipment harness, Reu grunted something unintelligible. It was a small, humorless reaction, followed by, "That's some security system."

"Yeah, no kidding." Looking around the area, Markham tried to do a count of the soldiers who were visible. "Did everybody get out?"

The sergeant was holding his radio close to his ear. "I'm getting a count now." After a moment, he nodded. "We're all good. No casualties." Then he cocked his head. "What are the odds that we'd all get out before it blew?"

Markham pondered the observation. "Good point." Pivoting on his heel, he took in the scene of both structures, which had completed their collapse and now lay amid an expanding cloud of dust and smoke. A few telltale flames licked at some of the rubble, but the destruction appeared to be otherwise contained. "Between that and simply incapacitating our people when it would've been so easy to kill them, you have to wonder."

He recalled from his conversations with Heffron that her mysterious friends did not seem to employ any sort of lethal means in the course of their various tasks. They did not carry weapons, at least not in the conventional sense, the sole exception being the pen-like servo devices. Could those kill? Maybe that was true of the models employed by Koroma and other agents, but it was not the case with the specimen taken from Heffron herself. Could one reason for the destruction of Koroma's servo be to ensure its technology was not captured and exploited?

"We can still get a team in here," said Reu. "Sift through the rubble. There might be something worth salvaging."

"Go ahead and call them in. We'll do it just to cover all the bases." Markham shrugged. "Maybe we'll even get lucky."

He did not expect that anything of true value would be recovered during any excavation of the site. There would be bits and pieces of destroyed components, but the technology itself would have been rendered utterly, irretrievably inert as part of the agents' evacuation plan.

It's what I would've done.

Shifting his M4 rifle so that it hung suspended by its sling from his shoulder, Reu asked, "What's our next move, sir?"

"Heffron and whoever else was here," said Markham, gesturing toward the ruins of the barn and the teleportation technology it had once contained. "They got away. We just need to figure out where they ended up."

Reu frowned. "Any ideas where they might be?"

Shaking his head, Markham released a long, slow sigh. "Based on what we know of their capabilities? Anywhere on the planet."

Or, maybe they went even farther than that?

18

Los Angeles, California
November 20, 2032

Her eyes opened, and Kirsten Heffron jolted to a sitting position. Within seconds, she regretted that abrupt action as pain shot through her left shoulder, making her flinch and sending her crashing back to the couch she now realized she was occupying.

"Natalie? Mestral?"

She winced at the words as they left her parched throat. Coughing, she closed her eyes, as even that simple action sent another wave of pain through her wounded shoulder. Allowing her body to adjust to sudden wakefulness and the other protests it was issuing her, Heffron remained silent and prone on the couch, looking up at a mobile display of the solar system. A few dozen foam spheres were suspended by white twine from the ceiling, each painted to approximate the sun along with all of the planets and at least some of the larger moons. Hanging between the orbs representing Earth and its moon was a small, spindly construct that Heffron recognized as the International Space Station.

Where the hell am I?

"Miss Heffron."

Looking away from the display, Heffron turned her head to see Mestral crossing the room, which was an office of some kind. A flat-screen television hung on the far wall, and two battered, gunmetal-gray desks of the sort that were ubiquitous in government office buildings were pushed against the wall across from her couch. Laptop computers, each set into a docking station with its own smaller flat-screen monitor, were active, and both desks were littered with books, maps, charts, and assorted papers along with pencils, colored markers, and other administrative debris. Whatever wall space was not blocked by filing cabinets and books was adorned with posters of planets and star maps, newspaper clippings and pages taken from magazines, notes and various scraps of paper, and what Heffron realized were mock travel posters to the Moon, Mars, Jupiter, and Saturn. Creased and dog-eared posters tacked to a bulletin board celebrated the films *2001: A Space Odyssey*, *The Day the Earth Stood Still*, and *Apollo 13*.

A clock on the wall told her that it was 12:45. She recalled that it had been just after 6:30 in the morning when the farmhouse was attacked. Had she lost consciousness due to her injury? That was likely, she decided, but how long had she been out of it? There were no windows in the office, so Heffron had no idea whether that meant early afternoon or the middle of the night.

At least I'm not dead. I've got that going for me, which is nice.

"How are you feeling?" asked the Vulcan as he stepped closer. Now standing before the couch, he knelt beside her and reached toward her before pausing. "May I examine your wound?"

Heffron nodded, and it was only when Mestral again reached toward her that she realized her sweatshirt was gone, and that she now wore a heavy flannel robe. With a gentle touch, Mestral moved aside part of the robe's collar in order to inspect where she had been shot, and Heffron saw that the skin there, though reddened and slightly swollen, showed no outward signs of the bullet's entry into her body.

"Are you in any pain?" he asked.

"It only hurts when I move, or breathe, or think about it." To her surprise, she felt no pain when Mestral's fingers touched her skin where the wound had been. "Actually, it's not that bad at all. What did you do?"

"A medical kit was among the emergency supplies staged at this location." He did not look away, but instead continued to examine her shoulder. "The kit contained a tissue regeneration unit, which is quite useful for injuries of this type. I was able to begin treatment shortly after our arrival, so your blood loss was minimal. However, I have administered a medication that will accelerate blood cell creation in order to restore what was lost. There may be some residual muscular discomfort for the next twenty-four to forty-eight hours, but you will otherwise make a full recovery."

Smiling, Heffron rested her right hand on his arm. "Thanks, Doc." She allowed him to help her to a sitting position, and was surprised that even the lingering pain from her shoulder was already weaker than it had been just moments ago. With a push from the couch's armrest, she rose to her feet and took in their surroundings. "What is this place? It looks like the basement at the Pentagon."

Having risen to his feet, Mestral replied, "We are at the Griffith Observatory in Los Angeles, California. It is early morning here, as we are eight hours behind Arran. You were asleep for approximately one hour and fifty-four minutes, while I tended to your wound."

"Los Angeles?" So, this had been the emergency escape destination programmed into the Beta 7 computer, but what was its significance? "Is this some kind of safe house?"

"In a manner of speaking." Looking around the room, the Vulcan cocked his right eyebrow. "However, it has been some time since I last visited it, and I am uncertain as to how our arrival will be received."

"I'm guessing you won't be all that welcome."

Both Heffron and Mestral turned at the sound of the voice to see a woman standing in the doorway leading from the office. Heffron guessed the new arrival to be about the same age as her, if the wrinkles around the eyes and mouth and the gray streaks in her short black hair were any indication. She was dressed in khaki pants, a dark blue sweatshirt, and running shoes, and while she carried no purse or other bag, there was the silver fountain pen in her right hand that gave Heffron pause. It was pointed at her, but not without any real malice or intention. After a moment spent appraising them, the other woman slipped the pen into her pocket, her expression turning from uncertainty to one of disapproval.

"What the hell are you doing here, Mestral?" When she spoke, her voice sounded as though it belonged to a much younger woman, though there was also a faint, raspy quality, which communicated her age. "I mean, besides tripping the silent alarm and activating the Beta 7. What, you didn't think I'd notice that kind of thing, even in the middle of the night?"

Clasping his hands behind his back, the Vulcan replied, "I apologize for the intrusion. We were forced to make a hasty exit from Arran after our presence there was discovered." He gestured to Heffron. "May I introduce—"

"I know who she is," snapped the other woman. "We've never met, but I know exactly who you are, Director."

Surprised by this, Heffron eyed their visitor. "Okay, that's nice, but who are you?"

The woman jammed her hands in her pants pockets. "I'm surprised you've never heard of me. I'm Rain Robinson, and I was really hoping I was done with all of this crap forever."

Sitting at one of the desks, her hands warming as they cradled a ceramic mug of what might well be the best coffee she had ever tasted, Heffron regarded Rain Robinson. The other woman remained silent as Mestral continued to work with the Beta 7 computer console tucked behind the basement office's brick walls. She drank from her own cup, her gaze drifting to Heffron every so often before returning to the littered desktop before her. It was obvious that she was lost in thought, perhaps recalling whatever unpleasant memories that had been spurred by this sudden intrusion into her realm and her life.

"I'm sorry about this," offered Heffron, hoping to break the awkward silence. "None of the other agents ever mentioned you before."

"That's because I was never an agent," replied Robinson, keeping her attention on her coffee. "I didn't stick with it all that long, and when I left, I asked that Roberta and Mestral and the others just forget about me."

Heffron thought that unusual. "But you have . . . equipment here. One of their computers, and one of those . . . vaults."

"My one concession for old times' sake. I didn't leave

on the best of terms, but that didn't mean I hated everything about the job." She nodded toward Mestral. "He's still my friend, and so was Roberta. I allowed them to install all of that stuff, so they'd have a safe house if they ever needed a place to hide."

"Turns out we needed it," said Heffron.

Robinson rested her mug atop the desk, spinning it slowly with her fingertips. "It was bound to happen, sooner or later." She looked up from her cup. "Being found, I mean. I'm honestly surprised it took them this long." Her eyes narrowed. "Them. You. Whatever."

"I'm not like them," replied Heffron, irritated by the remark. "I was always grateful for the insight and help you provided. Your colleagues, I mean." She paused, recalling that last horrific moment before the transport vault swept her and Mestral from the barn on Arran. "I'm sorry about Agent Koroma."

That, at least, appeared to have some effect, as Robinson's expression changed to one of sadness. "Me too. She was a good friend. They were all good friends." The grief clouding her features seemed to darken. "Well, most of them, anyway."

Before Heffron could react to that, she saw Mestral approaching them from the Beta 7. The Vulcan's expression, as always, was unreadable.

"I have dispatched a message off-world, alerting Agent Koroma's . . . superiors . . . of the current situation and requesting instructions. I have also confirmed that the farmhouse and barn were destroyed per the evacuation protocol. All traces of Aegis technology have been sanitized, including Agent Koroma's servo. There should be very little for Majestic 12 to salvage, let alone exploit."

Robinson snorted. "I wouldn't be so sure. Those

people have been at their game almost as long as we've been at ours, and without the benefit of a supposedly benevolent superior alien race helping them out. They've had more than eighty years to capture, study, and exploit whatever alien technology manages to find its way here, and from what I can see, they've gotten pretty good at it."

"That was our mission," said Heffron. "We were mandated to figure out a way of defending ourselves against alien attack." Leaning back in the desk chair, she shook her head. "Lord knows that for everything we managed to do, we're still nowhere near being able to fend off something like that, if and when somebody decides to drop that kind of hammer on us."

"We're not that important." Pushing herself from her own chair, Robinson grabbed her mug and crossed the office to where a coffee pot sat atop a small table. "No, really. We're just one small, insignificant, out-of-the-way planet in one corner of the galaxy. Do you have any idea how many other worlds are out there, with resources and technology that make ours look like we're a bunch of cavemen wandering around clubbing each other with sticks?"

"Then why do so many alien races seem so interested in us?" asked Heffron. "Why have they been visiting us for at least a century, and probably longer?"

Documented cases of extraterrestrial sightings and encounters went back to the 1800s, but most records before the turn of the twentieth century were unreliable, at best. She had never seen anything to confirm such activity prior to the 1900s. Despite decades of work on the part of Majestic 12 and its various offshoot organizations and groups, there was no concrete evidence to support the notion that ancient structures like the pyramids in Egypt or South America or other strange constructs and markers scattered around the world were linked to alien influence. The possibility was still there, and perhaps one day conclusive proof would be found. In the meantime, people like Heffron would have to go on seeking answers. All those who toiled in secret to answer the questions about humankind's status in the universe or just to prevent their home planet from alien invasion would also continue searching for the truth. Even those civilians who harbored questions or fears about such things would look for whatever information presented itself, and when that failed they would invent their own.

Because we have a ridiculous need to feel significant in the universe. How's that working out for us?

Robinson poured coffee into her mug. "I said we were unimportant. That doesn't mean we're not interesting or amusing or occasionally useful in some way. Or, maybe we're just convenient, depending on specific circumstances." She sipped from her cup before moving back to the desk. "And yes, there have been times where Earth or humans have played some role in larger events, even without our knowledge, or we were perceived as a potential future threat." With her mug, she gestured to Mestral. "His people were studying us back in the 1950s. Were we a threat to anybody back then?"

"No," replied the Vulcan. "However, humanity's development of nuclear weapons and demonstrated willingness to employ them on members of its own species, when coupled with the pursuit of interplanetary space travel, made it prudent in the eyes of my people to observe your continuing advancement."

"I think that's the nicest possible way anyone could

ever describe someone as a threat to interstellar peace." Robinson lowered herself back in her chair. "But Vulcan's one of few exceptions, right? I mean, sure, there's been the occasional visit by someone who thought our planet might make a nice new home, but how often was that really the case?"

Heffron replied, "At least once, that I know of from direct experience. I'm sure there were others."

Nodding, Robinson raised her mug. "Point conceded, but only because I've seen that sort of thing once or twice myself." She gestured to Mestral. "But from what you told me, we're pretty out of the way for that sort of thing to really grab somebody." Then she held up her hand, partnering it with a wan smile. "However, we know that's not always going to be the case, don't we?"

"Doctor Robinson," said Mestral, and Heffron caught the faint yet unmistakable hint of warning in his voice.

Rolling her eyes, the other woman swiveled her chair so that she could rest her feet on the desk. Heffron saw a flattened wad of dirty pink gum jammed into the tread of her left shoe. Leaning back in her chair, Robinson held her coffee mug in both hands and affected a smug smile.

"Come on, Mestral. The lady here knows what I mean. Isn't that right, Director?" When Heffron did not respond, Robinson continued, "After all, the whole reason for the Aegis being here is because we childish little humans aren't able to figure out our own problems for ourselves, and so we need a guiding hand every once in a while. That is, except when our mentors decide it's really in our best interests to get our asses kicked from time to time."

Mestral stepped closer. "Doctor, I do not believe this is the best time for this sort of conversation."

For the first time, Robinson's tone hardened. "Hey, you're the ones who showed up in my observatory in the middle of the night, dragging me back into everything I'd put behind me thirty years ago. You want to bunk here, you'll pay the price of admission, and that means getting to listen to me bitch about some things."

Thirty years, thought Heffron. Feeling her brow furrow, she considered the significance of that number. *Our asses kicked? What happened thirty years ago, that—*

"Holy shit," she said, startled to her the words coming from her own mouth. "Nine Eleven?"

Robinson sipped her coffee, her gaze shifting so that she appeared to be studying some point on the room's far wall. "Give the lady a cigar."

The attacks carried out on September 11, 2001, were the deadliest acts committed on American soil—until then, at least. Heffron, at that time a lieutenant colonel assigned to an unnamed organization attached to Majestic 12 at the Pentagon, was like many in her group trapped far belowground when American Airlines Flight 77, following its hijacking by five members of the al-Qaeda terrorist group, slammed into the building. Well protected far below the surface where the tragedy was unfolding, Heffron along with General Daniel Wheeler and the rest of his people had been forced to observe the rest of the day's heart-wrenching events play out above their heads as well as in New York and Pennsylvania via televisions and computer monitors in her unit's situation center. After nearly twenty-four hours spent in "the Trench," as the room was known by those who worked there, Heffron and her people were able to piece together enough of the horrific puzzle to know who was responsible well before that information was made known to the rest of the world.

"My father was in the North Tower," said Robinson, her voice cold and tense. "Managed to get most of his employees out of the building, then went back inside to look for stragglers. They never found him. Imagine how the world might have been in the years to come if those planes had been kept from hitting their targets. Maybe they didn't need to be hijacked at all." She shook her head. "Nope. Such overt action was apparently beyond the purview of my trusted friend and mentor, Roberta Lincoln, who didn't even know about the attacks until it was too late. No need to know, as the saying goes."

Listening to Rain Robinson give voice to something that continued to torment her even after all these years, Heffron wanted to offer some kind of sentiment or condolences, but words failed her. What must it be like, knowing you or the people you worked for possessed knowledge of future events, along with the means to affect the course of human history? How immense was the temptation to take active steps to shape that outcome? The responsibility to safeguard such information and abilities, along with the pressure to maintain a healthy perspective and not let that burden warp one's judgment, must be all but overwhelming. It would take a special sort of person to wield such power; people like Gary Seven and Natalie Koroma, bred and trained for this very task. Then there were people like Roberta Lincoln and Rain Robinson, ordinary humans drawn into events beyond their comprehension, who had pledged themselves to the same arduous duty undertaken by Seven, Koroma, and others before them.

"Seven knew," said Heffron, putting the pieces together. "Didn't he?"

Draining whatever remained of her second cup of coffee, Robinson set the empty mug on the desk. "Of course he knew. He always knew, or at least he knew more than he let on, and certainly more than he told any of us. Even after he retired and left Roberta to run things, he'd still drop in every so often. You know, just to remind her—and me—who was really in charge. It wasn't Roberta, and it sure as hell wasn't me."

"What did he do?" When Robinson did not answer her question, her expression once again taking on that faraway look, Heffron turned to Mestral, who despite his composed demeanor still appeared uncomfortable with the conversation.

"Yes," he said. "Mister Seven knew of those events, and what it would mean for the people of this country and—ultimately—the rest of the planet. At least, he knew enough. Even he did not always possess complete knowledge of a particular event, let alone its ramifications. On many occasions, this reticence on the part of the Aegis to give him more information weighed on him, and there were times when he was not certain he was taking the correct action. This was especially true on that day."

Heffron frowned. "He came back to Earth because of Nine Eleven?"

"In a manner of speaking. His mission was very small in scope, requiring him to prevent a single person from boarding one of the planes ultimately used in the attack. The Aegis tasked him with carrying out the assignment, rather than giving it to Miss Lincoln or Doctor Robinson. It was their contention that Mister Seven possessed the necessary detachment from the events to carry out the mission without . . . exceeding his mandate."

"Exceeding his mandate." When Robinson repeated the words, they were laced with contempt. "Rescue one person, who would go on to make significant contributions to human history. Shaun Christopher was worth saving, but Daniel Robinson wasn't."

The name was familiar. "Shaun Christopher, the astronaut?" Heffron recalled the man's career, which concluded more than a decade earlier with his successful command of the first manned mission to Saturn. "Wow." She looked to Robinson. "Doctor . . . *Rain* . . . I'm truly sorry."

Robinson waved a hand in a dismissive gesture. "Not your fault. You weren't the one with the book of secrets."

She glanced to Mestral. "I don't even blame Roberta, or you, Mestral. Neither of you had any idea, and that's the only reason you're still welcome here, but Seven?" She paused, blowing out a long breath that signaled she was wrestling to keep her emotions in check. "He knew. I don't care what he told me. He had to know."

"In my experience," said Mestral, "Mister Seven was not given to lying, at least not to the people who worked with him."

"Maybe not lying," countered Robinson, "but he could definitely keep certain truths to himself. Even Roberta did that, sometimes, but never on that scale." Her expression fell again. "At least, not that I know of."

A tone from the Beta 7 caught their attention, and Heffron watched Mestral cross the office to the advanced computer's console. Without saying anything, the Vulcan swept his hands across the station's flat, smooth interface before tapping a series of illuminated keys. As he worked, the entire workstation seemed to die. The bars of multicolored light disappeared, the display monitors went dark, and even the console's backlighting faded before the entire unit disappeared from view as the displaced section of brick wall returned to its proper position.

"Whoa," said Robinson, rising from her chair. "What the hell just happened?"

Straightening his posture, Mestral replied, "I . . . am not certain. The alert we heard was due to a transmission being received from off-world, but it was not a message. I was only able to examine it for a moment, but it appeared to be a protocol for the Beta 7 to terminate all systems support for current operations here on Earth and then deactivate itself."

"They ordered the computer to turn itself off?" asked Heffron. "Why?"

Mestral said, "I do not know. I attempted to countermand the directive, to no avail." He looked to Robinson. "I am sorry, Doctor."

"Figures." The other woman's expression was one of disdain. "Terminate all systems support? They're pulling out and leaving us holding the bag. Bastards."

Folding his arms, Mestral said, "It would seem a logical course of action. After the incident on Arran, our presence here is compromised. Majestic 12 knows about us, and they also know that we escaped. They will not stop looking for us, and it appears they were able to track us to our previous location. Whether they have obtained sufficient information about our technology and abilities to pose a threat remains to be seen."

"Well, I was thinking bigger picture," said Robinson. "I mean, the Aegis has been here in one form or another since the 1950s, right? In all that time, they've never done anything like this, and humans have put this planet through plenty over the years, but they're leaving *now*? Something's not making sense."

Heffron could not believe her ears. "Seriously? They hung you out to dry? What the hell are we supposed to do now? Maybe something's coming that they know they can't stop, or feel that they shouldn't even try."

That's pretty encouraging, isn't it?

"The Aegis? Those saviors of humanity?" Robinson rolled her eyes. "Perish the thought."

"For the time being," replied Mestral, "it seems that maintaining a low profile is the most prudent course of action available to us."

Sighing in exasperation, Robinson said, "It's been a while since I had a roommate. It's a good thing I like you two, or else I'd kick both your asses to the street."

19

Sralanya
2386

Picard watched T'Ryssa Chen pace her fiftieth circuit of the holding cell, if his count was to be trusted. In all fairness, he was unsure of his own figure. Losing track of time was easy in a place such as this, with no windows or timepieces. It was without doubt a deliberate measure on the part of his captors and part of a preplanned strategy for dealing with prisoners that would disorient them and make them more receptive to interrogation.

It might be working.

"Lieutenant," he said when it appeared Chen might begin her fifty-first trip around the room. "Perhaps you should have a seat. The rest might do you some good."

Chen smiled. "Thank you, sir, but I'm not really tired."

"But watching you is exhausting your captain."

Her smile turning to an expression of embarrassment, Chen moved to take a seat next to him. "Sorry, sir."

Along with Chen, Picard was relieved to be reunited with the rest of the away team. Lieutenants Dina Elfiki and Austin Braddock along with Glinn Ravel Dygan occupied seats on one of the four benches lining two of the holding cell's walls. Like him, the other members of the away team had been relieved of their communicator badges as well as any weapons or other equipment they may have been carrying. The communicators were the biggest loss, as without them there was no ready way to contact the *Enterprise*. If they were being held in an underground facility, the starship's sensors might have difficulty locating them through whatever interference was being produced by the surrounding rock and mineral deposits.

The room they occupied was unremarkable, with stone walls, floor, and ceiling colored a uniform pale gray. Lighting panels set into the ceiling provided ample illumination, and the only exit was a heavy metal door set into the forward wall. The benches, each fashioned from a single piece of unidentified metal with no joints, right angles, or sharp edges, were secured to the floor against the side walls. An angled section of wall jutted out from the room's far corner, providing a modicum of privacy around a hole in the floor that served as the holding cell's lavatory.

Noting that Braddock had said little since Picard's unceremonious arrival, he said, "Mister Braddock, I'm sorry about Lieutenant T'Sona. She gave her life defending mine, without hesitation. Presider Hilonu assures me that her remains will be treated with respect." She had told him about the postdeath rituals observed by many Eizand, which involved cremation and interment in a special vessel that could, she promised, be delivered to the *Enterprise* at a more appropriate time.

"Thank you, Captain." The young security officer swallowed before reaching up to wipe his forehead. "She was a good officer and an even better friend. I know she could come off sounding aloof, but once you got to know her, you realized she had a wicked sense of humor." A small smile brightened the man's features. "Even for a Vulcan, she had one of the best deadpan deliveries."

One aspect of command with which Picard had never been comfortable was dealing with the death of a crewmember. He could in time come to accept it as an unfortunate aspect of a chosen life, but that did not ease the accompanying pain, in particular when it involved someone sworn to serve under his leadership. It did not matter how well he knew an individual officer—it was impossible to know each of the more than one thousand beings assigned to the *Enterprise*—for that lack of familiarity did not lessen their loss. It was no different when it came to those horrific occasions when he ordered subordinates on missions that led to their deaths. He never undertook such action lightly, and the repercussions of those decisions would always haunt him. Picard was grateful for that burden; it reminded him of the sacrifices made by those who answered the call to service and the tremendous costs that duty sometimes exacted.

"What about the *Enterprise*?" asked Chen. "I don't care what Hilonu said. You just know Commander Worf is doing everything he can to find us."

Picard said, "If she's to be believed, the *Enterprise* encountered difficulty with the planet's orbital defense network."

Sitting across from the captain, Lieutenant Elfiki said, "If those satellites used their EMP generators, Commander Worf may have had no choice but to break orbit, rather than risk the ship being incapacitated."

"According to Hilonu, that's more or less what happened." Picard recalled the terse report the presider had offered, following the message she sent to the *Enterprise* to warn them about taking us into custody. He was confident that Worf, whose diplomatic skills had evolved to rival his command abilities, would also be employing restraint, at least for the moment. The first officer would be assessing the situation and determining a course of action that would avoid or at least minimize possible casualties, in the hopes of salvaging any chance of brokering peaceful relations with the Eizand people. Crafting such a solution would take time, which meant that Picard and the away team would have to be patient.

Here's hoping Hilonu and her people are equally tolerant.

"Captain," said Elfiki, "can it be true? Is it really possible that we—Earth, I mean—could be responsible for what happened to these people?"

It was a question Picard had been pondering since Presider Hilonu's startling revelation. "There's strong evidence to suggest it, Lieutenant, but I'm not yet convinced. However, if it is true, then we are obligated to find out everything we can about what occurred here, and do everything in our power to balance the scales with the Eizand."

"Three hundred years ago," said Braddock, shaking his head. "It seems impossible, sir. I mean, we were barely able to leave our own planet back then. How could we possibly have managed something so advanced?" His expression turned sour. "And so terrible."

Picard nodded. "That's the rub, isn't it? I suppose it's possible that someone on Earth found and was able to exploit some piece of alien technology and use it for such a purpose, but that doesn't give us a reason."

"It couldn't have been a sanctioned action," said Chen. "I understand that Earth was having its share of problems during that time, but that's what makes this illogical. Earth and humanity were embroiled by all sorts of internal strife, including the Third World War. How would they have had time or resources for something like that?"

Braddock added, "There's certainly nothing in any of the history texts. According to everything I ever read, our space program slowed down considerably after the Mars missions of the mid-twenty-first century and didn't really pick up again until after first contact with the Vulcans."

Sitting next to Elfiki on the bench with his hands clasped before him, Glinn Dygan replied, "History is usually written by those in power, Lieutenant; all governments have their secrets. A lack of record does not mean that event did not happen."

"Dygan has a point." Picard offered a small, wan smile. "After all, history doesn't record my witnessing humans' first contact with the Vulcans."

Chen crossed her arms. "Point taken, sir. Still, this? It's just so beyond anything that makes any sense."

"On that, we agree," replied Picard, "but Glinn Dygan makes a valid observation. Why would such an action take place, and why would it be carried out in secret?"

The Cardassian said, "There have always been groups and organizations that have operated in the shadows, working clandestinely and often without accountability while striving for what they perceive to be a greater good. In many of these cases, the ends, in their mind, justify the means. Sometimes, these groups take the form of the Obsidian Order or the Tal Shiar. Even Starfleet Intelligence carries out covert missions in the name of security, Captain."

"But even those groups answer to someone," replied Elfiki.

"What about groups like Section 31?" asked Braddock. "We know they've been around in one form or another for more than two hundred years."

Picard nodded. "And perhaps longer." His own encounters with the mysterious shadow organization were few, but all were memorable, including one or two instances he would prefer to forget and even was ashamed to acknowledge. The group, which was active even before the Federation's founding, had been involved in countless acts and decisions from behind the proverbial curtain, guiding and influencing and even coercing the history first of Earth and later the entire Federation. Even today, and despite a greater awareness of its existence and activities, the group remained couched in shadows, and pinning down the group or anyone affiliated with it continued to be a daunting task.

"When I was first offered command of the *Enterprise*—the predecessor to our current ship—I read the official logs of every captain of a ship named *Enterprise* dating back to the twenty-second century. Jonathan Archer, the captain of the first starship *Enterprise*, with the first propulsion system capable of achieving warp five, had a lot to say regarding his own encounters with Section 31. Even then, he expressed concerns that such a group, despite whatever noble intentions had led to its creation, ultimately could undermine the principles that had brought together the people of Earth and Vulcan, and later the Andorians and the Tellarites and indeed the entire Federation."

He wasn't wrong.

"Could something like Section 31 be behind whatever happened here?" asked Elfiki. "Regardless of what it became, the group was formed with a mission of defending humanity from external threats. It wasn't a bad idea, but the lack of accountability probably doomed them from the start."

Rising from the bench, Picard straightened his uniform before beginning to pace his own circle around the room's perimeter. "There have been stories about such organizations, created for similar reasons by every national power on Earth dating back centuries. Nothing substantiated, but can every account be fiction? Most likely not."

Was it possible that a forerunner to Section 31 was responsible for the calamity visited upon the Eizand? Might such a group, perhaps born out of genuine concern for the safety of Earth and operating with autonomy and anonymity, grow over time to become so corrupted that it undertook the sort of horrific preemptive action inflicted upon the Eizand, for whatever reason? The answer to that question was too troubling to contemplate.

And yet, it's not impossible, or even out of the question.

The sound of the holding cell's door unlocking made everyone rise from their benches. Picard could sense the anticipation, particularly from Lieutenant Braddock and Glinn Dygan, both of whom seemed ready to pounce at the first opportunity. Despite their enthusiasm, he doubted that, even with their Starfleet unarmed combat training, they could take a guard detail that likely was prepared for just such a situation.

"At ease, gentlemen," he cautioned. "If they'd wanted to harm us, they could have done so by now."

Tell that to Lieutenant T'Sona.

The door opened outward without benefit of automation, doubtless to prevent accidental breaching in the event of a power loss, and a tall, thin Eizand male wearing the uniform of a Tevent Coalition soldier entered the room. Picard recognized him as Janotra, the soldier in charge of this facility's guard detachment. He was followed by five more soldiers dressed in similar fashion, and each of them had unlimbered sidearms from their holsters. While the other five moved into a protective formation around Janotra, he eyed Picard. His weapon's muzzle was pointed at the floor.

"Captain, I have been ordered to escort you to Presider Hilonu."

"Where are you taking him?" asked Braddock, taking a step forward and earning a stern glare from the soldier.

"As you were, Lieutenant." Picard's sharp command was enough to halt the security officer, who looked to him and nodded in acknowledgment. Turning his attention to the guards, the captain raised his hands. "I'll go with you without trouble. There's no need for this to be any more unpleasant than it already is."

"Captain," said Chen, but did not continue when Picard eyed her. Instead, she nodded in silent understanding.

"You're in charge, Lieutenant Elfiki," he said, proceeding at Janotra's direction from the holding cell into the long, stone corridor. With the cell door once more secured, the Eizand guard made a simple gesture for Picard to begin walking. No further words were exchanged, leaving him alone with his thoughts.

Now what?

"Valmiki Goswami. Meredith Harper. Park Ji-hu. You have been charged with committing wanton acts of aggression against this planet and all of the Eizand people. You represent a race of beings that can only be deemed a threat to our very existence, and we are compelled to act in defense of our world and to seek justice for the uncounted millions of Eizand who have perished through direct result of your actions. After hearing your testimony and weighing the

evidence presented against you, this tribunal has found you guilty. Punishment for your heinous crimes is death, and sentence is to be carried out immediately without delay or reprieve."

There could be no mistaking the fear and defeat on the faces of the three humans as they stood alone on a raised podium before a stone wall. Picard heard a low murmur like the muted voices from an audience somewhere nearby, but no one else was visible on the recording. All three were bound by cables or chains that kept them standing against the wall.

The humans, two males and a female, wore what Picard guessed were standard jumpsuits or flight suits common to Earth astronauts of the early to mid-twenty-first century. Each garment was adorned with different patches and other markings, including a simple white stripe over the left breast pocket, with the wearer's last name rendered in English. One of the males, who appeared to be of Indian descent and whose name tag identified him as Goswami, looked around as though searching for someone or something, but there was a lethargy to his movements that suggested he might be drugged. His companions exhibited similar behavior. None of them spoke, or so much as lifted their heads in a final expression or remark of defiance.

A row of six soldiers stepped into view. Their clothing was different and yet evocative of the uniforms now worn by members of the Tevent Coalition military. Knowing what he was about to witness, Picard wanted to look away, but forced his gaze to remain locked on the screen. The three humans, as though realizing for the first time that their end was at hand, began to shift in their restraints, but there was no way for them to escape. Each of the approaching soldiers wielded a long-barreled rifle. Someone still not visible on the screen issued a sharp, military-style command that Picard could not understand, and all of the soldiers raised their weapons to aim at one of the humans. He tried to brace himself for what was about to occur, but there was no time for that as each member of the execution detail fired in unison, their weapons unleashing hellish streams of bright crimson energy. Two beams struck each of the humans in the torso, and their bodies convulsed in the face of what was obviously a brutal assault. Goswami remained silent, though the woman and the other man cried out in agony as the beams continued to tear and burn their flesh and clothing. Over the sound of the rifle reports, Picard heard the low rumble of the audience, and—though he was not certain—he thought it was approval.

The vile display lasted for several seconds before the soldiers reacted to another voice command and ceased fire. Against the wall, the tortured remains of all three humans, their skin and clothes scorched almost beyond recognition, hung limp in their restraints, and Picard felt his gorge rise as he saw wisps of smoke rising from the ravaged bodies. The sounds from the unseen audience were growing now, along with Picard's anger, and he almost flinched when the mounting noise stopped as the image halted.

"In hindsight, it was a barbaric form of execution, having evolved over generations from methods that were even more heinous. Fortunately, we discontinued the practice soon after this incident. Capital punishment is now a much more humane means of dealing with those deserving of such harsh penalties. Thankfully, it is a rare occurrence. I suppose you might call that progress, after a fashion."

Picard turned from the screen and its haunting image to face Presider Hilonu, who stood on the far side of the windowless, bland circular room in which he had been brought from the holding cell. She was dressed in a simple maroon gown that covered her from neck to feet, and one of her long, thin hands still rested on the control pad set into the wall behind her. Near the door leading from the room, a pair of soldiers stood in silence, hands resting on holstered weapons and watching Picard's every movement.

"My people once embraced similar forms of justice," he said, "though we too learned that it was not an effective deterrent. It seemed only to serve a need for vengeance, and we eventually did away with the practice altogether."

Hilonu stepped away from the control pad. "In time, I can see our people taking a similar path. A significant portion of the population is already in favor of such a change, which I honestly find heartening."

In time, Picard thought. *But not yet.*

"I do wish to thank you," he said. "My people and I have been treated with care and respect."

Moving to stand just beyond an arm's length from him, the Eizand leader clasped her hands before her. "I would like nothing more than for that treatment to continue, Captain, but a great deal of that decision rests on your shoulders. I need to show that your people admit to and regret the actions taken against our world. All Eizand must see justice for the harm inflicted upon them."

"I assure you that I do regret what happened here, Presider. What I cannot say with any honesty is that I understand it. I don't know why the action was taken or who was responsible." Picard nodded back toward the screen, though kept himself from taking in the paused image. "However, I can see to it that an investigation takes place. If we can identify those people, we may be able to learn where they came from and who sent them here."

Hilonu said, "Is it your assertion that these criminals were not human?"

"I can't assert anything of the sort without evidence or more information." Pausing, Picard drew a breath while collecting his thoughts and trying to plot a course of action. "What was done with their bodies?"

"Like your Lieutenant T'Sona, they were reduced to ashes and placed in ceremonial vessels. For a time, they were displayed in one of our museums that chronicled the war. As you might imagine, the exhibits detailing the conflict's beginnings are of great interest." Hilonu's gaze shifted to the screen. "I suspect those events will receive even more attention and study, given your arrival."

Picard said, "If we could have access to those remains, we might be able to identify them using records in my ship's computer or information available to me from my superiors. We can solve this mystery, Presider, for all time."

"Are you not afraid of what your efforts might reveal?"

"I do not fear the truth, Presider. If Earth was responsible for inciting the war that engulfed your planet, then the Federation will want to do everything in its power to see that tragic wrong is corrected. Indeed, we are willing to render assistance now, regardless of the circumstances. All I request is the opportunity to answer the questions you've posed for generations."

For the first time since entering the room, Hilonu smiled. "As I told you before, Captain, I find it easy to trust you, and I take comfort in your words. It is obvious that what you have seen here troubles you, and I sense a genuine desire to help us. That is comforting, to a point, but I hope you can understand my position. I am bound by a duty to seek justice in this matter not just for the Tevent Coalition, but all the Eizand people." As she spoke, Picard noted that the anger that had threatened to seize her during their last meeting was absent, replaced by worry and even a hint of resignation.

"Because of that duty, I am compelled to act in accordance with our laws. You will stand trial, Captain, and answer for the crimes of your planet."

20

U.S.S. Enterprise
2386

I don't care what the doctors say. Bionic eyes can get tired.

Leaning back in his chair behind the desk in his small office, Geordi La Forge rubbed his temples, sighing at the momentary sensation of relief. He knew that it was not the ocular implants serving as his eyes that gave him discomfort, at least not by themselves. Instead, fatigue along with hunger and worry was conspiring to make him feel as though his efforts to this point were fruitless. How long had he been at this? Three, maybe four hours? He had spent that time working alone as well as with members of his staff, in an effort to understand the Eizand weapons technology that had sent the *Enterprise* running away from Sralanya with its tail tucked between its legs.

Or its warp core tucked between its nacelles. Whatever. Not that it matters. Three or four hours later, and we're nowhere. Good job, Mister Chief Engineer.

Closing his eyes, La Forge listened to the low, gentle thrum of the *Enterprise*'s warp engines, which despite all manner of sound dampening systems was still audible anywhere on the ship. It was most pronounced here, mere steps away from the heart of the vessel's central power source. Years of starship duty had long ago inoculated him to the ever present drone, and he even became uneasy on those rare occasions when the warp core was inactive and the ship took on an unnatural silence. Only with the immense power plant on line and functioning normally could La Forge feel at ease. In fact, if he dimmed the lights and sat here long enough, tucked away in the relative privacy of his office with his eyes closed, he might very well be able to drift off to—

"Bridge to Commander La Forge."

Lurching himself upright in his chair, La Forge opened his eyes at the sound of Worf's voice booming through the ship's intercom.

"La Forge here. I know why you're calling." Rising from his seat, the chief engineer moved around his desk and exited his office into the main engineering area. All around the massive chamber, members of his staff were hard at work, monitoring various workstations along the bulkheads or near the large, pulsating cylinder that was the *Enterprise*'s warp core. "I can't say I have much new to report, Commander. We're still dealing with the effects of that last bout with the Eizand weapons. Until we come up with a way to defend against them, I can't recommend taking the ship back to the planet. The only thing I see working is destroying the satellites before they can get close enough to do us any more harm. Of course, we know there are people on some of those things." Sensors had already revealed that while most of the orbiting constructs were automated, more than a dozen were larger and contained small numbers of Eizand, with the satellites functioning more like space stations than remotely controlled drones.

"I have considered that," replied the first officer. *"However, Captain Picard would not want me to take such action except as a last resort, if for no other reason than to avoid casualties. For the moment, I am prepared to enter-*

tain less extreme options. Can we lower the intensity of our phasers?"

Reaching the master systems display table in the center of the engineering section's primary work area, La Forge leaned over the console, resting his hands atop its smooth black surface. "I thought about that, and I've already looked into it. The problem is, the ship's phasers are powerful enough that setting them to not destroy the satellites outright also drops their effectiveness to the point that they wouldn't incapacitate the EMP generators. I'm still looking for a workaround. Another problem is that we really don't know what kind of range those pulse generators have. I'm willing to bet it's more than what we need to get into transporter range." He tapped the tabletop interface, and the table's array of status displays and data readouts flared to life. It took him only a moment to get up to date on the current status of every major shipboard system.

"Worf, we're still not fully recovered from that last attack. Shield generators are only back to eighty-five percent, and I'm putting the warp core through a level-two diagnostic. I'm worried about the power fluctuations we got last time. If we go back in there and the warp core is disabled, we'll be in serious trouble."

Having been forced to leave orbit around Sralanya to escape the Eizand energy weapons, the *Enterprise* was now far enough from the planet that obtaining sensor locks on the away team was all but impossible thanks to the distance. Unless or until La Forge and his team could craft a miracle to defeat or at least mitigate the effects of the energy weapons, taking the ship back to Sralanya was fraught with risk. Under other circumstances, it might well be a chance worth taking, but La Forge knew that there were larger concerns, not just with the away team but also any potential relations between the Eizand people and the Federation. If there was a peaceful solution to this situation, the captain would be expecting his crew to find it before resorting to less polite methods.

"Understood. Do you have an estimate for completing your research?"

Sighing, La Forge replied, "At this point, I honestly don't know. Let's say two hours. I know that's not what you want to hear. We're doing everything we can to figure this out. I'll keep in touch."

"Acknowledged. Worf out."

The connection closed, leaving La Forge to contemplate his report. Two hours, tacked on to the time he had already spent working this problem, seemed like an eternity. He knew it had to feel that way for Worf, who was dealing with this issue and everything else that had spun out of the developments with the away team's detention on the surface. The first officer's anxiety would only be heightened by not knowing the whereabouts or condition of Captain Picard and the others. The Klingon would be stewing over being out of touch with the captain, given that he had likely protested Picard's decision to lead the away team. Diplomatic protocol and the need to offer positive initial impressions aside, such duties were the purview of the first officer, which Worf was not prone to shirk. La Forge knew without doubt that his friend was questioning his own decision not to push the point with Picard, and now was blaming himself for what had happened down on the planet.

The longer this takes, the angrier Worf's going to be. We need to get on with solving this thing.

"Commander."

Looking up from the systems display table, La Forge was surprised to see Taurik standing several steps away, hands behind his back and wearing his uniform as though it were any other duty day.

Except that today was most certainly not like any other duty day.

"Taurik," said the chief engineer, holding up his hand, "what are you doing? You know you're not supposed to be down here."

The Vulcan nodded. "Yes, sir. However, given the unusual circumstances that have arisen and with the captain off the ship, I felt it prudent to offer my assistance to solving the technical issues we are facing."

Stepping around the table, La Forge said, "Look, I get it, and damn if I don't appreciate your initiative, because in all honesty we could use you, but the captain's orders are still in effect even when he's not aboard the ship." La Forge had been as surprised as anyone upon hearing that Picard had relieved Taurik of duty and confined him to quarters. There had been no explanation, which was certainly the captain's prerogative, but even that act was outside Picard's normal behavior. Whatever had riled the captain to this degree, La Forge did not see countermanding his orders as a wise course, regardless of the current situation. "Have you cleared this with Worf?"

Taurik replied, "The commander has been consumed with his duties since the captain's departure and the subsequent developments on the planet's surface. Therefore, I felt it inappropriate to disturb him."

Reaching up to rub his forehead, La Forge said, "Taurik, I don't understand everything that went on between you and the captain, but I know it has something to do with orders you got from Admiral Akaar and Starfleet Command. Worf told me that much. Whatever it is that's made Captain Picard mad at you, I promise you that disobeying his orders is not the way to get back in his good graces. As for Worf, if he finds out you went against those orders, he'll be angrier at you than the captain."

"I was obeying the orders of a superior officer," said Taurik. "I regret that this has placed me in a position of conflict with the captain. That was not my intention, and I have proceeded as I considered appropriate with respect to the safety and security of the ship. My skills would be useful in resolving this issue, and it is therefore logical that I render assistance and deal with any ramifications once the situation has been alleviated."

If it were anyone else, La Forge might think the person was looking to shift blame from themselves, but from a Vulcan it was a simple statement of fact, onc with which La Forge was uncertain he could argue. The engineer wondered what he might do if he found himself in a similar predicament, caught between two respected officers issuing conflicting orders. Regulations provided clear, concise answers to such questions, and in this case the rules favored Admiral Akaar.

On the other hand, there was something to be said for simple respect, which in this instance La Forge was unsure the admiral had extended to Captain Picard. By giving Taurik orders to follow and establishing a chain of command that carried with it the possibility of bypassing Picard, Akaar might well have damaged the captain's relationship with Taurik, compromising the Vulcan engineer. It was also, in La Forge's mind, disrespectful to Picard and his ability to command the *Enterprise*. If anyone had earned the benefit of any doubt, it had to be Jean-Luc Picard.

I'd side with the captain, every time.

"Taurik, I understand and appreciate where you're coming from, and the fact that you're here shows you're looking to do the right thing. I'll talk to Worf about getting you back to work, but for now the best way to demonstrate loyalty to the captain is to obey the last order he gave you. I promise you we'll work this out somehow."

The Vulcan appeared to ponder this for a moment, and his right eyebrow lifted. "I will respect your wishes and Captain Picard's orders." He turned as though to exit the engineering area, but Taurik paused and returned his gaze to La Forge. "May I at least study the problem from the computer terminal in my quarters? I may be able to provide assistance, but my access to the ship's engineering and technical databases was suspended when I was relieved of duty."

La Forge grimaced. Such action, while benign and perhaps ultimately helpful to his efforts, would still violate the spirit if not the letter of Picard's order. However, that was a hazard he was willing to negotiate. The captain, though stern, remained a fair and principled officer, and he would judge the situation on its merits before making any decision.

"If you can't ask permission, you can at least ask forgiveness."

"I beg your pardon, sir?"

Only then realizing he had spoken aloud, La Forge cleared his throat. "Never mind. I'll see what I can do, Taurik. We can use all the help we can get."

"Thank you, Commander. I will begin my research

immediately." Pivoting on his heel with his hands still behind his back, Taurik left the room, leaving La Forge alone at the systems display table with only his thoughts for company.

Can this day get any weirder?

Sralanya

The fruit, whatever one was supposed to call it, tasted pretty good.

Reaching up with her free hand to wipe juice from her chin after taking a bite of the greenish, pulpy sphere, T'Ryssa Chen regarded her repast, such as it was. The selection of provided fruits was plentiful and varied in addition to having a pleasing taste, but Chen had no idea if what the away team had been given to eat possessed any nutritional value for humans, or human-Vulcan hybrids, or Cardassians in the case of Ravel Dygan.

On the other hand, it's not poisonous. I guess that's something.

"What are these things called again?" she asked.

Sitting on the bench next to Chen and peeling her own piece of the green fruit, Dina Elfiki replied, "The guard called them *kervala*. Please don't ask me to spell it." She gestured toward the large bowl sitting on the floor in the center of the holding cell, which contained several *kervala* as well as other fruits of different shapes and colors. "Or any of those, either."

The Tevent Coalition soldiers overseeing them, in particular their leader, Janọtra, had taken steps to ensure the food provided for the away team was compatible with their digestive systems. With little to no recent information to go on, Janotra provided Lieutenant Elfiki with one of the team's tricorders so that she could scan the fruits and other foodstuffs and make proper determinations. Once she was satisfied that the selection would not harm or even kill her or her shipmates, the tricorder was taken away, stored along with the rest of their equipment at some unknown location. Only when the Eizand soldier had come and gone during that exercise did Chen think about the oddity of that interaction.

"Even without the universal translators in our communicators, we could understand them," she said, around a mouthful of *kervala*. "They must be wearing some type of similar technology, but I didn't see anything obvious."

Elfiki replied, "They are. It's part of the chronometer they wear on their wrists."

"When did you determine that?" asked Glinn Dygan.

"When we were doing our tour of the city." She shrugged. "It makes sense. If they were sending probes and ships into deep space three hundred years ago, they would've developed some kind of language facilitation or translation technology, in order to understand communications broadcasts from any planets they found."

"Like Earth," said Chen.

The science officer pointed at her. "Exactly."

From where he sat on the bench opposite Chen, Austin Braddock held up his own piece of fruit. "Can we use that to ask them to send down something else to eat?" The security officer had taken three of the *kervala* from the bowl and eaten them with haste, and now was wiping his mouth with the back of his hand. "Those taste good, and all, but a steak would be better."

Chuckling, Elfiki replied, "I'll see what I can do."

Further conversation was muted by the sound of the holding cell's door being unlocked, and the four *Enterprise* officers stood as one to face the entrance as the heavy metal hatch swung away. Four Eizand soldiers entered the room, followed by Janotra, who remained near the door as his companions stepped deeper into the cell.

"What's going on?" asked Elfiki.

Janotra replied, "You are being moved."

"To where?" Braddock remained still as he posed the question, though Chen noticed him tensing as one of the guards moved toward him while holding a pair of wrist restraints.

"You have been treated well to this point," said Janotra, his expression unreadable. "However, do not mistake our benevolence with weakness or a tolerance for disrespect. Do as you are instructed, and you will not be mistreated."

"Everybody take it easy," said Elfiki.

Chen saw her lock eyes with Braddock for an extra second, as though trying to convey to him not to do anything rash. The security officer seemed to get the message and offered a subtle nod as the guard secured his wrists in front of him with the thin metal restraint band. For her part, she caught a glance from Glinn Dygan, who appeared as though he might be ready to take a chance on disabling one of the guards and perhaps getting his hands on a weapon. She shook her head just enough to communicate that he also should not do anything that might cause more trouble for the team.

"The transport is waiting," said Janotra, once his charges were secured.

At the lead guard's direction, the soldiers indicated

for Chen and the others to move from the cell into the corridor, which looked just as dreary and poorly lit as she recalled from her transit from the surface after being taken into custody. However, she remembered coming from the direction opposite the one Janotra now indicated for them to go.

Hope this doesn't mean they're about to make us disappear. Forever.

Under the watchful eye of their guards, Chen and the others made their way down the passage. Their every footfall echoed in the dim corridor, pressing home the point that they were traversing an underground tunnel. Eyeing every door and wall panel they passed, she looked for anything that presented itself as a potential avenue of escape, but nothing looked promising. The passage made a turn, and the group found themselves approaching a large door, with two more Eizand soldiers standing behind a console.

"Janotra?" asked one of the guards, his expression one of puzzlement as he stepped around the console. "What is the meaning of this?"

Gesturing to Chen and her companions, Janotra replied, "I have been instructed to move these prisoners to a more secure holding facility until their captain's trial gets under way."

"I was not aware of any such transfer." The other guard's features continued to cloud as his apparent confusion deepened. "Do you have an authorization order?"

"Yes." Janotra reached for a pocket of his uniform, but then Chen saw his hand moving instead for the sidearm in its holster.

Oh, holy hell.

"Wait!" The other Eizand guard, still standing behind the console, was reaching for his own weapon even as he shouted the command, but by then the sound of the first shot was howling in the contained space.

Chen flinched as the bolts of bright red energy streaked past her to strike the guard in the chest, driving him backward into the stone wall. His companion had drawn his weapon and was aiming in the direction of Janotra, and Chen had only an instant to realize she was standing between the guard and his target before she felt something slam into her from behind.

"Get down!"

It was Braddock, grabbing her and pushing her out of the way just as the guard fired. Chen felt the impact of the energy bolt striking the security officer as they both fell to the ground, then everything exploded into chaos as more weapons fire and shouts of alarm filled the corridor. The air forced from her lungs from her impact with the unyielding stone floor, it took Chen an extra second to realize that Braddock, who had landed partially atop her, was not moving.

"Braddock? Austin?"

The lieutenant's body was limp, all but pinning her to the ground. Shifting her position, Chen managed to work her way out from under him. That was when she saw the ghastly wound in Braddock's left side, just below his armpit.

"Braddock!" Kneeling beside him, Chen rolled him onto his back. His eyes were closed, and she pressed her fingers to the side of his throat, searching for a pulse. She found nothing. "Damn it, Austin!"

"Your friend is dead," said a voice behind her, and

Chen whirled to see Janotra and one of his guards, weapons in hand and standing over the fallen forms of their companions. The two soldiers who had been stationed at the massive door were also down.

"We must leave," Janotra said before walking up to Elfiki and undoing her wrist restraints. His fellow guard repeated the same action with Glinn Dygan.

"What the hell is going on!?" asked Elfiki. The science officer had moved to kneel on the other side of Braddock's body, confirming that he was dead.

Stepping closer to Chen, Janotra reached for her hands and removed the band around her wrists. "We need to move quickly. Central Control will send someone to check on this station when the guards fail to make their next scheduled report. We must be gone from here before then, or we will all die."

Uncertain what to make of this bizarre development and still reeling from the loss of Braddock, Chen scowled as she rubbed her wrists. "What are you babbling about? Who are you people?"

"There is no time for this." Janotra was growing more agitated by the moment. "If they capture us, we will all be executed. We have to get you away from here. Only then can you help us."

His tone one of open accusation, Dygan asked, "Help you?" The Cardassian fixed Janotra with a stern, menacing glare. "Help you to do what?"

"To find the truth," replied the Eizand soldier. "Find the truth and reveal it to all our people. For generations we have been living a lie."

21

The Pentagon, Washington, D.C.
August 27, 2039

It was like watching a nightmare come to life.

Standing with arms crossed before the large monitor that dominated his office's front wall, Gerald Markham watched the scene being broadcast to him from the other side of the world. Figures in oversized protective suits walked around a hellish landscape, as though moving about on some distant planet. Background radiation was interfering even with the shielded, secure communications link connecting him to his people at the scene, resulting in a distorted, static-filled picture. In the screen's lower left corner, a digital readout told him how long this operation had been active.

"They've only been on site for twenty minutes," he said aloud. "Why does it feel like a month?"

Sitting in a nearby chair, her ubiquitous computer tablet resting in her lap, his assistant director, Heather Burden, replied, "With the radiation at those levels, they can last another forty to forty-five minutes before they'll have to move to a safe location."

Markham snorted. "They're in China. 'Safe location' is something of a relative term, don't you think?" Rubbing his forehead, he asked, "What are they saying on the news channels?"

"Pretty much variations on what they've been saying all night." Burden studied the scroll of data streaming across her tablet. "The fires are still too intense for anyone to get too close, and the radiation threat makes the entire area a hot zone. At the rate things are going, that entire complex is going to melt before this is all over. The probe is a total loss, and there are still about a dozen people who've gone missing. That's just the immediate problem, though. The explosion and resulting fire are releasing all sorts of toxic shit. That whole area's going to be a quarantined zone for at least a decade."

"A damned shame, if we're being honest. The Chinese were really starting to put together a comprehensive program. They were set to send a manned mission to Mars next year. There's no telling how long something like this will set them back."

And it's all our fault.

"Any indications that anybody knows about our people?"

Still looking at her tablet, Burden replied, "Not from anything being broadcast. Our liaison team in China made sure our people were covered going in, and they'll make sure no traces are left behind when they pull out. Nobody else has the kind of gear needed to get that far into the affected area, so our team should be okay. It's getting them in and out that's the tricky part."

"No kidding." Markham drew a deep breath. "The last thing we need right now is an international incident. We'll have a hard enough time as it is, convincing the Chinese we didn't sabotage their launch."

Markham began the previous day with a mixture of enthusiasm and anticipation that was tempered by the grim realities of his job. Arriving early at his office to watch the video footage being streamed from the Jiuquan Satellite Launch Center in China, he beheld yet again the thing of beauty that was the *Xuanzang* probe. China's first unmanned survey craft designed for travel beyond the solar system was readying for its epic journey to the stars. Markham had followed the craft's development for years, watching both as a space enthusiast as well as with the critical eye of someone in his chosen if unsung profession. Whereas efforts by the United States to expand its own space exploration programs had stagnated in the wake of the ill-fated *Ares IV* mission, other nations around the world were continuing to make progress.

Chief among those making rapid advances were India and China, who had been partnering for space-based projects for years. That relationship was an outgrowth of the two countries already being members of the Eastern Coalition, which had come together nearly twenty years earlier and counted among its signatory nations Kazakhstan, Pakistan, Russia, Singapore, and Vietnam. China and India had been at the forefront of a combined space effort, making several exchanges of technology and personnel in order to assist each other's programs. Such cooperation had seen to it that it was an ECON-based mission that was the first manned effort to return to the Moon, nearly fifty years after America's last landings in the early 1970s. The shared scientific effort was just one aspect of the thawing of relations between the two countries, which had been strained for decades but now were strengthened by mutual ties to the Coalition. Rivalry between the ECON and the United States was also on the upswing, on par with the tensions that stressed American interactions with Russia as well as China and

North Korea in the early twenty-first century. Military and foreign policy experts within the current presidential administration were forecasting continued deterioration in relations between the U.S. and the ECON in the coming decade as the world continued to undergo a shift in global economic power as well as control and consumption of natural resources.

However, none of that had mattered to Markham yesterday morning. For a few brief, precious moments, he was able to forget the reality of the world in which he lived and focus instead on a flight of pure science and fantasy. He was even hopeful that a successful *Xuanzang* might somehow motivate the world's most powerful nations to come together and work toward a common goal.

Then reality had reasserted itself, as Markham gave the order to see the probe destroyed on its launch pad. With his single command, disaster had been visited upon the *Xuanzang* rocket, with the world watching as years of work was consumed by flame.

For the good of humanity, he reminded himself.

"Director Markham," said a female voice over a speaker hidden in his office ceiling. *"The ground team leader is asking to speak with you."*

Glancing to Burden, who only shrugged, Markham said, "Put her through."

A moment later, one of the suited figures on the screen moved toward whoever was controlling the camera recording everything from the site. The curved faceplate of the person's helmet was reflective, providing Markham only with a reverse image of the camera operator.

"Hello?" said a female voice, sounding distant and weak as it was channeled through her helmet com-

munications system and the satellite link. *"Director Markham?"*

"This is Markham. Who am I talking to?"

"Doctor April Hebert, sir. You asked to be notified when we had something worth reporting."

"Time's short, Doctor. What've you got?"

Hebert held up a large piece of twisted, scorched metal. There were no visible markings and no other easy means of making any sort of visual identification. *"We're still picking up pieces like this, and there are a hell of a lot of them. They don't belong to the* Xuanzang *rocket or anything else you'd expect to find in China, sir. We've only got our portable scanners with us here, and two of them have already failed thanks to the radiation, but I'm willing to say now that this is definitely EZ31 material. More accurately, it contains elements of those compounds. If this isn't a reuse of original elements, then it's a pretty damned good approximation."*

"Just as we suspected all along," said Burden.

Markham felt a weight settling upon his shoulders as everything he had feared for the past twenty hours and indeed the last five years was coming to pass. It had been that long since the last recorded sighting of an unidentified craft in low Earth orbit, which Majestic 12 satellites had confirmed as being Eizand in origin.

Then the vessel disappeared.

With American military planes moving to intercept the craft over the Pacific Ocean, the target slipped below radar. At first believing it to have crashed at sea, Markham and other MJ-12 supervisors deployed assets to the region in search of the ship or any wreckage or alien specimens that may have survived. Days of hunting the elusive craft were rewarded with nothing. Where had the ship gone? What about its crew, assuming there was one? The idea of one or more aliens running free anywhere on Earth sent MJ-12's senior leadership into a frenzy, with personnel and other resources allocated across the planet with orders to hunt down and secure the ship and any passengers or crew it may have carried. Those efforts went unrewarded, and theories began to circulate that perhaps this ship had employed some manner of self-destruct system to prevent its capture. Unconvinced of this notion, Markham saw its merits. If the Eizand were stepping up their surveillance of Earth, and still searching for their lost probes as well as the one manned vessel Majestic had captured, then it stood to reason that they would take steps to protect themselves. Without proof in the form of wreckage, there was no way to to be sure this had indeed happened, and because of that, Markham and his people remained vigilant.

That persistence paid off when intelligence agents working in China soon reported unconfirmed rumors of the secretive government now possessing some form of alien technology. Confirmation was a much more difficult proposition, coming less than a month ago as the *Xuanzang* probe and its accompanying rocket were entering the final stages of assembly before beginning the lengthy series of diagnostic checks in preparation for launch. The proof had been slim, in the form of a single small piece of metallic composite smuggled out of the Jiuquan Launch Center by an undercover Majestic operative, but it was enough to send Markham scrambling.

The probe could not be allowed to launch.

With the constant threat of the Eizand returning, either to find their missing ship or to attack Earth itself, time was short. Paranoia remained high, fueled by the disappearance of the *Arex IV* command module seven years earlier to the apparent loss of the *Charybdis*, the third failure by NASA to send a manned spacecraft beyond the solar system. Communication and computer telemetry with the vessel had been lost only months earlier, two years after the ship's launch. There was no way to ascertain whether the *Charybdis* experienced systems malfunctions or catastrophic failure, and there would be no opportunity to send another ship after the wayward vessel for at least another year. Had the vessel suffered from a critical design flaw, encountered some form of heretofore unknown stellar phenomenon, or been the victim of deliberate action? If the latter, were the Eizand to blame, or was this the fault of some other alien race? Such questions, though they could not be asked in a public forum, were the focus of much discussion within the hidden halls of Majestic 12's leadership.

As for the *Xuanzang*, a ship constructed with components from an Eizand ship could not be allowed to leave Earth. Not yet. Majestic engineers were hard at work on their own version of such a craft, but the task was being carried out in absolute secrecy. Markham had not even told Burden, his trusted right hand, about this initiative, which was under way after being initiated nearly a decade earlier. There would be only one chance at such a launch before the Eizand became aware of humanity's exploitation of their more advanced technology, and Markham and Majestic were going to make the most of that lone opportunity, provided China or some other world power did not first screw up things for the entire planet.

Hence, the "accident," perpetrated by Majestic, and

made to look as though the *Xuanzang* rocket had succumbed to a simple yet catastrophic malfunction, one with massive, lingering consequences. A single small explosive charge placed by a clandestine MJ-12 agent was all that was needed. The resulting detonation forced a chain reaction that ended up destroying the nuclear reactor that was to power the spacecraft's ion plasma propulsion engine. There was no massive explosion as one might expect from a nuclear weapon, but the blast was enough to destroy the rocket as well as the launch gantry and surrounding infrastructure. All of this was followed by the massive fuel fire that still raged, along with an enormous amount of radioactive fallout and debris. The entire area had been quarantined until the fire died down, but the lingering radiation was enough to keep out anyone who did not possess the necessary protective equipment. In this regard, Majestic 12 had the edge.

What concerned him about this operation was the potential for interference from other outside forces. They had seemingly dropped off the face of the Earth, though Markham knew that at least one and perhaps more of the agents he had sought for years remained at large. Following Kirsten Heffron's escape from custody and the director's disappearance years earlier, and in the aftermath of the assault on their secret base of operations off the coast of Scotland, the agents went into hiding. All vestiges of their advanced technology were destroyed before it could be taken into Majestic 12's possession for study. Markham knew they were out there, somewhere, likely still poking their noses into matters around the world. Would something like the *Xuanzang* attract their interest? Perhaps they were monitoring the launch, but from far away and beyond MJ-12's reach. What would their reaction be to today's "accident"? That remained to be seen, but Markham could not wait for the enigmatic troublemakers to show themselves.

"Doctor Hebert, how much longer do you think you'll need?"

On the monitor, the figure in the bulky suit turned as though looking for other members of her team before replying, *"We'll have to leave here in about half an hour. That's the limit of protection these suits can provide in this environment, but we have enough replacements to make three, maybe four more trips back if necessary. There's really not much more for us to do here, though, sir. This place is an inferno. By the time anybody with regular equipment can get in there, any evidence we might be worried about will be long gone."*

"I'd rather not risk another trip. We're pushing our luck as it is, and you've done remarkable work, Doctor. Get your people out of there."

Hebert touched her hand to her helmet's faceplate, mimicking a salute. *"Understood, Director."*

"Do you think the Chinese will figure out it was sabotage?" asked Burden.

Shrugging, Markham turned from the monitor and moved toward his desk. "Hell if I know. So far as we've been able to figure out, they had no idea we knew they'd recovered that Eizand probe. That might be the one thing working in our favor. On the other hand, they're paranoid, and they're always accusing us of one thing or another. I figure the president will be getting an earful about this from the Chinese president, regardless, assuming he hasn't already."

This sort of saber rattling was nothing new and in

fact had been on the uptick in recent years, thanks to everything from trade disputes and economic sanctions to incidents involving military vessels in disputed waters. Both sides were guilty of these transgressions, and until now both leaders had managed to smooth all ruffled feathers and maintain a semblance of civility. How much longer would that last?

Good question.

Settling into the chair behind his desk, Markham said, "It could be months or years before the Chinese can make any sort of educated guess about what happened."

Burden rose from her chair near the monitor and approached his desk. "Yeah, but we can't rule out one of their investigators or forensic scientists or engineers finding some shred of evidence that gives them the idea they were sabotaged."

"Nope, we can't, but proving it is a whole other kettle of fish, let alone pulling together enough information to level a formal accusation, at us or anybody else." That was of little comfort, as Markham was well aware that in the world of political brinkmanship and ever-stressed diplomatic relations between global powers, accusation and innuendo were two of the most powerful weapons in any government's arsenal.

"If they do find something," said Burden, "then there's a good chance we're all going to war."

Markham offered a humorless laugh. "If that happens, then we'll likely end up making things a hell of a lot easier for the Eizand."

And won't that be grand?

22

Sralanya
2386

Flanked by a pair of male Tevent Coalition guards and with his hands bound in front of him by the now-familiar restraint bands, Picard sat on a bench along one wall of the personnel transport's passenger compartment. Roused well before dawn after enduring only a few brief hours of fitful sleep, he felt himself being lulled by the ground transport's gentle movements and the hum of its propulsion system as it proceeded on its antigravity cushion.

It would be easy enough to drift back to sleep, but he was doing his best to keep track of their journey, which he suspected would end up being a futile endeavor. The vehicle's passenger area had no windows, and whatever changes in direction the transport undertook were without sharp turns or sudden slowing or acceleration. How long had they been on the move? Fifteen minutes; twenty at the outside, Picard guessed. He could not be sure if they were even still in the city.

"Where are you taking me?" It was the fifth time he had asked the question of his escorts since entering the vehicle. He made a point of employing the exact same phrasing and tone each time, refusing to offer the guards any hint that he was growing tired of posing the query. For their part, the two Eizand soldiers seemed to be growing irritated, though neither had ordered him to remain quiet. Until he received a reaction, Picard was content to keep needling them with questions.

It'll pass the time, if nothing else.

He had already examined the passenger compartment's interior. Besides the aft hatch through which he had entered, the only other features were the benches along both sides and a small communications panel set into the forward bulkhead. He and his guards were the only passengers. The rear hatch, he had observed during his loading process, could be opened or closed from the inside, but only with an octagonal key or access card each of the guards carried in a pocket of their uniform. Other than with assistance from outside the vehicle, the only way Picard was getting out of here was through the guards, which seemed an unlikely proposition.

Deciding to change tacks, he asked, "What about my people? Are they being moved as well?" Again, he received no reply, though one of the guards at least glanced at him. It was progress, Picard decided, if only a small portion.

The appearance of the guards in his holding cell had come as a surprise. All they had told him was that he was being transferred to another, more secure location to await his trial, and that time was of the essence. Having already been segregated from the rest of the away team, Picard's first questions to the guards were about them and their current condition, but he was ignored then just as now. He wondered about the idea of being moved to a "more secure location." Was the implication that his former holding area was somehow vulnerable? Perhaps his captors were anticipating the *Enterprise* attempting a rescue operation, assuming the crew had found a way to deal with the planet's orbiting satellite defenses. Even without the use of transporters, due to interference from one source or another, a security detail from the starship would be more than capable of taking control of whatever base or installation was his current destination. Presider Hilonu would be doing everything in her power to prevent that from happening. She needed Picard for the trial she wanted held and also required the away team to use as leverage to ensure his cooperation. It therefore seemed obvious that the Eizand leader would be taking no chances.

Where was the presider? Picard had not seen her since their last meeting, following his separation from the away team. Would she not appear again until his trial got under way? As for whatever legal proceedings Picard soon would face, would they be broadcast around Sralanya? He knew the *Enterprise* would be monitoring all planetary broadcasts, if for no other reason than just one more means of attempting to track the away team.

A shift in the transport's movements pushed Picard back against the passenger compartment's sloping starboard bulkhead, and he shifted his feet to better brace himself against the deck. His two guards also were surprised by the odd maneuver, with both Eizand reaching with free hands to steady themselves.

"What was that?" asked one of the soldiers.

His companion shook his head. "I do not know." He pushed himself from the bench, moving toward the front of the passenger compartment just as the transport lurched again, this time to port. Picard was able to keep steady in his seat by sticking out his right leg and planting his heel in a groove running the length of the deck, but the guard did not fare as well. Instead, the Eizand stumbled and rammed his shin into the opposite bench.

Snapping a stream of invective Picard did not understand, the guard reached for a handhold to keep from being knocked off his feet.

Picard flinched as something slammed into the vehicle's starboard side, behind his back. The effect was immediate as the transport lost power and began decelerating. Despite his best efforts, Picard felt himself dragged toward the front of the passenger compartment, pushing him into the other guard who was still seated on the bench. The second soldier, still standing at the time of the strike, stumbled forward and slammed face-first into the front wall. Picard heard bone snap and the guard whimpering as he dropped to his knees, reaching to cover his face.

"Ambush!" shouted a voice through the communications panel. *"We are under attack!"*

Who in the hell would be attacking a prisoner transport and why? Were the assailants after the guards, the vehicle, or him? Locked inside, he was a sitting duck. These and other questions and thoughts raced through Picard's mind as a second salvo punched the side of the transport, and this time he had to grab on to the edge of the bench to keep from being thrown to the floor.

You need to do something.

His stomach lurched as the transport halted with no warning, and Picard and the guard started to come up off the bench. Whereas the Eizand tried to arrest his motion by reaching for the bulkhead behind him, Picard allowed the inertia to carry him forward. With his hands still clasped together, he swung upward, his fists smashing into the underside of the guard's jaw. The strike was enough to snap the soldier's head back and into the bulkhead, and he grunted with surprise and pain. He attempted to push himself to his feet, one hand making a clumsy move for his holstered sidearm, but Picard gave him no quarter. Following his first attack, he lashed out at the guard again, chopping at his face with the edges of his hands. The blow was enough to drop the soldier back onto the bench and he toppled over.

"Stop!"

Ignoring the voice of the other guard, Picard scrambled to grab the weapon from his unconscious companion's holster. It took two tries to pull the sidearm free, and it required effort to wield the unfamiliar pistol with his hands still locked together. He spun, leveling the weapon's muzzle at the other guard in time to see the wounded Eizand, pale gray-blue blood streaming from his broken nose, struggling to push himself to his feet. The soldier had already drawn his weapon and now was attempting to take unsteady aim at his prisoner.

Picard fired.

The pistol bucked in his hands as it unleashed a single energy bolt, which was blinding and deafening inside the cramped passenger compartment. His aim was true and the bolt struck the guard in his left shoulder, spinning him around and pushing him against the forward wall. The soldier slumped against the bulkhead, dropping his own sidearm and rolling over onto the deck.

A quick check confirmed that the guard was merely unconscious, for which Picard breathed a sigh of relief. He had not wanted to harm the Eizand, but killing him would have only made an already tense situation far more uncomfortable.

The sound of metal against metal from behind him

made Picard turn and drop to one knee, aiming the awkward pistol at the transport's rear hatch. A moment later the door swung open and faint daylight streamed into the compartment.

"Captain Picard?"

The call was in halting Standard, as though its speaker was unfamiliar with the language, but it was enough for Picard to drop his weapon's muzzle toward the deck as first one, then a second Eizand head poked through the doorway. One of the new arrivals was a female, but the other was a male that Picard recognized.

"It is him," said Janotra, the guard who had overseen the away team's original incarceration. He looked away, toward someone Picard could not see, before redirecting his attention back inside the vehicle. "Are you injured?"

"What is the meaning of this?" asked Picard. He felt his grip tighten on the pistol.

Janotra replied, "You are safe, Captain. I am here to take you to your people, but we must leave quickly. They will send soldiers and others to investigate, and we must be gone from here before they arrive. We have no wish to harm anyone beyond what is absolutely necessary and otherwise unavoidable."

Allowing himself to be helped from the transport, Picard handed his weapon to Janotra. He saw that the ambush had occurred on an undeveloped road well away from the activity of Ponval. The cityscape was visible in the distance, many of its buildings' lights still glowing as dawn approached. A narrow, winding road cut through grassland, and a trio of ground vehicles, each featuring an antigrav system like the transports, were parked in the shadows beneath a canopy of towering trees. Several

Eizand moved about, and Picard noted how their uniforms and equipment were far less clean and polished than what he had seen in the city. These were not regular soldiers, he decided.

Realization dawned, and Picard scowled. "You're the dissenters Presider Hilonu mentioned."

"Yes," replied the Eizand. "A few of them, at least. There are many more of us, Captain, scattered around the world."

"I don't understand. Why are you fighting your government?"

"Because it is based on treachery and deceit." Janotra took Picard by the arm and led him toward one of the vehicles. "Our world's history is one of tragedy, Captain, but many of us have come to believe it was as much of our own making as it was influenced by outside forces. There are those who are unwittingly ignorant of this, and still others who have chosen to bury the unpleasant truths. We mean to set the record straight."

That gave Picard pause. "Wait. Are you saying that you don't believe my people were responsible for the war?"

Janotra shook his head. "That I do not know, but with your help, we hope the truth will soon be known to all."

Chen was the first to see him, and Picard was almost knocked off his feet as she eschewed all manner of Starfleet protocols and convention by wrapping her arms around him in a firm hug.

"Lieutenant," said Picard, though he did not resist his own instinctive return of the embrace.

"You can court-martial me later, sir, but it's damned good to see you."

With that undignified greeting out of the way, Picard took stock of Lieutenant Dina Elfiki and Glinn Ravel Dygan before the science officer updated him on the team's liberation from their holding cell. Fleeing from Ponval, they along with Janotra and other Eizand dissenters had ventured into the mountains far north of the city before arriving in this network of underground tunnels and caverns. Picard had been given the same treatment, leaving the scene of his own escape via ground vehicles before switching to a small airborne personnel craft and flying deep into the mountain range. After landing and camouflaging the shuttle, Picard's rescuers escorted him on foot the rest of the way, entering the subterranean hideaway through a concealed entrance at the bottom of a narrow ravine.

Finally, with Elfiki's recounting of their journey to this unlikely sanctuary complete, Picard listened to her report about Austin Braddock's death during the away team's escape.

"I'm sorry, Captain," she said. "It happened so fast, and there was so much confusion."

"He saved my life, sir," added Chen, her eyes moistening. "It was over in an instant. I don't know if he even knew what he was doing, or if he was just acting on instinct, or . . ." Her words trailed off as she reached up to wipe a lone tear that had begun running down her cheek.

Dygan placed a hand on her shoulder. "He knew, Lieutenant." The Cardassian offered a small smile. "He acted out of duty and training, but also out of loyalty to his shipmates. Remember that."

Nodding, Chen reached up to pat his hand. "Thanks."

"Captain Picard."

Turning at the sound of the new voice, Picard saw Janotra standing at what he perhaps considered a respectful distance as the captain reunited with his officers. The tall, lean Eizand soldier had exchanged his Tevent Coalition military uniform for looser, more comfortable-looking clothing. He was accompanied by another Eizand: the female Picard had seen during his liberation from custody.

"This is my assistant, Renli," said Janotra, gesturing to his companion. "She oversees our supplies, including scouting for new sources of food, water, weapons, and other necessities. She also plans raids into Ponval or other, smaller cities or settlements to provide us what we need."

Picard asked, "You steal what you need?"

"Sometimes, yes." Janotra grimaced. "It is not something we are proud of, Captain. It is a tactic of last resort, and even then we do everything possible to ensure that those suffering a loss due to our theft are not innocent bystanders or those who cannot afford to lose whatever meager possessions they have acquired. Instead, we focus our activities against government or military entities."

It all sounded so very altruistic, and Picard attempted not to render summary judgment upon these people until he heard more of their story. At first, they seemed to be a band of rogue bandits, but such people would not have taken the trouble to free strangers from prison. There was more here than met the eye, Picard decided.

"If you are hungry or require rest," said Renli, "we

can provide for your needs just as we have for the rest of your group. I promise you will be treated well."

Chen said, "They've taken great care of us."

Drawing himself up, Picard said, "Thank you for your offer and for looking after my people. What I require is an explanation for our release and access to my ship."

Janotra nodded. "Your second request presents some problems, as any attempt by us to establish a communications link will surely be tracked by the Coalition's rather extensive monitoring and surveillance apparatus. I am not saying such communication is impossible, but it will require additional planning and coordination on our part in order to keep Coalition forces from discovering our location."

"Fair enough," said Picard. Though he was uncertain he should take everything Janotra told him at face value, there was something to be said for exercising patience and restraint for the time being, in the hopes of learning more about these people and what they were doing here.

"As for why we extracted you from detention," said Janotra, "the simple answer is that we need your help, Captain. We need your help to unlock the truth of what happened to us. It affects you as well. It is our hope that if the reality of the war is revealed, the divisions that continue to plague us even after so many generations will finally begin to dissolve."

Chen asked, "You mentioned that your people have been living a lie. What does that mean?"

"Are you saying the astronauts from Earth weren't responsible?" asked Elfiki.

"We know that they played a role. What remains unclear is the extent of their involvement."

Indicating for Picard and the others to follow them, Janotra and Renli moved out of the small cave where the away team had greeted one another and into a connecting tunnel. As with the caves, the ceiling here was low and the floor uneven. Picard saw how lights strung on cables provided illumination in the otherwise dark spaces. He ran his hand along a stone wall, feeling its network of craggy grooves and wondering how long ago this underground passage had been created.

As they walked, Janotra said, "Many of the war's contributing factors were in play long before their arrival, such as our endless squabbling over natural resources and territorial boundaries. While the Tevent had ready access to vast deposits of mineral ores and other resources, the Galj and Yilondra nations also controlled their assets." The Eizand soldier shook his head. "Disagreements and distrust over access to resources was a constant source of ever escalating conflicts. Given the unwillingness of any of the major participants in these disputes to negotiate or even honor existing treaties, all-out war was inevitable."

Picard asked, "But what about the astronauts? What does any of this have to do with them?"

His expression now one of sadness, Janotra replied, "They were the perfect means to an end, Captain."

"They were scapegoats?" asked Chen.

Janotra frowned. "I do not understand your reference, Lieutenant, but if it means they were treated unfairly, that is not inaccurate."

"But what of their trial?" asked Glinn Dygan. "Are you implying that was a miscarriage of justice?"

"It was worse," said Renli. "It was theater, designed to distract the masses and inflame their emotions at a time when our people were still reeling from the effects of global war. After having their civilization almost ripped from them, the Tevent Coalition government was able to march these three criminals before an audience of hundreds, with millions more watching on news broadcasts, as they were executed for their supposed deeds."

Unwilling to simply accept what he was hearing, Picard said, "Even if what you say is true, it still doesn't give me a reason. Why would the Tevent Coalition have to pursue such a—"

Wait.

Janotra nodded. "Yes, Captain. The Tevent started our war."

"Damn," said Elfiki.

Renli replied, "There were many who believed war was inevitable, and opinions differed on which of the three powers would launch the initial strikes. Tevent leaders at the time attempted to portray the conflict as the Galj and Yilondra combining forces to threaten Coalition interests; there is equal evidence to suggest the Tevent government pursued unduly aggressive policies with respect to territorial expansion and protection." She held out her hands. "In the end, all that matters is that war finally came, and our entire planet suffered for it."

"Whether your people provided the trigger for the war is another matter," said Janotra. "Several theories were put forth, establishing a case for a version of events that was rather convenient. The precise timeline has always raised questions for those willing to consider them. In the aftermath of the initial strikes, when the trial was under way, Tevent forces moved on Galj and Yilondra targets while people's attentions were elsewhere. By then, it was too late."

The group resumed their traversing of the tunnel, with Janotra eventually leading them into another, somewhat larger chamber. Picard saw stacks of storage containers, tools, and other items, including an array of computer and communications equipment sitting on worktables along the rear wall. Although Picard did not recognize the function of every component, there was enough here for him to glean some understanding.

"I know that our story must seem outlandish," said the Eizand soldier as they entered the room. "I cannot expect you to simply believe me. The truth is that we have no proof of these allegations. Finding evidence has been one of our goals for quite some time. Thankfully, there are others, like me, who have inserted themselves into the Coalition government and military at various levels, working in secret for years to locate the proof we seek."

"There must be something," said Picard.

Renli replied, "As generations passed, leaders changed, and people forgot, it became harder to believe that such evidence existed at all. However, one of our people alerted us to a possibility just a few days ago, before your arrival. That prompted us to take a chance on raiding one of the Coalition archive annexes."

"That is what Presider Hilonu mentioned," said Glinn Dygan. "When we first met her, there was talk of such a raid."

Picard nodded. "Yes, she did talk about that."

"Do you think Hilonu knows about this evidence or what it represents?" asked Chen.

"I do not believe that the presider, or even anyone on her staff, knows the truth," replied the Eizand. "However, she does have advisers who will attempt to shield her from this, to protect her from a political standpoint. We hope that if the evidence we have found is conclusive, we can use it to convince Hilonu that our cause is just."

Elfiki asked, "What kind of evidence are we talking about?"

Moving to one of the storage crates, Janotra pulled open the container's access panel, revealing a cache of computer or electrical equipment. It took Picard a moment to realize that some of the components did not appear to be Eizand in origin. Sitting among a section of console or workstation parts were at least two keyboards bearing English lettering, along with another panel of status gauges and controls labeled with similar script.

"Is that what I think it is?" asked Chen.

Janotra replied, "This is a computer core from the Eizand ship that originally visited your world and eventually returned to us, modified for use by humans. We have attempted to access it, but it is encrypted using methods we do not understand."

"Captain," said Elfiki, "if this has a record of the ship's flight from Earth, maybe with personal logs or journals—"

Already ahead of his science officer, Picard nodded. "The truth about everything may be right here."

23

Vandenberg Air Force Base, California
September 6, 2044

Gerald Markham glanced at the clocks on the Spaceflight Operations Center's curved forward wall. Positioned in a row above the array of ten giant high-definition display monitors that dominated the wall, each clock was labeled with a different time zone from around the world, with the range of times spanning fourteen hours from California to Japan. Now, however, the only clock that concerned him was the one that matched his wristwatch and was set to local time.

Markham always found it fascinating that in a room teeming with state-of-the-art computer and communications equipment, people who staffed facilities such as this one continued to rely on analog clocks for keeping track of the hour. With a small smile, he recognized the irony of questioning the SpaceOps clocks while sporting his own archaic timepiece. The watch, with hands instead of a digital readout, possessed no special features beyond a backlit face. It was a throwback, much like himself. He had never held any particular interest or enthusiasm for timepieces beyond their obvious usefulness, though he had developed a fascination in recent years not just for clocks and watches, but also calendars and any other sort of timekeeping tool.

Of particular interest was their ability to count down toward zero—to nothingness.

"Holding at T minus five minutes," said a voice over the SpaceOps intercom system. *"All controllers maintain readiness levels."*

Standing at the rear of the SpaceOps chamber, Markham glanced around the room. His vantage point gave him an unfettered view of the entire floor, which was arranged in tiered fashion with four rows of nine workstations each, curving outward as they faced the wall of monitors. The highest tier, where Markham stood, had an additional trio of workstations behind the row of consoles on this level, where the flight director and other high-ranking personnel could be found during active missions. The consoles were streamlined, with docking stations for laptop computers, tablets, phones, and other devices that would be swapped out or moved to other stations as required by the needs of a specific mission. Despite this latest delay, Markham noted that every workstation was occupied, with people either sitting at computer terminals or moving between consoles to exchange information.

Centered on the array of screens at the front of the room was a giant image of a spacecraft secure in a weblike cradle. The image, fed to them from camera systems all around the orbiting dock facility, displayed the ship it protected in all its glory. *Peacemaker 1*, as it was known in Majestic 12 circles, was an ungainly conglomeration of disparate components that scientists and engineers had somehow convinced to play nice with one another. Rather than relying on heavy-lift launch systems that could not escape public scrutiny and curiosity, *Peacemaker* was assembled in space, with components lifted to orbit under the auspices of building a new permanent space habitat to replace the International Space Station, which had sustained damage several years earlier and was now incapable of supporting a crew. While that new station was being built, it provided cover for *Peacemaker*'s construction. It was an approach that allowed Majestic and its subordinate organizations to evade detection, which was of enormous benefit when considering the spacecraft's cargo and mission. That aspect of this endeavor was embodied in the oversized cylinder that had been affixed to the front of the alien craft. At first glance, it reminded Markham of the body of an old Saturn V rocket from the 1960s or 1970s, or the larger orbiting satellites—many secret from the general public—from the United States as well as the Soviet Union during the same time period.

"What's the holdup this time?" asked Markham, allowing a hint of irritation to creep into his voice.

Standing at the workstation normally designated for the flight director and dressed in the dark, formal uniform of a United States Navy admiral, Geoffrey Stanton replied, "We're still waiting for the all-clear on that final cryo systems check."

Despite being unhappy about the report, Markham said nothing. A problem with the cryogenics support systems aboard the spacecraft could scrub the entire mission. The system, despite surviving a prolonged battery of rigid testing and other quality assurance checks, was still facing its first use in an actual operational scenario. A modernization of technology first developed during the last century, cryogenic suspension support systems had come a long way since the ill-conceived experiments conducted in the 1990s. For one thing, the version carried by this ship benefited from all the lessons learned during those initial trials, as well as enhancements from equipment used by the Eizand crew. Despite all of this preparation, this was to be the system's first practical test.

The ship's crew—Commander Valmiki Goswami, Lieutenant Meredith Harper, and Lieutenant Park Ji-hu—were already in hibernation, tucked in for their journey as just one of the hundreds of thousands steps to be accomplished prior to launch. The ship would be piloted by the onboard computer guidance system for the duration of the journey, with Goswami and his crew only emerging from cryogenic sleep as the vessel approached its destination. If the system malfunctioned in flight, the crew would die, so if there was a chance for technicians to rectify any issues or concerns without aborting the mission, Markham supported that action.

You've been waiting almost fifteen years for this day. A few more minutes won't kill you. Well, maybe they will.

"But everything else is checking out?"

Stanton shrugged. "So far, but that thing is a tight ball of about three million parts, all designed to work in close formation with each other while doing its level best to bend the hell out of at least four or five laws of physics as I understand them." He gestured toward the monitors on the front wall. "I won't breathe easy until it's away from this planet and on its way to be someone else's problem."

Peacemaker was a miraculous union of human and Eizand technology, a great deal of which Markham made no attempts to understand, instead trusting such matters to the dedicated, talented Majestic engineering and science staffs. While much of the Eizand spacecraft salvaged in 2031 was still usable, several of its internal systems had been retrofitted or replaced in order to support a three-person human crew. This included food storage, environmental control, computer and other electronic interfaces, and the cryogenics systems that would sustain the crew for the majority of its decades-long voyage. Once free of its orbiting support gantry, the ship would set off for deep space, traveling well away from Earth and maneuvering into a course that would take it out of the solar system before onboard computers sent *Peacemaker* on its extended voyage through the cosmos at speeds faster than light itself. Even with the fantastic engine powering the vessel—a propulsion technology that Majestic scientists only partially understood—the journey would take almost two decades to complete.

For a brief moment, Markham regretted the knowledge that he would not live to see the ship and its crew achieve the goal for which they had been training for years. He would not be an active member of MJ-12 by the time *Peacemaker* reached its destination; he had thought he might at least still be part of the information loop, and thus notified when the mission he had put into motion more than a decade earlier finally came to fruition.

That was now an impossibility.

Feeling an urge to cough, Markham reached for a handkerchief in his pocket and held it to his mouth. The fit was brief, yet painful, with each cough feeling like someone punching him in the chest. He glanced at the handkerchief after pulling it from his lips and saw the dark flecks staining the white material. There were more of them today, and they were darker.

Well, shit.

His doctor had given him the news a week earlier. What had begun as a routine physical almost a month ago quickly escalated into a series of tests, screenings, and evaluations by specialists from more fields than Markham could count. All of that ultimately was boiled down to a prognosis delivered by his personal physician, whom he had known for more than twenty years. The cancer in his lungs was spreading, and there was nothing more to be done, except use his remaining time to ensure his affairs were in order, finish what he could of the work he had started, and try to die with at least some of his dignity still intact.

You win some. You lose some.

He folded the handkerchief and put it in his pocket, straining to clear his throat.

"Are you all right, Mister Markham?" asked Stanton.

"I'll live."

For now.

Glancing around, Stanton leaned closer to Markham and said in a low voice, "Sir, may I have a word with you in private?"

Markham eyed the admiral with skepticism, but nodded and allowed Stanton to lead him from the floor and through a pair of doors leading from SpaceOps into a connecting corridor. The lighting here was brighter than inside the control center and Markham blinked a few times, forcing his eyes to adjust.

"What can I do for you, Admiral?" he asked, forcing himself to fight back what felt like another oncoming coughing bout.

Again, Stanton looked around, checking the corridor as though ensuring they were alone. Then he said, "Mister Markham, I've been director of the I-31 group for five years. When I was briefed on the unit's activities and this project in particular, you'll recall that I offered some initial concerns, and it's a topic you and I have revisited from time to time."

That much was true. Markham recalled his first meetings with Geoffrey Stanton, who soon after his promotion from captain to rear admiral was notified of his assignment to the Pentagon. On paper, Stanton's duties listed him as assigned to the Office of Naval Operations for Plans, Policy, and Operations. A far-reaching organization within the navy's already Byzantine organizational structure, it was a viable cover for Stanton's actual assignment as director of Initiative 2031. Upon learning of I-31's mission and long-term goals, Stanton offered a number of nuanced viewpoints. Although in favor of assuring American—and indeed, global—security in the face of extraterrestrial threat, the admiral provided a fresh, outside perspective that made Markham consider whether his own thinking had made him entrenched in his views and therefore blinded to other possibilities. Rather than shut down Stanton, Markham instead encouraged the decorated officer to continue offering his unbridled thoughts, and there had been a number of spirited late-night conversations over brandy over the ensuing five years. However, Stanton had never wavered on one crucial point, in that he did not favor a preemptive aggressive action against any target, indigenous or alien, without proper cause or provocation. This also spurred numerous discussions, and each man found himself working to move the other's viewpoint, if only the slightest bit.

Despite whatever disagreements Stanton many have raised, he continued to carry out the tasks given to him and I-31, which included overseeing the *Peacemaker* project and bringing that endeavor to the point they now all awaited: launch day. The admiral still voiced his concerns in private to Markham and balanced this task with others designed to provide less extreme options in the event of "otherworldly engagements," as Stanton liked to call such scenarios.

"What's your point, Geoff?" asked Markham, before covering his mouth with a fist to stifle the single cough he could not suppress.

Stanton drew a long, slow breath, sounding like air escaping from a tire as he exhaled. "My point is that we're here, at the moment of truth, and I don't know that I feel right about what we're about to do."

"Are you serious?" The question came with such force that it prompted another coughing fit. Markham retrieved his handkerchief and covered his mouth, doing his best to keep from spitting more blood into his hand. He ignored Stanton's hand on his arm, getting himself under control before glaring at the admiral. "After all these years, and everything we've talked about doing to keep this planet safe, you're getting cold feet at the precise instant we're getting set to launch this thing?"

"I've had all those years to think about it, sir. You know where I stand on our security. I'm as much in favor of doing what's needed to protect ourselves, but this is different. It's always been different."

Markham snorted. "They came at us first, Admiral. Have you forgotten that? Twice, that we know of, but how many other times have they come here, sizing us up? What about *Ares IV*? The *Charybdis*? The space station? How many more times do we have to get smacked across the nose before we're allowed to hit back? How do we know the next time they come won't be when they're coming to crush us?"

"We don't know any of that, sir," replied Stanton. "We've never been able to conclude what happened to the *Ares* or the others. Even if by some chance all three of those were the result of alien attack, how can we know it's the Eizand?"

Rolling his eyes, Markham said, "We know the Eizand know about us, Admiral. What we don't know is how much they know about us or what our vulnerabilities are. We've got one chance to do something decisive, and that's it." He pointed toward the doors leading back into SpaceOps. "We can't stop. Not now."

"With all due respect, Mister Markham, I disagree."

"Then you can take your concerns to the president. This was her idea."

No, Markham decided, it was not that simple. That they were standing here today was as much his own doing as anyone else's. "Look, I'd have been perfectly happy to leave well enough alone, and hey, if the Eizand had come looking to talk or asking for help, then maybe we could've worked something out, but that's not why they came. We know they were looking for a new planet because they've done an even better job of screwing up theirs than we've done here. They weren't looking for help, or friends. They want our planet. Sooner or later, you have to wonder when they'll decide we're just in the way." He shrugged. "The way I see it, this is an 'us or them' situation. If we can't win the Eizand's hearts and minds, then we'll burn their damned house down, and the president agrees with me."

The current president of the United States had inherited Majestic 12 and all of its ongoing operations from her predecessor, and she had taken the time to review all of the provided material and spent weeks consulting with MJ-12 leadership before arriving at her decision earlier in the year. Most of her questions had revolved around the weapons platform the *Peacemaker* would be transporting across space to the Eizand homeworld. The space-based nuclear weapons package was the latest iteration of a concept first tested and deployed in the 1960s during NASA's *Gemini* manned spaceflight program. Such weapons lost favor with government leaders following a near-tragic mishap in 1968, but the United States, China, and Russia quietly resumed their development in the 2030s, not long after Majestic 12 and rival organizations from other countries concluded that the tragedy that befell the *Ares IV* mission to Mars might have been a deliberate attack or act of sabotage by an alien enemy. Majestic's plan for the weapons package was simple: travel to the Eizand home planet, deploy the weapons package against selected targets based on information retrieved from the alien ship's original onboard computer files, verify that bombardment was successful, and return to Earth. Astronauts Goswami, Harper, and Park had trained for years for this mission. They knew the stakes and were committed to carrying out their duty regardless of the personal sacrifices they would make by returning to Earth nearly fifty years after their departure.

Armed with all of this knowledge, the president had confirmed her commitment to the task less than an hour ago, giving the astronauts a final send-off via teleconference before the *Peacemaker* crew entered hibernation.

A buzz from Stanton's pocket forestalled any response the admiral might offer, and he extracted a smartphone and held it to his ear. After a moment, he lowered the phone and looked to Markham. "Cryo systems check out. We're a go for launch."

"Let's get on with it, then."

Would this crazy scheme work? There was no way to know if the efforts of uncounted men and women over the course of decades would bring success or failure. Predicting the ramifications of the bold plan being put into motion today was impossible. Gerald Markham could be sure of only one thing: after a lifetime spent defending his country and—indeed—his planet, he would never know whether that effort was wasted.

Ain't that a kick in the ass?

Kansas City, Missouri
September 6, 2044

Thanks to Mestral's continued tinkering, the Beta 7's main display now showed an image of *Peacemaker 1* as the vessel pushed out from its orbital cradle. For some silly reason, the imagery reminded Kirsten Heffron of a bullet leaving the barrel of a gun.

Well, you're not wrong.

Video feeds from the orbital docking facility, itself one of several clandestine projects created over the years by Majestic 12, showed the vessel and its ominous cargo pushing away from Earth, plunging forward into the darkness of space. Leaning on her cane and with a shawl pulled around her narrow shoulders in a feeble attempt to ward off a chill, Heffron said nothing. Instead, she was listening to one of the audio feeds into which Mestral had tapped, and which now broadcast everything currently taking place in the Spaceflight Operations Center at Vandenberg Air Force Base.

While the facility was not classified, Heffron knew for

certain that the mission currently being overseen there was perhaps the most secret military endeavor since the Manhattan Project. The parallels between that clandestine operation and this new effort were not lost on her. Both were conceived for comparable purposes and, it was arguable, created for similarly misguided reasons.

A little late for that kind of musing, isn't it?

Pushing away the troublesome thought, she recalled her memories of the operation center's layout while listening to the current audio feed and the various controllers calling out status updates with every passing minute. Then, a voice in clear authority declared the launch a success, and the mission now officially under way.

"That is Admiral Stanton," said Mestral from where he still stood next to the Beta 7 console. "He has been the director of the group you once led for quite some time now, though the details of his assignment since being transferred to Majestic 12 are somewhat difficult to find."

"That's the way we liked it," said Heffron, her gaze still fixed on the screen and the image of *Peacemaker 1* as it continued to travel away from Earth.

The super computer sat exposed in the nook he had fashioned for it behind the basement's brick wall. The nondescript ranch house southeast of the Kansas City metropolitan area sat on three acres of land, providing a nice buffer from prying eyes for Mestral and Heffron, allowing the pair to live in relative quiet. It had taken Mestral months to quietly transport the computer and other equipment from the Griffith Observatory in Los Angeles once Rain Robinson made it clear that she wanted nothing more to do with the Aegis or any of its "toys," as she put it. Robinson held no ill-will toward Mestral or Heffron, but having them in her home and at the observatory had proven too much for her to bear, bringing with it the memories of her father's loss and the anger and disappointment she still felt toward Gary Seven and his unseen masters. Robinson had allowed Mestral and Heffron to take whatever they wanted, on the condition that they left her alone from that point forward.

Heffron could only feel sadness for the other woman. They were so close in age, and with lives shaped in so many ways by the same external factors, even if the details were markedly different. Both had devoted their lives to causes they considered worthy, only to turn away in the face of betrayal.

Life sucks mighty hard sometimes.

"So, what happens now?"

Turning from the Beta 7, Mestral replied, "There is nothing more we can do. The ship is presumably bound for the Eizand home world. Stopping it was beyond our abilities, and our attempts to alert the Aegis were unsuccessful."

"Or they heard us and just ignored us," countered Heffron.

"That is a possibility."

Even though he had been able to disassemble the Beta 7 and put it back together after relocating it to this suburb on the edge of nowhere, Mestral had not enjoyed similar success with the transporter system, which had gone inert years earlier following his and Heffron's chaotic arrival at Rain Robinson's feet. The Aegis, at least so far as Mestral and Robinson had been able to determine, were responsible for the unit's deactivation. Despite finding a way to restore operation to the computer, the transporter resisted his every effort, leaving Mestral and Heffron with eyes and ears to monitor events around the world, but no means of inserting themselves into things.

Probably just as well, thought Heffron. Now seventy-six, her days of gallivanting around the world in search of alien or other threats were long behind her. Even Mestral, with his extended Vulcan lifespan and superior physiology, was beginning to the feel the onset of aging. The brutal truth was that they were too old and without the necessary equipment and support to carry on any assignments the Aegis might have had in mind for Earth. The mysterious benefactors had ceased all communication, refusing to answer any requests for help or information and leaving Mestral, Robinson, and even Heffron herself high and dry. Was that because there was nothing more to be done here on Earth? Had the Aegis accomplished the goals that justified this entire decades-long endeavor? Perhaps they had failed to achieve those objectives, and instead had thrown in the towel, leaving humanity to fumble along the road to whatever future fate awaited it.

There's a comforting thought.

"Is there anyone else we can call for help?" asked Heffron. "Maybe your people?"

"It is an interesting notion, but I am afraid the communication equipment at our disposal is not sufficient to reach Vulcan. Any message we send will not arrive for decades, by which time *Peacemaker* will have reached its destination."

She gestured toward the computer monitor. "We've done a fabulous job trashing our own world and only recently figured out a way to travel to other planets. We have absolutely no idea what we're doing, but there we go, wandering about in the dark, and acting like we own the place."

Clasping his hands behind his back, Mestral arched an eyebrow. "It is a concern my people had during our initial surveys of Earth."

Heffron shook her head. "Right. We're nowhere close to being ready to do something like this, but here we go anyway, and for our first trick, we're going to attack another world. Hell of a way to introduce ourselves to the rest of the galaxy, isn't it?"

24

U.S.S. Enterprise
2386

He did not want to sleep. There was still so much to do, and he felt guilty pausing even for a moment.

Just a few minutes. A quick nap, to make Doctor Crusher happy. That's all I need. I can handle this.

"You're not sleeping, are you?"

Staring at the ceiling above the bed, Geordi La Forge sighed. "No."

"Do you want me to get you something?" asked Tamala Harstad, lying next to him on the left side of their shared bed. "As it happens, I'm a doctor."

"So I've heard." He shifted his position in an attempt to get comfortable, resting his right forearm across his face. "Let me just lie here a minute. Maybe I can drift off."

Harstad chuckled. "Are you kidding? I can hear your brain turning from here. I know you're thinking you'll just lie here nice and quiet for a few minutes with your eyes closed and the lights down low, and that'll be enough. It won't work, Mister Chief Engineer. Even you know it won't work. You didn't even get undressed."

"I took off my boots."

"And thank you for that."

Closing his eyes did nothing to help La Forge relax. His mind was still conjuring images, building and disassembling pieces of diagnostic results and other data fed to him in rapid fashion by the ship's computer over the past several hours. The unending stream of information had wormed its way past his eyes and deep into his brain, which now was fighting to continue the work he had been forced to suspend at the behest of the ship's chief medical officer. Somehow, in that manner she had perfected over years spent working as a doctor, Beverly Crusher knew that he had been working almost around the clock and was well into his second day before she appeared in the engineering section, ordering him to get some sleep before resuming his duties. He had pleaded to continue working, citing as justification the urgent need to locate Captain Picard and the rest of the away team but that only compelled the doctor to reduce the length of his mandatory rest period.

"You have a staff, don't you?" she had asked, in response to which La Forge remembered thinking that he did indeed have a staff, even if his assistant chief engineer was confined to quarters. With Taurik out of the picture—at least, officially—it fell to the rest of his team to fill that gap, and that meant La Forge spending more time in engineering, working on the problems the *Enterprise* currently faced.

"One hour," said Harstad. "That's all she wants out of you."

La Forge frowned. "It's too long. I can't stand being here while my people are down there, carrying my weight."

He felt Harstad rest a hand on his chest. "I know, and I understand, but you won't be helping anybody if you don't take care of yourself."

Reaching over to caress her hand, he said, "Okay, Doc. I get it."

Even though sleep would not come, it was still good to relax and to do so with Tamala at his side. Living together had taken some getting used to, but he had come to enjoy having someone to "come home to" after a duty shift. Their schedules and the demands placed on them were such that they were not always in synch with each other. Her duties often required her to work delta shift, whereas his role as the *Enterprise*'s chief engineer made it so that a strict adherence to a duty schedule was a nice idea only infrequently realized. Even with those challenges, they still found time for each other.

"Your gears are turning again."

Despite his fatigue, La Forge laughed. "Yeah, but it's not what you think."

"Uh-oh."

He was rolling toward her when the door chime sounded, causing him to cast a wary look in that direction.

"Really?"

The chime beeped a second time before he could push himself from the bed and smooth his uniform tunic.

"Come in."

The door slid aside in response to his command, revealing Taurik standing in the corridor. As always, he was dressed in a Starfleet uniform that was irritatingly free of wrinkles.

"Commander La Forge. I hope I am not disturbing you."

"You are," said Harstad from behind him, though La Forge heard her playful tone and the chuckle that punctuated the reply.

La Forge aimed a dismissive wave in her direction. "Ignore her. Look, Taurik, you know what the expression *confined to quarters* actually means, right?"

"I am familiar with the term. However, I feel that my decision to disobey that instruction is justified, for I believe that I may have a solution to the Eizand weapons."

That was enough to make La Forge forget all about sleeping. "What?"

"Until now, our focus has been on defending the *Enterprise* against the electromagnetic pulse generators. Alternatively, we have explored how to disable the satellites with the EMP weapons, but our phasers would either destroy their target, or else be ineffective."

La Forge tried not to scowl. "I know all of this, Taurik."

Unperturbed, Taurik continued. "Something that has not been considered, at least so far as I am aware, is using our shields to act as a countermeasure against the pulse generators."

"Our shields can't hold out against those . . ." He allowed the rest of his sentence to die on his lips as his mind, having taken the extra needed second to process what Taurik had said, caught up to his mouth. "Wait, you're not talking about protecting the ship. You mean using our shield emitters as weapons?"

Taurik's eyebrow rose. "Imprecise, but essentially correct, Commander. The Eizand EMP generators operate on a very narrow band of frequencies. If we modulate our deflector shield emitters to a comparable frequency and broadcast that energy toward the satellites at the time they are firing at us, we may be able to initiate a feedback pulse that would disable the weapons, but leave the rest of the satellite undamaged and operational."

"Yeah, but the strain against the shields might be too much to handle while defending the ship. We could blow out some or even all of the emitters."

"I have considered that possibility. Routing power

from the warp engines to the deflector shield generators may prove sufficient."

Now La Forge grimaced. "Or we could overload the generators, and then we'd be a sitting duck." Even as he expressed his doubts, he was turning over Taurik's proposal, trying to see it from different angles. How had he not considered something like this before now?

Because you've had your hands full, and you're tired, and Doctor Crusher's going to be mad at you. Again.

"I have not had an opportunity to test my theory using a computer simulation," said Taurik. "However, I could do so from engineering."

"How did I not see that coming?" La Forge made no effort to hide his sarcasm, but Taurik had a point. For something like this and with so much at stake, a test was needed. Several tests would be better, but he still had no idea how much longer they would have to devise a workable solution, but he figured time was a commodity in very short supply.

"Okay, let's go." Sleep would have to wait. La Forge could already feel a renewed surge of adrenaline beginning to course through his body. This was just what he needed to feel energized all over again. "How did you work this out without computer access?"

Taurik replied, "I considered the issue while meditating."

"I'm going to have to try that one of these days."

"I would be willing to assist you."

"Later. Come on." Satisfied now that they had something new to try, La Forge followed the Vulcan to the door. He knew he was taking a gamble so far as enlisting Taurik's help, but the simple truth was that he needed his fellow engineer if he had any hope of crafting a solution to the current problem. In his head, he was already devising not only his apology to Worf and Captain Picard but also the instruction set he would need for the *Enterprise*'s main computer to realize his simulation parameters.

"Excuse me," said a voice from behind him. "Mister Chief Engineer, sir?"

Pausing in the doorway, La Forge looked back to see Harstad crossing the room toward him, a large smile brightening her features as she offered him his boots. Only then did he remember to look down and see his socks. He leaned toward her, planting a kiss on her cheek.

"Let's just keep this between us, all right?"

"My lips are sealed."

Sralanya

The tunnel opening and connecting passageway afforded Picard a view of the cavern below. In gentle fashion, the rock walls sloped the two-meter distance to the larger chamber's floor before leveling out, providing a relatively flat, open area for members of the group to congregate. The area had been converted into a barracks of sorts, with rows of makeshift cubicles formed from stacking storage containers and other items used as dividers. Narrow walkways separated the rows of cubes, and inside a few of the spaces Picard could see crude bunk beds or, in some cases, blankets and padding arranged on the floor. A pond occupied the compound's far end, with tubing running from a series of scaffolds erected around its perimeter to provide water. He watched as individuals or small groups of Eizand filled buckets or other containers of varying sizes to transport water to some other area of the subterranean compound.

"Where does the water come from?"

Standing next to him on the ledge, Janotra replied, "Underground springs. Deep enough that they were spared contamination from the war. There are subsurface rivers and springs running all through these mountains."

Despite not attempting to keep an accurate count, Picard found himself noting the number of Eizand in easy view. At least a hundred, perhaps more, assuming there were other areas within the caverns suitable for housing members. "Surely all of these people didn't defect from the Tevent army."

Janotra shook his head. "Not all of them were soldiers. In fact, many of them are not of the Tevent Coalition. Our group is home to descendants of those who fled from the Yilondra as well as the Galj during and after the war, along with a good number of Coalition soldiers who left the Tevent military forces. We are all united by a common purpose, Captain. We all want to see the truth revealed and shared with the world."

Footsteps from the tunnel behind him caught Picard's attention just as T'Ryssa Chen emerged from the adjoining cavern. Her uniform was rumpled and her hair somewhat askew, and there were visible circles under her eyes, indicating it had been some time since she had slept. Picard could sympathize, as fatigue had long since taken hold of him. A fitful nap on a thin mattress in one of the smaller caves had done little to provide rest, though Janotra and his companions had been forthcoming with food and water.

"Captain," said Chen. "We've found something you

need to see." There was no emotion in her voice, and Picard could not decide if that was just another symptom of her weariness or if she was attempting to remain composed in front of Janotra.

The three of them moved to the cave where Chen and Dina Elfiki had been working. Picard found the science officer and Glinn Ravel Dygan hunched over a low table, which was covered with a mishmash of equipment in various stages of assembly. Picard recognized only odd components, including a rectangular computer monitor that had been removed from its casing and now stood propped against part of a storage container, with wires and cabling connecting it to a manual interface panel as well as a small, portable generator. Noticing the tricorder in Elfiki's hand, he gestured to the device.

"Where did you find that?"

Elfiki replied, "You can thank Renli. She managed to get her hands on one during our breakout. It's definitely making this process easier." Pausing, she turned toward Picard. "You know, we could use this to get a signal to the ship, sir."

Picard had already been thinking along those lines. Although not equipped for voice communication, the tricorder's data transmission capabilities could be used to attract the attention of *Enterprise* sensors.

"Good idea, Lieutenant, but we should probably hold that card in reserve for the moment." He looked to Janotra. "I suspect any communications signals would be traceable and would attract unwanted company."

The Eizand nodded. "You are correct, Captain. Coalition forces do employ a vast array of monitoring equipment. They will be scanning for any such transmissions. We observe strict communications discipline when in or near our various camps." He pointed to Elfiki's tricorder. "Also, I do not believe any signal you attempt to send will penetrate the surrounding rock. You will almost certainly have to get closer to the surface."

"Very well," said Picard. "We'll wait until a more opportune time." He indicated the computer equipment on the table. "Lieutenant Chen said you'd found something."

"Yes, sir." Elfiki rested her free hand on the computer interface panel. "According to Renli and some of the others, this equipment was taken from the Eizand ship that returned here after visiting Earth back in the twenty-first century. It's a terminal that originally was tied to the ship's onboard computer, but it also was portable, with its own memory core and data storage platform. All of this was salvaged from the ship and placed in storage."

"The Tevent military made sure all of this was quarantined and stored in a secure archive facility," added Janotra. "The computer records were used during the trial proceedings of the three humans."

Elfiki nodded. "Right. Everything aboard the ship was modified for use by the astronauts, including the computer. If they couldn't interface with something, then they substituted their own components, like this computer terminal. It's not the central core, so it only has whatever was entered into it or transferred to its own data storage, but it does have personal journals, copies of status updates from the main computer, and records of visual and audio messages transmitted to and from the ship. There are sections of the storage core that are damaged. I can't tell if it's just from age or if something actually happened to it, but there's still a lot here to access. Everything's encrypted, and so far as I can tell, no attempt has ever been made to decode it." She shrugged. "If I had to guess, I'd say no one bothered."

"A more likely explanation is that our scientists simply did not possess the knowledge or expertise to counter your encryption procedures," offered Janotra.

"Is there a record of anything transmitted from Earth after its departure?" asked Picard.

The science officer replied, "Other than some navigational data for course adjustments or corrections very early on, there's nothing."

Glinn Dygan said, "It is possible the crew was operating under orders to restrict communications for security purposes."

"Very possible." Picard studied the computer setup. "I take it you've had some luck with the decryption?"

Chen said, "Oh, yeah."

Her hands moving in slow, deliberate fashion as though she was still acquainting herself with the interface, Elfiki pressed several controls on the panel. A moment later the computer monitor's image shifted to show what could only be the cramped interior of a vehicle. Picard likened it to a shuttlecraft's cockpit, but this space was even more confining, with rows of switches, gauges, and other displays covering most of the available bulkhead space.

"According to the date-time stamp on this entry, the crew's been out of hibernation for about a day," said Elfiki. "Computer logs show that the ship is on course to Sralanya. There's been no contact with Earth, so they're acting on whatever orders they had before launch."

Picard studied the imagery, trying to absorb everything. There was a mixture of technologies crammed into the cockpit, featuring components of obvious human origin affixed to or interfaced with pieces that had to have been part of the Eizand vessel's equipment. Sandwiched between all of that were two human males and a human female, who Picard knew were Valmiki Goswami, Meredith Harper, and Park Ji-hu.

"This is incredible."

So absorbed was he by the centuries-old imagery that it took him an extra few seconds to realize that someone somewhere in one of the nearby tunnels or caves was shouting in alarm.

"They have found us! Coalition soldiers are coming!"

25

U.S.S. Enterprise
2386

Frustrated with sitting in the command chair and doing nothing as others around him were able to focus on their tasks, Worf had taken to strolling the bridge's perimeter. It was a habit acquired long ago, soon after accepting Captain Picard's offer to serve aboard the *Enterprise* as his first officer. He found the ritual to be calming, if not outright relaxing. It also served a dual purpose, in that it allowed him to get an informal update on the status of the ship's various systems just by wandering past each of the bridge stations. The officers on duty were long accustomed to his routine and gave him no mind as he stopped at this or that console, looking over the odd shoulder to see what he might be missing.

The port turbolift doors parted and Geordi La Forge stepped onto the bridge.

"Almost there," said the chief engineer in lieu of an actual greeting as he moved to one of the engineering stations at the rear of the bridge. Tapping a control on the workstation's interface panel, he said, "Computer, transfer engineering to the bridge."

In response to his command, the workstation flared to life and displayed a compact version of the master systems display La Forge would normally monitor down in the engineering section.

"You've found a way to defeat the Eizand weapons?"

Without looking away from the console as he worked, La Forge replied, "We think so. We're setting up the final adjustments now. I figured you'd want to know the minute we're ready, and I can monitor everything from here while Taurik oversees things from down there."

"Taurik?" Worf shot an irritated glance at his fellow officer. "Commander Taurik was relieved of his duties by the captain."

"Yeah," said La Forge, "but he's the one who came up with the initial idea. We've been working on this for hours, Worf, and we think we can get past the Eizand satellites and not kill everybody in our path."

While diligent when it came to obeying rules, to say nothing of the orders issued by his captain, Worf was not so bound by protocol that he would not give La Forge and Taurik a chance to prove themselves. Both officers were owed at least that much.

Tapping strings of controls, La Forge said, "We've reconfigured the deflector shield emitters to fire a feedback pulse on the same frequency as the EMP generators. When they hit us, we'll hit back, and the feedback should overload the weapons. There's a hitch, though."

"Of course there is."

La Forge ignored the remark, keeping his attention on his instruments, before saying, "Because of the reconfiguration, our shield emitters won't be able to provide us with the same level of protection. If we're dealing with a handful of satellites at the same time—say a half dozen—it'll get a little bumpy, but if they decide to really gang up on us, we could be in trouble."

Recalling the previous encounter with the weapons, Worf asked, "Can't we outrun them?"

"To a point, but if we have to retreat out of transporter range, then retrieving Captain Picard and the others becomes a problem again, and after we try this, they'll be onto us."

Worf turned his attention to the main viewscreen and the image of Sralanya it displayed. The *Enterprise* was still maintaining a safe distance from the planet, giving it time and maneuvering room in the event any of the Eizand military craft attempted to make a move toward them. So far, the patrol vessels seemed content to avoid doing anything that might escalate the current situation, but Worf knew that would change the moment he ordered the starship back to the planet.

"Commander Worf," said Lieutenant Šmrhová from the tactical station just behind the captain's chair. "I'm picking up an incoming burst transmission from the surface, on an encoded Starfleet frequency." Then she turned from her console to look at Worf and La Forge. "Sir, it's an emergency data transfer from a tricorder. The only thing it contains is a topographical scan of the planet's surface and a set of coordinates."

Every Starfleet officer was familiar with a standard tricorder's various methods of transferring information to another data collection point, whether another tricorder or a starship's main computer. Designed as a failsafe feature in the event of unexpected calamities in which the transfer of important data was critical to a mission's success, the emergency burst transmission feature was intended for use when it became apparent that the tricorder would soon lose power or otherwise become inoperative or even seized by a hostile party. Enabling this last-ditch measure would quickly exhaust the unit's power supply, so officers were instructed not to use it except as an extreme last resort.

"The away team," said La Forge. "They must not have their combadges, and they're sending up a flare."

Nodding in agreement, Worf gestured to Šmrhová. "Scan those coordinates."

"Aye, sir." A moment later, she reported, "I've got a low-power transmission. It's weak, but I can compensate." A few more commands entered to her console resulted in the bridge's intercom system erupting with the voice of Lieutenant T'Ryssa Chen.

"—en to Enterprise. *If you can read this, we could sure use a hand down here!"*

Worf moved to the command chair. "Conn, set a course back to the planet. Full impulse. Stand by all weapons." He glanced over his shoulder to La Forge. "Are your modifications ready?"

"They will be," replied the engineer, already turning back to his console. "I hope."

As he settled into the captain's seat, Worf fixed his attention on the image of Sralanya. The planet was growing larger on the viewscreen with every passing moment.

In front of him at the flight controller station, Lieutenant Faur called out, "I'm showing two ships along our present course, sir."

"Sensors show they're Eizand security vessels," added Šmrhová. "They're moving to intercept, but we'll get to the planet first."

"We will deal with them as necessary," said Worf. It was not the patrol ships that worried him. His primary concern was the satellites and the barrier they represented between him and the away team. Would the scheme hatched by La Forge and Taurik work, or was he placing the *Enterprise* in even greater danger?

There was only one way to find out.

Sralanya

Picard did not see the soldier until it was almost too late.

"Get down!" he shouted, pushing aside Dina Elfiki and leveling the Eizand pistol at the first figure to step into view.

The Coalition soldier and his companion were rounding a bend just as Picard fired, catching him in the chest. Falling backward off his feet, the soldier dropped to the tunnel's rock floor even as the other Eizand reacted. Picard, weighed down by the equipment pack he carried on his back, stumbled and fell against the tunnel wall as a burst of energy from the soldier's weapon chewed into the rock behind him. Bits and flecks of heated stone peppered his back, and he flinched as one piece of shrapnel landed on his left hand. Even as he shook off the momentary pain he fired his pistol, forcing the soldier to retreat around the bend in the tunnel.

"Captain, are you all right?" asked Elfiki, who crouched on the other side of the passage, pressing herself against the wall. Like Picard, she carried a pack laden with some of the computer equipment she had salvaged from the work area and held an Eizand sidearm in her hand.

Holding up his free hand to indicate silence, Picard pushed himself to his feet. He advanced up the corridor, the muzzle of the pistol leading the way as he maneuvered forward. The sound of something rubbing against the tunnel wall was coming from just around the bend, and before he could think about it he lunged ahead. Around the corner was the Eizand soldier, trying to backpedal in response to the unexpected new threat. The barrel of his weapon was coming up as Picard fired his pistol. Falling against the rock wall, the soldier crumpled and slid unconscious to the ground.

"We have to keep moving," he said, studying the fallen Eizand. This far into the subterranean passages, he and Elfiki were still somewhat isolated from the assault force that was now storming the dissenters' hideaway. The raid itself was a surprise, but reacting to such an occurrence had been part of the rebels' plans. An early warning from lookout patrols had provided sufficient time to mobilize the dissenters and prepare to repel the attack, and also allowed Picard to send T'Ryssa Chen and Ravel Dygan to the surface in search of help from the *Enterprise*.

Janotra, prior to leaving them in the work area, had given them instructions on how to reach the surface through a smaller tunnel that was away from the caverns and the paths connecting them. The passage had been cut through the rock with explosives years ago, intended as one of several emergency evacuation routes in the event of cave collapses or an attack like the one they now were experiencing. These contingency tunnels were not referenced on any maps of the underground area, just in case such documents were captured, but at least two Coalition soldiers had found their way here. That they were alone was wishful thinking at its finest. The only choice for Picard and Elfiki was to seize the computer equipment and invaluable secrets it held, and make a run for the surface in the hopes that the *Enterprise* would be waiting to beam them to safety. All Picard had to do was not get lost in this underground labyrinth, but protecting the computer and its data was of the utmost importance.

A map would certainly be useful now.

Following Janotra's designated path took them on a gradual incline as the tunnel began angling toward the surface. Picard could hear the sounds of fighting, with yelling voices interlaced with weapons fire and other noises he could not identify, growing louder as they progressed. He paused when part of the wall on the passage's right side opened up to give him a bird's-eye view of one of the larger caverns.

Below, all was chaos.

"Damn," said Elfiki, peering around the edge of the stone wall to take in the scene. There were dozens of Eizand rebels and even more Coalition soldiers scattered across the chamber, chasing or fighting one another. Numerous bodies from both sides littered the ground, and while some weapons fire still echoed through the cavern, much of the skirmish had devolved to hand-to-hand combat. Picard saw that the Coalition troops had a definite advantage. From what he could see, the attack on the underground sanctuary was turning into a rout.

"We can't stay here," he said. "The Coalition will have control of this place before too long."

Elfiki shifted her pack to a more comfortable position on her shoulders. "How much farther do we have to go?"

Gesturing up the gently sloping tunnel, Picard replied, "Perhaps two hundred meters, assuming we don't run into anyone else." What would they find on the surface? Had Chen and Dygan made successful contact with the *Enterprise*? Or would a squad of Coalition soldiers be there, ready to take them back into custody? Picard had no intention of being arrested again.

That will be the day.

An energy burst from behind him slammed into the rock over his head, and Picard spun around while dropping to one knee. Shielding his head with his left arm, he raised his weapon and searched for a target just as the whine of a second shot howled in the tunnel. Another bolt of red-white energy was almost blinding in the passage's dim illumination, and Picard had the presence of mind to drop to the ground as the shot passed over him. To his right, Elfiki returned fire, not truly aiming but instead attempting to force their attackers to seek cover by sending shot after shot back down the tunnel.

"I guess they found the secret passageway," she remarked.

Scrambling to his feet and trying to ignore the protests of his back under the weight of the pack, Picard pulled at the science officer's arm. "Let's go."

More weapons fire screamed from somewhere behind him, obliterating chunks of the tunnel walls. This time, Picard did not stop to return fire but instead fired to his rear as he pushed Elfiki ahead of him. The suppressing fire worked, but only for a moment before he heard warning shouts followed by more shots. Leading the way, Elfiki found another turn in the passage but stopped, releasing a cry of surprise. Picard whirled in that direction, searching for threats, but saw only Janotra.

The Eizand dissenter was worse for wear. Blue-gray blood caked the left side of his head. His left eye was swollen shut, and his clothing was dirty and torn in several places. Walking with a limp, he rested the barrel of his rifle atop his left forearm while aiming with the weapon down the tunnel, past Elfiki and Picard. Without saying anything, Janotra fired, holding the rifle steady as multiple shots screamed down the passageway.

"Keep moving," he ordered, and Picard and Elfiki moved behind him, proceeding down the tunnel. Seconds later, Picard heard him hobbling after them.

Elfiki dropped back to help him. "Are you all right?"

Janotra sagged as he used his left hand to steady himself against the wall while continuing to walk. With a cough, he replied, "I . . . am injured. The Coalition is moving quickly. I must get you to . . . safety."

"Are you sure you can walk?" asked Picard. The Eizand's condition seemed serious. How far could he travel with such injuries?

"That . . . is not important now. Getting you to safety is . . . the priority."

With Elfiki assisting as best she could to keep Janotra moving, Picard took the lead, increasing his pace as they continued their ascent. Was it his imagination, or was the uphill slope getting more pronounced? The passage itself seemed to be narrowing, and for a moment he feared they had taken the wrong route to safety and would instead become stuck here.

Then he rounded another bend, his shoulders rubbing against rock in the tightening passage, and in the distance he saw a small circle of bright light.

Picard smiled.

Almost there.

26

U.S.S. Enterprise

Alarms wailed across the bridge. Alert indicators flashed at every station, amplified in the weak glow of emergency illumination. The deck shifted and trembled beneath his feet, and even with the benefit of artificial gravity and inertial damping systems, Worf still felt his stomach heave as the *Enterprise* withstood the full force of yet another assault. Despite himself, Worf realized he was gripping the arms of the command chair with such strength that he might very well rip them from their mountings.

From where he still stood at the aft engineering station, Geordi La Forge shouted to be heard over the din. "Initiating feedback pulse!"

Seconds later, the lights dimmed even further as power was drawn from across the ship and fed to the deflector shield emitters. On the screen, Worf saw the combination of energies as the electromagnetic resonance bursts collided against the *Enterprise*'s shields, and the deflector emitters struggled to handle the assault even as La Forge channeled vital power to the feedback pulse. The risky maneuver was already having an effect on the ship as energy from the EMP weapons began bleeding through the compromised shields and attacked the *Enterprise* itself.

"We got three of them that time," said La Forge. "Three are partially incapacitated, but still in it." Worf heard the engineer curse before adding, "I'm not sure how many more of these we can do before we have to pull back."

"Power drains across the ship," reported Ensign Jill Rosado, who was manning the ops station in the absence of Glinn Ravel Dygan. "It's not critical, but it'll be a problem the longer we stay here."

Worf grunted, unhappy with the report, but for now there was nothing to be done. "Acknowledged. Conn, continue evasive maneuvers."

"Aye, sir," replied Lieutenant Faur, her voice sounding harried. The senior flight controller had her hands full guiding the *Enterprise* back to the planet and now was attempting to keep the massive starship from falling victim to too many of the Eizand satellites. Despite her best efforts, it was impossible to avoid them now that whatever controlled the devices seemed to have figured out the strategy devised by La Forge and Taurik.

"I think they're onto us," said the chief engineer, confirming Worf's thoughts. After a successful first attempt had seen three of the unmanned satellites rendered inoperative thanks to the feedback pulse, a second bout against six of the devices only managed to disable four, forcing Worf to order the ship's phasers brought to bear. It was an option he was willing to undertake for any of the satellites without living crews, but now even those, which were far fewer in number and yet just as dangerous, were beginning to converge on the *Enterprise*'s position. The remaining two drones were destroyed, but the chink in the starship's proverbial armor was exposed along with the potentially fatal flaw in this entire scheme.

"We're starting to lose the power battle," said Ensign Rosado. "It's taking more energy each time we repeat the process, and the shield generators are taking the brunt of the abuse, and they can't recharge fast enough. At this rate, another couple of rounds and the generators will fail."

"Engineering to bridge," said the voice of Commander Taurik. *"Be advised that we are experiencing fluctuations in the antimatter containment system."*

Stepping away from his station, La Forge called out, "How bad is it, Taurik?"

"The fluctuations are minor," replied the Vulcan without hesitation, *"but given the fluidity of our present situation, caution is advised."*

Worf pushed himself out of the command chair. "Bridge to transporter room. Do you have a lock on the away team?"

Over the intraship, the transporter officer on duty, Lieutenant Statham, replied, *"I've got four non-Eizand life signs at the designated coordinates, Commander."*

"How much time do you need to complete transport?"

"Fifteen seconds should do it, sir."

"Stand by." Moving so that he stood just behind Faur, Worf said, "Lieutenant, can you guide us clear of all satellites for that long?"

The flight controller looked up from her console. "Scans show twenty-one more of those things in position to intercept us within the next three minutes, sir. About half of them are close enough that they could be on us in less than a minute if we slow our speed to get a decent transporter lock."

"It is a risk we will have to take. Initiate the necessary course adjustments." Turning from the conn and ops stations, Worf looked to Aneta Šmrhová at the tactical console. "Lieutenant, attempt to hail Lieutenant Chen again."

The security chief nodded. "Aye, sir. We may have better luck now that we're closer." She entered the necessary commands to her console before reporting, "Channel open, Commander."

"Lieutenant Chen," said Worf. He returned his gaze to the main viewscreen, which now showed the planet Sralanya all but filling the image. "Stand by for transport."

Instead of Chen, everyone on the bridge was surprised to hear the voice of Captain Picard. *"Number One, I need you to beam Lieutenant Chen, Glinn Dygan, and one Eizand male back to the* Enterprise. *Notify Doctor Crusher to be ready for an incoming emergency. Then, you'll transport myself and Lieutenany Elfiki directly to Presider Hilonu's office."*

Taken aback by the unusual request, Worf nevertheless set aside his surprise and instead replied, "Captain, our situation here is deteriorating. To this point, we have managed to avoid firing on any manned ships or satellites, but if we remain in orbit much longer, we may be left with no choice."

"I want to avoid any casualties if at all possible. Once you've completed transport, withdraw to a safe distance until you hear from me."

Before Worf could respond, he heard what could only be the sounds of energy weapons fire ringing through the open channel.

Still gripping the clunky, primitive radio transceiver with his free hand, Picard dropped behind a rock jutting from the side of the gentle mountain slope, raising his Eizand weapon and returning fire. His shot went wide, but he saw one of the remaining soldiers sticking his head up and around the boulders that were providing the assault troops their cover and concealment. He fired again, sending the soldier scurrying back out of sight. Lying unconscious on the hillside were a half dozen troops, all incapacitated thanks to the weapons carried by the four *Enterprise* officers.

"The Tevent assault force has pinpointed our location," said Picard into the handheld radio's microphone. "More are coming. We can't afford to be taken into custody, Mister Worf."

"Understood," said the first officer, his voice sounding tinny and distant through the radio's speaker. *"Stand by for beam out, Captain."*

Kneeling next to Picard and doing their best to tend to Janotra's injuries, Chen and Elfiki leaned over to cover the Eizand dissenter's stricken form when more weapons fire echoed across the hillside. Positioned several meters away behind another rock outcropping, Ravel Dygan aimed his Eizand weapon and fired. The Cardassian was rewarded for his efforts with another Coalition soldier falling to the ground.

"Do they want to capture us or kill us?" asked Chen.

Picard's attention was divided between Janotra and the troops attempting to maneuver closer without exposing themselves to return fire. "I honestly don't know at this point. If they want to take us alive, then their tactics are rather sloppy."

"Well, that's encouraging, sir." Chen was using a piece of her blue uniform undershirt to bandage the wound on the side of Janotra's head. The Eizand rebel had fallen unconscious, succumbing to his injuries.

"Captain," said Dygan, and when Picard looked in his direction the Cardassian was pointing his free hand toward the sky. "Do you hear that? It sounds like an aerial vehicle."

Damn.

Now able to hear the sound, Picard agreed with Dygan. "Something's coming, all right." Being caught out in the open would be suicide if the assault force was able to bring air assets into the hunt.

"Cover would be good right about now," said Elfiki.

She reached for the pack that had lain next to her feet after she and Picard emerged from the underground passages and sought refuge with Chen and Dygan at what they hoped would be an extraction point. Picard had been thrilled to learn of Chen's success in using the tricorder's emergency data transfer protocol to attract the *Enterprise*'s attention. The Eizand radio given to her by Janotra was also a huge help, allowing first Chen and then him to make contact with the starship.

Weapons fire from somewhere higher up on the hillside tore into the ground near Picard's feet, making him draw his body into a ball while searching for the source of this attack. More shots rang out, with Dygan returning fire as best he could, but the tide of this skirmish was turning in even greater favor of the Coalition troops.

"Hey. Wait!" shouted Chen just as Picard watched a transporter beam coalescing around her and Dygan as well as the wounded Janotra.

As he hoped, the *Enterprise* transporter scanners were able to distinguish between the human and nonhuman members of the away team, given that none of them had combadges for identification, focusing on extracting Chen and Dygan as well as Janotra. In seconds, all three were gone, and Picard had only enough time to sling his own pack over his shoulder before he felt the familiar tingle on his skin as the transporter found and claimed him. The hillside along with the advancing Coalition troops disappeared in a shower of sparkling light, replaced mere heartbeats later by the interior of Presider Hilonu's office. He and Elfiki materialized facing the window overlooking the Ponval city, the last lingering tendrils of the transporter were releasing their hold on him as he turned to his right in order to see the Eizand leader standing behind her desk. Her expression was one of shock, violation, and mounting anger, as she reached for something on her desk. Raising his weapon, Picard pointed it at her.

"Don't."

Freezing in midmotion, Hilonu glared at him. "How dare you intrude on my inner sanctum? What is the meaning of this insolence?"

Staring past the muzzle of his phaser at the presider, Picard could not help thinking about Lieutenant T'Sona, who had given her life in this room in order to protect him. The tragic waste of her death angered him, and it required physical effort to rein in that emotion. There would be time for mourning later, but understanding and acceptance would take far longer.

Damn it.

Behind him, Picard heard another set of transporter beams flaring into existence near the door leading from Hilonu's office. Six columns of energy coalesced into the forms of Lieutenant Rennan Konya and a detachment of *Enterprise* security officers. All six officers were armed with phaser rifles and wearing tactical equipment vests over their Starfleet uniforms, and each member of the team wasted no time aiming their weapons at Presider Hilonu.

"Good to see you, Captain," said the ship's deputy chief of security in greeting. "Commander Worf sends his regards. Thought you might need some backup, sir." Stepping closer, he reached into a pocket of his vest, extracted a communicator badge, and handed it to Picard. "He also mentioned you might need one of these."

Affixing the combadge to his own uniform jacket, Picard smiled. "The commander is most efficient when it comes to such things." He nodded in the direction of the door. "See to it that no one comes in here."

"Aye sir," replied Konya before turning his team toward the door.

"Captain Picard," snapped Hilonu. "This behavior is outrageous! Do you actually believe I will stand here and do nothing? You are already scheduled to be tried for the horrors your people inflicted upon mine. Do you wish to add endangering the life of a senior Tevent government official to your quest?"

Picard removed his backpack, grateful to be out from under its weight. "I promise that you are in no danger, Presider. We have no desire to harm anyone, even in self-defense, but we will protect ourselves if provoked." Indicating for Elfiki to begin arranging the equipment for use, he said, "As for why we're here, it's a simple matter, really: we're here to offer you the truth about your planet and your people, in the hopes that you'll broadcast it to your world. The question is, are you afraid to face what this information may tell you?"

"I am afraid of nothing," said Hilonu. "I certainly do not fear anything you can present me."

Picard gazed upon her with sadness. Watching her

body language, listening to the inflection in her voice, and seeing the anger burning in her eyes was enough to tell him that Presider Hilonu had no idea what he was talking about or why she should care. He regretted what he was about to do, but the fate of this planet's entire population, and its interactions with its interstellar neighbors both known and unknown, demanded he do so.

"With all due respect, Presider, after watching this, you may want to reevaluate your opinion."

27

Near Sralanya
April 19, 2063

The world outside the windows was breathtaking.

Valmiki Goswami remained as captivated by the lush green-blue orb as the first time he had lain eyes upon it, mere moments after emerging from hibernation. Despite obvious differences in the shapes and sizes of the land masses, the planet was remarkably like Earth. Below the blanket of clouds that only partially obscured its oceans and continents, Sralanya teemed with life. It was still too far away to see such details, but Goswami imagined dark clusters dotting the landscape, indicating immense cities visible even from orbit as described in the mission briefings. Billions of beings, going about their lives in much the same manner as the people he and his companions had left behind. What were their thoughts, their goals, their dreams? Had anyone paused to admire the simple beauty of a flower, or an animal running in the wild, or a sunset?

Did anyone suspect they were supposed to die today?

"Val? You all right?"

Glancing over his shoulder, Goswami saw Meredith Harper standing a few steps away, drying her still-wet red hair with a towel. The tiny, coffin-sized shower was one of the few extravagances afforded to them in the ship's cramped berthing area, and she had taken advantage of it following her own emergence from cryogenic suspension. Now she wore a standard gray one-piece jumpsuit, the front of which was unzipped far enough to reveal a blue T-shirt underneath. Over the jumpsuit's left breast pocket was a white label with her last name in red block letters, and an American flag adorned her left shoulder, as opposed to that of India on Goswami's own suit.

He forced a smile. "Sorry. I guess my mind wandered."

"Yeah." Harper stared at her towel. "Mine too. You'd think after napping for twenty years, I'd be more alert."

The hibernation process responsible for sustaining *Peacemaker 1*'s three-person crew since the spacecraft's departure from Earth nearly twenty years earlier had performed in accordance with all specifications as well as the hopes and dreams of the engineers who had designed and constructed the system. Goswami understood how it worked, thanks to the time he had spent studying it as part of his training, and so possessed a working knowledge of its operation. While he could make some rudimentary repairs on his own or with the aid of instructions from the ship's computer, that was as far as his understanding took him. All he knew now was that it had worked, and he and his fellow astronauts were alive.

Despite the rigorous preparation for this mission, Goswami was still coming to terms with the notion that he along with Harper and the crew's third member, Park Ji-hu, had aged mere weeks thanks to the hibernation process, while nearly twenty years had passed on Earth. By the time they returned to their home planet, many of the people they knew would be aged or even dead. Children born just prior to *Peacemaker*'s departure were now young adults, perhaps attending college or serving in the military or simply lying around the house, annoying their parents while glued to some gadget or other distraction. What events of note had occurred during those years? How had technology and society advanced during that time? Was war still a constant specter, or had the nations of the world figured out a way to live in harmony? Perhaps the alien invasion Goswami's superiors had feared finally came to pass, making his mission here irrelevant.

Wow. Some pretty thick irony there.

"I guess you've seen it," said another voice as Goswami and Harper were joined by Park. His close-cropped black hair also still damp from his shower, he wore a jumpsuit like those of his companions, but with the flag from South Korea on his left shoulder. "It's absolutely gorgeous. I've already had the cameras angled for some great pictures."

Goswami nodded. "Almost like home."

"So," said Harper, exchanging looks with her friends. "Are we really going to go through with this?"

"Well, we did come all this way." Goswami intended the reply to carry a bit of levity, but it came out flat and even a bit sardonic, and he felt guilty about even attempting to make a joke at all. This was serious business, after all. The fate of an entire world—perhaps two—was at stake.

Five years of training and preparation, overseeing and participating in every step of mission planning down to the smallest detail, had brought the *Peacemaker*'s crew to this moment. The plan had been under way long before Goswami's selection as commander of the mission, originated from deep within the bowels of the intricate web of secrets that was Majestic 12. Neither Goswami nor his fellow astronauts had even met anyone from the clandestine organization that had come up with this notion. For security reasons, intermediaries saw to it that the *Peacemaker* crew had all the information they were required to have at the appropriate times during their training, without there ever being a need to meet with those overseeing the entire affair. Even their meeting with the president of the United States, less than a week prior to the ship's departure, had avoided discussing mission specifics, which Goswami found comical given the chief executive's authorization for the launch to go ahead as planned.

It was as though no one wanted to talk about attacking a planet and perhaps wiping out an entire civilization.

Valmiki Goswami did not set out to command such a mission, and it was not among the goals he had in mind upon applying to the astronaut candidacy program in 2035 while serving as a lieutenant and an aviator in the United States Navy. Despite his Indian heritage, he enjoyed joint Indian-American citizenship, born in California while his parents lived there under a guest worker visa program. A military career seemed like the fastest way to attain his dream of flying, and eventually applying to NASA, where he hoped one day to participate in a mission to the Moon or one of the system's other planets. Joining a top secret, all-but-invisible shadow government organization tasked with searching for signs of extraterrestrial activity on Earth and creating defenses against possible alien invasion was not in his original plans. Still, there was no denying the draw of such a fantastic challenge, especially when presented with incontrovertible proof that such threats were real.

Like Goswami, Meredith Harper and Park Jin-hu were both military veterans who had made the transition to NASA's astronaut corps. All three were selected for the *Peacemaker* mission after meeting a lengthy list of criteria, including technical knowledge, experience, and accomplishments in a number of skill areas. Each also possessed an unwavering commitment to the security of their country and their planet. The mission they were being asked to carry out was one that required a particular mindset and fortitude. Could they, at the moment of truth, visit mass destruction upon an enemy in defense of their own civilization? A battery of psychological tests and interviews indicated they could indeed rise to this commitment.

But that was not going to happen today.

Making their way to the *Peacemaker*'s cramped cockpit, Goswami maneuvered himself into one of the two forward-facing seats positioned before the slanted canopy. There was just enough room for the three astronauts in and around the equipment and other components stuffed into the tiny compartment. One of the consoles separating the two forward seats, a piece of retrofitted hardware with a computer setup the crew could use to access the vessel's own systems, was so large that Goswami and Harper had to climb over it to reach the cockpit chairs. Behind them, a third position had been installed for Park, whose station oversaw all of the ship's power and life-support systems along with other processes like communications and emergency procedures.

From where Goswami now sat, he could look down the length of the massive cylinder fitted to *Peacemaker*'s forward docking collar. Twice the diameter of the massive center fuel tanks that had powered Space Shuttles to Earth orbit during the late twentieth and early twenty-first centuries, the weapons platform was essentially the largest six-round gun ever created. Half a dozen Titan V missiles and their support systems were crammed into the massive tube, which possessed no propulsion capabilities of its own. All control over the platform was routed to the *Peacemaker* cockpit and one of the computer terminals separating Goswami and Harper.

Sralanya was visible in all its splendid grandeur, and he had to take another moment to admire the planet as it hung alone in space. The very idea of harming this jewel, let alone allowing such devastation to be inflicted by his own hand, filled him with rage and disappointment. The anger was fueled by the knowledge that he was here at the behest of cowards who lacked the conviction to do their own dirty work, but instead sent others to carry out directives born of fear and ignorance. His dissatisfaction, however, was reserved for himself.

"I can't believe I ever went along with such a stupid idea. What the hell was I thinking?"

In the beginning, it was an abstract notion, a scenario developed and tested and theorized to every imaginable limit. Goswami likened it to the military officers who once sat at the bottom of missile silos, prepared to launch intercontinental nuclear weapons against distant targets at a moment's notice. For all the testing and make-believe, there were no stakes, and neither were there consequences. In Majestic's case, it was all just another simulation in an endless series of games designed to create strategies for countering an alien invasion. A preemptive strike was justified if one's entire world was on the line, right?

Only after the simulations turned to actual mission planning, and he watched the *Peacemaker* spacecraft being assembled in orbit and fitted with the nuclear weapons platform the ship would push to an alien planet, did the horrific reality of the task he had volunteered to perform begin to grip him. That Goswami had allowed himself to be a willing part of such a malicious venture, and that he once believed it to be a righteous cause in the name of protecting his home planet, only furthered his anger and self-loathing.

"I'm initiating the course correction," he said, tearing his eyes from the beautiful planet beyond the *Peacemaker*'s cockpit. "Stand by for platform separation."

Uncounted hours of training in a mock-up of the ship guided his hands over the controls, which were a hybrid of Eizand and human technology. It was a simple matter to fire maneuvering thrusters in order to induce a pivot that turned the ship so that it was no longer facing the planet. Satisfied with the vessel's new attitude, Goswami reached for the row of switches and status indicators dedicated to the weapons package. Habit made his fingers drift over the controls that would begin the process of arming the platform's six missiles, but he pushed past those to the next set of six switches and began flipping them in sequence. A light illuminated behind each control. He was just activating the last one when an alarm began buzzing in the cockpit.

"What the hell is that?" asked Park.

Goswami tapped the console. "It's a master alarm for the platform arming controls." He frowned. "Something's not right here." As he stared at the rows of switches, each of the toggles he had just activated flipped themselves back to their previous positions, and their associated indicators went dark. Next to them, the controls for the arming package flipped in unison, accompanied by all six lights activating.

"It's the computer," said Harper, her face all but buried in the console and pair of keyboards and monitors that comprised her own workstation. "It's initiated some kind of override protocol." Scowling, she muttered a string of colorful profanity. "I've never seen these routines before. This procedure wasn't here during any of our simulations or prelaunch checks."

Park said, "Are you kidding me? They installed new procedures and didn't tell us? Why would they do that?"

"It's a failsafe," said Goswami as realization struck. "Son of a bitch. Majestic probably stuck it in there, in case we got cold feet. Maybe it was a fallback if we were incapacitated or killed during the trip out here." He tapped the console, attempting to reset the arming switches and reactivate the separation controls. Nothing registered. It was as though that portion of the control panel had gone dead. "How long until the arming process completes?"

Harper checked her readouts. "About five minutes. Same as if we'd gone through the process by the book." She snorted. "Guess you can't rush greatness or insanity."

"Can you disable the procedure or find a way around it?"

The crew's designated computer and software expert, Meredith Harper had learned her trade first as a network systems officer and later a cyberspace operations officer. There was, in Goswami's experience, nothing she could not do if given a keyboard and sufficient time.

"Are you asking me if I can hack Majestic's super-secret doomsday program?" she asked. "Yeah, I think so. It helps that I know one of the people who wrote some of the mainline software." When neither Goswami nor

Park asked the obvious question, she added, "I look at her in the mirror every morning."

Goswami had activated a countdown timer on his console, which now read less than four and a half minutes. "Whatever you're going to do, faster would be better."

"Hey," said Park. "Something else is up. We're transmitting."

"To whom?" asked Goswami. Was it possible *Peacemaker*'s computer was sending information back to Earth? How long would such a signal take to even reach home from this distance? Decades, he guessed.

"It's aimed at the planet, on a wide broadcast across multiple frequencies." He toggled a pair of switches. "Listen." In response to his actions, the cockpit's recessed speakers came to life, and Goswami heard his own voice.

"—and security of all our people, we are forced to answer these unprovoked actions against our planet. We cannot tolerate interlopers or invaders from other worlds, including yours."

Goswami felt a knot of dread forming in his gut.

"Oh my god. That's . . . that's got to be something they recorded during one of our training runs, right?" As part of their repeated simulation training exercises, each of the *Peacemaker* astronauts had performed their assigned tasks down to the smallest detail. For Goswami, that meant reciting a set of prepared remarks that were similar to whatever message he would end up sending to the people of Sralanya just prior to launching the weapons package. Given what he had planned to do upon *Peacemaker*'s arrival here, he had hoped to have something profound to say. It would never measure up to those immortal words uttered by Neil Armstrong from the surface of the Moon or Shaun Christopher upon reaching Saturn, but he had hoped they would serve a noble purpose, rather than the agenda of those who sent him here.

Instead, the people of Sralanya were hearing the preface to their destruction.

"I think I've got it," said Harper, blowing out her breath. "It's not pretty, and I'll have to do some serious cleaning up in this code when this is all over, but I think I can get us around this."

"Three minutes," said Park, pointing to the timer on Goswami's console.

Feeling his stomach tightening, Goswami asked, "What now?"

Her fingers moving almost too fast to follow, Harper typed extended strings of indecipherable commands to her terminal. Line after line of rapid-fire text filled her screen. From what Goswami could tell, she was rewriting entire sections of whatever subroutine had been embedded into the ship's computer, or simply substituting the offending code with entirely new pieces of her own creation. He did not care about the details, so long as it worked.

Harper stabbed at the Enter key with one finger and all of the script on her screen vanished, replaced by a technical schematic of the weapons package. On the console between them, Goswami saw all of the indicators on the platform's arming panel go dark.

"That's it?" asked Park.

"I think so. Try the separation sequence again."

With tentative fingers, Goswami reached for the control panel. "Here we go."

He flipped each of the switches for the platform separation sequence, watching with increasing relief as the indicators above each toggle lit up as before. "That's it."

"Push the button," snapped Park. "Before the damned thing changes its mind."

"Yeah." Goswami reached for the switch marked *Commit* and flipped it.

The effect was immediate, with the entire cockpit jerking as explosive bolts fired around the collar linking *Peacemaker* to the weapons platform. Through the cockpit canopy, the crew watched as the massive cylinder disconnected from the rest of the ship and began falling away. Within seconds the entire construct was visible, the act of its separation pushing it into a slow tumble as it drifted in the void.

"It won't get caught by the planet's gravity," said Harper. "Will it?"

Goswami shook his head. "We're still far enough away that it shouldn't." Manipulating the controls for the thrusters one again, he guided the ship back to its original heading, centering Sralanya once more in the cockpit windows.

"Hit the radio," he said, taken once again by the sight of the planet. "Let's try to fix this somehow."

Behind him, Park replied, "Go ahead, Val."

Clearing his throat, Goswami said, "People of Sralanya, I bring you greetings from the planet Earth. The craft we have used to travel to your world is actually one you sent to us some time ago. We have returned it to you, in what we hope is a gesture of peace. I regret the earlier message that implied a threat to your planet. Rest assured, that is not the case. We intend no harm toward you and welcome the opportunity to establish peaceful contact."

"Not bad for off the cuff," said Harper.

A string of low-pitched beeps from her console made her shift in her seat, and she pointed at another row of indicators. "Uh-oh. Look at this. Lidar's showing a couple of pings." She looked to her companions. "It's a pair of ships, heading right for us."

"You're sure?" asked Park.

Harper nodded. "Oh, yeah. No doubt about it."

The three astronauts said nothing, waiting in nervous silence to see what happened next. Within moments the ships moved into view, approaching from opposing angles and converging on the *Peacemaker*. According to the light detection and ranging, or lidar, system, the new arrivals were less than fifty kilometers away, but even from that distance they looked enormous. Their curved, wedge-like shapes gave them an ominous, predatory appearance Goswami found unsettling.

"I don't know about this," said Park.

As the *Peacemaker* carried no armaments, it had no means of defending itself should Eizand ships decide to attack, not that Goswami had any desire to start a fight. Their situation was precarious enough without adding to the trouble.

We're the aliens here. Remember?

Now it was they who were trespassing. In light of that, and particularly the events of the past few moments, he knew that the best option was cooperation, honesty, and respect. The safety of Earth itself might well be hanging in the balance, based on what he did right here and now.

No pressure, right?

28

Sralanya
2386

Silence hung in the room as the visual recording faded, leaving behind only the blank computer monitor. Standing to one side, Picard watched Presider Hilonu's face go through a gamut of expressions, from shock to disbelief, doubt to anger, and confusion to sadness. With the *Enterprise*'s assistance, Dina Elfiki was able to channel a broadcast of the computer core's revealing visual record across the planet. The Eizand leader had said nothing throughout the playback of the visual record, and neither had Picard pressed her with questions or his own observations from watching the recording. He knew that Hilonu would have to come to her own conclusions, on her own terms, if there was to be any hope of convincing her to question everything she had accepted since childhood as immutable truth.

"I . . ." she began. "I do not know what to say, Captain. All of this is . . . rather overwhelming. I can only imagine what people around the world must be thinking and feeling at this moment."

Picard nodded. "I understand, Presider. It is rather a lot to absorb all at once."

Millions of Eizand had watched the archival footage of the *Peacemaker*'s actions. The file had come to an abrupt end soon after the crew learned of the approaching ships, and despite Elfiki's best efforts, that portion of the computer core's data storage matrix was damaged beyond repair. This would raise obvious questions as to the fate of the astronauts as well as the events that transpired following their capture, but Picard suspected this revelation would spur a host of investigations as the Eizand people demanded a full accounting of the events that had shaped their civilization for generations.

A tall order, that.

In truth, Picard was having trouble keeping his own emotions in check. A wave of immense relief flooded over him upon learning that the *Peacemaker* crew had not carried out the mission that had sent them here in the first place. There remained many questions, and uncounted more would be asked in the coming days as Hilonu and all the Eizand people were forced to reevaluate what they knew of their past. At least now there could be mutual cooperation as they sought answers.

"I honestly do not know how to proceed," she said. "There is so much to say, and so much to do. Never in my life did I dream I would ever have to face something like this." She looked to Picard. "However, I am gratified to know that my initial feelings about you were correct, Captain. You are a being of noble character, and I am relieved to know that you are but one representative of a race who values such things."

Picard replied, "I do my best to meet that standard, Presider, but there are those who are far more adept at it."

"It will be difficult, leading my people as we all attempt to make sense of something like this, but it must be done." She turned to him. "I am hopeful that you would be willing to help me educate our people about yours."

Standing next to the captain, T'Ryssa Chen replied, "We'd be honored to assist in any way we can, Presider." The lieutenant, according to Worf's rather harried update following the transport of Picard and Elfiki to Hilonu's office, had insisted on being beamed down as well. Chen argued that as the ship's contact specialist, it was her place to be at the captain's side in a situation such as this, and relations with the Eizand people were about to undergo a major shift, one way or another. Worf agreed with her reasoning and managed to transport Chen to the surface before maneuvering the *Enterprise* away from the planet.

"Such graciousness," said Hilonu, her voice low and humble. "Such forgiveness, in the wake of all that has happened. Those three humans, in a single moment, demonstrated more compassion and respect for our people than those we once trusted to lead us. Everything that happened afterward, that is our burden. We are to blame for our own fate." She shook her head. "Most remarkable."

"We still don't know how the war was started," said Elfiki. "There are no other visual records dated later than what we've already seen. Whatever happened after the crew was captured is anybody's guess. All we know is that they did jettison the weapons platform. We didn't detect any objects of that size or configuration drifting anywhere in the system, so it's a good bet that whoever captured the *Peacemaker* seized the platform as well."

Moving to where Elfiki stood before the makeshift computer setup, Hilonu said, "Tevent Coalition forces took the ship into custody. It stands to reason that they acquired your weapons. The narrative we have always been taught is that the humans attacked us and our response was a catastrophic overreaction." She paused, her expression turning to one of sadness. "If events did not play out in that fashion, then we as a people now face considerable questions about our own history."

The door to her office opened, and Lieutenant Konya entered the room, accompanying a young Eizand male Picard recognized from his previous visits as one of Hilonu's aides. He carried an electronic tablet, and he appeared anxious.

"Sorry for the interruption," said Konya, "but the presider's assistant says he has some urgent business for her."

"What is it?" asked Hilonu, motioning for the aide to join him.

The young male, obviously nervous, replied, "We are being contacted by several world leaders, Presider. All of them have seen the visual records. Many are demanding answers. There have been calls for investigations, meetings, one has even suggested a summit of all national leaders."

"I need to speak with our military commanders." Hilonu walked toward her desk. "They need to be alerted." She looked to Picard. "I suspect that emotions will be in turmoil, at least until there has been time to reflect on what we have seen. We need to be in control of that response."

Picard nodded. "Agreed." Then he tapped his combadge. "Picard to *Enterprise*."

Over the open channel, Commander Worf responded, "Enterprise. *Worf here, sir.*"

"Status report, Number One."

"We are maintaining a safe distance from the planet. We've taken some damage, but Commander La Forge reports it is manageable, and repair teams are already working. I can report that we did not endanger any of the manned satellites orbiting the planet. However, we are prepared to return to the planet to extract you even with the defensive systems still active."

"I will order the defense network to discontinue its protective measures," said Hilonu. "Your ship will be free to approach our world without further obstruction, Captain."

Thankful that no casualties were suffered, Picard allowed himself a sigh of relief.

"Thank you, Presider. Mister Worf, are you continuing to scan broadcast transmissions on the planet?"

"Yes, sir. There are a number of news reports and other transmissions pertaining to the broadcast. World leaders are contacting one another, and there have been several attempts to reach the Tevent Coalition leadership."

"What about military responses? Has there been any escalation in that regard?"

"None that we've been able to detect, sir. In fact, several leaders of smaller nation-states have explicitly ordered their military forces to remain in place or stand down. These directives appear to be in concert for calls to gather government leaders."

Buoyed by the news, Picard turned to Hilonu. "Presider, it seems your counterparts around your world are as interested in finding the truth as you are."

"Are they as afraid of the truth as I am?" asked Hilonu.

"Maybe," said Elfiki, "but that doesn't sound like it's necessarily a bad thing."

Chen added, "Exactly. It sounds like they want the same thing you want, Presider: answers, instead of doing something hasty and regrettable, and understanding what really happened and maybe keep it from happening again."

Hilonu nodded. "Hasty and regrettable. That appears to be at the heart of all that we did to ourselves. And if we do not like what that truth reveals? What then?"

"Your people are most fortunate, Presider," replied Picard. "They survived annihilation and forged themselves a second chance through sheer force of will. The Eizand are strong and determined. I find it difficult to believe that you won't find a way of getting through this."

She lowered her gaze to her desk, resting her hands atop its surface, and Picard watched her shoulders sag as though she only now was beginning to comprehend the weight of everything that she soon would be facing. There were challenges ahead, and she would need to be strong and patient in order to guide those who had looked to her for leadership and wisdom. Picard imagined her counterparts in offices like this around the world were contemplating similar thoughts, and wondering how they would rise to the tests and trials that lay ahead for all the Eizand people.

But they did not have to do it alone.

"Presider," he said, "this will not be an easy revelation for the Federation to accept either. Our people will also have to acknowledge and recognize our role in what happened here, despite it occurring long before there *was* a Federation. As a citizen of Earth, I pledge our support to you and your people. The path to the truth is a long one, but we can travel it together, if you'll allow us to walk with you."

For the first time since the meeting began, Hilonu smiled. "I cannot speak for other leaders, or even other citizens, but I know that I would welcome that, Captain." She walked to the window, and Picard moved to stand with her, taking in the view of Ponval. Below them and beyond the grounds of the Tevent Coalition capital, hundreds of Eizand citizens now stood at the fences, or were making their way in this direction. There were no loud or unnerving protests. There was no murmur of discontent. Instead, they all seemed to just be standing there, waiting to hear from their leader.

"I need to make a statement," she said, gesturing to her aide, who remained by her desk. "As quickly as possible. We need to project calm and confidence. The people will expect as much, and should accept nothing less." As the assistant left the office to carry out his assignment, Hilonu regarded Picard. "That was an easy first step. The ones to come will be much harder."

"But the destination is worthwhile, Presider. As is the journey."

Hilonu returned her attention to the crowd gathering outside the capital. She placed her hand on the window, and Picard heard the sounds of reaction from the congregation below. The people wanted answers, and it fell to their leader to provide them.

After a moment, she said, "It occurs to me that what happens today, and in the days to come, may very well define my legacy for all time as a leader of this nation. Nothing else I say or do will be so remembered."

"Perhaps not," said Picard. "However, you have a

unique opportunity to help shape the course of history not just for those who elected you, but for all Eizand. There are no greater ambitions to pursue."

Hilonu's gaze remained on the people outside her window. "And where do we go from here?"

"Forward, Presider Hilonu," said Picard. "Always forward."

29

U.S.S. Enterprise
2386

Positioned atop a table along the far wall of the small sickbay conference room Beverly Crusher had appropriated for this purpose, the trio of ceremonial urns seemed to radiate a simple yet undeniable somberness that was more than sufficient to communicate their purpose. Picard had already seen the vessels following their extraction from the catacombs beneath the city of Ponval, but it was only now that the captain was gripped by the solemnity of what they represented. Each was an unadorned black oval, with a flared base to provide stability. Their exterior showed no obvious visual evidence of seams or other means of opening, and neither were they polished or otherwise reflective. Indeed, the urns seemed to absorb the light, remaining unrelentingly black and at total odds with the room's color schemes and other gleaming surfaces.

"Not much of a legacy, is it?"

Picard glanced over his shoulder to see that Beverly had entered the room. Wearing a blue medical smock over her uniform, she stood with her hands in the light jacket's pockets.

"No, I'm afraid not." He returned his attention to the urns, which provided nothing in the way of insight as to the people whose remains they now held. "Were you able to learn anything new?"

Beverly frowned. "Not much more than we already knew. Starfleet Command went through every historical data bank there is and confirmed that there were three astronauts named Goswami, Harper, and Park in service to the international space agencies during the mid-twenty-first century. However, the records from that time are pretty scattershot thanks to the war. No family connections were found, but that's not unusual by itself. A mission of the sort they volunteered for would've meant leaving behind nearly everyone they knew and loved, so viable candidates likely had no ties."

"And they also were part of a clandestine group engaged in secret activities," replied Picard. "It's entirely possible that any record of their mission and even their entire existence was deliberately destroyed decades if not centuries ago."

The tragic irony of this situation was not lost on Picard. Humanity's involvement with Sralanya corresponded so closely to Earth's official first contact with the Vulcans. That latter event had positively changed the course of his homeworld forever, even as astronauts Goswami, Harper, and Park carried death and destruction to another people. While they may not have actually caused the devastation that had gripped the Eizand, their actions had set into motion a sequence of events that should never have been allowed to unfold in the first place.

"We might not be able to change the past," said Beverly, "but we can influence the future, and hopefully for the better."

Picard could take some solace in knowing that the Federation would be doing all that was possible to heal the wounds inflicted so long ago upon this world, and with hard work and trust earning a new ally. Even as the *Enterprise* maneuvered away from Sralanya and back toward the Odyssean Pass, he had left behind a team of sociologists who were already working with Hilonu and the Tevent Coalition as well as other world leaders to assess what long-term aid might be provided to the Eizand.

"I've been informed by Starfleet Command that a dedicated first-contact team is already en route," he said. "They should arrive in about eight weeks." It was a necessary first step, the first of many along what was hoped to be a new bond of friendship between the Federation and this newly discovered civilization.

You mean rediscovered.

He gestured to the urns. "We won't be able to confirm their identities, will we?"

Shaking her head, Beverly fidgeted with her hands still in her smock's pockets. "Not without something to match against their DNA, or perhaps facial recognition from the visual data Hilonu gave us. Federation and Starfleet historians are still searching; we may get lucky."

"You're talking about public records," said Picard. "But we already know that Starfleet has access to information that's obviously not generally available. That's why we were in this mess to begin with." He had to wonder as to the nature and scope of the secrets to which Admiral Akaar and others were privy. How old was some of that information? Centuries, to be sure, but all the way back to before the Third World War? To a time before humans had even made any meaningful leaps beyond the boundaries of Earth, but were still fighting each other and entertaining various flavors of paranoia about threats from around the world as well as from others hidden among the stars? How dark were the chapters of human history that seemed destined to remain concealed from view and immune from judgment?

"I'll take what I can get," replied Beverly. "Whatever helps put this matter to rest forever is fine by me."

In addition to excavating and transferring the remains of the three astronauts to the *Enterprise*, Presider Hilonu also had delivered to Picard all remaining personal effects and other artifacts taken from the three humans during their incarceration. There was precious little in the consignment, and according to Beverly almost nothing that might aid in providing definitive identification. This, coupled with the fragmentary prewar records of the early to mid-twenty-first century ensured that researchers and historians faced a formidable challenge. It also was a task that could not even commence until the astronauts' remains were returned to Earth.

"I've asked Mister Worf to prepare a runabout for transport back to Federation space," said Picard. "Three members of the crew are due for rotation, so they'll serve as escorts for the remains, including those of Lieutenant T'Sona." Starfleet observed rigid protocol when it came to the handling of remains, with procedures designed to accommodate numerous species as well as religious beliefs and personal preferences. While the rules were in place for those attached to Starfleet, extending them to cover any remains in the care of a starship's crew was a long tradition. The three crew members Picard was sending aboard the runabout *Roanoke* would see to the proper transfer of the remains to a liaison from Starfleet Medical, who in turn would work with a civilian representative acting to identify the astronauts and see to it that they were interred in accordance with the wishes of any known descendant. Lieutenant T'Sona's ashes would be escorted to her family on Vulcan. A memorial service for Lieutenant Austin Braddock was scheduled for later in the day, after which the security officer's remains would be sent into space in accordance with his wishes.

"What happens if no one's able to find a link to any relatives?" asked Beverly.

"Then the Federation Council will likely see to it that they're given whatever final respects and honors are their due, which may prove to be its own unique challenge." Given the astronauts' role in this unfortunate chapter of both human and Eizand history, and despite their ultimate actions in defiance of everything that had led to their traveling to Sralanya, Picard suspected putting this matter to rest would prove to be politically sensitive.

I don't envy the poor bureaucrat who's about to inherit this rather sticky wicket.

"Captain Picard."

Standing at the entrance to the room was Taurik. As always, his features were stoic, and he stood ramrod straight as Picard acknowledged him. "Commander."

"I was informed you wished to see me immediately, sir."

"That's right."

With a final glance to the urns, Beverly turned and left the room without another word, leaving the two men alone. Picard studied the Vulcan for another moment, deciding how he wanted to start this new conversation, but there was really only one thing to say.

Gesturing for Taurik to follow him from the conference room, Picard said, "I'm told that your assistance to Commander La Forge was invaluable. Your actions had a direct impact on the successful outcome of our mission. Thank you."

Taurik bowed his head. "It was my duty, sir. I know that by doing so, I disobeyed your orders to remain confined to my quarters. However, as the situation evolved I felt it prudent to—as I have heard it described—ask forgiveness, as I was unable to request permission."

Hearing such an explanation from a Vulcan almost made Picard laugh, but he managed to fight back the impulse at the last instant. "Yes, Mister La Forge has already given me his side of the story. I will tell you what I told him: I will always value loyalty and initiative, Commander, particularly when it comes to the safety of this ship and its crew."

Now standing in the middle of the sickbay's patient examination area, Picard sighed. "I've never doubted your loyalty to me, Mister Taurik. Not really. My concerns with your current role are that you might be placed in an untenable position between two superior officers and forced to choose between contradictory orders. That's unfair to you. However, I cannot discount the possibility that your unique knowledge may one day prove of vital importance as we continue our exploration of this region."

"I am still unable to offer any insights about the information I saw in the Raqilan weapon ship's computer files, sir. Admiral Akaar and the agents from the Department of Temporal Investigations were very clear on that point. Unless or until circumstances make it necessary, I am forbidden from disclosing any aspects of future events."

Picard nodded in understanding. "Yes, I understand. Just as I trust your loyalty, Commander, I also have full faith in your judgment. This business with Admiral Akaar is mine to deal with, and it was improper of me to subject you to my frustrations. I hope you can forgive me."

"I hold no animosity, Captain." Taurik raised his eyebrow. "I would hope the reasons are obvious."

Now Picard laughed. It was small and quiet, but needed, and he felt better for it. The strain of the mission and having to navigate the uncertain waters separating him from Admiral Akaar seemed to fade, if only a tiny bit.

"Somehow, Mister Taurik, we'll figure this out, one way or another." He gestured toward the sickbay's exit. "You may return to duty, Commander."

"Thank you, sir." The Vulcan offered a final, formal nod before turning and exiting the room.

"Well, that was easy enough," Picard said to no one, now that he was alone. He gave brief thought to dropping into Beverly's office, but decided against that notion. There was still one more conversation to have.

"I've been reading your report, Captain. Given the mess you were dealt, you handled things exceptionally well. My compliments to you and your crew."

Sitting behind the desk in his ready room, Picard stared at the face of Leonard James Akaar as displayed on his desktop computer screen. The admiral was sitting at the desk in his office back at Starfleet Headquarters on Earth, and Picard knew thanks to a computer query that it was very late in the evening in San Francisco, well after normal working hours. Despite the hour, Akaar seemed as fresh and alert as if he had just reported for duty. Only his expression gave away anything, along with the underlying tone of disapproval behind his words of praise. There could be little doubt as to what was bothering Akaar, so Picard opted to let the other man bring it up on his own terms.

"What of the astronauts' remains?"

"The runabout *Roanoke* left the ship less than an hour ago. It's a long journey back to Earth, but hopefully by then more information about their identities and activities can be confirmed." Deciding there was nothing to lose from some gentle probing, Picard added, "I'm hoping that whatever resource provided you with insight into what we would encounter out here can also shed some light on these other questions."

Akaar's expression was cold and hard. *"To be honest, this situation is one big jumble. Temporal Investigations is involved, but not because of anything relating to what you just went through. Even their records are stitched together from different sources, mostly owing to what they learned about alien activity and time travel here on Earth during the twentieth and twenty-first centuries. You know about some of that, obviously."*

"Indeed I do, sir."

"They're the only group that seems to have anything resembling a full picture, but rest assured we have people combing through every file and computer record we can find. I've even sent a team to our classified archive at Aldrin City." Akaar grimaced, seemingly at the very mention of that facility. *"I'm almost afraid to hear what they might find up there. It seems like every time something comes out of that place, it makes our lives a lot more difficult."* The admiral's expression seemed to grow even more dour. *"I only wish that was the biggest problem I had to deal with right now."*

Uncertain as to where this was heading, Picard frowned. "I don't understand, sir."

Akaar leaned closer, his eyes narrowing as he stared out from the screen. *"Tell me about Min Zife, Captain."*

The request was so abrupt and so unexpected that

Picard had no time to control his reaction. He felt his mouth open in shock in response to hearing the former Federation president's name spoken aloud.

"What about him?"

Settling back in his chair, Akaar rested his hand on the desk. *"He was removed from office. He didn't step down for the good of the Federation and then disappear quietly into exile. That's the story that was fed to the general public, but that's not what really happened. The truth is that he was forced to abandon his office without due process, without articles of impeachment being presented, and without any sort of formal investigation into his actions. Yes, those actions were heinous and cost millions of lives, and President Zife deserved to face a trial for what he did and allowed others to do, but he was denied that, wasn't he, Captain?"*

Damn.

Picard supposed he should not be surprised. He had always known that this day would come and that the sins of his past would come forward demanding retribution. President Min Zife, during the Dominion War, had seen fit to arm the people of the planet Tezwa, an independent world near the Klingon border, as part of a fallback strategy should Federation forces find themselves retreating in the face of a Dominion advance. The act was a direct violation of the Khitomer Accords, to which both the Federation and the Klingon Empire had been signatories for decades. Such a breach, if discovered, would give the Klingons cause to declare war against the Federation, leaving massive sections of both the Alpha and Beta Quadrants ripe for conquest by other interstellar powers such as the Romulans and the Tholians. When the weapons were used years later against Klingon vessels, Zife and some of his trusted allies initiated a massive cover-up of their actions on Tezwa, attempting to steer blame for the attack away from the Federation and onto the Tholians. Only the actions of the secretive, renegade group Section 31 had uncovered the truth.

"With Zife's crimes revealed and knowing that bringing them to public attention would only provoke the Klingons to retaliate against the Federation," said Akaar, *"you and a few other officers decided to take matters into your own hands."*

Picard nodded. "Reluctantly, but yes." His voice was quiet and sounded feeble, even to his own ears. "At the time, it was believed that forcing President Zife to step down and allowing him to live in exile was the best course of action for the Federation."

"It was a damned coup d'état. You forced him from office at the muzzle of a phaser. Yes, the ends were justified, but the means were deplorable, and despite your best efforts, the whole story's public. Everything, Picard. It's all out there, including all the players. The next time you're able to access the Federation News Service, you'll be able to read how Section 31 lied to your faces. Zife never went into exile, Captain. He and his collaborators were assassinated— murdered*—right there in the Monet Room just as soon as he was done delivering his final speech."*

Picard blinked several times, unwilling to accept what he had just heard. "What?"

"Two centuries worth of Section 31's dirty laundry has been tossed into the open, thanks to a nosy investigative journalist who hit the mother lode. On any other day, I'd be happy, because it might just mean that group is finally getting what's been coming to them for a long, long time. However, the list of people they've recruited, corrupted,

blackmailed, and simply disposed of in order to continue their games behind the scenes is staggering. People in this building, Picard. Members of my own staff have been implicated. Respected officers, like Edward Jellico, William Ross, Alynna Nechayev, Owen Paris, and you.*"* The admiral shook his head. *"You, of all people."*

"I'm not proud of my part in that affair, Admiral," said Picard, "and I'm prepared to answer for my actions, but I did not suggest, sanction, or stand by while President Zife was assassinated. That was not part of the bargain."

He had regretted his part in the ousting of a duly elected Federation president, regardless of the crimes of which he was guilty. There could be no denying the enormity of Zife's transgressions and the very real possibility of all-out war with the Klingons. With extreme trepidation and the knowledge that he was acting for the greater good, Picard had gone along with the plan to oust the president and send him far away to live out the remainder of his life in obscurity. It was not a good choice, but it was—by far—a lesser evil than sentencing millions if not billions of Federation and Klingon citizens to death. That, at least, had been enough for Picard to swallow such a bitter pill, but murder? How had that even happened?

Section 31, of course.

Akaar continued to glare at him. *"Yes, the information revealed so far shows that, so we can't hang a charge of conspiracy to commit murder on you. That doesn't mean you're out of the woods, though, not by a long shot."*

"Very well, Admiral." It hurt Picard to even say the words. "Where do we go from here?"

"The fact that you weren't involved in Zife's assassina-

tion gives me some wiggle room. Not much, but enough. Jellico, Nechayev, and the others are bigger problems, but you at least are out of reach and perhaps out of mind. I may be able to mitigate the damage."

"I don't require another cover-up, sir. I will accept whatever punishment is deemed appropriate." In truth, it was something he should have done a long time ago, but even coming forward to confess his role in Zife's overthrow might bring unwanted attention to the Tezwa affair and still end up attracting the Klingons and giving them reasons to pursue vengeance.

Akaar held up a hand. *"It's not that simple. We're only a year removed from President Bacco's assassination. We've had dishonor and corruption polluting the ranks of Starfleet and the halls of Federation power for far too long. The public doesn't need another scandal right now, and particularly not when it involves one of the genuine darlings of Starfleet. That's you, in case you were wondering."*

Mulling this over, Picard supposed he could understand this line of reasoning. Even if his punishment was not to be made a matter of public record in order to avoid rousing the ire of the Klingon Empire, surely there remained some means of submitting himself for penance?

"So, we can't do anything to you publicly, but here's the reality: You can forget any thoughts or dreams about ever making admiral. I know you said you never wanted a promotion and you wanted to stay in command of the Enterprise. *Well, this is for real now. Captain is the highest rank you'll ever obtain."*

Picard said, "I've been a captain for more than fifty years, Admiral. I've had my opportunities for advancement. If I haven't done it by now, then chances are good I never wanted to do so in the first place."

"Well, that Jim Kirk cowboy act's not going to work for you, or me, either. Yes, I need you where you are, and your skills and experience are invaluable, but I can learn to live without them. My biggest concern, Captain, is one of trust. Can I trust you?"

"Absolutely."

"You'll have to convince me, Picard. Until that happens, and assuming I can provide cover and keep you from getting filleted by the media, you're on a very short leash and I'm holding the other end. We'll discuss this at length later, once we've had time to analyze the full effect of the Section 31 data dump. Just do your duty, and remember my warning." Akaar made a jerking motion with his fist, indicating an imaginary leash he had just yanked. *"We're done here. For now, anyway."*

He said nothing else before the connection was severed and his face disappeared from the computer screen.

In some ways, Picard was relieved that the truth about Min Zife was finally coming to light. He had not celebrated the president's removal from office, instead seeing it as an action necessary to prevent a costly and needless war that would have been the Federation's fault. Likewise, he took no joy from learning the disgraced president's true fate. If the data exposed by this journalist helped to bring Section 31 and its activities out into the open and onto its knees, then Picard could live with the damage to his career and status.

But what of the wall that now had been thrown up between him and Akaar? How far did that barrier extend into the halls of power at Starfleet Command and the Federation government? Picard had spent a lifetime building a reputation as an officer of the highest ethical standards. How much of a hit would that standing absorb? Could it endure the heightened scrutiny that would soon be coming his way? Might it cost him command of the *Enterprise* and perhaps even a dismissal in disgrace from Starfleet? Is that what the future held for him?

Only time would tell.

ONE LAST THING

30

New York City
June 7, 2067

"We are at T minus fifteen minutes and counting for liftoff of Friendship 1. *Mission Control reports all systems are go, and launch is expected to proceed on schedule."*

Cloaked in darkness save for the beams from the array of floodlights bathing it in their brilliant white glow, the rocket stood silent and waiting. Just visible on the horizon was the first thin ribbon of pink, signaling the approach of another dawn. By the time the first rays of the sun shone across the waters of the Atlantic Ocean and the wetlands of Florida's west coast, the rocket would be gone. Until then, it remained flanked on one side by the enormous red gantry that provided physical support for the rocket as well as conduits for fuel and electrical power. All of those connections would be severed during the last moments before the rocket's launch, at which point the craft would be on its own as it climbed toward the stars.

"Even at this early hour," continued the voice of the female news anchor, *"our reporters on the ground tell us that the bleachers at all of the observation gantries are packed with onlookers. People are lining the causeway across the Indian River from the launch site, all of them eager to get a glimpse of history in the making as we send our first truly interstellar craft into deep space in search of intelligent life. We know it's out there, and we've already made friends*

from another world who came here, to our planet. Now it's our turn to extend the hand of friendship."

Mestral stood before the large rectangular monitor that was the centerpiece of the Beta 8's control panel, regarding the images being transmitted from Cape Canaveral. The supercomputer was culling telemetry from satellite transmissions, surveillance cameras scattered around the high-security launch site as well as the visitor areas of the Kennedy Space Center, and even the portable cameras held by the hundreds of observers packing the stands. After sifting through the litany of data at his fingertips, Mestral had settled on the main video feed being transmitted by the United Earth Space Probe Agency. It was obvious that the fledgling organization, a successor to the various entities that had overseen spaceflight for their respective countries dating back more than a century, was doing everything to avoid incident with this, the first launch under their auspices.

For a moment, Mestral imagined he could still feel the breeze on his face and the tinge of the salt air in his nostrils and on his tongue. Standing on the gantry before setting to work on his modifications to the *UESPA-1* rocket—or *Friendship 1*, as it was being called for the sake of the viewing public—his view of the Atlantic Ocean had been similar to what he recalled of the Voroth Sea during holiday excursions to the city of T'Paal on Vulcan. The Florida warmth had also been a welcome change from the cooler climate of the northern United States, where he now spent most of his time, and for a brief moment he considered a permanent relocation to the more inviting region. Even after more than a century living here, Mestral could not escape the occasional yearning for the desert heat of his home planet. It was a sensation that seemed to grow more acute each year as he aged, and that it was mirrored by elder humans offered him mild amusement.

"It seems you've been busy."

Startled by the voice behind him, Mestral turned toward its source. Was his hearing finally succumbing to age, or was his unexpected visitor just that stealthy? Mestral decided it was the latter upon recognizing the new arrival, who stood just outside the open doorway leading into the otherwise hidden vault containing the transport mechanism. The man, a human, was stoop-shouldered and he used a polished black cane to support his gaunt, withered frame. He wore a tailored, dark gray suit with a black shirt and matching tie. His skin was pale and deeply lined, and though his hair was full, its original pigment had long ago surrendered to stark white. Steel-gray eyes burned with a fierce intelligence and wisdom, though Mestral also thought he sensed weariness there as well. He estimated him to be nearly one hundred forty Earth years of age, well beyond a normal human's lifespan but doubtless aided by superior genetic engineering and advanced medical care on the mysterious alien world he called home.

"Mister Seven," said Mestral. "It is agreeable to see you again."

Stepping away from the vault, even with the cane in his left hand, Gary Seven moved with a grace and speed that belied his advanced years. He smiled as he closed the distance and extended his free hand.

"Good to see you again, too, Mestral. It's been a long time." There was a raspy quality to the man's voice, though it did not stifle the comfortable authority and calm self-assurance that had been a hallmark of Gary

Seven's personality since Mestral's first meeting with the genetically engineered human nearly a century ago.

The Vulcan took Seven's proffered hand, something he would never have done before encountering humans. It was yet another simple gesture that had long ago become second nature as part of Mestral's efforts to blend into human society.

Smiling as he studied the images scrolling past on the Beta 8's monitor screen, Seven turned and indicated Mestral's attire with a nod. "As I said, you've been busy, and it looks like your efforts were successful."

Mestral looked down at himself, studying the light blue jumpsuit he still wore, and ran his fingers across the distinctive blue arrowhead patch sewn into the garment's left breast pocket. The symbol for the United Nations, stitched in white thread, emblazoned the arrowhead's center. It was with some fascination that Mestral noted the emblem's similarity to the one he had seen worn by James Kirk, Spock, and other members of the *U.S.S. Enterprise* crew during his sporadic encounters with them. He had first seen the symbol almost a century ago, on the occasion of his unexpected and intriguing travel forward from 1968 to the *Enterprise* in the twenty-third century.

As for this logo, it had had only recently been adopted to identify UESPA, the multinational organization that had evolved as a successor to NASA and the European Space Agency along with similar groups from Japan, India, China, and a host of other countries around the world. The symbol also represented an ideal as well as a promise for the future. Memories and scars of the Third World War were still fresh enough that they could not be completely forgotten or healed even in the wake of the realization that humans were not the only intelligent life in the cosmos. This new space agency represented the hope that the people of Earth could finally put aside their differences and push away from their own planet while in pursuit of common, constructive goals for the betterment of all humanity. For reasons he could not fully articulate, Mestral found it somehow gratifying that the icon chosen by UESPA leaders to denote their organization would survive across centuries. From the available evidence, the symbol would progress alongside humanity's continual reach beyond the confines of their world, eventually coming to embody an even greater, interstellar entity with a simple mandate of exploration and discovery.

And so much of what humans hope to accomplish stands ready, Mestral reminded himself as he studied the monitor's image of the rocket. *Waiting to be sent on its way.*

"I believe I was able to make the proper reconfigurations in the probe's onboard computer software," he said. "I was just about to confirm that when you arrived." Turning to the Beta 8's main console, he said, "Computer, assess my updates to the probe's onboard control systems. Verify all corrections are in place."

After a moment during which the supercomputer offered nothing but a stream of flashing digital dots and lines across one of the console's smaller status monitors, the advanced mechanism's feminine voice replied, *"All updates to onboard computer software have passed validation tests. Systems are operating within expected parameters."*

Satisfied, Mestral nodded. "Excellent." In truth, he knew even before leaving the gantry that his updates had been correct, but he still welcomed the independent confirmation.

"Good thing," said Seven. "You were cutting it a little close to the launch time with that stunt."

"It was a necessary risk, given the security around the launch complex," replied Mestral. "I was forced to wait until all support personnel were clear of the area before transporting onto the gantry."

The Beta 8 had detected a flaw in the *Friendship 1* computer software that, if left uncorrected, would have issued a false abort and self-destruct signal mere moments after liftoff. Mestral was only aware of the problem because he had been monitoring the launch, and—motivated by simple curiosity—instructed the supercomputer to conduct a scan of the probe and the rocket that would carry it away from Earth.

Such a setback would have been costly just with respect to the loss of equipment and the years and resources that had been expended to bring to fruition the vision put forth by the *Friendship 1*'s mission planners. To suffer such a catastrophic failure during its first launch would have dealt UESPA a severe blow with regard to public perceptions and government oversight. Both of those groups harbored no small number of critics who had from the beginning denounced the unmanned interstellar exploration initiative as an obscene waste of time and money. In the minds of such people, efforts of this sort might well be better expended toward the goal of continuing to heal the world and its people of the wounds they had suffered during the war.

Upon detecting the fault, he had conducted his own investigation of the onboard software and determined that a correction was critical if the probe was to survive. Updating the defective software was easy enough, though it could not be done remotely, necessitating an onsite interaction prior to the probe's launch. With less than an hour before launch available to him, Mestral had scanned the entire launch gantry and immediate area, ensuring that all UESPA support and security personnel were well away from the vicinity before using the apartment's hidden transport vault to put him on the gantry. Once there, it was an easy matter for him to disable or reorient the various surveillance cameras for the few minutes he needed to access the probe and make his modifications to the craft's onboard systems.

Shifting his stance so that he once more faced the aged human, Mestral clasped his hands behind his back. "Based upon a review of your initial assignment as an active agent here on Earth, you subjected yourself to similar jeopardy during your very first mission. I was merely following your example."

"Well, things were a lot simpler in my day." Seven offered another wry grin. "Not so many cameras and other surveillance equipment to deal with. It's a lot harder to be a good spy or saboteur these days. Or, if you're one of us, an agent for positive change."

Mestral nodded. "Indeed."

His smile fading, Seven stepped closer to the computer console, resting a wrinkled hand upon its smooth, black surface. "Mestral, I heard about Rain Robinson and Kirsten Heffron. I'm sorry, particularly about Rain. I regret that we were never able to settle our differences. She was a natural for this kind of work."

Both Robinson and Heffron had died of natural causes less than a decade earlier, having never again involved themselves in any of the work begun by Aegis agents in the 1940s. Mestral had respected Robinson's wishes to never again be contacted, and he had helped

Heffron find some measure of peace with a new identity and relocation to Denver, Colorado.

Seven continued, "I also never got a chance to thank you, personally, for agreeing to return to the fold after all this time. I know it probably wasn't an easy choice to make, given the circumstances."

"Actually, I arrived at the decision without a great deal of effort. Despite whatever considerations motivated your . . . benefactors . . . to distance themselves from their interests here, their desire to influence positive change for Earth is commendable. I have spent more than a century observing humans, and I have seen them at their best and their worst." He gestured to the Beta 8's monitor. "They are poised to be their best once again, and this time the effects carry the potential to be farther reaching and longer lasting than anything they have accomplished to this point. It is a wondrous time to be here, both as an observer and as someone who can offer the occasional discreet hand of assistance."

Mestral paused, weighing how his next words might be received. "However, there is an argument to be made that the Aegis, by inserting itself into humanity's affairs, might well be causing more harm than good. Also, I am forced to wonder how an agency that apparently has foreknowledge of the future—including those involving Earth and its people—could be caught by surprise with respect to events unfolding on this planet. That would seem to be . . . an inconsistency."

Seven replied, "If you're asking me whether the Aegis is all knowing, my truthful answer is that I don't have the first damned clue. Even after all this time, there's still information they keep from me." He shrugged, and for a moment the small smile returned. "The reality is that even though I do hold some knowledge of what will happen in the years ahead, I've never had the full picture. Even when I was an active agent, on Earth or elsewhere, I was told just enough to carry out my assignments, and if I was lucky there may have been some additional context to help me make a better decision."

"But these conservative measures on the part of the Aegis," said Mestral. "Given the knowledge they apparently possess, and their obvious interest in seeing humanity evolve to something more than they are, it is illogical that they would not take a more direct role. And at a time when it seemed Earth would most benefit from their guidance, they elected to withdraw. If they knew what was to come, and yet chose to do nothing . . ." He let the sentence trail away, watching Seven frown. The older man's brow furrowed, and the creases along his face seemed to deepen.

"The Aegis was never in this to hold humanity's hand, Mestral, and neither did they ever want to make all the hard choices for these people." Seven brushed his hand along the Beta 8's console, and his expression appeared wistful, as though he was recalling memories from long ago. "They see the potential humans carry within them, individually as well as a race, and they know the sort of influence they'll bring to the interstellar table in the decades and centuries to come. However, in order to do that—to be the people they need to be in the years ahead, they first have to learn how to get out of their own way."

Mestral replied, "It sounds as though the Aegis sees itself as a parent."

"I don't know if they'd appreciate the comparison, but it's good enough for me." Seven gestured toward the monitor, and the rocket it still displayed. "For whatever reason, and they've never seen fit to share that with me, they want humans to succeed. It's more than being a parent, actually, but it's obvious they feel some kind of heightened, maybe even personal stake in what happens here." He shook his head. "Maybe one day they'll tell me what that's all about. As for me and the other agents, our job wasn't to drive the car, but to make sure the car traveled the right road. If the engine overheated or hit a pothole and blew out a tire or ran off the road into a ditch, they had to be allowed to make the necessary repairs. Even if they drove off a cliff, we had to let them do it, and that's enough car metaphors for one day."

Mestral cocked an eyebrow. "Indeed."

"If humanity is going to succeed, it'll have to keep doing its own heavy lifting, and that means making mistakes and learning some hard lessons along the way." Seven sighed. "And a global war is one hell of a lesson."

If Seven was right, then how painful must it have been for his enigmatic overseers to step back and watch as Earth plunged into yet another worldwide conflict that had resulted in millions of deaths, millions more wounded, and left a civilization on the brink of collapse? With the knowledge they had to possess, it was unfathomable that the Aegis was unaware of the war and its effects.

They naturally would also have known about the Vulcans.

Just as Mestral suspected they might do at some point many years after his own decision to remain here, his people had sent emissaries to Earth, and while the relationship between the two worlds was a new one, Mestral knew from his dealings with Captain Kirk and Mister Spock that it was an alliance that would only strengthen and deepen over time. Now, however, the people of Earth were still learning how to accept with humility the hand of friendship Vulcans had offered.

He found it interesting that the Aegis, as inexplicably as they once removed themselves from Earth's affairs, had returned with equal ambiguity, at least in some form, not long after the arrival of the Vulcan ship. Although he had never experienced any direct contact with Gary Seven's unknown sponsors, Mestral received a message nearly four years earlier, directing him to this Manhattan apartment where he had found the storehouse of advanced technology along with instructions and a request to "resume his assignment." The message itself had been short and to the point, not bothering to mention that he had never actually been designated as an official Aegis agent. Intrigued by the possibilities and with nothing else to do, he had accepted the offer. As for this new base of operations, it was not the same residence or even the same building in which Mestral had first come to know Seven and his human protégée, Roberta Lincoln, nearly a century ago. That building along with a significant portion of that area of the city had been decimated during the war, and reconstruction efforts were still under way. There seemed to be something of a cyclical nature to how the Aegis operated, returning to New York. Perhaps this new location had even been selected by Seven himself.

"Since you are here," said Mestral, "does this mean I can expect to be joined by a team of actual Aegis agents? After all, I am approaching an age where this sort of activity might not be the most prudent course."

"I passed that point decades ago, but to answer your question, a new team is in final preparations and should be here within the next few days."

"Is there a reason for this change of attitude?"

Seven replied, "We weren't meant to avert World War III, or even the actions that sent the Eizand ship back to its homeworld, but there are still things we can do to help the people of Earth as they move into this new age. They'll find their own way, but that doesn't mean we can't lend a hand now and again. There's still a lot to do, even with the amazing turnaround we're seeing since the Vulcans came. Humans now know without doubt that other civilizations are out there, waiting. Many of those civilizations are potential allies, while others will be enemies. Unfortunately, and as you know from your own experiences here, there are humans who will view everything and everyone not of this planet as a potential threat. They'll continue to create clandestine groups like Majestic 12, Initiative 2031, and the Optimum Movement, and allow themselves to be controlled by their uncertainty, their paranoia, and their fear, which will only grow deeper the farther humanity moves into space."

Considering the aged human's words, Mestral said, "Then we can expect to be busy for some time to come."

There would be much to do, he knew, and much of it would be accomplished without the people of Earth being any the wiser. Just as he, Gary Seven, and so many others had done for more than a century, he would continue to move behind the scenes, hopefully affecting positive change for humanity and his adopted planet. Like those who had come before him, Mestral would carry out this necessary work standing not in the limelight, but instead from within the protective veil of history's shadow.

ACKNOWLEDGMENTS

Many thanks to my editors, Ed Schlesinger and Margaret Clark, who continue to indulge me when I veer off on these weird tangents and harangue them with things like, "No, I really can connect all these dots. *Honest!*" Their patience for my antics is endless.

Thanks once again to Greg Cox, author of some of my all-time favorite *Star Trek* novels: *Assignment: Eternity*, *The Eugenics Wars: The Rise and Fall of Khan Noonien Singh* (both volumes!), and *The Rings of Time*. I've endeavored to keep my twentieth- and twenty-first-century tales in sync with these novels in particular, and Greg has always supported my efforts to expand this little corner of the *Star Trek* literary sandbox.

Thanks also to Kevin Lauderdale, author of "Assignment: One," which appeared in *Star Trek: Strange New Worlds 8*. While the details of his tale don't mesh with *The Eugenics Wars*, the basic premise was such that I still wanted to include it in this story, while making it consistent—at least in the broad strokes—with Greg's books as well as mine. Kevin understood my desire and gave me his blessing, and it's always nice to pull together a few threads as we keep weaving new patches into the *Star Trek* storytelling quilt.

Finally, thanks to the readers who've told me how

much they've enjoyed *Star Trek: From History's Shadow* and *Star Trek: Elusive Salvation.* I wondered if I had one more of these stories in me before moving on to something else, and it was you all who made me decide to give it one more go.

ABOUT THE AUTHOR

Dayton Ward understands and forgives readers who skip over these "About the Author" pages. It's easy to gloss right past them. Besides, a lot of them can be kind of pretentious, with the author listing everything they've ever written along with the names of every cat they've ever rescued from a tree. Dayton hates being that guy, even though he digs cats.

But if you've made it this far, let Dayton know by visiting him on the web at www.daytonward.com, where you can read about all the stuff he's written and thank him for sparing you the pain of yet another long, drawn-out "About the Author" page.